THE BAD BOY SERIES COLLECTION

BOOKS 1 - 4 OF THE BAD BOY SERIES

S. E. LUND

ACADIAN PUBLISHING LIMITED

BAD BOY SAINT

NEWSLETTER

Sign up for S. E. Lund's newsletter and get advanced notice of upcoming releases, sales, and free books!

She hates spam and will never share your email.

S. E. LUND NEWSLETTER SIGN UP

CHAPTER 1

CELIA

THE CALL CAME in at eleven in the morning on a Thursday.

Nothing bad happens at that time of day, and Thursday is just another day of the week. That's what I thought, so I didn't worry and let it ring through to voicemail. I had pages and pages of journal articles to read for my class at two in the afternoon and couldn't afford to waste any time. Our professor expected us to be familiar enough with the material so we could discuss, answer questions and ask them. Not just any questions. Smart questions. I had to be in the top five percent of the class to keep my ranking, and so I tucked my cell into my book bag and turned the page in the article.

So far so good for another three minutes of reading the dense material, but then my cell rang once more, the shrill ring irritating me, making it hard to concentrate on the text in front of me. It rang five times and then went to voice mail once more, so I sighed and turned another page. Less than a minute later, it rang again and I knew I couldn't ignore the call any longer.

I took the cell out of my bag and checked the caller I.D.

1

Massachusetts General ICU.

Adrenaline jolted through me. My mother and stepfather were out of town on one of those river cruises up the Danube, so it wasn't them.

It could only be Graham.

Graham must have been in an accident.

I answered the phone, my heart thumping in my chest.

"Hello?"

Sounds of people talking, monitors beeping. That wasn't good. Finally, someone came on the line.

"Sorry," a female voice said. "I didn't think you were going to answer. Is this Celia Franklin?"

"Yes, this is her."

"Your brother Graham is in ICU here at Mass General. You should come down as soon as possible."

I gasped, covering my mouth. "What happened? Is he going to be okay?"

"He received a brain injury during a fight and is being kept sedated for now so you should come down as soon as you can."

"Is he going to die?"

"He's currently in serious condition, and he's very sick, but no. He should recover barring any unseen complications."

I closed my eyes and exhaled, relieved that he wasn't dead or dying. "I'll be right there."

I ended the call and tried to calm myself but my hands were shaking.

My older brother by five years, Graham was my financial manager and my slave driver, watching over me to make sure I didn't stray too far from the straight and narrow. He'd taken over that role from Spencer, my bastard of a stepfather, when I'd left home at nineteen to escape the household from hell. Luckily, I had an inheritance from my father and used the interest to fund the dorm I lived in. A tuition scholarship covered the rest.

I texted my best friend, Amy.

CELIA: I need you to take me to Mass General. Graham's been in a fight and he's unconscious. They want me to come right down. I'm freaking out right now. Where are you?

There was no answer and I wondered if she was in class. I checked her schedule, which I kept on my laptop, which showed that she was in between classes so I knew she'd answer as soon as she could.

I frantically ran around my dorm room, pulling on a sweater over top of my yoga pants and bra. Finally, my cell dinged, indicating an incoming text.

AMY: OMG I'm so sorry I didn't check my cell. I'll be right there!

I responded immediately, relieved I wouldn't have to take a taxi.

CELIA: Thank you. I don't know what I'd do without you.

AMY: Hold on. I'm on my way right now. Be there in five.

I went to the small bathroom and brushed my teeth, washed my face, and then gathered up my hair into a topknot. When I glanced in the mirror, I saw a face white as a ghost, and haggard from staying up late too many nights to get on top of my classes. I needed sleep but it appeared that I wouldn't be getting any for a while.

I pulled my laptop into my book bag, grabbed a couple of articles I'd need to read for classes tomorrow, and stood at my window to wait for Amy.

Then, I realized I'd have to miss my contracts class, so I texted my Prof.

CELIA: Sorry, but I have to miss class today. My brother is in ICU at Mass General.

I didn't expect a response, so I went down the stairs to the front of Kirkland House and stood on the sidewalk, my nerves all jangling. When would Amy be here?

Most importantly – what the hell happened to Graham?

He didn't get into fights. He was an investment advisor in a startup he and his friend Mark formed a couple of years earlier.

He managed an investment fund. Stocks. Bonds. Securities.

He didn't *fight…*

Not even with Spencer, our bastard of a stepfather, who beat the crap out of both of us when we were kids.

Graham took it in silence, unlike me. I always rebelled. It cost me many a slapped face, but I could not accept his authority.

After my father died in the car crash that disabled my mother, Spencer tried to become our replacement father, but neither Graham nor I accepted him in that role.

I *hated* him. When I was nineteen, I decided that the last time he'd hit me was the last time I'd take any more shit from him. That was it. I never went home again, and I never had to take anything from him again.

I aimed to keep it that way.

Amy finally drove up in front of the building in her old jalopy of a car – an eighties Austin Marina, dark green, dented and held together by duct tape and wire. I hopped into the passenger side, my book bag in hand.

"Oh my God, Celia," she said, her eyes wide as we drove off. "What the hell happened? It's not like Graham to get into a fight."

I fastened my safety belt and leaned back, my eyes closed. "I have no freaking idea. Maybe he was mugged?"

She shrugged and made a face. "Possible. But his office is in the swanky part of the city."

I shrugged, at a loss about how Graham could have gotten into a fight. "All I know is that the ICU nurse called and said he'd been in an 'altercation' and was being kept sedated. He must have a concussion."

"I can't believe it. What do you suppose happened? I didn't think investment bankers got into fist fights."

"Me neither," I said and watched the streets pass by. The world seemed so normal, with people walking down the sidewalks, going about their business. My brother was in ICU and the hospital called and said I should get down right away.

That wasn't good.

"Do your parents know?" she asked as we waited at a stoplight.

I shook my head. "Honestly, I won't call them until I know what's happening. They're in Germany right now and so it's late at night for them. The last thing I want is to scare my mother. She wouldn't be able to sleep if she thought Graham was dying or something."

"Do you think he's dying?"

"No, no," I said quickly, "but if my mom got a call late at night, she might freak out. You know what she's like."

Amy rolled her eyes. "I know," she said. "She can't handle any stress. It's probably best you wait and see how Graham is. But you should call her if things are bad."

"I will."

She reached out and took my hand in hers, squeezing. "I'm so sorry. You must be freaking out."

"I am." I forced a smile and nodded. "Thanks for being here." I stared at her while we drove down the street. "Your hair is pink and blue," I said with a smile.

"Do you like it?" she asked, running her hand over her pigtails, which bounced perkily when the car drove over bumps in the road.

"You look like Harley Quinn."

She laughed. "That's the effect I was going for."

We drove on, and my smile faded when my thoughts turned from Amy's love of Joker's main squeeze to my brother Graham. There was nothing left to do but wait until we got there to find out what the hell happened.

Finally, after what felt like ages, we stopped in front of the Mass General entrance and I got out of the car, slinging my book bag over my shoulder. I leaned in to the open window and caught her eye.

"Thanks for this."

She nodded. "Do you want me to park and come in?"

I glanced around at the busy parking lot. "No, that's okay. I know you have classes this afternoon."

"I can cancel if you want. I can stay with you."

I shook my head. "I'll call you if I need you. Go on. One of us should attend class."

"Okay," she said doubtfully. "You text me and keep my up to date with what happened and how Graham's doing. You know I always had a crush on him."

"*Eww*," I said and made a face of mock disgust. "I know you had a crush on my brother. You still do."

"I do," she said with a sigh. "Tell him I hope he gets better soon."

"I will."

She blew me a kiss and drove off so I went into the hospital and worked my way through the maze of hallways and elevators until I found the ICU. I went through a set of double doors and down a busy hall with a row of individual rooms with big glass windows so the nurses could watch the entire ward.

People lay on beds, the heads raised, and some were intubated, tubes either in their mouths or through tracheotomies. Wires and tubes ran from their bodies to machines, and telemetry recorded their heart rates and respirations. The beep-beep-beep of the ECGs was like a cacophony and it set my nerves off. My hands actually shook.

I went to the nursing station and stood at the counter, waiting for someone to notice me. The nurses were busy consulting a chart or on the phone. Finally, a man in scrubs with a stethoscope around his neck turned to me.

"Can I help you?" he asked. An older man in his fifties with thinning grey hair, he had a kind face and warm brown eyes.

"Yes, I'm here to see Graham Parker. I'm his sister, Celia. Someone called me and said I should come right down."

He nodded. "Yes," he said and pulled up a screen on his monitor. "I'm Doctor Malone. Your brother is in Room 12. Just down the hall."

"How is he?"

He stood and came over to where I was at the counter. "He's been beaten pretty badly and was unconscious when the EMTs brought him in. He has a concussion, some cuts and bruises and internal injuries. We had to wire his jaw shut because it was broken. I'll take you to see him."

I followed him down the hall. While we walked, he recounted what happened.

"According to your brother's friend, Graham left with three men in a van he met outside his office. They must have beaten him up and then dumped him in the back alley behind his building. Your brother's friend called the ambulance and they brought him here."

We went into a tiny room and it was hard for me to believe it was Graham for his face was beaten so badly that he was almost unrecognizable, his eyes swollen shut and already turning blue-purple. His head was wrapped with white bandage.

"Oh, my God," I cried and covered my mouth. "What did they do to him?"

"He's lost a few teeth. And they did this," the doctor said and lifted up Graham's gown to reveal a large bandage. He peeled back one edge and lifted the bandage up. Underneath were several letters carved into his abdomen, the edges bloody and held together with butterfly sutures where there weren't stitches.

The letters read '7 DAYS'.

"Seven days?" I stepped closer. "What does that mean?"

The doctor reapplied the bandage to cover the wound. "I have no idea. Is it a deadline for something? Did he owe any money to someone?"

"He's an investment banker. He doesn't get into fights."

Tears sprung to my eyes as I examined Graham. What on Earth happened to him? Who would do this to him?

"Someone sent him a message," Doctor Malone said. "He's out of immediate danger. Now, we'll watch to see if he regains consciousness. We're going to take him for another CT later to make sure he's okay."

I thanked him and stood at Graham's side for a while, watching him breathe.

After about ten minutes, Graham's friend and business partner Mark showed up with a cup of coffee in his hand.

"Celia," he said and glanced at Graham. "Thank God you're here."

"You have to tell me what happened," I said and grabbed his arm. I didn't want Mark to tell me in front of Graham so I pulled him down the hallway to the small alcove with chairs and a kitchen for family. We sat on the chairs beside each other.

"Tell me," I said, my throat choking from emotion. "What the hell happened to Graham?"

Mark leaned back and took a sip of his coffee. "Honest to God, I thought they killed him."

"Who are they? Why would anyone what to kill him?"

Mark made a face of discomfort, like he didn't want to have to tell me.

"Tell me!"

He sighed. "Some thugs who looked like they came out of Eastern Promises showed up at the office. A guy named Stepan went into his office and I heard some shouting. Graham went outside with him and got into a van on the street. The van drove away and I thought nothing of it, because Graham seemed so calm. I guess they beat the shit out of him and dumped him behind the building in the back alley. I went out back for a smoke and when I found him, I called 9-1-1 right away. They were there in three minutes but who knows how long he was lying there in the back alley? He was gone for half an hour at least."

"And the thugs?"

He shook his head. "I talked to the cops and gave them a description of the men and the van. The detective said it sounded like the Russian mob."

"The Russian mob? What the *hell*..."

We sat in silence for a moment while I tried to figure it out. I had this sense he knew more than he was telling me.

I turned to him. "What was Graham doing talking to the Russian mob? You guys weren't laundering money for them or anything, were you?"

Mark shrugged, but didn't meet my eyes. "He lost your money."

I frowned, adrenaline flowing through me. "He what?"

Finally, Mark turned to me, his face red. "He invested your money and lost it all. He was swindled, Celia. He was so upset, because he knew you relied on that money for school."

"What did he do?"

"He went to a loan shark to get it back because he knows you need the money for your dorm. He couldn't afford to pay the interest. To put them off, he gave them the money back, and was supposed to pay the interest back this week. He didn't have it."

I covered my eyes and took in a ragged breath. *Graham...*

"Why didn't he tell me?" I asked, my eyes filling with tears.

"Why do you think?" Mark said, turning to me. "You trusted him to manage your inheritance. He lost his money and yours in this pharmaceutical startup that was supposed to give a big return due to some great new genetic tech advance, but the company went bankrupt and he lost both your funds."

"Oh, God, why did he do that? My trust fund was supposed to be put in a safe investment."

He raised his hands. "He thought he had this sure thing and wanted to double your money so you could start your own firm when you graduated if you wanted. He borrowed and was going to use it to leverage some extra money, but he failed. His investments lost money. All he could do was pay back the loan shark the principal. No interest. The beating was to make sure he remembered to pay the interest."

"How much?"

"Thirty percent."

My jaw fell open. "Thirty percent interest?"

Mark lifted a shoulder. "That's actually a good rate. The problem is that if you don't pay on time, they break an arm or leg to give you an incentive."

"What's he going to do? Can he afford to pay thirty percent? That's..." I sat and calculated the interest. My inheritance gave me a nice stipend of two grand a month before taxes. That paid my room and board and a little left over for spending. If he lost my entire inheritance...

"That's one hundred and fifty grand for your fund alone, not to mention some that he invested from his own money," Mark said quietly.

I sat in stunned silence, unable to grasp what he told me.

"I guess I better get a job." I shook my head and felt tears threaten but I couldn't feel bad for myself when Graham was so badly hurt.

"Graham's so sorry about losing your money," Mark said, turning to me. "He was sick about it. He was going to cash in some of his investments to pay the interest but he can't cover all one hundred and fifty grand. He could only come up with ten grand in cash. He gave that to Stepan but it wasn't enough to stop the beating."

"Why did he go to a loan shark? My *God*, Mark, even I know you never get mixed up with them."

"He freaked. You were starting law school and he has big debts. He thought he was investing your money in this sure thing..." He sighed and finished his coffee.

A nurse came down the hallway to where we sat. "Celia?" she said, peering around the corner. "Your brother's waking up."

I jumped up and went to his room, where a nurse tended to him, offering him some water from a glass with a straw.

I went to the other side of the bed and took his hand in mine.

"Hey," I said, my eyes brimming. "You're waking up."

He nodded almost imperceptibly. He tried to say something, but he had his jaw wired and I could barely make out what he said.

I leaned down and put my ear to his lips. "What did you say?"

"I lost it all," he whispered. "I'm so sorry."

I glanced at him and saw tears slipping down his cheeks.

"Shh," I replied and stroked his cheek. "I know. Mark told me. Don't worry about that. You've got to get better. That's all that matters."

He shook his head slowly. "Go to Hunter."

I frowned.

Hunter. There could be only one Hunter.

Hunter Saint.

"I can't," I said and shook my head. "You know better than that."

"Go," he said through gritted teeth. "Go to him."

"No, Graham, he hates us. He hates *me*."

Graham shook his head slowly. "No," he said. "*Go* to him."

"That's like going from the frying pan into the fire." I wiped tears off my cheeks. "He's as bad as this Stepan goon who beat you up."

"No," Graham said. "He's not."

My brother's former oldest and best friend, Hunter was now an enemy, thanks to Spencer, and there was no way Hunter would help.

"I'm so sorry," Graham said again, tears overflowing from beneath his swollen eyelids.

"Shh." I squeezed his hand again. "You go to sleep. I'll figure something out."

"Go to Hunter," Graham whispered again. "Don't call Spencer. *Don't.*"

"But I have to tell Mom you're in the hospital..."

"No," he said and squeezed my hand hard. "Don't tell Spencer. Go to Hunter."

I didn't reply. Hunter was the last person I wanted to go to but did I have any other choice?

CHAPTER 2

Celia

THERE WERE whispers about Hunter's family. In the school halls, in the playground. In my own house. "He's Irish," my grandmother said when she saw him the first time. "Stay away from that one. The Saints are trouble, the lot of them. I heard they have pirate blood in them, no doubt about it."

My stepfather said the elder Saint brothers were dirty, corrupt, mixed up with organized crime, and their sons weren't far behind them, destined to be just as criminal as their fathers.

I didn't care. At nine, I was intrigued by the drama and had no idea what 'organized crime' meant. Besides, Hunter was what my nine-year-old self considered a total hunk.

He was everything an adolescent girl could desire: buff from years of training at his father's club, Saint Brothers Gym and Boxing Emporium, with longish dark hair that flopped in his eyes, pale skin, and blue, blue eyes.

Hunter had a sexy smile that turned my insides to mush. Back then, I didn't know why I liked him, but I did, sensing something in him that would one day send women into paroxysms of lust.

"Pretty Boy Saint," they called him in the fighting circuit, because he still had a perfect face, his nose straight and his features symmetrical despite fighting since he was ten. My stepfather called him "Bad Boy Saint" but to me, he was just Hunter.

The man of my dreams. The only one I wanted.

Hunter's older brother Sean had hoped to go pro, and had taken up mixed martial arts. He was fierce-looking with his busted nose and glistening muscles, pumped from working out, tats across his chest and back. But he'd been in one too many fights where he'd gotten knocked out, and was no longer able to fight. He'd suffered brain damage and was now reduced to being the caretaker at the gym.

Hunter's younger brother Conor was fast becoming a skilled boxer, but back then, it was Hunter everyone placed their bets on to go to the Olympics. He was quick on his feet and fast with his hands, or so Graham told me as we stood at the side of the ring and watched Hunter practice, kicking and punching his trainer's gloves.

When Hunter was done, he leaned over the ropes and looked at Graham and me where we sat on the sidelines. He was a sight to behold with his hair wet from exertion, his fair skin pink and his muscles pumped.

"Hey, Celia, you wanna try?" Hunter asked, giving me a crooked smile.

"Yes," I said, jumping up without hesitation. I'd do pretty much anything Hunter asked. I turned to Graham. "Can I?"

He shrugged. "Go ahead," he said with a grin. "Be gentle with him. Don't want him to lose that pretty-boy smile."

I climbed up and through the ropes to stand in front of Hunter, who was almost two feet taller than me. Even at fifteen, Hunter was built. He had on a pair of black boxing shorts and his chest was bare. His hands had been wrapped in cotton tape and his skin gleamed with sweat. He took some smaller boxing gloves from the side of the ring and tied them onto my hands. I couldn't help but stare at him while he fastened them, in awe and somewhat breathless at being so close to his beautiful and unmarred face.

He must have known how impressed I was, because he glanced down into my face, his blue eyes twinkling.

"Excited?" he asked, as he finished tying one glove.

I nodded, at a loss for words, as usual.

He showed me a few stances and how to guard my face, then I punched his practice glove a few times to get my bearings. When the instruction was over, he put the practice glove down and stuck out his chest, his hands on his hips.

"Okay, Celia. Take your best shot."

"You want me to…" I said, stammering. "To hit you?"

He nodded. "Go for it. Hit me as hard as you can. I can take it."

I held my gloves up and jabbed at his abdomen. To my utter shock and horror, he fell back, dropping to the floor in pain.

At first, I was appalled—I didn't think I'd hit him hard. Then I realized he was faking me out, and I frowned.

"*Hun-ter!*"

When he saw the look on my face, he doubled up with laughter. On the sidelines, Graham laughed out loud, enjoying Hunter's little game at my expense.

Hunter got up and came over, rubbing my head playfully. "It's okay, Nibs," he said, using my nickname. "You'll get better. Everyone has to start somewhere."

Nibs. I hated that nickname. My cheeks grew hot with embarrassment that Hunter knew it and, even worse, used it. I'd received it because of my flat chest and noticeable nipples, which seemed to always stick out at the worst times. My stepdad Spencer wouldn't let me get a real bra, saying I was too young, so I had to cover my chest instead. I spent a lot of time with my arms across my chest.

"Don't *call* me that," I said, fighting not to pout like a child, but it crushed me to have Hunter—of all people—know my nickname.

"It's okay," he said, his voice soft. He bent down and looked in my eyes. "One day you'll have real tits and no one will call you Nibs. I heard that the longer you go without getting them, the bigger they'll be. Then all the guys will be lining up to be your boyfriend."

"I hope so," I said, mortified that Hunter was talking about my non-existent breasts, but somewhat mollified at the thought that I had a nickname-free future where boys might line up to date me.

"Now, hit me for real." Hunter stuck his chest out again. "Put everything you got into it."

I tried again and this time, I landed a punch with a solid *thwack!*

"See?" Hunter said with a chuckle. "You can do it. You learn to fight and no guy will ever mess with you, boobs or no boobs."

I nodded, then he led me over to a punching bag.

"Hit this for a while. Graham and I have to go out back for a minute."

"Okay," I said, and proceeded to punch the bag instead of him. He hopped out of the ring and he and Graham went out back—to do what I had no idea—and I was alone with the punching bag. I hit it listlessly, no longer interested now that Hunter was gone.

While I was punching the bag, imagining Hunter returning to spar with me some more, my stepfather showed up, entering through the front doors of the gym. I stopped hitting the bag and watched as he scanned the gym floor looking for Graham.

When he saw me, his face changed from usually-grumpy-Spencer to really-angry-Spencer.

How I knew that face...

"What the *hell* are you doing here?" He stomped over to the ring. "What are you doing with boxing gloves on? Don't you know you could get your teeth knocked out? We spent thousands of dollars on those braces." He jerked his arm. "Get out of there."

I jumped down from the ring and stood silently while he unlaced my boxing gloves, his hands roughly pulling them off before they were properly untied, hurting me.

Even at nine, I knew that was his intention. Spencer liked to hurt me, spanking or slapping me at every opportunity.

"Where's your brother?"

I shrugged.

"Don't tell me he's left you here. How many times have I told him to be responsible? That boy…"

"He's out back with Hunter," I said finally, not wanting Spencer to punish Graham. Then I bit my lip, realizing I should have kept my mouth shut. As much as I hated him, I was also afraid of Spencer. He had a mean streak and you never knew when he might snap and haul off and whack you.

"You stay here," he said, and forced me down on the bench beside the ring. "I'll be right back."

In a few moments, Spencer entered the gym from the back, one hand circling Graham's bicep, pushing him ahead. Graham and Hunter had been out back, smoking in the back alley behind the gym —and not just tobacco cigarettes, either. Smoking a spliff, Graham called it. Marijuana. Not a good idea when your stepfather was the assistant DA.

"Let's go," Spencer said and pointed to me. "You're both in trouble."

That was the last time I went to Saint's Gym for almost ten years.

CHAPTER 3

PRESENT DAY...

CELIA

I SAT in the cramped ICU room and watched Graham sleep.

I had to decide what to do. My biggest concern was paying back the loan shark Graham went to. How would I pay back one hundred and fifty grand? As if that wasn't enough to worry about, I needed the money to fund my room at Kirkland House. At fourteen grand a year, it was expensive. I'd have to find another part time job if I wanted to stay.

Graham's breathing was slow and deep. I watched him, fearing that something would go wrong and he'd go into a coma or cardiac arrest, but he seemed stable enough.

I needed a drink, my mouth was so dry from anxiety about Graham. I left the ICU room and found that Mark was still waiting in the alcove.

"How is he?" he asked when I plopped down beside him.

"He's sleeping now, but he was okay. He told me to go to Hunter."

Mark nodded. "His best friend from his MBA?"

"They were friends from the time they were in middle school. Best friends until a few things happened and now they're officially enemies. Our families are enemies."

"He's rich," Mark said. "His family's got lots of money."

"It's dirty," I said and ran a hand through my hair, which had fallen out of my makeshift bun. "Besides, there's no way Hunter will be happy to see me, even if I'm begging on my knees."

"That's a lot of money to pay back," Mark said smiled sadly at me. "Maybe you need dirty money to pay back dirty money. He might charge you less interest that the usual loan shark. Better terms since you're old friends."

"I don't know..." I sighed and went over to the vending machine in the alcove. I reached into my bag and removed some quarters to buy a bottle of water. It fell into the bottom of the machine with a heavy thud. I took the bottle and sat back down beside Mark.

"I have to figure out how to pay for my room at Kirkland House," I said and opened the lid to the bottle, taking a big drink. "Or find a room to rent. Oh, God, when Spencer finds out Graham lost my trust fund..."

Mark nodded. "Spencer's not likely going to step in and save the day."

"He couldn't afford to anyway," I said and imagined how much Spencer would freak when he learned what Graham did. Mark knew our family dynamics well enough from being Graham's business partner. "It's not like they have thousands lying around even if Spencer was willing to help, which he won't be."

Spencer was the new DA and while he had a nice income, he couldn't just pull up one hundred and fifty grand on short notice. He'd probably disown Graham when he found out what he did with our inheritances.

I shrugged, numb about what to do. "I can get a second job."

"And go to Harvard Law?" Mark said doubtfully. "Graham said

your scholarship was based on your grades. Can you keep them up and work two jobs?"

"Looks like I'll have to."

We sat in silence for a few moments.

"Loan sharks are dangerous, Celia. They'll kill Graham if he doesn't pay up," Mark said quietly. "Maybe you should go to Hunter."

"I know they're dangerous," I said and shook my head, although that was starting to seem like our only option. "He'd laugh in my face."

"I thought you and Hunter..." Mark said, his voice trailing off suggestively.

I turned and made a face at him. "You thought what?" but I knew what he meant. Hunter and I had a thing once upon a time. Or should I say, I had a thing for Hunter.

"You and Hunter hooked up. At least, that's what Graham told me. Spencer freaked." He raised his eyebrows.

"Graham should keep his mouth shut."

I frowned, remembering back almost four years to the one night – one amazing night – with Hunter before all hell broke loose between Spencer and me. Between Spencer and Graham.

I never saw Hunter again until his brother's funeral last year, and even then, I didn't say a word to him. He never once met my eyes when I stood off to the edge of the crowd gathered for Sean's funeral. I didn't have the guts to go up and give my condolences, so I only observed from afar. Even Graham didn't have the balls to go to his former best friend in person, sending a card instead.

Hunter hated us both.

"Hunter hates me for good reason."

"You broke his heart?"

I shook my head. "No," I said and made a face. "It's because of me that Spencer went after his family. Spencer's a nutcase, in case you didn't realize it. He had a vendetta against the Saints, and made them pay. It's because of Spencer that Sean died. It's because of Spencer that his uncle's in prison."

"I never met Spencer," Mark said and leaned back in his chair. "But Graham's told me a lot about him. And you."

"We're the family from hell," I said and drank down half my bottle of water. We had such a nice life before my father died. Then some drunk driver went down the wrong side of the freeway and hit my parent's car head on. My dad died and my mom was disabled. Spencer worked with my Dad and he just seemed to take over and my mom was so damaged physically and emotionally that she let him.

I looked at my bottle of water and wished it was something stronger. I needed a drink at that moment, but that would wait until I knew Graham was out of danger. Then, Amy and I would go out to a bar and get drunk.

"Well, I've got to get back to work," Mark said and stood up. "Tell Graham to take it really easy and not to worry about work. I've got things covered at the office."

I stood up and Mark gave me a brief and awkward hug. Then he left me alone with my worries.

I went to the nursing station once more to find out more about how Graham was doing.

"When can he go home?" I asked the doctor.

"We'll do another CT tomorrow and see how he is, but he's regained consciousness and seems to be okay in terms of his function. We'll know more tomorrow morning after the CT but you can expect he'll be in ICU for at least another twenty-four hours. Maybe on the neuro ward for a few days and then rehab."

"Thank you," I said and went back to my brother's side to start my vigil.

I spent the rest of the afternoon at Graham's side but when eight o'clock came around, I decided to go home. Graham had woken a couple of times during the afternoon, but he was sleepy and the pain meds they gave him made him doze with not much to say.

I kissed his unbroken cheek. "I'll be back tomorrow morning. You sleep now and get better, okay big brother?"

"Call Hunter," he whispered.

"I will," I said and squeezed his hand. "You sleep now."

He moved his head just slightly, enough to signal yes, and then he went back to sleep.

On my way out of the hospital, I texted Amy and she was there in twenty minutes to pick me up. I stopped in the cafeteria and picked up a bag of chips to eat for my dinner. Finally, Amy drove up.

"How's Graham?" she asked when I got inside the passenger seat.

I told her what happened, including the loss of my entire inheritance. She was suitably horrified.

"Oh, my God, Celia. As if Graham being beat up wasn't enough. What are you going to do?"

"I have no idea. I need to find one hundred and fifty grand, and fast."

"Jeeze," she said and we sat in silence for a moment. "Now what?" she asked as the car idled. "What do you want to do now?"

"Get drunk," I said, feeling like I could cry.

"My exact thoughts. Where to?"

"The Brass Lantern and quick," I said. I was exhausted but on edge at the same time. "I need a drink or three."

"The Brass Lantern it is," she replied and off we drove.

CHAPTER 4

Celia

I'D WORKED as a bartender part time for the past two years at the Brass Lantern, a pub that many Harvard students frequented, and it was my pub of choice when I was off work. I knew the entire crew and got drinks at a discount, so of course, given my new status as impoverished non-trust fund baby, I had to watch my pennies.

Amy and I slid onto stools at the bar and faced Dean, the bartender working that night.

"Hey, Celia," he said and smiled at me and Amy. "What can I get for you?"

"Margarita," I said. "Make it a double."

"Make that two," Amy said and nodded to Dean.

"Whoa," he said. "You two mean business. What's up? First week of law school got you down already?"

I shook my head and watched while Dean poured my drink. When he placed it in front of me, I took a long gulp. "Graham's in ICU."

"Oh, man, that's rough," Dean said. "What the hell happened? Car accident?"

I took another sip. "Bad business deal."

Dean made an alarmed face. "Oooh, that's not good. What happened? I thought he was a wizard with money. Doesn't he have this really hot investment startup?"

"Yeah, but let's just say he made a few bad investments and got into trouble."

"Sucks," Dean said. "Will he be okay?"

"They're keeping him in ICU overnight and then he'll be admitted to the neurology ward to watch him for a few days. He's going to need a lot of rehab."

"Well, you give him my regards."

I nodded and Dean went back to pouring drinks.

I turned to Amy. "What they hell am I going to do?"

"Go to Hunter," she said. "Graham's right. He's got lots of money."

"He's got lots of hate on for us, too," I said.

Amy shrugged. "What other choice do you have? Spencer will freak when he learns that Graham lost your money."

I shook my head. "Hunter hates us."

"Hunter had the hots for you. That's what Graham said."

"Hunter's a manslut," I replied, remembering Hunter from before. "He never has the same woman twice and he's never alone. The man must have slept with hundreds of women in his time. I was nothing but another piece of ass to him. Fresh, young and willing."

Amy took a sip of her drink. "Go to him," she said and sucked on the slice of lime. "Ask him for the money. Otherwise, those loan sharks will come back for Graham. And maybe you, too."

I had to admit she was right.

"Hey, Dean," I said. Dean came right over. "Do you need any relief bartenders? I need a second job."

"You know we're always short," he said. "Go look at the schedule and put yourself down for a few more shifts. We have openings and I've been pulling double shifts so it'd be great if you're available."

I nodded. At least I'd be able to pay for a rain coat in case I became homeless but even with extra shifts at the bar, there was no way I could scrape together enough money to afford to stay in Kirkland House, let alone pay for Graham's debt.

I had no idea how I could manage two jobs *and* Harvard Law at the same time... If I couldn't convince Hunter to lend Graham the money for the loan shark, I'd have to go to Spencer and that would be a nightmare.

I'd avoid that at all costs if I could.

THE NEXT MORNING, I went to Mass General first thing to check on Graham. He was better, and had a clean CT so they were going to transfer him to the neurology ward to watch him for a few days as soon as his bed opened. He was still sick enough that he was taking some version of morphine, but he had passed the night successfully without any regression and so the doctor was optimistic he would be discharged from the neuro ward to a rehab ward in a few days.

I spent the morning watching him sleep in the ICU while they got his room on the neurology ward ready, drinking coffee and reading over a few journal articles I brought along on case law for my law class in the afternoon. I felt good enough about Graham's progress that I could leave him in the hospital and go to class. It was a huge relief because I didn't want to get behind, but at the same time, I wanted to be sure Graham was on the mend before I left him alone.

He woke up close to noon and blinked several times, like he was trying to remember where he was.

"Hey, big brother," I said and leaned down to kiss his cheek. "How are you? You've been sleeping all morning."

"Hey," he managed through his gritted teeth. "Sorry."

"No worries." I smiled and squeezed his hand. "That's what I'm here for."

"Did you call Mom?"

I shook my head. "I was a good girl and obeyed your order not to. We should probably wait until we figure out the loan shark thing before I call. She's on the cruise and I don't want her to feel like they have to fly back or anything. If you weren't getting better, I would have called though."

He moved his head slightly to indicate agreement.

"Did you call Hunter?"

I sighed. "Not yet." I felt bad that I didn't contact him but it was the very last thing I wanted to do in life. "He won't want to talk to me, Graham. You're being too optimistic that he'll be willing to help."

"He has money," Graham managed. "He'll help. Call him."

I frowned, not wanting to deal with this. Of course, I had to deal with this. Soon. That '7 Days' carved into Graham's chest was a clear message.

"I'll try," I said. "But I doubt he'll agree to speak to me, considering what happened."

It wasn't just that I'd been mean to him four years earlier. It was that Spencer caused their family irreparable harm. The kind of harm you couldn't forgive.

Why would Hunter even consider speaking with me, let alone lending us the money we needed to pay back the loan shark?

"You really think Hunter will help you? After what Spencer did?"

"He will. Call him. Right away, Celia," he said, his voice full of urgency. "I'll be dead in less than a week if you don't."

"Do you really think they'll kill you? They'd never get any money from you if they do."

"They will," he said and his voice was starting to sound strained. I had to move closer to hear his voice. "They'll come after you for the insurance money. You're my beneficiary."

I sat back in my chair with a thud. "Oh, God. I never thought of that. Should I call police? Maybe they could protect us."

"No, don't bring the police into this. They think it's just a mugging."

"I really should call them," I said, all my instincts telling me to trust the police.

"No. The mob will kill me, Celia, no matter what you do. They'll get their money, one way or another. If I can't pay, killing me would solve their problems. Call Hunter. He'll help."

I could text Hunter if his cell was still the same. If he didn't answer, I could always go down to the gym and see if he was in the office. Worst case scenario? I'd have to go to the club he managed in person and confront him if he didn't answer my texts.

"Okay, but I hope you're right," I said, feeling sick to my stomach at the prospect of seeing Hunter again after everything that happened between us and our families.

But I loved my big brother. The reality of the situation with the loan shark was finally sinking in, now that I could see Graham would recover. I'd do anything to save his life.

"Please, Celia," Graham whispered through clenched teeth.

"I'll do it," I said and squeezed Graham's hand again. "I'll text him right away."

"Thank you," he replied and squeezed back. Then he went to sleep, as if the strain of talking about this was too much for him.

I didn't blame him. I felt this sense of doom hanging over me as well. Usually, my first instinct would be to call Spencer and the police. Maybe Graham was right — the mob would get their money no matter what I did.

I never thought about how Graham's actions could hurt me personally, other than seeing Graham harmed. I never thought they'd kill him. Most of all, I never imagined that I'd become their next target and that killing Graham might be the easiest way for them to get their money back.

I WENT to my criminal law class in the afternoon, but was quiet and didn't offer any comments or ask any questions. I was distracted by my situation and what I had to do. My professor must have noticed it because he asked me to stay behind as we began filing out.

A balding man in his sixties with half-eye glasses that perched on the end of his nose, Professor Markham looked like a kindly grandfather but he was a slave driver when it came to class participation.

"Ms. Parker," he said in a slightly annoyed voice. He stood behind the huge desk at the front of the lecture hall and looked me over when I stood in front of him. "You were silent today. Not your usual MO. Didn't you read the material? You know I expect full participation in this class from every student."

"I'm sorry,'" I said and exhaled. "My brother's in ICU at Mass General. I guess I'm distracted. I did read the material, but I'm afraid it didn't take."

He frowned. "Is he okay?"

I nodded. "He'll be discharged to a ward this afternoon, but he's got a bad concussion, broken bones, and internal injuries."

"Sorry to hear that. That's totally understandable. Car accident?"

I shook my head. "Mugged."

"Don't worry about the class," he said and waved his hand in dismissal. "Take some time off if you need it. Just contact your profs and let them know you have a family emergency."

"Thanks," I said but I stopped before leaving.

"Can I ask you a hypothetical question?"

He turned back and nodded. "Sure. Ask away."

"Say the mafia was trying to collect on an outstanding debt. Say someone went to a loan shark for money and couldn't pay the interest. Would you pay the debt and leave it at that, or would you go to the police? Could the police protect you?"

"That's more than one question," he said and smiled. "Is your brother in trouble?"

"No, I was just watching this old episode of Law and Order," I said, my cheeks hot with embarrassment.

"Hypothetically, if the cops felt they could use your case to get someone big in the organized crime hierarchy, they might spend the money to protect witnesses. If it was some low-life thug? Not so much. They can't afford to provide 24-hour protection for a witness unless it's a federal case. In that case, if the person could pay off the debt, they would be better off. If not, go to the police and hope they take it up to a higher authority, like the FBI or DEA."

"Thanks," I said and smiled. "My stepfather is DA. I probably should have asked him, but I was curious."

"Anytime," he said. "You interested in criminal law?"

I nodded. "My dad was a prosecutor."

"I knew him well," Professor Markham said. "From your grades, you're a chip off the old block."

"Thanks," I said. "I hope so."

Finally, he turned back to his files. I left the lecture hall, glad that I had asked him. Maybe Graham was right. Maybe it was better — *safer* — to go to Hunter than the police.

I was also glad I had a good enough reputation that I got the benefit of the doubt from Markham. I didn't plan on missing any more classes, but it was nice to know my profs would be understanding if I needed to.

I walked across campus to my dorm and when I got into my room, I sat down at my desk and looked at my cell, reluctant to contact Hunter, but resigned to doing so. I scanned my contacts and came upon Hunter's number. I remembered all our old texts and I regretted immensely that I'd broken it off when I did.

I called up his number and sent him a text. For all I knew, he had a new cell number and the text wouldn't go through.

CELIA: *Hunter, sorry to be contacting you, but I need to talk to you about Graham. Please reply or call me as soon as you get this.*

I sent the text and waited to see if it went through. Sure enough, it did and so I waited, hoping he'd reply right away.

Nothing.

I opened my binder and started reading through my notes for my first class the next morning, but my mind was distracted, wondering when Hunter would reply.

An hour passed, with me checking my cell every few moments, but Hunter either didn't check his messages or he decided to ignore me.

I couldn't blame him.

How he must hate me…

∼

AMY CAME OVER LATER for supper and we went to the cafeteria. We got our food and sat at a table, munching down our tacos and drinks, surrounded by the other students at Kirkland House.

"So, did Hunter reply to your text?"

I shook my head. "Nope. I didn't think he would. He must hate me. I'd hate me if I were him."

"He doesn't hate you," Amy said. "I'm sure if he knew what happened, he'd offer to help. You and Graham have known him forever, right? That has to count for something."

"You'd think," I said doubtfully. "But he didn't answer."

"What did you tell him?"

I shrugged. "Nothing. I just asked him to contact me and that I had something to talk to him about Graham."

"Tell him that Graham's in the hospital. He'll respond if you do that."

I nodded and took out my cell.

CELIA: Hunter, Graham's in the hospital. He was beaten up pretty badly. I need to talk to you about him. We need your help.

I showed Amy and she nodded. "He'll respond. He was Graham's best friend forever until Spencer butted in."

"Yeah, but can you forgive a family that's responsible for your brother's death? I don't think I could..."

"All you can do is try."

We ate the rest of our meal, with me worrying how I was going to get the money together. It was Hunter or Spencer.

Neither option was going to be easy...

I DECIDED to go to the hospital that night and see how Graham was doing on the new ward. He had his own room and was sleeping peacefully when I showed up. I sat on the chair beside his bed and waited for him to wake up. The room was tiny, but it had a window and the light from the setting sun were warm on my face. I checked my cell for Hunter's response but there was none.

Finally, Graham woke up and smiled as best he could when he saw me.

I stood and bent over to kiss him on the cheek. "Hey, there," I said and smiled back. "How are you feeling? You look much better. Except for the double black eyes and broken nose and jaw wired shut and head wrapped in bandage."

He smiled, his eyes amused. He must be feeling better. "I'm good. Did you talk to Hunter?"

I sat back down. "I texted him twice but no response."

"Go to the gym and see him."

"I will," I said and took his hand. "You don't worry about this. I'll go after I leave here. He must be still mad about everything and decided to ignore my texts."

He nodded slightly in response. "Don't blame him."

"Neither do I."

We visited for a while before I broached the police. "Did the police talk to you about this? Did you tell them why you were beat up?"

"They came in when you were gone. I told them I was mugged."

"You didn't tell them that you owned the loan shark money?"

He shook his head very slightly, his eyes narrowing. "Don't tell them anything about it. I could get into big trouble. Spencer will go nuts."

"But your life's in danger," I said in protest. "They might be able to protect you."

"No, Celia," Graham hissed through his teeth. "Don't talk to the police. Go to Hunter. He's the only one who can help me now."

I sat back in my chair, resigned to it. He was probably right. The police didn't dole out money to victims of extortion or exorbitant interest rates on loan shark loans. In their minds, Graham would be just a victim of crime who brought it on himself. They'd be more interested in finding the loan shark than protecting Graham. I doubted they'd post a guard on the ward outside Graham's room, no matter what.

"I'll go to the gym on my way home," I said and that seemed to satisfy Graham. He closed his eyes, and so I talked about my classes and how the semester was going while he listened.

When it was time for me to leave, I leaned over and kissed him on the cheek once more.

"Don't worry, big brother," I said softly. "I'll go to Hunter. Maybe if I get down on my knees, he'll help us out. It might make him feel good to see me grovel."

"I'm so sorry," Graham said, tears in his eyes. I had said it in a joking manner, but it must have hurt him. "I'm so sorry you're cleaning up my mess. I never meant any of this to happen…"

"Shh," I said and kissed his cheek once more. "I'll let you know how it goes. You get your sleep."

He nodded and I left him with his eyes closed, his head turned away from the door as if he couldn't bear to look me in the eye.

CHAPTER 5

CELIA

I LEFT the hospital and took a bus to South Boston where Saint Brothers Gym and Boxing Emporium was located. I hadn't been there for four years, and felt a pang of regret as I walked down the street to the building. Once upon a time, I went to the gym with Graham on a regular basis to watch Hunter, Sean and Conor boxing, and once upon a time, I went there with Hunter, hand in hand after a late night of talking. I'd been in love with Hunter all my life, and he was the one boy and then young man I dreamed of when I thought of having a boyfriend, falling in love and getting married.

Now, we were like sworn enemies and it hurt to realize how far apart Graham and I had become from Hunter.

I approached the entrance, a knot of anxiety in my gut over having to face Hunter – or worse, Hunter's dad. Spencer's vendetta against the Saint family had led directly to the arrest of Hunter's Uncle Donny. When the FBI came for him, Hunter's older brother Sean resisted, and he was shot by police.

Back then, I watched the news reports in horror and knew at that moment that my faint hopes of someday reuniting with Hunter were totally dead. There was no way he'd ever want to talk to me, let alone hook up again. Not after what happened to Sean.

I walked into the gym with a great deal of fear and reluctance, and almost turned away at the last minute, but Graham needed me to do this. I took in a deep breath and steeled myself for what might happen.

The gym was filled with young men and a few women working out on various pieces of equipment. A half dozen stood around the boxing ring watching a couple of fighters sparring. I looked around for Hunter, but didn't expect to find him in the gym itself. He was the business manager and so I went to the back, past the fitness equipment and boxing ring to where the office was located.

Down a long hall, past the washrooms, was the small, cramped office filled with old furniture. It was like a relic from the fifties. Not much had changed since the last time I had been in the office when I was a kid and Hunter and Graham were best friends. I spent so many afternoons at the gym once school got out and Graham was responsible for me until supper. So many Saturdays and Sundays Graham dragged me along to watch the two of them work out or spar. Even the smell of old leather and sweat was familiar and elicited a strong pang of melancholy and sadness that it had all gone so spectacularly wrong.

The office was empty. Not even Conor or Mr. Saint were there. I sighed, upset that I wouldn't get the chance to at least talk to Hunter. I saw a sticky note pad on the desk and decided to leave a message for him in case he came by later.

Hunter, I was here to speak with you.

Graham asked me to come by and talk to you.

He needs your help.

Please call or text me.

Celia

I left the sticky on the computer screen and then thought I should go upstairs where Hunter lived to see if he was there. I'd been upstairs only once four years earlier. It was a fantastic apartment above the gym, and had been renovated with the top of the line fixtures and furnishings. I'd spent most of the night in Hunter's bedroom, but had never gone back.

My memories of that night returned as I climbed the stairs to the floor, my heart in my throat at the prospect of seeing Hunter again. I hadn't talked with him since that fateful night that set all this in motion, although I did see him from a distance at the funeral for Sean.

What would he say if I showed up at his door?

I went to the apartment and stood at the front entrance, my heart racing. Behind the door, I heard laughter – a woman's soft high voice and then a man's low voice, deep, and amused.

Was it Hunter?

If it was him and not Conor, he was there with a woman.

I turned away and crept back down the stairs, for as much as I needed to speak with Hunter, there was no way on Earth I would dare interrupt him if he had a woman with him. Besides, I hated the idea that he was with someone else. There was still this silly part of me that would always be in love with him, no matter what.

I hated that part of me, but it was a part I couldn't deny.

I left the gym quickly, having not run into anyone who recognized me and gave a huge sigh of relief once I was outside. I was a coward after all, afraid to face Hunter.

He'd find my message and know I was there. He'd know it was serious so I hoped he'd call me the next day.

I took the bus home and flopped down on my tiny sofa once I was back inside my dorm room. On the coffee table were a half-dozen articles I needed to read for the next week, but my heart was just not into it.

I took out my cell and checked once more for any messages, but there was none so I wrote another text.

CELIA: Hunter, I really really need to speak with you. This is a life or death matter.

I hoped that would convince him to contact me. He understood life and death matters – probably better than most. He'd been a MMA fighter. After the blowup with Spencer, he'd joined the Marines. He'd become and officer and then seen combat. He'd seen his brother shot down by police...

There was no response by midnight when I finally threw down the last journal article and decided to call it a night.

I knew what I had to do.

I had to go to the club. Tomorrow was Saturday. I had to work at noon for four hours, and I had to see Graham, but Hunter spent Saturday nights at his uncle's club in South Boston, working as a night manager. I'd go to the club and confront him. Maybe if I showed up in person, he'd realize how serious this was and stop avoiding me.

I went to sleep with a sense of gloom. What if Hunter refused to help us?

Graham seemed so sure of his old best friend but I wasn't.

The feud between our two families reached back more than a decade. Even farther back because the two families had been on opposite sides of the law and were adversaries. I hoped that Graham's situation would soften Hunter's heart and convince him to help us.

We had four days before the loan shark would expect to be paid. I had to contact Hunter and soon or who knew what they'd do to Graham and then to me to collect their debt?

ON SATURDAY MORNING, I visited Graham before I went to work. He was feeling much better and was sitting up by the side of the bed briefly with a nurse at his side.

"You're getting him up already?" I asked, hoping that meant he was ready to come home. "Will he be coming home soon?"

"Not for a while," the nurse said and helped Graham lie back down. "He's still got a few days to go on the neuro ward. Once we get the catheter out, and he's able to walk around the ward a few times, the doctor will consider releasing him to the rehab wing. He had serious internal injuries and broken bones. He'll need extensive rehab."

I nodded and sat on the chair beside Graham. The nurse administered him a dose of pain meds and before I could talk to him, he dozed off in a morphine haze. I checked my cell to see if Hunter had finally responded, but nothing.

I had to go to the club and see if I could confront him.

Honestly, I didn't blame him that he refused to respond to me, but I had to talk to him.

I spent an hour with Graham, reading several articles in my book bag I'd brought so I could read while he slept. Then, I went to work and took a bartender shift over the lunch hour. Later in the afternoon, after I choked down a quick lunch at work, I went back to the hospital and sat with Graham until dinner when I went back to my dorm.

When I arrived back at Kirkland House, Amy popped in to see me. "Hey," she said. "How's big bro?"

"On the mend. Still catheterized so he's not being released to a rehab ward until it's out."

"Ow," she said and made a face. "That's gotta hurt. Poor bastard."

"I know. They bruised his kidneys and bladder, I guess."

"So, what's the plan?" she asked and plopped down on my bed. "You going to the club tonight?"

I nodded. "Yep. After supper. I'll go and see if Hunter's there. From what Graham told me, he's usually there on weekend nights, managing the club. I'll go early and try to see him."

"Do you want me to come along for moral support?"

I shook my head. "No," I said and sighed. "This is something I have to do myself."

"Okay, but if you change your mind..."

"I won't."

She and I had dinner together in the dining hall, and then I watched some television, working up the nerve to go to the club and confront Hunter. I had this low level of anxiety about seeing him. Scratch that – it was a high level of anxiety, and I felt a little sick to my stomach.

I could only imagine the look of hate on his boyishly beautiful face when he saw me – the outright contempt in his pale blue eyes. Eyes that once stared into mine during the most intimate moment of my life.

An intimacy I'd never been able to rekindle with anyone else since.

~

AT EIGHT, I popped into the washroom and brushed my teeth, fixed my hair and checked out my image in the mirror. My long dark hair was pulled back into a pony tail. I didn't wear makeup besides a bit of gloss. I wore my hoodie and jeans and my Blundstones.

I looked like an average college student and not a damsel in distress approaching the local hard-hearted head of an Irish mafia family for money to pay off loan sharks...

I still could barely believe that had become my reality.

I kept putting off going and decided to drop by Graham's hospital room before I went, just to give him a break from being alone all evening. He was watching television when I arrived and had this expectant expression in his eyes when I walked in.

"Did you talk to Hunter?" he asked through a clenched jaw.

I shook my head. "I thought I'd stop by and see my big bro first," I said and leaned down to kiss his cheek.

"Go tonight," he said. "He'll have to get the money. It might take time."

"I will," I said, my stomach lurching at the thought. "As soon as I leave."

That seemed to satisfy him and so I sat on the chair beside his bed and we watched the game on the tiny television for a while.

"What happens if Hunter won't give you the money?"

Graham turned his head and looked in my eyes. "Then we'll tell Spencer. But don't tell them until you talk to Hunter. I don't want to ruin their vacation for nothing. If he helps, I won't tell Spencer."

I kissed Graham's cheek. "Don't worry. I won't tell him either. We've all suffered enough shit from him."

I left him at nine and made my way from Mass General to *The Venue*, the music and dance club Hunter's Uncle Donny owned in the waterfront district. When Donny went to prison, Hunter took over and managed it. Located on Seaport Boulevard, it was just a block from the water in an old warehouse. In the center of the block, it dominated the street, and there was already a lineup to get inside even that early on a Saturday night. Things didn't usually get busy until after ten, but tonight was busier than normal.

I checked out the line and saw there was a bouncer at the door admitting people a couple at a time. I bypassed the line and went to him, hoping that if I dropped Hunter's name, he'd let me in ahead of other people.

"The line ends there." A big beefy guy with a shaved head and a business suit pointed to the end of the line with his pen. He appeared to be taking names or checking names off a list on a clipboard. "But you're not getting in dressed like that so go home, little girl."

I frowned. "I'm not here for the club. I'm here to see Hunter," I said, trying to display all the dignity I could muster.

"You and a dozen other hopefuls. Now go. Grow up a bit and come back when you know how to dress."

I checked out the people in line and saw they were all dressed up, the men in suits and the women in sexy dresses with high heels, their hair and makeup impeccable. By comparison, I appeared what I was – a college student with no social life and no clue what one even looked like.

"I'm a friend of Hunter's," I said. "He'll want to see me."

"What's your name?" the bouncer asked.

"Celia," I said. "Celia Parker." But I knew that my name wouldn't ring a bell with the bouncer.

He glanced over his clip board. "I checked my list, Celia Parker, and you're not on it, so get. Go home."

"Hunter will be mad when he hears you turned me away."

He laughed and checked me over. "I highly doubt that, little sister, but you dream on. Now, I have work to do, letting these very attractive people inside."

With that, he turned away and I saw smiles on the faces of those people at the front of the line.

I felt like a complete idiot. Of course, I didn't expect there would be a lineup this early. I thought I'd be able to just walk right into the club and go find Hunter in the back or wherever it was he spent his time.

I walked away, found a taxi driving down a side street, and took it back to my dorm in Cambridge.

I'd have to dress up if I wanted to see Hunter that night. I knew what I had to do. I had to call in the big guns.

CHAPTER 6

Celia

AMY GLANCED AT ME, her eyes narrowed. "I could have told you that you'd never get in looking like that," she said, her voice amused. "Look at you – faded boyfriend jeans, Blundstones, a grey hoodie? What were you thinking?"

"This is me," I said and shrugged. "This is who I am."

"Who you are is awesome, underneath that student getup. Now, let's look in your closet..."

She checked out my closet and took various skirts and blouses and shook her head sadly.

"When was the last time you went on a date?"

"Months ago, and you know it."

She laughed. "I do know it."

My romantic life was dismal, so I didn't have a lot of sexy numbers that I could wear to *The Venue* to impress the very discerning bouncer at the front door.

"You can borrow my red dress," she said and pulled me into her room. "With your black hair and fair skin, you'll be a knockout." She

43

opened her wardrobe and removed this red dress with deep plunging neckline that fell just above the knee. "Wear these shoes and put on some eyeliner, you'll have Hunter eating out of your hand."

"Hardly," I said with a grim laugh. "Remember it's me asking for money from him. If anything, it'll be me eating out of his hand."

I changed clothes and then sat in front of her desk while she brushed my hair and straightened it with a flat iron until it was shining.

When she was finished, she stood behind me so that I could see myself in the mirror over her desk. "Your hair looks like black silk."

Then, she proceeded to paint me up so that I was practically unrecognizable.

"Kitten eyes are all the rage. That stupid bouncer won't be able to resist you now." I checked myself out in the mirror and sure enough, I looked like someone else.

Someone who fit in with the rest of the crowd at *The Venue*.

I slipped on Amy's black pumps with the straps around the ankles and turned in a circle for her.

"Perfect," she said. "When Hunter sees you, he'll realize what he lost back then."

I shook my head. "He'll hate me. He'll look at me with total contempt. I can see him now." The very thought of it made my stomach churn.

"I'm coming with you," Amy said. Then, she proceeded to get dressed herself in something hot – a black dress that looked great against her blonde hair. She applied her makeup quickly like a pro, and within half an hour, we were out the door and into her little Austin on our way to the waterfront where I would once again try to get past the bouncer.

By the time we got there, the lineup was even longer than before and so Amy and I stood at the end and talked while we waited for the line to move. It was slow going. The place was popular and was one of the in-spots on a weekend night.

The weather was warm and the sounds coming from the depths of the club made my heart rate increase. What would Hunter think when he saw me? Would he even be there or would this be a total waste of time?

By the time we got to the front of the line, the bouncer looked us over and motioned inside with his jaw. He didn't recognize me, and I was happy I took Amy's advice and changed clothes.

We entered the building and made our way past the cashier where we paid the cover charge and then went inside. The EDM was blaring, the fog machines were pumping out the fog on the dance floor and laser lights bounced off the walls.

Amy turned to me, a frown on her face. "You look like you've seen a ghost.

I hadn't seen a ghost.

I'd seen Hunter.

Hunter Saint. The middle brother of three. The Fighting Irish Saint Brothers, they were called by those in the business.

All six feet four inches of gorgeous Hunter Saint.

There he sat on a sofa on a raised dais in the rear of the huge room. He leaned back, his arms on the back of the sofa, his legs spread, surveying the club like he owned the world. Beside him sat an equally well-dressed man leaning forward, his elbows resting on his knees. He was speaking to Hunter and Hunter nodded occasionally, lifting a glass of some beverage to his mouth every now and then. On the sofa beside Hunter sat a beautiful blonde and her friend, who were leaning close and talking to each other.

She must be Hunter's most current fuckbuddy. Despite everything, a surge of jealousy filled me.

Hunter looked just as drop-dead hunky as the last time I saw him. His hair was a bit longer, but there was nothing that could disguise that fair skin, pale blue eyes with thick lashes and chiseled features. Impossibly handsome with a touch of boyish beauty that made my heart skip a beat.

Pretty Boy Saint was his nickname when he fought in the MMA circuit when he was younger, before he finished his MBA and joined the Marines.

The last time I saw him at the funeral for Sean, Hunter was still in the Marines and had his hair buzzed so short on the sides you could see his scalp. Whitewalls the Marines called it. Now, his hair was longer, below his collar, tucked behind his ears. He looked like what he was – a wealthy owner of a mobbed-up business in South Boston.

When I last saw him, he was on leave for the funeral, and still had that upright straight and narrow look to him like the red-blooded American hero that he was. Soon after the funeral, Hunter got out of the Marines on compassionate grounds to take over the business in Sean's place. Mr. Saint, their father, had suffered a heart attack a few years earlier and Sean had been the manager instead of him, but with Sean dead, Hunter had to step in.

Conor was no manager and was busy with the Olympic boxing circuit, so it was left to Hunter to take over.

I knew how much Hunter must have hated that. He had wanted to take the family business out of the bad influences in Boston – the family mafia ties in other words.

Now, he was in the middle of it.

It had been over a year since Sean died and I wondered how things had gone for Hunter and his dream to make his family's business completely legit. I doubted much had happened to change that, but I knew that was Hunter's eventual goal. According to Spencer, the Saints were still involved in money laundering for the Russian mob, and were still tied into the protection racket.

Hunter never wanted that for himself.

What a nightmare...

Now, I was supposed to go up to him with all that between us, and ask him for one hundred and fifty thousand dollars to save my brother's – and possibly my life.

"I need a drink," I said and turned to Amy. "Preferably a double."

"Coming right up," she said and pulled me over to the bar.

"Two Margaritas, doubles," she said to the bartender.

"Two Margaritas coming up, doubles for the pretty ladies," the bartender said, winking at me. We watched him pour the drinks and then place them on the bar for us. I took mine and drank half of it down in one gulp.

"Hey," Amy said, laughing. "Slow down. We have time."

"I need liquid courage."

"Relax," she said and took a sip. "He'll see you in that dress and be like putty in your hands."

"Hardly. More like he'll have me kicked out of the place."

"You're crazy," she replied, but she didn't sound so sure.

We turned to watch the dance floor, which was cramped with dozens of dancers pressed together, writhing to the music.

I finished the rest of my drink and took in a deep breath.

"Wish me luck," I said and put my empty glass down. "I have to go and face the music."

"Do you want me to come?" she asked, being the helpful friend she always was.

"No, you stay here." I squeezed her arm. "I have to do this alone."

I left her at the bar and walked over to the back of the club where Hunter was sitting. As soon as I got within ten feet of the dais, two big burly men approached me and stopped me from getting any closer.

"Can I help you?" one of them asked, his arms crossed. The two of them standing there was like a wall had suddenly materialized between me and Hunter.

Big Bodyguard Number One was dressed in a tight-fitting grey suit that strained at his huge muscles. His hair was buzzed short and he looked like a military guy stuffed into a suit. He even had a microphone in his ear, the coil reaching back behind his ear and down his neck beneath his jacket. The other bodyguard was similarly dressed but had a shaved head and glasses.

Did Hunter need bodyguards?

"I want to speak with Hunter," I said. "I'm an old friend."

The man checked me out, his eyes roving up and down my body from my feet to my chest and back.

"Hunter has a lot of lady friends," the man said dryly. "In fact, he's with one right now. I need a name or you're not going anywhere except out of the club."

"Tell him it's Celia," I said. "He'll know me."

The man turned to the other man. "Do you know of any Celia?"

47

The other man shook his head.

Bodyguard One turned back to me. "You'll have to do better than that. I've never heard Mr. Saint mention anyone named Celia."

"He wouldn't, but we go back a long way. Tell him Celia's here and needs to speak with him about her brother. Like I say, he'll know who I am."

The man finally nodded and turned back to the dais. The other bodyguard stepped in front where he had stood and blocked my view of Hunter and his guests. I peered around his massive frame and watched while Bodyguard One went up to the dais and bent down to speak with Hunter.

Immediately, Hunter turned to where we stood and frowned. He saw me. I know he did. Then, he turned away.

Just like I knew he would.

He said something and Mr. Bodyguard One turned back and returned to where I stood again.

"Mr. Saint's busy at the moment," he said officiously. "You can contact his personal assistant Amanda at the gym if you have any business to discuss."

I sighed. "Please tell Mr. Saint that it's not about me. It's about my brother. Tell him we need his help."

Mr. Bodyguard Number Two crossed his arms so I had two of them standing in front of me.

"In case you didn't understand," he said, his voice low and menacing. "Mr. Saint is not interested in what you have to say. Please leave or we'll have to escort you out of the facility."

I skipped around them both before they could respond, and practically ran up to the dais.

"Hunter!" I called out, but before I could reach the stairs, Mr. Bodyguard One had me in a bear hug.

"Jesus *Christ*," I heard Hunter mutter. He finally glanced in my direction and saw me standing there, my arms held back behind me by Mr. Bodyguard One. Hunter's expression was icy.

Full of hatred.

"Sorry, Mr. Saint," Bodyguard Two said when he reached Hunter.

Hunter stood and buttoned his suit jacket. He took in a visible breath as if he was trying to control his anger and then said something to the blonde woman, who turned to glance at me, a frown on her pretty face.

Then, he walked casually over to me.

He gave me a cold stare, his eyes moving over my body and finally resting on my face. I was totally upset by then, my breathing heavy, and I felt close to tears. I was sure my face was beet red from embarrassment, but I had to talk to him.

"Hunter, I need to *talk* to you," I managed, trying to meet his eyes but he seemed intent on avoiding mine. "It's about Graham."

"What makes you think I care about anything to do with you and your family?" he said, his voice steely.

"Graham asked me to come and speak with you," I said, not wanting to reveal everything in front of the two bodyguards. "Can we go somewhere private?"

"Graham thinks he can send you to me like some kind of peace offering?" Hunter said, his blue eyes half-hooded. "I'm not biting. Now, I'm busy." He motioned to the bodyguard who still held my arms. "Take her outside."

"Hunter, please!" I said, my voice finally breaking, tears springing to my eyes. "Graham's in the hospital. I need to talk to you in private."

He turned back and finally met my eyes – really looked in them for a change.

God, he was beautiful. His jaw so square, a tiny cleft in his chin, straight nose despite fighting for years, light blue eyes and thick eyelashes. His golden-brown hair was longish and fell onto his cheek and down behind his neck.

He gestured to the bodyguard with his chin. "Let her go," he said. Then, he turned to the back of the building and started walking. "Follow me," was all he said.

I straightened my dress and followed him, barely able to keep up due to my high heels and ineptitude in walking while wearing them. Hunter went through a door to the back, past a kitchen filled with chefs and cooks in white uniforms who were busy pumping out appetizers. People nodded to Hunter as he passed, showing deference to the boss. They looked at me with curiosity.

We went farther back into the bowels of the building, down a long dim hallway to the business office.

"Hunter, I'm sorry to bother you but--."

He held out his hand to stop me from talking. When he opened a door to a darkened room, I was a little afraid to follow him in. I stood just outside the door and peered in, watching as he went to a desk and turned on a banker's lamp, the brass shade casting a dim glow over the room.

"For God's sake, come inside," he said and came back to the door, grabbed my arm, pulling me in.

He was angry. I could see it in his face. Usually beautiful, his light blue eyes were now dark with anger. He was still the most desirable man I had ever seen.

In that moment, as we stood only inches from each other, his face shoved next to mine, I remembered another night when he'd been even closer. A night when his expression had been one of pleasure and affection, instead of contempt and hatred.

My breath caught in my throat, and tears sprang to my eyes.

"Quit with the tears," he said dryly. "I'm not moved by tears. I don't care if Graham's dying. Why would I care? My brother died right in front of my fucking eyes, Celia, or did you forget that little fact?"

"I could never forget," I said, my voice breaking. "I'm so sorry..."

I covered my face with my hands and sobbed for a moment, and he did nothing and said nothing. I was so overwhelmed with emotion, fear for Graham and fear for myself, guilt for how I treated Hunter years ago and for Spencer's role in Sean's death, and fear of Hunter's wrath...

I wiped my cheeks and watched him. He slipped his hands in his pockets and glanced away, not looking at me, a muscle in his jaw pulsing.

"Hunter borrowed money from a loan shark to pay back my inheritance that he lost on a bad investment. He thought he could turn it around and pay me back and the loan shark, but he couldn't and they

50

beat him up," I said, the whole story pouring out of me between sobs. "They broke his nose, broke his jaw, broke his leg, and punched out his teeth. He has internal injuries and a serious concussion and will be in rehab for weeks. They carved 7 Days on his chest with a knife and said if he didn't pay the money back by Wednesday night, they'd kill him. Then, they'll come after me for his insurance money."

"Oh, yeah?" Hunter said and tapped his foot, not looking at me. "That's what happens when you invest money that you can't afford to lose. I thought Graham was smarter than that. I guess not."

"Look, I didn't *want* to come to you," I said, frustrated that he was so uncaring, "but Graham insisted that you were the only one who could help."

"Yeah," he said, and turned to look in the other direction, his breathing faster now, like he was close to losing it. "It must have been hard for you to come to me and ask for help. You couldn't get me out of your life fast enough. Funny, but I thought there was always something special between us. I guess I was a huge fool."

"Hunter, it wasn't like that," I said, but of course, that's what he would think. I intended for him to think that about me and about what happened between us.

I had to.

"I wish you could understand…"

Hunter didn't say anything for a moment, like he was considering whether to help Graham or not.

"Who does he owe money to?" he asked finally.

"Some guy named Stepan," I said, repeating the name Graham had given me. The fact Hunter was even asking gave me a glimmer of hope that he'd help. "That's all I know."

"Stepan, huh?" Hunter said and smiled grimly. "You don't mess with the Russians. They mean business."

We stood in silence for a moment and I tried to gain control over my emotions.

Finally, he spoke again, his voice tired. "I know the Russians. If you don't give them the money by Wednesday, Graham will be dead. You can count on that."

Then he turned to leave and I stood alone in the room.

I followed him to the door. "You're just going to let them kill Graham?" I said, unable to believe he'd be so callous.

He stopped at the door, his hand on the knob. He turned to look me in the eye.

"Tell me, Celia," he said and tilted his head to the side. "Why should I help?"

I went to his side and looked up into his face, into his eyes, which were cold, guarded.

"Because you and Graham were best friends all your life. From the time you were in middle school and all through college. You were going to go into business together."

He was quiet for a moment, his gaze moving over my face.

"You might think that would count for something," Hunter said softly. "You might think that would mean he stood by me when I needed him. Instead, he went into business with someone else. He did nothing to stop Spencer from going after my uncle. Sean *died*, Celia," he said, his face red, his jaw clenched. "Sean's dead because of Spencer. Maybe if Graham dies, Spencer will know how it feels to lose someone."

He turned and walked away. Before he got too far, I replied, my voice breaking.

"Yes, he died because of Spencer," I said, my eyes filled with tears once more. I followed him down the hallway. "Not because of Graham! You *know* Spencer," I said and grabbed hold of Hunter's arm. "You know what he was like with us. With me. There was nothing either of us could do."

Hunter pulled his arm away like he couldn't stand my touch. I covered my eyes once more.

"Graham should have thought about the cost before he went to the Russians," he said finally. "He should have come to *me* if he needed money."

"How could he?" I said, wiping my eyes, which had now become smeared with the silly eyeliner Amy had applied to make me kittenish.

I was sure I looked more like a raccoon by then. "He knew you blamed him for what happened to Sean."

"I don't blame him," Hunter said quietly. "But he turned his back on me when I wanted to go into business with him. *You* threw me away like I was a bad apple when there were so many other fresh shiny ones to eat."

"I didn't do that," I said, but of course, that's what he would think. How could I explain?

I got down on my knees, unashamed to be begging. "Will you help Graham?" I asked, my hands folded in prayer. "Please!"

He turned to me, his blue eyes dark with emotion. He didn't tell me to get up. He didn't come to me and take my hand, make me stand.

"Tell me why I should, Celia," he said, his voice soft. "What do I get out of this?" He stared at me, waiting, his hands on his hips.

At that moment, I would have done anything for him if he helped save Graham's life.

"I'll do anything you want, Hunter," I said, my voice breaking. "Anything. Name it and I'll do it."

He'd know what that meant.

He shook his head. "What can you do for me that I can't get from any number of other women?" he asked, his eyes moving over me as I knelt before him. "Women who'd enjoy it, not hate every minute."

Of course, he was right. He was so gorgeous, he could get any woman he wanted. Gorgeous and rich. And powerful in South Boston. I was a first-year law student. I was going to be a pauper even if Hunter paid back the money for Graham. I'd have to work two jobs to afford my dorm...

"Anything," I said, my eyes filled with tears.

He took in a deep breath. Finally, he exhaled. "I'll pay the debt," he said softly. "As for your offer, I'll consider my options. How much does he owe?"

"One hundred and fifty thousand."

Hunter whistled. "That's a lot of high priced call girl services, Celia." His eyes narrowed. "At five hundred a pop, that works out to..." he said and smiled, icily. "Three hundred hours of being my fuck toy."

My traitorous body warmed at that. Was he *really* going to make me fuck him as payback? Not that I would mind, because I remembered him. *God,* I remembered him...

I remembered his beautiful naked body, his deep and passionate kisses, his skill, but I knew it would be hate fucking on his part.

"Are you really going to hate fuck me in payment?" I said, throwing caution to the wind.

He bit his bottom lip. "Hate fucks are pretty good, Celia. You should know. Isn't that what you did to me?"

"No!" I said, my fists clenching. "That was never what happened between us. Why would you even think that? "

"Graham gave me that idea." Hunter met my eyes. "He told me you wanted Greg, not me, but I was easier. As soon as you got Greg, you threw me away like trash."

"No, *no*," I said. "That's not true. I never—"

"Stop," he said and chopped his hand down. "It doesn't matter anyway so no more lies."

He started walking down the hall once more. On my part, I struggled up onto my feet, my knees killing me from the hard floor.

"I'll contact Stepan and pay the debt. As for you," he said and opened the door back into the club. "I'll think of what I want from you, if anything. But you better make it worth my while."

I went through the door and Hunter passed me. He stopped when he got to the dais and turned to me.

"You should go home, Celia. Your makeup's all messed up and I'm sure one of your frat boys is waiting for you. We'll be in touch. You can count on that."

Then he went back up to the sofas where his woman and the other man he had been sitting with were waiting. As I watched, Hunter bent down and kissed the blonde woman on the mouth, lingering there for a long while, like he wanted to show me that he was with someone else.

I turned away and walked back to the bar where Amy was waiting.

"Celia," she said, her eyes wide. "Your makeup..."

"I know," I said, on the verge of tears once more. "Let's get the hell out of here."

I led the way and Amy followed me. When we reached the car, Amy stopped me and grabbed my arm.

"Don't keep me hanging, Celia. Did he agree to help or what?"

I nodded. "I got down on my knees and begged. He's paying Graham's debt," I said and plopped into the passenger side. I slammed the door and leaned back, my head against the headrest.

"You got on your knees? Tell me," she said when she got in the driver's side. "What did he do? What did he say?"

"I think he said I had to be his high class call girl to pay off the debt. His sex toy or something. Three hundred hours of services."

"What?" she said, her mouth open. "You're kidding, right?"

I shook my head. "I don't think so. Maybe he was joking, but he seemed serious."

"Oh, my *God*," she said, facing forward, like she was imagining it. "He's really really hot and all, but still… You're going to be his sex toy?"

We sat in silence for a moment as it sunk in. "How can that be good?" she asked finally, turning to me. "I mean, if you hate someone, how can it be enjoyable?"

I shrugged. "He said hate fucking was actually pretty good."

"I can't believe it," she said, her mouth open.

Then, out of the blue, she laughed. When she looked at me, she covered her mouth.

"I'm so sorry, but I can't help it."

"Amy! It's not funny…"

"I know," she said and laughed even harder. Her laughter was infectious and soon, despite everything, or maybe because of it, I laughed out loud as well.

"Oh, my God, Amy… I'm going to be a fuck toy."

"That's a first," she said. "He's seriously hot, though. I'd do him."

"Every woman would do him," I said sardonically. "Probably most our age already have."

"Not me," she said and we laughed even harder. Then, to my

surprise, my laughter turned to tears and I sobbed out loud. The relief that Hunter was going to pay back Graham's debt, and the loan sharks and his 'goodfella' hitmen weren't going to kill Graham, finally hit home.

I covered my eyes and cried, the remnants of my makeup smeared on my cheeks and hands.

I wouldn't have my inheritance and would still have to work my butt off to afford to continue in law school, and I'd have to service Hunter like some call girl, but Graham would be alive.

CHAPTER 7

Five Years Earlier

Hunter

Saint's Gym sat between two old warehouses in Boston's historic district. It had been in our family for almost a hundred years, ever since my great-grandfather immigrated from Ireland and established his family there.

Both my father and grandfather were boxers. My great-grandfather started the gym and my father had a run at the middleweight championship decades earlier, but had to withdraw due to an injury. My older brother Sean had been a boxer and MMA fighter, but had a traumatic brain injury and had to stop fighting. Now, he managed the gym but he was really a caretaker, unable to really handle running the business. My younger brother was a boxer and Olympic hopeful.

Some Irish families sent their boys to seminary to become priests. My family sent us to the ring to become fighters. Our family was known as the Fighting Irish Saints. We fought our hearts out, scrappy, dedicating our lives to the pugilistic art.

That was the story, anyway.

The real story was that we'd been fighting for generations to keep out of the organized crime world, but had mostly failed—even more so under my Uncle Donny's leadership, or lack thereof. He laundered money and collected protection money for the Russian mob to keep them from burning down the business. My brother Sean provided muscle for the Romanov family, breaking legs and arms or whatever body part the family needed to get the money they were owed.

I refused to become involved. The exception to the family rule, I'd given up boxing and the family business after my grandfather burned to death in a crash outside of Boston—a suspicious single vehicle rollover and fire which my father claimed was the result of his mob ties. As a sixteen-year-old at my grandfather's funeral, I decided I would go clean and extricate myself from my family's business and influence.

After receiving an MBA from Harvard, I planned on starting a business with my best friend Graham. If all else failed, I'd join the Marines like my mom's father – the side of our family that wasn't tied to the mob. The side I wanted to emulate.

That weekend, I felt good about my life. It was Saturday and I'd been out surfing and when I arrived back at the beach outside our family house on Cape Ann, a considerable crowd of my friends from Harvard had arrived. It was the last week before we closed the beach cottage and I wanted to party hard.

When I saw Celia, I thought once again how hot she had become – so different from the skinny girl with braces and glasses who grew up before my eyes into a stunner.

Greg, one of my friends from Harvard Business, sat beside me at the makeshift beach bar. I'd pulled out all the stops for this final party before we closed the cottage down for the fall. I'd hired a bartender and had several kegs of beer brought in, several fire pits built, and a music system set up so we could party all night long.

Greg wolf-whistled when he saw Celia.

"Man, is she hot or what?" Greg said, turning to where she stood—a knockout brunette with dark doe eyes and a body that just wouldn't stop.

"She sure grew up. Girl's got it going on."

"And," I said, "she's officially off-limits."

"*Crap.*" Greg said, resignation in his tone. "Life's not fair."

Graham and Celia were regular fixtures at the gym when she was growing up. I'd treated her as my own kid sister, never expecting that she'd grow up to become a regular participant in my fantasies.

"She used to be skinny as a rake and had these thick glasses and braces."

"She's not skinny anymore," Greg replied. "She's built. Baby's got front *and* back."

I glanced around and surveyed the several dozen friends who were on the beach. Of all the women at the beach party, Celia was the one I wanted. The one I would pick, given the choice. Which I usually was.

I never wanted what I could have. It was always the one just out of reach.

That was the story of my family's life. We always bit off more than we could chew. Ambition and pride pushed us to achieve, but at a cost. I didn't want to think about any of my family's seedier connections, so I pushed it all out of my mind.

We watched as Celia ran out into the surf wearing her wetsuit and carrying her board. She caught wave after wave like a pro. Graham taught her well. He'd been a serious surfer who surfed every weekend during the summers. Until I was sixteen, I'd spent my summers boxing in the amateur MMA circuit, so I hadn't been part of Graham's life except during the school year.

I'd lost touch with Celia when she went away to boarding school, but the three of us reunited at Harvard when Celia started her freshman year and Graham and I were finishing up our last year of our MBAs. She was still Graham's kid sister and so she was untouchable.

Which was pure hell, because that was all I could think of when we were together.

When Celia finished surfing about half an hour later, Greg and I watched as she returned to the beach chairs where the party was being held and removed her wetsuit.

"She's seriously hot," Greg said once more, his voice appreciative. "Like, get her drunk and party hard hot."

My back stiffened.

Greg wasn't the kind of man I wanted to hit on Celia. Although I was also mentally fucking her—and very guiltily, I might add—I didn't like the thought that a manslut like Greg was ogling her. Or should I say, *another* manslut.

I knew what I was.

I shook my head and took a sorrowful sip of my beer. "She's officially off-limits, in case you're too dull to realize it."

"What?" Greg turned to me. "She's all grown up, and very nicely."

"She's not on the market."

Greg frowned. "Graham said she's starting her sophomore year at Harvard. Isn't she nineteen?"

"I think so," I said, remembering something Graham had said the previous week. "Just turned."

"She spent four years at some Catholic boarding school upstate. Think of all the pent-up lust she must have."

"She's a nice kid, Greg, not some plaything. Graham wouldn't approve of you making any moves on her."

"Graham should back the fuck off, man. She's ready to go. I might go over and buy her a drink. In fact," Greg said, giving me a telling leer, "that's exactly what I'm going to do."

I stood, my hand on his shoulder. "She's off-limits."

He glanced at my hand. At almost a foot taller than Greg, I towered over him. While he spent most of his down time in bars playing the field, I spent a lot of mine in my family's gym. I could take him easily and he knew it. I hoped it wouldn't come to that, but I would if I had to.

"Oh, man," Greg said. "Cockblocker is *so* not a good look on you, Hunter. You're supposed to be my wingman. What the fuck?"

"It's Graham's little sister. She's not only sweet, she's brilliant and she's *not* fresh meat."

"You know, those words sound really strange coming from your lips." Greg took a long swig from his beer. "Graham's going to be gone tomorrow, and you're going to be gone, but I'm still at Harvard for another year, so..."

I straightened to my full height and glowered at Greg. He'd seen me in the ring before. He knew the damage I could do—and how fast I could do it. I was built and strong and he knew it.

"You won't touch her." I stuck my finger in his face. "And if you hadn't screwed around all the time instead of studying, you'd be graduating with Graham and me instead of repeating a year."

"Jeez. What are you, my dad? Chill, okay? I'll leave her alone. I'm not a rapist or anything."

"There are lots of fish in the sea." I motioned to the array of beautiful young women on the beach. "Take your pick but leave Celia out of it. I'm serious. She's not fair game."

Greg glanced around and appeared to consider.

"Later, bro." He punched me lightly on the arm and left me sitting at the beach bar.

Alone again, I turned around on the bar stool and considered Celia, who was towel-drying her long dark hair. She was officially nineteen, so by all rights she was a full-grown woman and could do whatever—or whomever—she wanted, but she wasn't a party girl. I knew that much from what Graham had told me about her over the years. Serious by nature, Celia was a bookworm who planned on studying criminal law at Harvard, following in her dead father's footsteps.

Her stepfather Spencer had practically kept her under lock and key during high school, and I could see why. She was a beauty. I hated to see my former frat brothers hitting on her, knowing how persistent they could be.

I turned back to my beer and considered my upcoming schedule. My father wanted me to stay in Boston and work with him, but I'd be drawn into the worst part of the business no matter what I did—organized crime. My father had intended to take the business legit, but he'd failed.

Graham and I were talking about starting a business together but I wasn't sure things would work out. Spencer hated me and my family. As the Assistant DA, he had a pretty good idea about us, but I wanted to be completely legitimate and not use any of my family's dirty money.

That had to count for something.

If things didn't work out with Graham, I'd sign up with the Marines like my grandfather on my mother's side.

No matter what choice I made, I couldn't have Celia anyway. While I was musing on the fact that I'd never have Graham's beautiful little sister, he sat down beside me at the beach bar.

"So, any news on your decision?" He grabbed a beer from the bartender. "You going to stick with your dad? I know he wants you to help Sean run things."

I frowned. "What about Innova?" I asked, mentioning the name Graham and I settled on for the business we were going to start together.

"You know what a hardass Spencer is." Graham took a drink. "I don't know if I can do it. Besides, it'll be hard for your dad not having you to help with the business."

I said nothing for a moment, too shocked at Graham's suggestion that we might not go into business together. I'd already filed papers to check for our business name but maybe I'd been wrong about Graham's commitment to our vision for an investment start-up...

He knew I didn't want to get mixed up with my father's business. I'd often complained about the business dealings that were bordering on criminal – or outright criminal – that he couldn't seem to escape.

"You're getting cold feet," I said softly.

"Nothing's been decided yet, but it's hard for me to come up with money."

"I thought you had your trust fund," I reminded him. We were going to use it as half our nest egg to start the business. I'd provide the rest.

"There are complications," he replied. "That's all I can say for now. You can still go on your own even if I can't join you right away. Besides, you said you might join the Marines if things didn't work out."

"I thought it was a sure thing," I replied, trying not to sound as disappointed as I was.

"Your dad needs you," Graham said. "Sean really has no mind for business. What happened to the old *I'll clean up the business* plan you had?"

"It worked out really well for Michael Corleone," I replied dryly, referencing the Godfather movie Graham and I had watched when we were kids.

"If you got involved," he added like it was a done-deal, "You could clean things up. Take the business legit. Cut ties with your uncle. Extricate the business from the mob."

I raised my eyebrows at him. "They don't tend to like it when you stop paying them protection money. I think my father understands my decision to start a business not at all tied to the gym, even if he's upset."

Graham made a face. "Go into the Marines, then. I'll miss you but we all have to move on, right?"

I drank down my beer and placed the empty bottle on the bar. "I may do that."

"Your dad will be upset if you do, but you gotta be your own man, Hunter," Graham said, and took a long swig of his beer. "Do you think Sean can manage?"

"I don't know," I said, and shrugged. "That's the one thing that's stopping me. He's distracted."

"Too many knock-outs." Graham shook his head. "Good thing you stopped fighting when you did or you'd be a lot uglier than you already are."

I laughed at that, despite the sick feeling in my gut that Graham was pulling out on me. I was called Pretty Boy Saint when I was— briefly—in the local MMA circuit. For whatever reason, I'd managed to avoid the kind of disfigurement other fighters suffered—

cauliflower ears, broken and bent noses, busted swollen lips like Sean and Conor. I had my share of scars from kicks and punches, but my bones had all remained intact.

"I see Celia is with you," I said, keeping my tone level. I had planned to tell him Greg was talking about hitting on her, but Graham interrupted me.

"Speaking of which, stay away from her." Graham turned to me, catching my eye, an accusing expression on his face.

I frowned, a jolt of adrenaline surging through me. "Like you really need to even say that."

"I know what a dog you are. Just keep away, okay? Spencer would love an excuse to come after your family. Believe me, any excuse. If you even touch Celia, you're going down."

I glanced away, hurt by his words. "I thought you'd ask me to look out for her."

"What am I? A fool?" he said, laughing. "I know you better than anyone."

"Then you should know I've never laid a hand on Celia and never would."

"Keep it that way."

We sat in an awkward silence, and I was at a loss for what to say.

Sure, I was a notorious bachelor, and hadn't dated seriously since I'd entered the MBA program. I'd tried love, but found it to be untrustworthy. You give your heart to someone, tell them your secrets, your fears, and they up and leave you for your frat brother.

I grabbed another beer and took a long drink, needing the warmth to wash away the anger and hurt Graham's words brought out. Not only had he given me a not-so-subtle hint that we wouldn't be going into business together, he was warning me off his little sister.

Like I was planning on banging Celia...

Yes, I'd imagined it. Practically every time I saw her I imagined it, but I would never hit on Celia even though she'd grown up to be this beautiful sexy woman.

I wouldn't touch her. I knew how her family felt about me and mine.

THE BAD BOY SERIES COLLECTION

"You're a hound," Graham said. "You can't deny that, even if you're my friend. Keep away." Graham stood up from the beach bar. "I'm going up the coast with a few guys to catch some bigger waves. Greg's going to watch over Celia for me."

"Greg?" My jaw dropped in shock. "He's as big a hound dog as I am. He's already said he wanted to hook up with her."

"He was just testing you. See what you said. I'm warning you: Stay away."

"Don't worry about me." I gripped my beer. "I'm not in the market for the girl next door."

"I'm counting on that," Graham said and held my gaze. "She's not that kind of girl, Hunter, and you know it."

I waved him off and he finally left me alone, carrying his board to his Jeep. I sat there fuming and thinking about Graham's stepfather. He had ample reason to dislike my family, and avoided being connected too closely with any of us despite my long friendship with Graham. Guilt by association and all. One day, I'd find a way to take the business totally legit, free from any association with my uncle and his wise-guy friends.

Still, it hurt that Graham felt he had to even say anything about Celia. Graham and I had gone to public school and college together. While his family's money was legit and mine was dirty, it was all green and got us both into the same schools. There was nothing his stepfather the bastard assistant DA could do about that, no matter how hard he tried. He had tried to get my uncle on racketeering charges, but failed. He had a vendetta against us, and a grudge because my uncle had broken his perfect record of prosecuting bad guys.

As I nursed my beer and considered my future, I felt someone sit beside me, and turned to see Celia. She'd sidled up beside me and taken the stool next to mine.

Damn. She was hot in that girl-next-door, girl-you-take-home-to-mother way. Her skin was tan and smooth, her bikini was tiny with a semi-sheer wrap tied around her waist, and her long dark hair was wet from surfing. I'd admired her form while she rode the board during several decent waves and now I was seeing it up close.

"Hey, Hunter," she said in that soft voice. "What's up?"

"Not much, little sis." I did my best to put on my big brother persona. "That was some nice surfing. You've got great form. Graham's taught you well." I tried to meet her eyes, but I couldn't help taking her in with a quick look from her feet right back up to her eyes once more, skipping ever so briefly over her delicious over-ample curves, which threatened to spill out over the top of her tiny bikini. She was lush, like a ripe fruit brimming with sweet juices—so different from the geeky dork girl with braces who used to hang out at the gym with Graham.

"You look upset," she said and frowned. "What was my big brother saying to you that's made you mad? "

"Nothing," I said and turned away from her too-probing expression. "Nothing's wrong."

There was no use in talking about it, so I shut it off and tried to be more positive with her. It wasn't her fault her stepfather wanted to ruin my life.

"How about you?" I asked, turning to her. "You're moving out next week. That must be exciting."

I honestly hated to think of her alone at Harvard without either Graham or me to look out for her. We'd been her wingmen for the year as she learned the ropes at Harvard, and now she was moving out of the house and moving into Kirkland House, the most prestigious dorm on campus.

Her big chocolate brown eyes took me in, her thick black lashes clumped and still wet. A light spray of freckles over her nose gave her this totally innocent look, in contrast to those bedroom eyes. She looked so delicious I was afraid I'd get a hard-on just sitting there looking at her.

"I'm excited. There's so much to do, and I'm so glad to be free of Spencer."

I nodded, understanding completely how she must be feeling. "Free at last, am I right? That's actually what Graham was talking to me about."

She narrowed her eyes. "Was he giving you a hard time? Telling you to watch over me?"

"Something like that. He was just worrying about you and all these sharks in these waters." I gestured to the bar with my chin. "And I mean the human ones, not fish."

"Sharks?" She laughed. "You have to remember, I grew up with Graham and you. I know all about men." She waved me off like I was being foolish, which I most definitely wasn't. I knew what might be in store for someone as sweet and innocent as her.

"Hey, Celia!" Greg ran up to where we sat, concern on his face. "I'm assigned to be your knight in shining armor and protect you from the likes of *him*."

He slid in between Celia and me, laying his arm on the bar like he wanted to separate us. In the process, he knocked over my beer, the contents spilling out and splashing all over Celia. She squealed at the cold and jumped up abruptly, foamy beer on her chest and arm.

"For God's sake." I pushed Greg out of the way and handed Celia several cocktail napkins, which she used to wipe off her arms.

"Sorry about that." Greg grabbed a cocktail napkin, trying to wipe the beer off her arm and shoulder.

"It's okay," Celia said, her voice soft, pushing Greg's hands away. "No use crying over spilt beer." She glanced at me, a grin on her lips.

I thought once again about how damn hot she was. Not only that, but she was wicked smart. Graduated top in her class, tuition scholarship to study at Harvard with the goal of getting into Harvard Law when she finished her undergrad. She was always a brainiac as a kid when I hung out at their place, with dark horn-rimmed glasses and her body hidden behind oversized clothes, her nose in a book. It was still hard to see her without the glasses and in her bikini.

"There's a shower over there." I pointed to it. "You could go rinse off."

"Yeah, great idea," Greg said, ogling her. Celia ran over to the outside shower and turned it on, hesitantly testing it.

"Oh, man, this is like a fucking dream," Greg said, standing and watching Celia. He said nothing for a moment as the two of us watched her like hungry dogs studying a bone we both wanted. Then he turned to me, a huge grin on his face. "I know, I know... Down, boy, right?"

"Right," I said, frowning at him. "I'm sure Graham didn't think you'd hit on his little sister."

"What he doesn't know won't hurt me," he said.

"He'll know," I said. "Count on it. You even touch her, she'll probably plow you one. And I'll tell Graham myself."

"Man, you are such a downer. I think she likes me. In fact, she might even let me plow her." He made this totally lecherous face that made me want to knock him flat, but I held back.

Finally, Celia stood under the stream of water. It must have been cold, because she squealed sweetly, laughing as the spray hit her. She shivered visibly, her arms around herself, squeezing her breasts together, which only made them even more irresistible, her hard little nipples like rosebuds...

"Damn, I may not survive this night," Greg said, and as much as I hated to admit it, I felt the same way. "Being her guardian..." Then he turned to me. "As for you, Graham doesn't want you within ten feet of her, so get lost."

"Get lost yourself." I gave Greg my most fearsome expression.

"Seriously, man." Greg tried to stand up to me. "He told me to keep you away from her."

"She's all grown up and can make her own decisions. As for Graham, we're going our own ways so what the fuck do I care what he wants?"

"I'm only saying." He walked backwards, his hands up. "He wants you to leave her alone."

"All right, all right." I took my beer to a beach chair a few dozen feet away from everyone else and plopped down on it.

Celia returned to the beach bar and spent some time talking to Greg. I felt jealousy coil inside me when I watched him lean in close to her. Graham was a fool if he thought leaving Celia in his care was the smart move.

About fifteen minutes later, Celia appeared by my side. She smiled when our eyes met.

"Can I come and sit with you?"

"Of course," I said and gestured to the chair beside me.

She put her drink down and proceeded to squeeze water out of her long dark hair. Man, she was a feast for sore eyes. I had several regular fuckbuddies with whom I had an agreement—sex and no strings—but I had to admit I wanted Celia. This week was the start of her new life away from home and I wished I could have been the one to break her in.

Celia took the beach chair beside mine, her voluptuous body on full display. And so, while Graham was off surfing, and Greg was scowling at me from the bar, Celia told me all about her week getting ready to start classes, moving into the dorm and getting her books and class schedule set up.

For my part, I listened with half an ear, planning to watch over Celia to keep Greg and every other hound dog away from her. He was the real threat, not me. If Graham was going to go off surfing, I'd spend my time fending off my former frat brothers hoping to get her drunk and take advantage of her.

I knew the drill. I'd seen it far too many times. Hell, I did it a few times myself.

For the rest of the afternoon, we talked in serious voices about our futures.

"So, it's too bad that you and Graham can't go into business together," she said.

Well, that confirmed it. A knot formed in my throat, and I had to cough to clear it.

"Yeah," I said, trying hard not to sound as disappointed as I felt. "It's a shame."

"Spencer's such a bastard."

"That he is," I replied and took a long drink of my beer. "Was it him that convinced Graham not to go into business with me?"

"Didn't he tell you?" she said, her eyes wide. "I thought that was why you looked so down..."

"More or less."

"What will you do?"

I shrugged. "I have no idea. Depends on if I can find some other partners. That or I'll join the Marines."

"You don't really want to join up, do you? You have an MBA. It'll be wasted in the military."

I shook my head. "They need MBAs, too. I thought Graham and I would start Innova, but I guess I was wrong."

"I'm sorry, Hunter. That must be disappointing. I guess it's your family ties that make it hard." She smiled sadly at me, her expression sympathetic.

"It wasn't like my father wanted to get mixed up in the mafia," I said finally. "He had no real choice with a brother like my uncle. I still feel this loyalty to my dad. He's tried. Believe me, he's tried all these years but I wanted to start a business on my own. Or join the Marines. I have no idea what to do now."

Celia reached out and took my hand, squeezing it in sympathy. I was surprised at her show of affection and squeezed back, my heart warming at the thought that she understood. She really understood.

"Whatever you decide, I hope you're happy," Celia said. "I know Graham will miss you if you leave Boston. Where do Marines train?"

"Parris Island. If I join, I'll be in the Marines for at least four years. I hope to see some action if I do. Maybe special operations."

"Oh, no," she said and frowned. "That sounds dangerous. You mean the guys who go in and do rescues and take out targets? Like Delta Force?"

"First Special Forces Operational Detachment-Delta," I said, correcting her. "Something like that, but with the Marines."

She nodded and listened while I talked about future plans, which I was making up on the fly now that I knew Graham was pulling out on me.

Celia was a rapt audience, and seemed to understand how torn I felt.

"I must be boring you silly," I said with a laugh.

"Not at all, Hunter." She gazed into my eyes meaningfully. "I'm fascinated. It would be so fantastic if you could go legit." She leaned closer. "Spencer strictly forbade Graham from going into business with you because of your uncle." She gave me a sympathetic smile and shrugged. "He told Graham to cut you completely out of his life, but Graham refused. You two have such a long history."

"Your stepdad hates me," I said.

"He does," she replied and turned away, sighing. "When Graham said he wanted to start a business with you, Spencer said you could take the boy out of the hood, but you couldn't take the hood out of the boy."

I frowned, hating the way Spencer thought of me and my family.

"He's an idiot, of course, and wrong." She reached over and squeezed my hand again.

Warmth for her spread through me once more. It had hurt when Graham suggested we couldn't start Innova together after all. If I couldn't go into business with Graham, after all the years we'd planned to, I'd be on my own trying to make my father's business legit, and I knew I'd get sucked into that vortex.

I squeezed her hand back and smiled. Celia was a hot one, but she was so damn smart and nice.

We released hands and I sighed, wishing Celia was someone I could keep in my life, but her stepfather would probably prevent that.

"You really want to be a Marine?" Celia said, sounding doubtful and I could see she didn't like the idea. "You'll get sent somewhere dangerous. You could die."

"I could die if I stayed and tried to take the business legit."

That was the truth. It was hard to break ties with the family. I was proud of what my father had built—at least, the legitimate parts. But I wanted to be completely clean.

I took a long sip of beer and gazed out over the ocean, thinking of the future, not sure what direction to take in the military. I sighed heavily, and then turned to her. Her beautiful big brown eyes were liquid and so deep.

In the back of my mind, I couldn't help but think that if she were anyone else, this little emotional moment would make it easier for me to seduce her. I hated myself for being so venal, but I was just as much a hot-blooded American man as any other.

"I'm proud of you," she said, "no matter what you do." She smiled at me.

I smiled back, glad that my sunglasses covered up my mist-filled eyes.

This could have been a great night. I wished Celia was anyone else but Graham's little sister. If she had been, I would be anticipating getting to know her much more intimately.

CHAPTER 8

Hunter

ALL AFTERNOON, each time she was alone for a few moments, guys walked up to her and tried to start conversations. She spent quite a bit of time with Greg, and while she did, I couldn't help but glare at them, trying to look as menacing at him as I could so he wouldn't get any ideas. When she was alone, I quickly inserted myself back at her side. We spent a lot of time together as a result. Later, when I gallantly tried to leave her, feeling like I'd overstayed my welcome, she grabbed my arm and stopped me.

"Stay with me," she whispered. "You're the only person I know here besides Greg. I'm not good at this mixer thing."

Of course, I couldn't say no. While Greg was busy talking up some pretty young thing, Celia and I ate our dinner together, and even danced together around the bonfire. I ignored all the other young women I could have been seducing, not wanting to leave Celia alone with Greg.

Finally, just after sunset, we lay on the beach on a blanket to watch the stars, the party continuing a few dozen feet farther up on the beach. She truly did want to watch the stars—the Perseid meteor shower. We lay on the beach, the sound of the waves crashing a few feet away from us drowning out the sound of the party. My mind was focused on the location in the sky where the comet tail was, and where most of the meteors would appear.

We saw a few, and they were impressive. Still, my mind kept wandering to her lying beside me in the dark. I couldn't stop imagining turning over and lying on top of her, my hands roving over her curves, squeezing a deliciously ample breast, and sucking on her tiny hard rosebud nipple, then moving down and sucking something else tiny and hard between her thighs...

Fuck.

Then, out of the blue, she rolled over on top of *me*, her hands on either side of my shoulders. When she leaned down to kiss me, I put one hand firmly on her shoulder to stop her. Believe me, it was the hardest thing I had done in a long while.

"Celia, *no.*"

Saying that took just about every ounce of chivalry I had in me, but I did it.

"Hunter," she said in a breathless voice. "Tell me you don't want me and I'll leave right now."

"Of course, I want you but I can't." I could see her eyes in the darkness and her brow was furrowed.

"Why can't you?"

"You're Graham's little sister." I shook my head. "He promised me that if I even touched you, he'd tell your stepdad and he'd be only too happy to come after me and my family."

"Dammit." She rolled off me, lying on her back, staring up at the sky. "Will I *ever* get kissed?"

"You've never been *kissed?*" I stared at her in disbelief. I'd assumed she'd had some sexual experience, given how hot she was. How could she fend off all the guys who must have been dying to get into her panties?

"Not a real kiss." She turned to look in my eyes. "I have the Gestapo as a stepfather. You know Spencer." She leaned on her elbow.

"He made me sign one of those chastity promises that I'd keep my virginity until I was married. I was at a girl's boarding school for four years. No boys. And Spencer's done everything in his power to keep me from having a boyfriend ever since."

I remembered that stupid chastity contract that Spencer forced her to sign when she was just a kid. I'd assumed she'd broken it.

"You kept your promise?" I was truly shocked she was still a virgin. "No way," I said, shaking my head. "Someone as, excuse my honesty, but someone as hot as you remaining a virgin all this time?"

Her voice shook. "Of course, I did. I had no opportunity to break it. Spencer kept me under lock and key at Sisters of Mercy Boarding School for Chaste Girls. He practically had one of those iron maidens made for me."

I laughed. "An iron maiden was a medieval torture device. You mean a chastity belt."

"Same diff," she said, her voice seething. "Even when I was in middle school, he never let me go to parties or dances unchaperoned. I never had the chance to be really kissed or anything." She turned to me. "I got one kiss on the cheek from a cute guy at New Year's Eve party once, but even then, Graham was there to butt in and keep it chaste."

"I can't believe it."

"I was going to hit Greg up, since he seems willing. I thought that, out of all the guys Graham knows, Greg would be the one who would be willing to show me the ropes."

"I hope you mean fighting," I said, totally shocked by the frankness of her words.

"No, silly," she said and pushed my arm playfully. "Sex."

"Oh, God, no," I said, horror filling me at the very thought. "Not Greg."

"Why not him?" she said petulantly. "He's perfect. He's mature and he's experienced. He's hot, too."

Then I turned to face her, serious now. "Don't throw your virginity away like that," I said, surprised at myself. "Find a nice guy who really likes you, Celia. Someone who loves you. It'll be so much better if you do."

"You sound like Spencer."

I laughed ruefully at that. "Please, no. Not him. But really, Celia," I said and cleared my throat. "Your first time should be special. You'll find someone at Harvard," I said, regretting that it wouldn't be me. "Someone serious and smart—like you. Someone who'll treat you the way you deserve to be treated. With respect. And love."

Celia was silent beside me, and I hoped she was reconsidering it. I remembered how sweet and dorky she was as a girl, and felt genuine sadness that she felt she had to have sex with someone like Greg to get rid of her virginity.

I said nothing for a long moment. I was completely torn. Here was beautiful Celia—supple, lush, sweet Celia. A virgin wanting to be deflowered. Of course, I would have wanted to be the one... if I were anyone else but me. Hunter Saint, one of the Saint brothers. The fighting Irish bad boys of Southie.

Just hours earlier, Graham warned me to stay away. Just hours earlier, I'd vowed to myself I'd protect Celia from the sharks and lechers I knew would be at the party.

"You've put me in a very bad position, Celia," I said, fighting to resist my demons, struggling to comply with the better angels of my nature. "Graham's worried about you. He's afraid you'll be hurt by one of the letches around here. He left Greg in charge of protecting you. And I feel like I have to protect you from Greg."

She sighed. "You were always nice to me when you and Graham were friends. None of his other friends would even speak to me, like I was invisible. You were one of the good guys."

"You were really smart." I remembered those times I'd talked with Celia about whatever science project she was working on at the dining room table. "But Graham would kill me if he knew I didn't stop you from being with Greg—or anyone else—just to lose your virginity. I promised to protect you..."

"I can look after myself," she said defensively. "Graham needs to focus on his own life. I'm not a party girl. I want to know how to do it, when I find someone good. I just want to get rid of this ridiculous virginity and not feel so much like a freak."

"You're not a freak. Unusual, but not a freak. Not at all."

She sighed. "So, you think I should wait?"

I didn't know what the fuck to say.

"See?" I could hear frustration in her voice. "Even you think I should get rid of it. I bet none of your girlfriends were virgins. Tell the truth—were they?"

"No." I sat up. "But you're not like them. You're definitely girl-friend material."

"Graham said you don't do girlfriends."

"I don't. I'm not in the market for a girlfriend, but I know there'll be guys at Harvard who will want to be your boyfriend. You should wait."

Graham was right. I wasn't into the whole girlfriend thing, prefer-ring casual sex. But Celia wasn't that kind of girl. She was serious. She was studious.

"You're so sweet," she whispered. "I'll be sad if you leave Boston to become a Marine. I won't see you for ages, no matter what you do."

"I'll miss this place if I join up," I said, not wanting to admit I wished I could stay and get to know her better. I fought with myself—oh, how hard I fought. "I'll miss Graham. And you."

Then she leaned over, her face next to mine, and I realized she was going to kiss me.

I pulled back. "What?" I said, like an idiot, but I couldn't let her kiss me, no matter how much I wanted it.

"Will you kiss me at least?" she whispered. "A real kiss?"

"Celia..." I said, shaking my head. "You know I shouldn't. I'm Graham's best friend. I'm supposed to protect you."

"Just one kiss," she said. "I promise. Girl Scout's Honor." She held up a hand, fingers spread into a V.

"That's a Vulcan greeting, not a Girl Scout's salute," I said with a laugh. I could see her smile through the gloom.

She liked me, despite what shit her big brother spread about me—

all of it true, no doubt. That made me feel warm inside. If she were anyone else, I'd be unable to say no.

"Look, I really shouldn't."

That was three times now I'd turned her down. I thought that was heroic, and I doubted I could turn her down a fourth time.

"Not even a peck on the cheek?" she said, sounding so disappointed.

We were sitting beside each other on the blanket and I wanted so badly to pull her onto my lap and kiss her, then take off her bikini top and suck on those delicious globes... But Graham's words kept ringing in my mind.

"Just one kiss and then it's the meteor shower," I said, laughing at myself. "No trying to seduce me with your hot body."

"So, you think I'm hot?" I heard the hope in her voice and couldn't believe she was unsure of her desirability.

"Do I think you're *hot*?" I grinned. "Damn, girl..."

She leaned over and I leaned over, and we kissed. Lightly. Gently. Just two mouths pressing softly against each other. Her eyes were closed, and mine were open, and despite my best intentions, I imagined fucking her as I kissed her, mouth open, sucking her tongue into mine.

Then a bright light blazed in my eyes.

"Hey, what the *hell?*" came a male voice.

Graham.

Crap.

Celia and I pulled apart and Graham pointed the flashlight directly at me so that I had to hold up my hand in front of my eyes.

"I told you my sister was off limits, man," Graham said, his voice nearly a growl. "What the *fuck?*"

"Hey..." Celia's back straightened. "I'm all grown up, Graham. I can kiss who I want." She looked back at me possessively.

"Not *him*." Graham scowled at me. "I told you he's a male slut, Celia. Besides that, his family is mafia. He's not the kind of guy you want to get tangled up with. *God*, it isn't even your first week away from home and you've already hooked up with the most notorious womanizer on campus?"

She stood up and brushed sand off her legs. "We didn't hook up. Besides, I can look after myself."

"I thought you could, but then I find you alone on the beach with *him*? Come on, Celia…"

"We were watching the meteor shower," I said defensively, standing beside Celia.

"Yeah, right." Graham gave a sardonic laugh. "Tell me another one, Mr. Comedy. I'll be talking to my stepfather, telling him what you did, so you better be prepared. As for you," he said to Celia, grabbing her arm, pulling her roughly away from me, "you come with me."

I wanted to defend her, tell him to let go, that she was an adult, but I said and did nothing. He was right to take her away from me. I was bad for her.

I stood and watched the two of them marching up the beach to the parking lot where Graham's Jeep was parked. Celia glanced back and waved at me.

Graham's threat to tell Spencer made my decision so much easier. I knew that if I wanted to have any kind of future, I'd have to make a clean break with my family. I'd join the Marines and to start a life completely divorced from them.

Little did I know how much that decision would cost me, and how it would drive me even more deeply into my family's clutches.

CHAPTER 9

CELIA

As we drove up the highway back home to Boston, I quietly fumed. My self-appointed champion and protector—one I had no need of and resented completely—sat beside me, quiet now that he had taken me away from the party.

He knew how angry I was that he decided to butt into my personal life. Hadn't I had enough of that from my stepfather? I though Graham understood that my moving from our family home to my dorm at Harvard was my escape from the tyranny of Spencer. My mother wasn't bad, but she was too tripped out on OxyContin to argue with him, and only too happy to have him run things so she could drift in her drug-induced haze.

It wasn't her fault. The car accident that broke her back and killed my father had left her immobilized with pain and almost paralyzed. It was OxyC or nothing and so she gladly dozed on her sofa all day, sleeping through soap operas so she was no longer in pain. Luckily, she had a legitimate reason to get prescription pain medicines, and so would never have to resort to heroin like so many other people addicted to prescription drugs did.

But she had been an absent parent to me and Graham for the past twelve years. That left it wide open for Spencer, bastard assistant DA, to rule over us like we were his own personal fiefdom. He seemed to take delight in his control over me, so that I was nothing more than a peasant under his authoritarian control.

I'd thought that when Graham took me to Hunter's family house on Cape Ann, I'd finally be free to be an adult. I had such a great day talking to Hunter and then, when I had some alone time with him, finally getting kissed—really kissed, and by my lifelong crush. Then, Graham butted in.

I'd never been so mortified in all my life as I was by the way Graham treated Hunter. It was really low.

Graham and Hunter had been the two best friends in all the world for most of their lives. Then Spencer, that bastard, got in between them, threatening to go after Spencer's dad unless Graham cut ties with Hunter completely after grad school.

I hated him.

If my mother had been healthy, there was no way she would have let him force Graham to cut Hunter out of his life. If they had started a business the way they'd always planned, Hunter would stay in Boston. They would have kept the business totally separate from the Saint family business, and done things right. No one wanted to be clean more than Hunter did. Hadn't Graham said that again and again?

Then Spencer put an end to that dream. And because of that, Hunter would now join the Marines...

WE ARRIVED at the house in Boston, and I rushed in without a word to Graham, I was still so mad. I thought I could slip in, say hi to mom, and then sneak into my bedroom without running into Spencer, who was usually holed up in his mahogany-lined office on the second floor, but I was wrong. My back was to the door while I unpacked my bag, so I didn't see him march into my room.

"What's this I hear about you and that Saint thug?" Spencer said, his hands on his hips. "Haven't I told you again and again that he's off limits? His family's corrupt and I don't want Graham to have anything to do with him or the brothers. Then Graham tells me that you were alone with him and were *kissing* him?"

I turned back to my bag, my cheeks hot. He strode over to the bed and grabbed me roughly, turning me to face him.

"Answer me! What did you think you were doing?"

"None of your damn business," I said, and straightened up, pulling my arm away. "I'm an adult and you have no authority over me so leave me alone."

He slapped me across the face, his hand landing with a solid *thwack*. I staggered back and held my cheek, my eyes filling with tears.

"I got you into Harvard, so I *do* have authority over you, you little *slut*," Spencer hissed, spraying saliva with each word. "You disobey me, you bring discredit to this family with any slutty ways, and I'll pull the plug and you'll never go to Harvard Law."

I turned back, tears streaming down my cheeks, and finished unpacking my beach bag. Spencer stood behind me, and I could almost feel the anger radiating off him. At times like this, when Spencer got violent, I knew not to say another word or I'd get a second slap—and maybe this time, it would be a lot harder.

When I was done, I slipped by him, making for the bathroom. I was so angry at that moment that I couldn't speak. I heard Spencer leave the room and I finally relaxed, glad I'd gotten off lightly.

Then I popped into my mom's room, only to find her asleep, the lights dim. I didn't want to wake her, so I carefully closed the door and went to the kitchen. Graham and Spencer were in the dining room, standing in the doorway leading to the deck. When they saw me at the fridge, Spencer came right over.

"I'm rethinking letting you go to live at the dorm after what you did tonight."

"My trust fund pays for that," I said quietly. "I have every right to move in."

I was surprised that Spencer didn't slap me, but Graham was standing there. Spencer was always more reluctant to hurt me when Graham was around and had started to stand up to him. Graham was taller and stronger than Spencer so he usually just yelled and shamed me instead.

"I told Graham to keep tabs on you. He has friends at the dorm who'll watch over you, so you'd better be good. If I hear one word about you sleeping around, drinking, or doing any drugs, you're cut off from this family or any help you might need getting into Harvard Law. I can get you in, Celia. I can keep you out." Spencer came closer, his finger pointing in my face. "And don't you even think about talking to that Saint thug Hunter. Do you hear me?"

I didn't answer. Beside me, Graham cleared his throat, like he was reminding Spencer not to hit me.

"I said, *did you hear me?*" Spencer shoved his face next to mine and I was unable to avoid looking in his beady little eyes.

"Yes," I said finally.

"Yes, what?" he asked, not giving an inch.

"Yes, *sir*," I replied, knowing he wouldn't stop until I called him 'sir.'

"All right then," he said and stood up, his hands on his hips. "Don't screw up."

I turned and left the kitchen, tears in my eyes.

THE NEXT EVENING, Graham drove me to the dorm, barely saying anything to each other. I wasn't sad—just really, really angry. I needed time to cool off after my fight with Spencer the previous night and the fact that Graham told him what happened.

When we arrived at the dorm, Graham helped me with my bags, following me up the stairs to the dorm's entry. Once inside, we made our way down the hallways to the rooms, past several large open areas where students were seated, talking and laughing. We found my room and I opened the door, hauling my things inside.

"Well, here you are," Graham said and glanced around the small bedroom. "You'll love it here. I know Spencer can be a bastard, but at least here you'll be free."

Despite everything, I couldn't say mad at Graham.

"Be careful," he said and came over to me, looking into my eyes. "Guys are a bunch of horndogs. Don't let them have anything until you know they respect you and care about you, okay?"

"I will," I said, wanting to make him worry less. "I understand."

He hugged me. When he pulled back, he frowned. "That's not pretty," he said, and touched my cheek. "He hit you too hard."

I held my hand up to my cheek. "Do I have a black eye?"

He shook his head. "The start of one. I can see where his hand hit your cheek. What a bastard."

He leaned in and kissed me on the cheek softly and then turned to go.

"Graham?" I said before he left. "Hunter turned me down. I was the one who wanted him to kiss me. I was the one who pushed. He refused me three times."

Graham said nothing for a moment, his back to me. "He should have refused you four."

Then he left and I was alone.

AFTER I WASHED the tears off my face and fixed a cup of tea with my new kettle, I unpacked, emptying my bags into my tiny chest of drawers. Once I was finished, I took out my cell and texted Amy, my best friend from high school.

CELIA: *I'm here.*

Amy: *Oh, Joy! How was the party? I wish I could have come...*

Celia: *Shit went down.*

Amy: *Why? What the hell happened?*

Celia: *Didn't even make it to the end of the night. Come over and we'll have some tea while I finish unpacking.*

Amy: Tea? I'll bring some beer.
Celia: Better bring some hemlock as well.
Amy: That bad? I'll bring some chocolate, too.
Celia: You are my savior...

I SMILED, glad that even if I hadn't been able to hook up with Hunter at the beach party, I was free now, on my own and away from Spencer. I'd be able to spend all my free time with Amy. She always lifted my spirits.

When she arrived, slipping in my open door, she reached into her bag and pulled out two beers.

"There you go," she said when I took one and opened it with an extra bottle opener I'd snagged from the kitchen at home. I opened hers and we sat on the tiny two-seater sofa. We clinked bottlenecks and then each took a sip.

"What the hell happened to you?" she said, leaning closer to peer at me. "Don't tell me. Some guy looked at you and Spencer the rat bastard decided to use you as his personal punching bag."

"He and I got into a fight." I felt my cheek. "Is there a mark?"

"Damn straight there is. He's such a monster. You could charge him for assault."

I shook my head. "He's Assistant DA. I doubt anyone would believe me."

She took her cell and snapped a photo of my cheek. "Evidence," she said and shook her head. "To add to my file. Just in case you ever want to press charges."

"If I did, no one would believe me. Spencer's a pillar of the community. A leader in the Church. The second most powerful attorney in Boston."

"I know," Amy said and wrapped her arm around my shoulder. "It sucks. Just put your head down and forget about Spencer. You're free of him now."

I nodded and took a sip of beer.

"I hope so."

. . .

MY FIRST DAY back at Harvard was exciting and tiring, rushing from class to class, getting to know the where all my classrooms were, meeting up with my fellow dorm mates, and of course, trying to keep up with all the reading and assignments. It was going to be a lot of work, but I welcomed it. I was so glad to be on my own and away from Spencer for the first time, I didn't care how much work I had.

Graham called me early Tuesday night and asked how things were going.

"Great," I said, plopping down on the sofa to rest. "I really like my philosophy class. It sounds great, plus I'm taking astronomy. I love it so far."

"You are such a geek," Graham said with a laugh. "Astronomy…"

I smiled at the gently chiding but proud tone of his voice. "What are you up to, now that you're a free man?"

"I'm going to watch Conor Saint in a fight at the gym tonight."

"What?" I said, surprised that he would go, considering what had happened at the beach party. "Why? I thought you and Hunter were on the outs."

"Nah," he said, sounding tired. "No harm, no foul. Besides, he's decided to join up. He's going to Parris Island in a few weeks. He'll be gone for who knows how long so I decided to go meet him for a drink and watch the fight for old time's sake."

"He really wanted to go into business with you, Graham. I hate Spencer so much…"

"Forget Spencer. You're a free woman now."

"When I talked to Hunter, he said if he joined, he wanted to go into special operations," I said, a sinking feeling inside of me. "He'll be doing dangerous things, going behind enemy lines."

"Yeah, but better that than stay here and get mixed up in the mob."

"I know," I said and chewed a fingernail. "Maybe Amy and I will show up, watch the fight with you guys."

"No, Celia. You should stay at your dorm," Graham said, his voice firm. "This is your first week of class and you don't want to start out on the wrong foot. You're in second year. You have to buckle down and study."

"I want to say goodbye to Hunter," I protested. "He was always really nice to me."

"I knew I shouldn't have said anything," Graham said and I could tell he was upset. "Hunter's not the guy for you, Celia. He's as much of a hound dog as any. Besides, he's leaving, so there's no future for you with him."

"I know that. I want to watch the fight. Conor's going to the Olympics one day."

"Yeah, *right*," Graham said, like he didn't believe me. He knew me better than that. I wanted to go so I could see Hunter one more time before he left. He'd been my schoolgirl crush for a decade. The older boy I'd always wanted to kiss—and more. "Do what you want," he said with a sigh. "I can't stop you."

"I *will* do what I want," I said. "I moved into the dorm to get away from Spencer and so I could do what I want and go where I want, when I want. You know, to be free."

"If you think Hunter is going to pay you any attention, you're wrong. He'll be partying with the boys and will be looking for a good time, not a girlfriend."

"I'm not going so I can be his girlfriend. I just want to say goodbye."

"Okay, but don't say I didn't try to warn you. You'll be disappointed when he's too busy to pay you any attention."

"Whatever," I said, and hung up. Then I texted Amy.

CELIA: *Wanna go watch a fight? It's Hunter's brother Conor. He's going to go to the Olympics. He's really good.*

It took a few minutes, but she responded.

Amy: Ooh. Is he cute? Will Hunter be there?

Celia: Who, Hunter? Could you possibly be referring to Hunter Saint, one of the Saint brothers? Just the most gorgeous hunk of man who ever put a pair of boxing gloves on my hands and let me hit him?

Celia: That Hunter? The brave Marine who wants to serve his country Hunter? The one who started to kiss me on Saturday night only to be rudely interrupted by my busybody brother? Why would you possibly think I wanted to go because of him? ;)

Amy: I'll be right over.

CHAPTER 10

CELIA

ABOUT AN HOUR LATER, after Amy and I had changed clothes and fussed with our hair, I took one last look in the bathroom mirror.

"You still have that bruise," she said, pointing to the bluish mark on my cheek from Spencer's hand. "Here. Cover it up with some of this." She handed me a tube of concealer.

"It's tender," I said as I applied the make-up. "Does it still show?"

She made a face. "It'll be dark in the gym. No one will see it."

"Okay," I said and tucked the tube back into my bag.

We left the dorm and took her car to Boston, arriving at Saint Brothers Gym in about half an hour. After we found a parking spot, we walked the rest of the way to the gym. It had been years since I was there, but it looked almost exactly the same. The gym had been in the family for decades and had that old-school feel to it. It had been a local hangout for kids from South Boston for years, and hopeful young boxers and fighters went there to learn how to fight.

There were other, newer gyms with boxing rings and stands for the weekly audience who came to watch practice bouts, but there was nothing quite like Saint's Gym anywhere else.

Amy and I were both excited to enter the gym, and when we arrived at around nine, there was already a decent-sized crowd gathered to watch the fights. I checked around to see if I could find Graham and Hunter, but didn't see anyone at first. Then, just when I thought Graham must have changed his mind, I saw him standing ringside, his arms on the railing surrounding the ring. He was alone.

I went over, Amy in tow.

"There you are," I said and threw my arm around his shoulder for a hug. "Where's Hunter?"

I glanced around, but then Graham smiled and gestured to the ring with his chin. "There."

I turned to look at the ring and there he was.

He was fighting.

"Why is Hunter fighting?"

"Conor's sick. People came to watch a fight, so Hunter stepped in. He's getting pummeled."

I glanced up and saw Hunter. He was bare from the waist up, had his hands wrapped in green tape, and was wearing a mouth guard, but it was him.

"What are they doing? Where are their gloves?"

Graham shook his head. "It's MMA, not boxing. If you don't like to see a man get hurt, you should look away now. Hunter's out-matched despite all his training."

I turned to Amy. "There he is," I said, making a face at her. "He's fighting because his brother's sick."

"So that's the infamous Hunter?" she said, frowning. When Hunter turned, we got to see him face-on. He looked fierce, his wrapped hands held up to protect his face. His skin glistened with sweat. He was bouncing around, staying just out of range of his opponent.

I stepped closer to the ring, alarmed that Hunter was losing. He looked fantastic, but what did I know about MMA? His opponent seemed beefier than Hunter, who, while buff, wasn't a heavyweight. All the years of training wasn't enough to give him the edge.

It was then I saw the amazing tribal tattoo on his shoulder and down his bicep. Green and dark blue, it was fantastic. I could only imagine running my hands over it, and then over the rest of his body.

When he caught my eye, he seemed to hesitate for a moment, and that was enough to give his opponent an advantage. In front of our very eyes, the other fighter clocked Hunter a good one, knocking him hard on the cheek. Hunter fell against the ropes on the other side of the ring, then flopped to the floor.

"Oh, my God!" I covered my mouth to keep from screaming out loud. "He's knocked out."

"Jesus," Graham said and jumped into the ring, going over to where Hunter lay. The referee went over to Hunter and checked him, but he was out cold. As Amy and I watched, Graham lifted Hunter and, finally, Hunter's eyes blinked open. He tried to get up but couldn't. The official called the fight for Hunter's opponent.

"He was looking at you," Amy whispered to me, making a face. "He got knocked out because of you, Celia."

"Oh my God," I said, a sinking feeling in my gut. "I think you're right. I distracted him and that was enough."

Graham and some other man lifted Hunter up and helped him out of the ring. I followed them into the back of the gym, worried about how badly Hunter was hurt.

"Hey, who are you?" one of the beefy guys who worked at the gym asked when I went into the changing room. "No girls allowed."

"It's Celia," Hunter said from inside. "Let her in."

The man stepped aside, so Amy and I went into the changing room and over to where Hunter sat on a bench. Some chunky guy in a shirt with the gym's logo on it was attending to his face. He wore a white cap and looked every inch the boxing promoter. I wondered if it was Hunter's uncle.

Hunter's nose was bleeding and he held a cloth to it to stem the flow.

"Looks like you might have finally broken that pretty-boy nose of yours, Hunter," the man said with a gruff laugh. "You're going to have to go to the hospital and get that fixed."

I stepped closer. "Are you okay?"

"I'm fine," he said with a nod. "I'll have to make it through worse at boot camp and there'll be worse in the future, so I better toughen up if I want to be a Marine."

"You *are* tough," I said firmly. "I'm so sorry." I knew he'd gotten hit because he saw me.

"It's okay," Hunter said, a grin on his lips. "It's nice to see you again. I didn't think I'd see you before I left for Parris Island. Big brother gave me such a hard time and all." Hunter gave Graham a look and the two smiled at each other.

"Just looking after my little sister," Graham said. Then he turned to me. "I'm taking Hunter to the ER so you two should leave. Say goodbye. You won't be seeing him again for a while."

"Goodbye," I said, and smiled sadly. "I hope you do okay in the Marines."

Graham pushed me and Amy out of the changing room, and I caught Hunter's eye before the door closed. He smiled and nodded at me, then turned back, bloody cloth still held to his nose.

"Go back to the dorm," Graham said to me, before he closed the door. "I'll call you and tell you what the doctor said. He'll be fine. Now, scoot."

"Okay," I said, and Amy and I left the gym, now that the fight was over and Hunter was going to the hospital.

"He's seriously hot," Amy said when we got back into her car for the drive back to the dorm. "Even with the bloody nose. I like his tattoo. And everything else. He reminds me of Heathcliff or something with that dark hair and fair skin, blue eyes. To think he took the fall because he was mesmerized by seeing you…"

"Oh, you," I said, although I completely agreed with her. "You are such a romantic."

I smiled inwardly at the fact that he had indeed taken a hit because he saw me. Part of me felt bad for Hunter, but a secret part of me felt elated. He saw me and couldn't focus on the fight.

That meant something, right?

· · ·

WE DROVE BACK to the dorm and went to our respective rooms, texting each other that we'd meet for coffee the next morning before our first classes.

I took off my clothes and got into my pajamas, then crawled into my tiny bed, picking up my Kindle so I could read the latest novel I'd downloaded. It was just after midnight when my cell dinged.

I pulled it out of my bag and checked my messages.

Hunter: Hey, Celia. Are you still up?

I almost dropped my phone when I realized Hunter had texted me.

Celia: Yes, I was just reading. How are you? Is your nose broken? I feel so bad that happened to you.

Hunter: That's what I get for paying too much attention to beautiful women.

Celia: I'm so sorry I distracted you. I feel responsible.

Hunter: Don't worry about it. It had to happen sooner or later. They won't be able to call me Pretty Boy Saint anymore, I guess...

Celia: Oh, no! Is it really badly broken? Are you in pain?

Hunter: No, it's not bad. The ER doc said it would be fine. Not broken. They gave me some nice pain meds so I'm good. In fact, maybe a bit too good, which is probably why I broke down and texted you when I know I shouldn't.

Celia: Oh, no, you should text me! I wanted to know how you are, so now I can relax and know you're okay. Will this prevent you from starting boot camp?

Hunter: No. I'm lucky it's not broken. If it was, they might have disqualified me at intake. The Marines have the highest number of broken bones in the service during boot camp so you should be in top shape to go.

Celia: I'm glad you're okay. I'll miss you when you go.

Hunter: I'll miss you, too. I'll miss Graham and Boston...

I didn't know what to write and there was silence for a moment. Finally, I texted him back.

Celia: Well, I hope everything works out for you, Hunter. Take care.

Hunter: You too, Celia.

I SIGHED and lay back in bed, remembering our kiss, wishing there had been so much more. I doubted I'd find another guy like Hunter. He was just everything I could want in a man. Hot. Sweet. Funny. Smart.

I tossed and turned in my tiny bed, wishing that he wasn't going away and that we'd get together, but I realized it was just another silly girl fantasy.

THE NEXT DAY was a blur for me as I ran from one class to another, with barely enough time to breathe. I didn't mind, because I got to return to my dorm room and to the peace and quiet – and most of all, the freedom from Spencer – that I felt there.

I met Amy for dinner in the cafeteria and then went back to my room to study for the next day. At around ten o'clock, my cell dinged and I got a text.

It was from Hunter.

My heart did a flip-flop when I saw his name.

Hunter: Hey, do you want to meet for coffee? I feel a bit lost.

I hesitated. What did he mean, lost? It was probably that he was still sad about him and Graham not starting a business together, and deciding to join the Marines.

I checked my watch. It was late and I had a class in the morning, but not until eleven. I could go out for an hour at least...

Celia: Sure. Can you come here?

Hunter: To your dorm?

Celia: No, you can't come here. I mean, can you pick me up? There are a few places we can go for coffee... I mean, if you really did mean coffee...

Hunter: LOL yes, I really did mean coffee. I wanted a chance to talk to you before I go away.

Celia: Great. I'll be waiting just outside the dorm.

Hunter: See you in fifteen or so.

Celia: Okay bye.

I RUSHED AROUND like a crazy person, getting dressed, checking my

THE BAD BOY SERIES COLLECTION

hair and brushing my teeth once more even though I had brushed them an hour before. I grabbed my bag and then left the room, took the hallway to the exit and stood outside, waiting for Hunter.

When his car drove up, a thrill of excitement raced through me. He got out and opened the passenger door and when I saw him, I felt a stab of pain at the sight of his face. He was starting to get a black eye and his nose was still very red.

"Oh, Hunter," I said and reached up to touch his cheek. "Does it hurt?"

He smiled and then his face changed. "What happened to you?"

I hesitated. He must have seen the bruise on my cheek and my own black eye.

"Oh, this?" I said and touched my cheek. "Spencer wasn't all that happy when Graham told him he found me kissing you."

"What?" Hunter said and bent down, looking more closely at me. He reached up and cupped my cheek, his eyes a mixture of anger and sympathy. He gently stroked my skin where the bruise was. "That bastard hit you?" He shook his head and I could tell he was upset by the tone of his voice. "What a coward. Why does he get away with it? That's assault. He should be charged."

"He's a big man in this town," I said with a sigh. "No one can touch him."

"Someone can," Hunter said. "I'm sure my uncle knows people who could have a little talk with him."

"Hunter," I said, stepping back. "I thought you hated that side of your family."

"Spencer shouldn't lay a hand on you." He took hold of my shoulders and looked in my eyes. "I'm so sorry I got you in trouble. I should have said no."

"No," I said, leaning in closer to him. "I'm glad you kissed me." I smiled at him and his expression softened. "I want you to kiss me again."

He shook his head sadly. "Celia... I don't want you to get in trouble because of me."

"You're going away," I said and put my arms around his neck. "I won't see you for maybe years. Besides, I'm free now. Spencer has no power over me here."

"We'll see each other," he said. "I promise. I have family here. There's Conor and Cam, and Graham. I'll come back every chance I get."

He carefully extricated himself from my arms, and opened the door to his car.

"Shall we go?"

I stood there, upset that he wouldn't kiss me, but I wanted the night to continue. I hopped in the car and he closed the door, then he got in the driver's seat beside me.

We drove to a nearly coffee shop and sat at a small table by the window. Outside, the streets of Cambridge were almost bare, with light traffic at that time of night. Hunter and I talked and talked, going over all sorts of things from our shared past.

He laughed when he talked about the first time he saw me, when I was nine and had braces.

"I never had a sister," he said, smiling to himself. "I thought Graham was so lucky. While I had brothers, he had you. Girls were always this mystery to me because my mother left us when we were kids. My step-mom is great but she was always focused on the business. I was mothered by my Aunt Carol, and while she was nice, she couldn't replace my mom."

I squeezed his hand. "My mom's been in a haze for years," I said. "Spencer's a beast to both Graham and me. Graham had to be my protector and parent."

"He was," Hunter said. "He'd kill me if he knew I was out with you tonight."

"Why?" I said, angry that Spencer and Graham thought they could tell me who I could be with. "Of all his friends, he should be happy I'm with you. You're going to be a Marine. You're honorable. More honorable than Spencer or anyone in his family."

He smiled at that. "That means a lot to me."

We drank decaf coffee and shared a piece of cheesecake, talking for an hour about my classes and what would happen at boot camp.

He seemed like he could be a real boyfriend, if only he was staying. I hated that he was leaving and I probably wouldn't see him for a long time.

We left and walked down the street to the car and I didn't want the evening to end. When he drove me back to the dorm, he got out to open my door like a real gentleman. We stood in front of the building and I shivered, not wanting to say goodbye.

I could tell Hunter was torn about being with me. I wanted to kiss him and he seemed to be fighting a similar urge. So, I put my arms around his neck, not caring anymore about what anyone—Spencer or Graham—thought about me being with Hunter.

I pressed my body against his and he groaned.

"Celia," he said with a sigh. "I'm trying to be a gentleman."

"You are, more of one than anyone I know."

Then I kissed him. He kissed me back, but it was hard for him to breathe because of his nose and he had to stop.

"Sorry," he said with a chuckle. "Not much of a kisser tonight."

"I don't care. Take me to your place," I whispered. "I'd take you to my room, but there are no guests allowed overnight."

"Celia..." He sighed. "What would Spencer do if he knew you'd come to my place?"

"To hell with Spencer," I said. Then I leaned up and kissed him again, making my kisses short so he could breathe. "Take me to your place. I'll stay with you tonight. You're leaving soon. I probably won't ever see you again."

"I'll be back on holidays."

"I always wanted you to be the one."

He shook his head. "Graham would kill me if he knew."

"He *won't* know," I said, and touched his cheek hesitantly. It was swollen, the black already blossoming beneath his eye. "Only you and I will know. Hunter, I want it to be you."

He closed his eyes and took in a deep breath, clearly fighting with himself. When his eyes opened again, I pressed my body fully against his.

"It's the least I can do, considering you got knocked out because of me." I grinned at him, trying to break the tension.

Finally, he smiled. "It's not a gift," he said softly.

"I don't care what it is. I want you. That's all."

He hesitated. Then he leaned down and kissed me, as if he wanted to test me to see if I meant it.

His kiss was deep and hungry, like he'd been waiting for a chance to really kiss me. It took my breath away, and when he pulled me even more tightly into his arms, my whole body shuddered.

This was what I wanted. I'd wanted it for years.

I kissed him back, my fingers running through his hair, over his back, my whole body pressed against his. When I felt his bulge against my groin, I ground against him, showing him how much I wanted him.

When our kiss ended, he looked in my eyes, held my gaze for a long minute, and then he took my hand and led me to his car.

I could barely think the rest of the drive to his place. He was staying at the apartment above his father's gym, in one of the spare bedrooms. We held hands the entire trip through Cambridge and then through Boston's streets to South Boston, where his father's gym was located.

The music was blaring and there was little conversation. What do you say when you know you're going to have sex with someone in a few moments? All I knew was that Hunter was taking me to his place. I'd spend the night with him. I was finally going to lose my virginity and it would be to the one man I had always wanted from the time I first saw him.

I'd had a crush on him since I was nine. It was right that Hunter was the first. I wished so hard that he wasn't going away and could stay in Boston so I could be with him, but this would have to do.

When we stopped at a light, he turned to me. "You can back out at any time," he said, holding my hand up to his lips. He kissed my knuckles and then turned to watch the road when the light changed.

"I won't change my mind." I had to clear my throat, my mouth was so dry. "I've wanted you forever, Hunter. Ever since I was nine and saw you in the ring."

He smiled. "Ten years?"

"Ten years," I said emphatically. "You're going away and I probably won't see you again. I can't stand the thought of you getting away from me if you want me, too."

"I do want you," he said, his voice throaty. "But I don't want to get you into any trouble."

"Spencer will never know. It's not like I'm going to tell him."

He nodded, just as we finally arrived at the building. After we parked, he opened my door, taking my hand and leading me to the back of the building to the apartment entrance. The back alley was dark except for a lone yellow light at the loading dock of the building next door.

As he opened the door to the building, I felt like fate had brought us both to that point. All my life, I'd known I wanted him to be the one.

I took in a deep breath and crossed the threshold.

CHAPTER 11

Hunter

I HELD Celia's hand the entire time, not wanting to let go in case she changed her mind. Part of me fought with myself, a silent internal battle that said I should take her back right now and never see her again. The other part—the part that was weak, the part that wanted to be happy—won.

There were three bedrooms in the apartment above the gym. Mine was in the corner of the apartment, facing the street. An ensuite bathroom was off to the rear of the large room. In the middle, a four-poster king-sized bed dominated the room, layered with silky sheets and thick comforters and pillows. It was ostentatious, but my stepmother had hired an interior decorator to do the apartment over when my father decided to sell our house in Cambridge and move downtown. The renovations had turned the apartment into a stylish home with all the appointments. It was nice—and would be a stark contrast to my new living quarters in the barracks when I went to boot camp at Parris Island.

I pulled Celia into the apartment after quietly unlocking the door when we reached the top of the stairs to the third floor. The apartment was dark except for a light over the kitchen island. My brother and father had gone to bed, so we had the place to ourselves, but Conor was a light sleeper, as was my father. I held my finger up to my lips to signal to Celia that we should be quiet.

Still, I wanted to grab a couple of beers from the fridge. I didn't plan on drinking, but maybe Celia might like something to help her relax. I knew from her kiss earlier that she was eager for us to fuck, but this was something that had to be handled carefully. It couldn't be rushed. As tired as I was, and as sore as my face was despite the pain meds, I wanted it, too.

We tiptoed down the hallway to my room. After I closed the door and locked it, she almost jumped me when I turned around, her arms going around my neck.

"Finally," she said, her voice breathless.

"Not so fast," I said with a smile, pleased at her eagerness, but wanting to slow her down. "This isn't something you rush."

She laughed softly and kissed me while I held her waist with one hand and the two bottles of Corona with the other.

"You're not nervous?" I asked, pulling away, taking her hand so I could lead her to the bed.

"I'm impatient," she said and sat on the edge while I stood in front of her and opened one bottle, handing it to her. She took it and waited while I opened the other, then we clinked our bottle necks together.

"To us," I said.

"To us," she replied. She took a long sip, like she needed some liquid courage. For my part, I took a miniscule sip just to drink with her. Then I took her bottle and put both down on the bedside table and stepped closer, so that I was standing between her legs while she sat on the edge of the bed. The mattress was high enough that we could put our arms around each other.

I kissed her, slipping my arms around her, pulling her against my body. She wrapped her legs around my waist, and that was all the encouragement I needed. I broke the kiss and pushed her down onto the bed, lying on top of her, taking her hands in mine and threading our fingers together. I watched her face for a moment, drinking in her features. I wanted to remember everything about this night—every expression on her face, every sight and sound and scent and taste.

She was so beautiful to me at that moment. Her long hair was spread out on the bed beneath her head. Her dark doe eyes were half open and dark with lust, her skin flushed with desire. Her body beneath me had all the right curves to make a man dizzy with lust, from her ample breasts to her small waist and very round hips. I couldn't wait to grab them and thrust into her when it was finally time.

She was so ripe and, I expected, so juicy that I was hard as a rock at the prospect of stripping her naked and eating her until she cried out loud.

Most of all, I wanted it to be memorable for her. I felt a great responsibility for her pleasure. Part of me was secretly glad she was still a virgin. She was old enough now, at nineteen, to know what she wanted and to be eager for it. If she had been younger when she lost her virginity, she might have been less in control, more open to manipulation by some randy boy her age who knew nothing about pleasuring a woman.

I still felt it would be best for Celia to be with someone who loved her, who wanted to be with her more than just a night, which was all I could give her considering my situation, but I cared about her. More than someone like Greg would have.

"You sure you want this?" I whispered into her ear. I kissed her neck and then pulled back so I could catch her eye. "You can say no and I'll stop at any time."

"Yes, Hunter, I want this," she said, frowning at me. "I want *you*."

That was all I needed. I kissed her again, deeply, claiming her mouth, sucking her tongue into mine while I ground my erection against her. I wanted to work her up as much as possible so she'd be panting with lust before I even took off her clothes.

I pulled off her sweater, revealing her lacy red bra, her breasts spilling out on either side. Then I unzipped her jeans and slipped them off, so that she lay on the bed, her knees hanging off the end, wearing only her bra and a matching lacy red thong.

God, the way her skin contrasted to the red of her underwear was amazing. She could have been a pinup girl with her curves, and my erection strained at my jeans at the sight of her. She bit her lip as if she were nervous and so I lay on top of her and pulled her lip down with a finger.

"Don't bite that lip," I said, my voice husky with lust. "Let me."

I kissed her again, taking her bottom lip in between my teeth gently, pulling on it just a bit before I kissed her deeply once more. While I kissed her, I ran my hands over her body, from her softly rounded hip to her waist, and then cupping one breast in my hand.

"You are so lush," I almost growled. I pulled down the fabric of her bra and kissed my way down from her jaw to her neck, and then over her collarbone. I glanced down and saw the full roundness of her bare breast pushed up from the bra, her nipple hardening in the cool air. I ran my tongue all around the curve of her breast then swiped it over the hard bud of her nipple. She groaned and arched her back, pressing her breast up towards my face.

I denied her, wanting to tease her for as long as possible. Instead, I blew on her wet nipple, enjoying the way she shivered, her skin all goosebumps, her nipple even more tightly erect. I repeated this with the other side, sliding the fabric down below her breast so that it was pushed up and out. I licked her skin all over without touching the nipple, leaving it until last, and she gasped once more when I quickly lapped my tongue over it.

"Please," she whispered, her eyes closed, her body writhing under me.

I smiled, enjoying her built-up desire.

"Be patient," I said, my voice firm. "I intend to make you beg for it."

She smiled at that, her eyes still closed. "Haven't I already done that?" Finally, she opened her eyes and met mine, her lips curved.

"Not nearly enough."

I squeezed her breasts with both hands, kneading them, then pushing them together before swiping my tongue over each nipple, one after the other. She inhaled deeply, her eyes rolling up in her head, her hands gripping the covers.

Finally, I took one hard bud into my mouth and sucked, indulging myself in what I had been imagining ever since I'd seen her at the beach party. I ran my tongue around and around, enjoying the way her nipple hardened beneath it. I stopped all motion and was rewarded when she arched her back, desperate for more contact.

"Don't stop," she whispered. I repeated my motions with the other breast, squeezing it, pulling her nipple into my mouth and running my tongue around the nipple before sucking hard. "Oh, God," she moaned, almost panting.

I continued to move from one nipple to the other until she was writhing beneath me.

Finally, I released her breasts and ran my tongue down her abdomen to her navel, which I circled, then lower to the lacy thong. Her thighs were already spread to accommodate me, and I pressed them open even wider. Her panties were damp, but I wanted them even more damp, so I ran my tongue over her, feeling the cleft between her lips, pressing my tongue hard against her.

She moved her hips, hungry for more sensation. I denied her at first, licking down her thighs and then up again. I could barely wait to pull off her thong, but enjoyed the visual of her lying there beneath me, her bra pulled down, her breasts jutting up, her nipples hard, and her thighs spread.

I pulled the fabric of her thong to the side, exposing her pussy. It was closely trimmed, the dark hair short so that I could see her inner labia and clit, glistening with moisture.

"So nice," I murmured, pressing her legs farther apart. "Nice and wet."

I licked her slowly, running my tongue up and over her labia without lingering on her clit and she shuddered, her body trembling.

"You like that, do you?" I said, my voice gruff with lust.

"Yes," she whispered, her eyes closed.

I studied her, hungrily taking in her nice wet pussy, on display for me, her red lace thong pulled to one side.

"Do you want me to lick you again?"

I waited, watching her face. She kept her eyes closed tightly and was breathing fast.

"Yes," she said, wriggling her hips like she was trying to tempt me. I smiled, enjoying her pent-up desire.

"Yes, what?"

She said nothing and then finally, she opened her eyes. "Are you going to make me say it?"

"Yes."

She bit her bottom lip once more. "Lick me again," she said, her voice barely above a whisper.

"What? I couldn't hear you."

She glanced down and caught my eye, which was my intention. I wanted her to see me with my face between her legs, my mouth so close to her clit. I wanted her to ask me to lick her. I enjoyed her saying the words.

"Lick me, please," she said, her voice louder now and sounding a bit desperate.

"Lick your what?"

I waited, wanting to see what she said.

"Whatever the hell you want," she replied, frustrated with the little game I was playing with her.

She clearly didn't feel comfortable saying 'clit' or 'pussy' out loud, so I said it for her. I wanted her to feel completely wanton.

"Do you want me to lick your pussy? Suck your clit?"

"Yes," she said, groaning audibly. "Yes."

"Say it," I said, kissing her inner thigh. "I want to hear the words."

She was panting now, her face flushed. "Lick my pussy," she said, her voice tortured. "Suck my clit."

I did. I licked her slowly and deliberately, then pressed my lips over her clit and sucked, my tongue rolling over the hard nub.

"Ohh," she cried out, her back arching. "Oh, *God*..."

I smiled again, pleased at the way she responded.

Then I stood and pulled off her thong, revealing her neatly trimmed pussy. I reached to her and sat her up, then unlatched the front closure of her bra so her breasts fell out free. They were fantastic, heavy and round, her nipples small and hard and calling out for attention.

I pushed her back onto the bed and lay on top of her once more, still fully clothed myself, enjoying having her naked beneath me.

"Aren't you going to undress?" she asked, her dark eyes wide.

I shook my head. "Shh," I said and held my finger over her lips. "Let me lead."

Her eyes widened at that. She knew what I meant. I wanted to control her. I enjoyed control during sex, but most of all, I enjoyed having her shudder beneath me, responding to my touch.

My own pleasure, my own orgasm, was the smallest part of this. That would come, but first I wanted to drive her crazy with lust so that when I finally entered her for the first time, when I filled her up, she'd be ready. So ready she'd pop with only a few thrusts.

I pulled off her so that she lay beneath me, her arms beside her head. I stood up, pulling her legs away from my waist, one hand on each of her knees so I could see her completely open. I ran my hands down the inside of her thighs, my fingers soft, slipping beside but not touching her labia, then up over her belly. She gasped, her breathing hitching in her throat. I touched her all over, her breasts, her nipples, her neck, up her arms to her hands, kissing her as I lay on top of her once more. I slid my hands back down again, stopping to touch her, slipping my fingers over her mound, sliding between her outer lips, my thumb finding her hard clit, the sensation making her back arch.

"You're so fucking perfect." I licked each nipple as I cupped her breasts, running my teeth softly over each one until they were hard, sucking each one in turn, each time making her gasp with increased desire.

I pulled her up farther on the bed, then spread her thighs once more and began to lick and suck her pussy. She groaned, her back arching. I slipped a finger inside of her then, and found her tight but nice and wet.

I stroked her while I tongued her clit, sucked it, slipping my finger in more deeply, wondering if I could stretch her enough so it wouldn't hurt when I replaced my finger with my cock.

She groaned when I stopped, moving her hips.

"Shh," I said. "We have to take it slow."

"Please..."

I smiled to myself. She was ready. "Please, what?"

"Please don't stop."

I lowered my mouth to her once more. "Tell me when you're close," I said, stopping my motions.

I touched her clit lightly then withdrew my finger. She strained, pressing her hips up, searching for the sensation. Her body was shaking, her face flushed.

Then I kissed her once more before rising and removing my shirt, my belt and jeans, and my boxers. I didn't need any stimulation—I was already hard as a rock and dripping.

"Do you have a condom?" she asked, her eyes opening as she lay back on the bed. I was already rifling through the bedside table, where I kept a box.

"Help me," I said and she sat up, her eyes wide when she saw my erection. "Have you ever seen one before?"

She shook her head. "Just pictures online. Porn."

"You watched porn?"

"Of course," she said, laughing softly. "We all did. Just to see what it's like."

I smiled, amused that this virgin had been watching online porn. What must she have thought about it? MILFs and creampies and facials?

"Touch it if you want."

She gripped me, her hand closing around my shaft.

"It's hot and hard," she said, smiling softly. Then she licked the head and I groaned out loud. "I always imagined doing that."

"I imagined you doing it to me."

That seemed to encourage her, and she took the head into her mouth and ran her tongue around the rim. My body tensed, my dick throbbing.

"Oh, that's so good."

She pulled back and looked up into my eyes. "Am I doing it right?"

"You're doing it perfectly," I replied, my hand in her hair to encourage her even more. She complied, sucking gently on the head, knowing enough to watch her teeth. I could have let her continue but my focus was her pleasure, so I gently pulled out of her mouth and handed her the condom.

"Place it on the head and unroll it," I instructed. She complied, taking the condom and doing as I said. Once it was in place, I pushed her onto the bed on her back and placed both her thighs over my shoulders, wanting to make her orgasm at least once before I entered her. I wanted her as wet and as swollen as I could get her. The more relaxed she was, the less it would hurt, and that was my goal. I wanted her first sexual experience to be good, so she'd want more and more after that.

It was purely selfish on my part. The truth was that I wanted her virginity to be mine. I'd be her first and I wanted her to remember me and this night all her life.

I continued licking and sucking her, a finger inside to stimulate her g-spot, and soon she was writhing under my mouth.

"Oh God," she gasped, her hands gripping the sheets. "I think I'm going to..."

Then her orgasm began. I felt it—her body clenching around my finger, her clit practically vibrating under my tongue. I continued to stimulate her clit, enjoying as her body trembled, her muscles all tensing. I watched as her nipples hardened and knew she was in total ecstasy.

She groaned, her hands reaching down to take hold of my head. "Stop, stop!" she cried out. I knew she'd become too sensitive, so I stopped licking her clit.

"Oh God, that was so good," she said, breathing hard.

I rose and leaned over her, staring down into her face. "You liked that, did you?"

She smiled, her eyes closed. "You can do that anytime you want."

"I might just take you up on that offer," I replied, kissing her mouth.

Now it was time to deflower her. I pressed the tip of my erection against her, pressing between the lips of her sex.

"If I continue, you can maybe come again," I said, and rubbed her clit lightly with the tip.

"Whatever you say," she said and opened her eyes.

I began to work her up again, this time using my cock instead of my tongue. I licked her nipples and bit them softly until they hardened into peaks. I ran my tongue all over her breasts and down her belly, licking her, slowly at first, then with more insistence until I felt her clit harden once more. She thrust against my mouth, hungry to feel my tongue on her.

I stood up and rubbed the head of my cock against her clit, the slick wetness of it feeling almost as good as her mouth. I thrust my hips, running my hard length against her, teasing the opening to her body with the head, repeating the motion, hoping to bring her to the edge.

I entered her finally, pushing the head of my cock past her entrance while I stimulated her clit. She took in a deep breath and waited. I pressed more firmly, slipping inside a bit more.

"Ohh," she said, her eyes widening. I pulled out and stroked her clit once more with the head, leaning down to suck her nipples.

I tried again to enter her, this time pushing deeper until I heard her sharp intake of breath.

I kept pulling out my cock when I heard her respond until I was a few inches inside her. Not my entire length, but enough that she was stretched. Then I stimulated her clit, determined to make her come with my cock at least partially inside of her. I wanted her to know what it felt like to come around my cock. To feel a cock inside of her when she orgasmed.

I kept still, not thrusting, and rubbed her clit in lazy circles with my thumb, one hand on her breast, squeezing her nipple between my fingers.

Soon, she began to move on me, just small movements as if she wanted to feel me deeper. I let her push on my cock more deeply while I kept my thumb softly circling her clit. Soon, as I had hoped, she tensed up and I knew she was close.

"Oh, *God*..." she cried out and I knew she had gone over the edge. Her body rhythmically clenched around the head of my cock, making me gasp with pleasure.

"That's it," I said with satisfaction and entered her more deeply, knowing she was in ecstasy. I began a slow thrust while she recovered, taking my thumb off her clit and focusing on my own pleasure now that I was filling her with my cock right to the hilt.

Watching her pleasure, feeling her body clench around the head, had brought me close enough that with only a few moments of deep thrusting, I was at the precipice myself. I leaned over her completely, my hands on either side of her shoulders, and watched her face. I wanted her to watch me come as I had watched her.

Pleasure spread from my balls to my gut and down my legs as I came, almost blinding me with its intensity. I thrust with each spasm and then collapsed on top of her. She slipped her arms around my neck and pulled me close as I panted, recovering.

"It barely hurt at all," she said, and when I pulled back to look in her eyes, I saw happiness there. She had been afraid of pain, but had felt little and had, instead, orgasmed twice.

"My work here is done if that's the case," I said with a grin, bending down to kiss her smiling mouth. "It'll only get better the more you fuck. You'll learn what you need. You'll be able to come with your partner if you're not afraid to do what works."

"Thank you," she said softly.

"Are you sore?" I asked when I began to slip out of her.

"Not too bad," she replied.

I gripped the edges of the condom so that it didn't slip off. On my shaft were a few streaks of blood, so I knew she had been a virgin. I would have liked to see no blood, but that wasn't always possible. Every woman's body was different.

I removed the condom, tied off the end and threw it into the waste basket beside my bed. Then I laid back down and kissed her, nestling between her still-open thighs.

"How are you?" I asked, resting on my elbows, my face above hers.

She smiled and raised her arms over her head. "I'm good. I didn't think I'd come when you did it. I thought it would hurt too much."

I shrugged. "It all depends on how ready you are. If you're not wet and aroused, you're not going to enjoy anything. It would be like rubbing your elbow. When you're aroused, it's like scratching an itch."

"God, no wonder they try to keep you a virgin," she said, closing her eyes and running her fingers through her long hair. "If I'd known how good it felt, I'd have been doing it all the time."

I laughed at that, pleased it had been so good for her. "I'm glad you waited."

She frowned. "But I would probably be a lot better at it if I had more experience, right? Wouldn't you prefer someone who knew what they were doing?"

I shook my head. "I enjoyed being the one. Your body is delicious, and I loved it when you came on my cock."

She wriggled underneath me. "I loved it when I came on your cock too. If it wasn't so late, I'd want to do it again. But I should get back to the dorm. I need my sleep."

I smiled at that. "A girl after my own heart. You could stay here if you want, but I understand. I'd love to do it again if you could stay. I'm in town for another week so maybe, if you want, we could get together again before I go. We could see how many times we could make you come."

She kissed me, her eyes twinkling. "I'm at your disposal. Besides, I need the practice."

"Need the practice..." I said with a grin. "What night works best for you?"

"Any night except Wednesday, because I have an astronomy lab."

"I'll text you. We have some time."

"Seriously, you could do me every night if they're like tonight."

I laughed. "I could do you, could I?" I bent down and kissed her deeply, glad that she was so relaxed and eager to be with me again.

We pulled apart finally, and I helped her off the bed. Beneath her on the sheet was a single smear of blood.

"I should keep this," she said with a grin, pointing to it, "and give it to Spencer as proof that I was a virgin on my wedding night."

"Look, by the time you get married, Spencer will have no power over you. Your husband will be glad he married you no matter whether you were a virgin or experienced. Only a small-minded religious zealot would expect a woman in her twenties to be a virgin."

"I hope so," she said. "I might give it to Spencer as a gift anyway, no matter who I marry. Shove it in his face."

"He's such a bastard." I shook my head, still angry that he'd had the nerve to hit Celia across the face. "I'm sorry you've had him as a stepfather all this time."

"I'm a free woman now," she said and raised her hands over her head, smiling. "He can't touch me." She shrugged and I hoped she was right. Spencer was pretty big in Boston. He seemed like the kind of man who would hold a grudge and try to get revenge. If he hurt his stepdaughter—slapping her across the face at her age—he'd do worse. I knew it.

"Try to stay under his radar even so," I said. "He's powerful."

"He's a sonofabitch." She got up and dressed, pulling on her underwear and other clothes.

I was sad to see her delicious body covered up. I usually didn't like it when women stayed the night, and encouraged them to go home early with some excuse or other, but I would have made an exception for Celia so we could fuck again. I would have loved to see her wake up to my mouth on her pussy.

We left the apartment and went to my car. While I drove her back to Cambridge, we talked about our lives, my time at boot camp and her classes. When we finally drove up to her dorm, I wished we weren't saying goodbye. Although she seemed pleased with the night, you never knew what people were really thinking. Would I see her again before I left? Did she want to hook up again or was she just being nice?

I knew I wanted to see her again. She was a delightful partner despite her innocence and inexperience. I hadn't realized how much I would enjoy being her first lover, and part of me wanted to be her only one. I would have time off now and then, and I intended to return to Boston to visit my father and brothers. Maybe I could see her as well, although I doubted anything more could develop.

She'd meet someone at Harvard and that would be that.

I had to settle for being her first.

"Here we are," I said, turning to her after parking on the street outside her dorm. "Thanks for a great time."

"It *was* great," she said and smiled at me, her expression a bit wistful.

"I hope you enjoyed it."

"I did," she said softly. She bit her lip. "From the time I first saw you when I was nine. I didn't know about sex at the time, but I knew about kissing. I wanted to kiss you. Later, I wanted you to be the first."

I leaned over and kissed her, surprised she had felt that way. "I never knew."

"You were too old. You didn't look at me that way but you were my crush."

I smiled, amused that she'd had a schoolgirl crush on me. "You let me know when you're free. I'll be right over. We can go out for supper, we can go to my apartment, your place. Whatever you want."

"I'll text you."

We kissed again and then she left the car and walked to the entrance to the dorm. When she got to the doors, she turned and waved at me. I waved back and then drove off once the door closed behind her, shocked that things had turned out the way they did. I'd imagined fucking her when I'd seen her at the beach party, but wouldn't have touched her to honor my friendship with Graham. But *she* had wanted *me*. She was all grown up. She had the right to choose who she wanted to be with.

I was glad she'd picked me.

CHAPTER 12

CELIA

I CLIMBED the stairs to my room and was surprised to see the door open. Concerned, I crept towards the door and peeked inside, worried that someone had broken in. On my sofa, I saw Spencer, sitting there with his arms crossed.

"Where the hell have you been?"

I frowned and pushed my way into the room, putting my bag down on the table. "What are you doing here? Who let you in?"

He jerked his head to the side. "Your next-door neighbor."

"Why did she let you in? She knows not to let anyone in when I'm out."

Spencer stood and came over to where I was. "I told her who I was and that I wanted to go inside and wait for you. Where the hell were you?"

"You could have texted me."

I went to mini fridge and took out a bottle of water, my heart pounding, fearing that Spencer was here to fight.

"Who were you with?" he said, his voice gruff.

"It's none of your business who I was with. A friend."

"Don't tell me it was that Saint thug."

I turned to face him. "Can you leave now? I'm fine. I need to go to bed and get some sleep. I have class tomorrow."

He stepped closer. "You've been drinking. I can smell it on you." He pulled me even closer and I struggled with him to get away. "You smell like sex."

His hand gripped my arm, squeezing so hard it hurt.

"Get out," I said, my voice low.

He slapped me. I expected it, and didn't care. When I recovered, my hand over my cheek, I tasted blood. It wasn't the first time he'd drawn blood, and unless I could escape him, it wouldn't be the last.

Mara, the girl who lived in the next room, peeked her head inside. She saw me standing with my hand over my cheek, tears in my eyes from the pain.

"Are you okay?" She saw my face. "Can I call security?"

"My stepfather was just leaving," I said, standing my ground. "Please leave," I said to Spencer, my voice firm.

"I'll leave when I decide."

"Leave now," I said, "Or Mara will call security."

"We're not done here," Spencer replied.

I turned to Mara. "Call security."

He pointed at me, his face so red that I thought he might explode. "You don't speak to me that way and you don't tell me to leave. I control your trust fund and I can stop paying for your room and board. Tomorrow."

"Go ahead," I said, my hands on my hips. "I'll get a job and live somewhere else."

He stepped closer, furious that I would stand up to him like that. "You'll regret this."

"So will you," I replied. "You better leave."

"I'm calling security," Mara said and held out her cell, showing that she'd dialed a number.

"You're a filthy slut," Spencer hissed and pushed by me, almost knocking me down. Mara stepped aside and watched as Spencer stormed down the hallway to the stairs.

"Are you okay?" she asked, coming over to where I stood. "Do you need to go to the hospital?"

"No," I said and rubbed my cheek. "He's done worse. I'm just glad he's gone."

"That's assault," she said, her brow furrowed. "He hit you. You could charge him with assault."

I shook my head. "He's the Assistant District Attorney, on his way to becoming DA. He's best friends with everyone who matters in the city. No one would believe me."

"Will he really stop paying for the dorm?" she asked, her arm on my shoulder.

"Yes," I said and shrugged.

"Where will you go?"

"I'll get a job. I'll find a room somewhere. I don't need to be here."

"That sucks," Mara said, and made a face of sympathy. "Maybe he was just mad and won't really cut you off. What happened?"

I went to the bathroom down the hall and Mara followed me. I splashed water on my face while she watched. "I was with my boyfriend. Spencer hates him. That's all."

"I didn't know you had a boyfriend." Her eyes widened. "Do tell, please."

"We just started seeing each other. He's going to Parris Island next week to become a Marine." I smiled, giddily imagining that Hunter was my boyfriend for real. Except, of course, he wasn't. I knew he wasn't the boyfriend type. He preferred to remain single, although he always had women around him, willing to keep him company.

Besides, I was just a kid compared to him. He'd finished his MBA and was going to become a Marine. He was a man. I didn't feel at all like a woman, even though I'd just been deflowered. Spencer tried to keep me a child because of his zealot commitment to protecting my virginity. He had to make sure I didn't damage his good name in the

119

evangelical community, where he held a position as leader of a Bible study group and "pillar of the community."

That was twice Spencer had hit me in the space of a few days. I knew I should go to my mother and tell her, but she was so fragile. Spencer was never violent with her—just Graham and me, telling us he couldn't spare the rod or he'd condemn us to hell. He had often told me that he hit me because he loved me, but I wasn't buying it. Spencer had stopped hitting Graham when Graham got big enough to fight back.

Spencer hadn't hit me for a while—not since Graham was strong enough to defend me, but Graham didn't always step in. Like Saturday night. Even Graham was mad at me for kissing Hunter. I was surprised that he hadn't stood up for me, but Spencer was holding the purse strings on Graham's start-up funding, so he might have been reluctant to make Spencer mad.

Spencer was a monster who dominated both our lives. How I hated him.

Mara finally left me alone, once she was sure I was okay. I had a quick shower and got into my bed, taking out my cell and checking to see if Hunter had texted me.

Sure enough, he had.

HUNTER: Hey. How are you? Any regrets now that you're back home?

CELIA: Not even the slightest doubt.

HUNTER: That's good. I wanted to make sure you were okay about tonight.

CELIA: Couldn't be happier. Only thing I would like more is another date before you go.

HUNTER: Count on it. Text me tomorrow when you want me to pick you up. We can come back here or go to your place. Up to you.

CELIA: Okay. Nite.

HUNTER: Good night.

I didn't want to tell him that Spencer knew we had been together. If I did, I knew Hunter would be honorable and never see me again. Instead, I lay back in bed, smiling, thinking of seeing Hunter again, and how we'd get some practice in. With that thought in mind, I turned off the bedside light and rolled up in my blankets.

I'd go looking for a job tomorrow so I could be free of Spencer, no matter what happened. I could handle a second job if that was all I could get. Tips were good so I hoped I could afford to find a house to share or a bed-sitting room somewhere in Cambridge if Spencer followed through with his threat. I'd hate to leave Kirkland House because it was a plum placement. I would hate to lose my place there.

But the most important thing was that I had a tuition scholarship which paid for my classes and books. I'd have to scramble to find a place to live if Spencer did cut me off. Once I was twenty-one, the trust fund would be under my control, and I couldn't wait for that. I'd be completely free of Spencer at that point.

I could ask for more shifts at the restaurant, but I could never get enough shifts to afford room and board or rent and expenses.

I fell asleep to that calculus—hoping I could afford to move out if Spencer followed through on his threat.

THE NEXT DAY, I woke up sore from the night before. It was a pleasant soreness, at least to me, because it meant I was no longer a virgin. I had a bath and then went to my classes, almost forgetting about Spencer and his economic tyranny. But it was brought back to me all too soon, when Spencer showed up at my dormitory after classes, while I was sitting at my desk reading over the next day's material.

The knock at the door interrupted my focus on an astronomy text calculating the distance to the moon. I went to the door and opened it, and Spencer barged inside, wearing his business suit, his briefcase in hand.

"What are you doing?" I said, angry that he felt that he could just come over without calling first.

"I'm here to save you from yourself," he said and stood by my desk.

"What do you mean?"

"I want to show you something," he said and reached into his massive briefcase. "Maybe it will help you see the light about your boyfriend."

"He's not my boyfriend," I said, angry that Spencer was back.

"Look at this," he said and handed me a file. "Read it over. Maybe this will convince you he's a thug, and no good for you if you want to ever make anything of yourself."

I took the file and opened it, thumbing through a dozen sheets of paper and photographs. Some of the names had been blacked out, but there was enough there that I could get the gist.

It was a police report about an assault that happened over a year earlier. The man in the very graphic photographs had been beaten almost to death, his leg broken, his arm broken, and his face beaten so badly, his eyes were swollen shut.

There were two mug shots included in the file.

One of Sean.

One of Hunter.

I covered my mouth and read the police report with horror. The man's wife reported that her husband owed Donald Saint money and that his nephews Sean and Hunter Saint had come to collect and had beaten him almost to death when he had no money.

"I can't believe it," I said and shook my head, my stomach feeling sick at what I saw in the photos.

"Believe it. I want you to promise you'll never see that boy again. He may seem all nice to you, but he's a thug underneath the pretty boy façade."

"I can't believe he actually beat someone up. He hates that side of his family."

"Apparently not enough to stay clean," Spencer said. "Blood is thicker than water, Celia. It's time for you to grow up and realize that. All that fighting he did as a kid made him and his brothers perfect for the protection racket that his uncle and father are involved in. If you want to be a prosecutor someday, you have to stay away from people like Hunter."

I shook my head, feeling a bit dizzy that Hunter had been involved in this kind of thing. He seemed so dead set against anything to do with his uncle.

"Stay away from him. Don't even talk to him again. If you agree, I'll keep funding you here at Kirkland House. I promised to fund you until you're twenty-one and I mean it. When you get control over your trust fund, you can do anything you want. I want you to get into Harvard Law. I'll even up your allowance so you can stop working. You have to be at least Magna Cum Laude to get into Harvard Law with any certainty, so I don't want you to focus on anything else—not work, not boys."

"I'm nineteen, Spencer," I said, frowning. "They're not boys. They're men."

"In age, yes, but not in terms of maturity. I don't want you to throw away your life over some jerk-off."

"Hunter is hardly a jerk-off and you know it. He's got an MBA. He's going to boot camp to become a Marine."

"His father is part of the Romanov syndicate, laundering money for them. His uncle runs a protection racket. Hunter can't escape his genes or his family."

"He's *not involved*," I said, angrily. "Why can't you understand that Hunter's leaving Boston to get away from his family's bad influence?"

"That police report says different. Stop seeing him. Don't see him again. If you stay away from him, I'll up your allowance and you can stop working part time. Make high honors and you'll be a shoe-in to Harvard Law. I have markers to call in. I can help you."

"I don't need your help, Spencer," I said, tears in my eyes. "I can do it on my own. I got into Harvard on my own."

"No, you didn't. I gave you the edge. If you disobey me, you'll get no money until you're twenty-one. You'll have to work two part-time jobs and you won't be able to keep up your grades. You won't make it. Is some thug worth it? Really?"

We stood there, facing off against each other. He had hit me for less than this before, but I wasn't afraid of him now. In fact, if he were to die tomorrow, I wouldn't care, except for how it would affect my mother.

"If you don't obey me, I'll call up my contacts in the Marines and get him thrown out of that. I can make a lot of trouble for Hunter, and I will—unless you promise me you won't ever see him again. I'll put a call in to the commander at Parris Island. If I want, I can get him kicked out before he even gets there. But I'd rather see him become a Marine than stay here and continue to bring Graham down or, God forbid, ruin you."

I fumed silently, my fists clenched.

"I won't see him again," I said finally, confused about the police report, and not wanting Hunter to suffer because I was being selfish. Maybe Hunter had beaten up that man. I was too upset to think but I knew that he was going somewhere and doing something noble with his life. He wanted to escape his family's dark heritage. I wouldn't be the one to force him back into their clutches.

"You have to promise," Spencer said, his face dark. "I don't want you to even call him or speak with him. He's a bad seed, Celia, and his family is no good. I'm breaking the law bringing this file to you, but I thought you needed to know what he's capable of. Don't think he wouldn't do that again – or worse – if he felt he needed to protect his family. I'm doing this because I care about your future. You have no future with him."

I turned away, wanting to hide my eyes, which were brimming with a mixture of anger and sadness. Anger that Spencer would stoop so low as to block Hunter from a career with the Marines; sadness because I really liked Hunter and believed him when he said he wanted to escape his family, but for him to do that to the man who owed his uncle money?

Spencer came around and peered into my face. "Promise me," he said, his voice insistent. "If you don't, I'll call my contact and turn over the evidence I have on Hunter and his family. There are more files like that one," he said and shook the file. "Like death threats. Prostitution. Gun running. If the Marines knew about his involvement in that, they'd turn him down, no questions asked."

I shook my head. "All right," I said, and exhaled. "I promise. I don't want Hunter to be hurt because of me. Don't report him to the Marines. It's his escape from his family."

"If I find out you're seeing him behind my back, I won't hesitate to call my contact. I mean it," he said, pointing his finger in my face.

"I won't," I said emphatically. "I'm not that selfish. He's leaving soon for Parris Island. I promise I won't see him again."

"Starting tonight," Spencer said, his frown dark. "Tonight."

I nodded. "Tonight. He'll probably email or text me, and I'll tell him I can't see him again."

"Do it now," Spencer said. "While I'm here. I want to see you do it."

I took out my cell and opened it to the messenger. I typed in a text to Hunter, my gut all knotted up.

Celia: Gonna have to cancel our plans. Too much work and can't afford to be distracted. Have to keep my grades up to keep my scholarship, so, thanks for everything. Have a good life.

I sent it and then showed it to Spencer, who grabbed my cell and frowned as he read the previous texts.

"Disgusting." He practically threw the phone back at me. "I'll be watching. I'll know if you see him. Believe me."

"You have someone watching me?"

"I have eyes everywhere."

Spencer gathered up the file and stuffed it back into his briefcase. Then, he headed for the door. Before he left, he turned back to me. "One day, you'll be happy I saved you from getting mixed up with him."

I didn't reply, too upset to even open my mouth. I turned away and, finally, Spencer closed the door and left me alone.

LATER THAT NIGHT, when I was sitting on the tiny two-seater sofa across from my television, I got a text from Hunter.

Hunter: Just got this. Are you okay?

I debated whether to reply, chewing my nail, torn about my response.

If I left the text unanswered, he might come over and check to see if I was okay. I knew he was concerned about Spencer having hit me in the past. I had to respond and find a way to make it clear I wasn't interested.

I had to just shut it off. I couldn't get the picture of the man in the hospital bed out of my mind. How could Hunter do something like that?

It was all there in the police report. Hunter never told me or Graham about it, at least that I knew of. Even if we had a great time together, I knew Hunter would be out with some new woman in no time flat. He was never alone for long, and probably had a list of women happy to spend their nights with him.

I bit my lip and tried to word my text just right.

Celia: Oh, sorry—I'm fine. I know we planned on seeing each other again before you go, but I finally got a date with Greg. Now that I'm no longer burdened with my virginity, I have a lot of lost time to make up. I'm sure you of all people can understand that! Thanks again! Have a great time at Parris Island!

There was a long pause. I wondered if he could see through my fake happiness. Part of me hoped he did and came to the dorm to check on me. The other part, the part that wasn't a selfish bitch, hoped he shrugged it off and found some floozy he knew to divert his attention on the off-chance that he was sad.

There was no answer.

I stared at my phone for a long while, wanting oh so badly for him to text me and to see him secretly, ask him about the police report, but what would that do? If Spencer did have eyes everywhere, he'd go after Hunter, maybe cost him a place in the Marines. I hated to think of that happening, no matter how sad I was that I had to completely give up on him and no matter how horrified I was from reading the police report.

So instead of happily waiting for him to come over and pick me up for what I expected would be a night of pleasure, I lay on my bed and silently cursed Spencer. I cursed Hunter's family ties. I should have used the time to study, since I wasn't going to see Hunter, but I couldn't do it. I'd already read the same paragraph in my astronomy text three times and still didn't understand it.

Someone else would come along who was as special as Hunter.

If I kept telling myself that lie, I might one day believe it.

Completely disheartened, I threw myself down on my bed and cried my eyes out.

END OF PART ONE

BAD BOY SINNER

THE BAD BOY SERIES: PART TWO

PREFACE

"They're a dark people with a gift for suffering way past their deserving. It's said that without whiskey to soak and soften the world, they'd kill themselves."

Steinbeck, on the Irish

CHAPTER 13

Hunter

ONE YEAR EARLIER...

I TRIED TO STAY CLEAN.

From the time I was in college, I did everything in my power to avoid being drawn into my family's business and becoming tainted by their ties to organized crime.

Despite my efforts, less than four years later, I found myself right back where I started.

Saint Brothers Gym and Boxing Emporium.

Four years had passed since I'd left Boston to join the Corps. After spending time in Afghanistan, and then with Special Operations Forces in Iraq fighting ISIS, I was on leave and ready for a term teaching at the Marine Corps Officer Candidates School in Quantico, Virginia.

Then everything changed.

We were standing around the ring at my father's gym watching my youngest brother spar with his trainer. Shorter than either Sean or me, Conor was more like my uncle than my father, who was taller and heavier. A lightweight boxer, Conor was fast, accurate, and on top of it all, smart. He not only felt it, the moves ingrained in his muscle memory, he also understood boxing at an intellectual level.

My uncle Donny was very pleased with Conor. Conor was the only one out of three generations who had a real chance, and he was working his way up in the circuit, undefeated in his last run at the title.

We were all so proud...

Just after nine in the morning, the FBI rolled up outside the gym and entered, armed for a takedown, moving fast. Many of the Agents had military training and the mission was conducted with military precision. Seven Special Agents entered the gym, shouting at the gym members to move to the sides of the building where they kept a watch over them. Connor was still in the ring. We were confused at first, uncertain what was happening and who the target was.

My father stepped forward to meet the Special Agent leading the team, who marched over to us. Two other Agents followed behind him, while the others fanned out inside the building.

"Can I help you?" he asked, his hands on his hips.

My father used to be an imposing man, but emphysema had made him weak. His back was stooped, his muscles wasted, his chest caved in. A small tank of oxygen hung in a harness around his shoulder. His hair was buzzed short, styled in whitewalls in solidarity with me. He appeared small and impotent before the Special Agent, a tall eagle-eyed man in an FBI blue windbreaker, who held out a warrant in one hand and a badge in another, practically shoving them into my father's face.

"Special Agent Vicars. I have a warrant for the arrest of Donald Cameron Saint."

He glanced around but he already knew my uncle was there and what he looked like. My dad examined the warrant and badge but barely had time to respond before my uncle stepped forward.

"What's the charge?" Uncle Donny was shorter and more vigorous than my father, with a shaved head and beady blue eyes. He looked like the street-scrappy former boxer he was.

"Three charges of extortion under the Racketeer Influenced and Corrupt Organization Act."

A RICO warrant. I knew what that was...

"Turn around, hands behind your back," Special Agent Vicars said, barking out the order like my former boot camp drill instructor.

My uncle held up his hands. "Not so fast," he said and reached for the warrant. The other Special Agents stepped forward and two of them pulled their guns out of the holsters, pointing them at my uncle.

"Turn around, now," Vicars repeated.

"I want to see the warrant," my uncle insisted. "It's my right."

One of the Special Agents grabbed my uncle and wrenched him around while the other pointed his gun at him.

It was then that cruel fate stepped in.

"Hey!" my older brother Sean said, his face red. "Let the man read the damn warrant!" Then Sean made a critical mistake. He pushed his way over to Vicars, determined to read the warrant to make sure it was legitimate.

I should have stepped in and stopped him, but I was more concerned with my father, whose face was white, his lips almost blue. He'd had a heart attack a few years earlier and I didn't want to see him stressed.

I should have stopped Sean, keeping him back from the arrest, but my focus was on my dad. I took him over to a bench beside the ring and sat him down, determined to go over and ask to see the warrant while they cuffed my uncle, but Sean made it there first.

Sean had a traumatic brain injury from too many knockouts. His emotions were on edge all the time, and he was often overwhelmed by anger. It clouded his judgment.

What happened next was so fast, it was over before I even realized it had started.

My uncle's hands were pinned behind his back, his face red from anger, as they pulled out the cuffs to take him into custody. Sean tried to get in between the Special Agent and my uncle. He thrust his chest out and held up his fists like he was ready to clock the Agent.

"Show us the warrant or get out."

"Get back," one of the other Agents said, stepping closer.

"I said, show us the fucking warrant!"

"Your lawyer can see it. Now step the fuck aside," the Agent said, taking out his sidearm and pointing it at Sean.

Why Sean did it, I'll never know, but he knocked the gun back with a chop of his hand.

It must have been his boxer instincts taking over. His ability to think critically and reason his way through life had been damaged by repeated trauma to his pre-frontal cortex, but the deep muscle memory was still there from years of boxing. And it was ready to go.

That was assault of a federal officer and it was all the other Special Agent needed. He was entirely within the law to do what he did.

But my brother was mentally disabled. He was emotionally disabled by his brain injury.

I ran forward, realizing at the last minute that it had all gone so terribly wrong, but before I could get to him, four shots rang out and my brother fell to the floor.

"Oh my fucking *God*!" my uncle cried out. "Jesus Christ, you shot him!"

"Get the fuck away," I said to the Agent who stood over Sean's body. Then, I knelt, covering Sean's body, trying to keep them from shooting him again. He had fallen face forward. I knew what that meant. He was out.

Maybe even dead.

I rolled him over carefully to check for gunshot wounds, and found three. One in his shoulder, one in his neck, one that appeared to graze his face. By some lucky chance, the wound in his neck must have missed the important veins and arteries, so he wasn't bleeding out. Nevertheless, I grabbed a towel from a table beside the boxing ring and pressed it against the wound. Sean's eyes were half-lidded, but he was unconscious.

"Sean," I said, leaning down to see if he was breathing. He was—

barely. I felt for a pulse, thankful for my training in dealing with battlefield wounds. I glanced up and motioned to the far wall, where a first aid kit was kept. " Quick! Call 911 and get the kit!"

One of the Special Agents spoke into his two-way, summoning the EMTs who were already waiting outside. Conor ran to the first aid kit and brought it to me.

"Sean!" my father gasped from the bench where he sat, trying to catch his breath. "Oh, God, Sean..." He struggled up and came to stand beside us, where the FBI Agent still had his weapon drawn.

"For Christ's sake, put down your weapon," I said angrily.

"He struck me," the Agent said, his arm still outstretched, the weapon still in his hand and pointed now at me.

"Put your weapon down," Vicars said, his voice quiet. The Agent finally complied, holstering it and shrugging his shoulders like it wasn't his fault.

In less than a minute, the two EMTs entered the gym, coming over to where I knelt beside Sean. I'd applied pressure to two of his wounds, and had elevated his feet to fight off shock, but Sean looked bad. His skin was pale, his pulse thready.

They assessed him and finally got him on the gurney and took him to the unit idling outside. An FBI Agent went in with him, because even if he was dying, he was still under arrest for assaulting a federal agent.

My uncle ended up in the back of the FBI armored vehicle.

I took my father and Conor to the hospital in my SUV, following behind the ambulance and several FBI cruisers. By the time we arrived at Mass General, they had intubated Sean and put pressure bandages on his legs to prevent shock.

We followed the gurney inside but were stopped at the admitting area in the ER.

"You'll have to register him," the clerk said. My father sat at the desk and answered the questions, providing them with insurance information.

"He shouldn't have resisted," Special Agent Vicars said to me, his voice low. "He struck a federal agent."

"Fuck off," I said.

I went to the door to the ER, trying to see where they had taken Sean. A nurse saw me and came to open the door. I introduced myself and said I was Sean's younger brother.

"Where are they taking him?"

"Right into the OR," she replied. "We'll keep you updated."

I nodded and reluctantly closed the door.

My father was wheezing on his way to the seating area in the ER. Lugging around the bottle of oxygen was too much for him and he passed out, crumpling in his chair, his head falling forward.

I called the triage nurse, and she came around the corner to where my father slumped in his chair.

"He has COPD?" she asked, feeling his pulse.

"Emphysema," I said. "He had a heart attack two years ago."

She called two orderlies over and they took my father to a room in the ER. I went inside with him, sitting at his side, waiting to find out if he'd had another heart attack or simply passed out due to stress.

For the next hour, I sat in his room with my head in my hands while they attached him to various machines to monitor his heart and breathing, his oxygen and pulse.

Later, an ER doc came into the room where I sat to give me an update. Sean was in a coma, his neck immobilized, his brain swelling.

The ER doc pulled me into the hall outside my dad's room.

"Your brother likely won't survive the next hour," he said, his voice grim. "If he does, he'll most likely have permanent damage to his spinal cord."

"If he survives, he'll be paralyzed?"

"Yes. Quadriplegic. That is, if he regains consciousness."

As soon as he said that, I knew Sean would die.

Conor was beside himself, a basket case, sitting alone in the ER waiting room.

Together, with Sean in surgery and my dad in the ER, we began our vigil.

· · ·

138

AFTER SEAN'S surgery was over and he was taken to the ICU, I spent all night watching him, listening to the hiss of the ventilator, the beep-beep of the monitors. I knew in my gut that he wouldn't make it.

My father stabilized and was discharged from the ER in the early evening after several tests showed he had no more damage to his heart. He didn't want to leave the hospital, and so he, Conor, and I sat beside the bed, taking turns holding Sean's hand. Finally, the doc in charge of the transplant team came to us, because my brother had indicated he wanted to be a donor when he died.

"What's the bottom line?" I asked. After my tour of duty in the Middle East, I was used to seeing death. "Does he have any chance of recovering?"

"I'm very sorry, but no," the doc replied. "His stats indicate he's not going to recover. His brain scan, his blood work..." He shook his head. "I'm very sorry."

My father bowed his head, pressing Sean's hand against it

I nodded. "Then we should take him off life support."

My father actually sobbed at that. It was the first time I'd heard him cry since I was a child at my grandfather's funeral.

My own eyes were brimming and all I really wanted to do was run down the hall and out of the hospital, escape all of it, but I had to be strong for my father and younger brother.

I had to be the oldest son now.

LATER, after they took Sean off life support and after we all said our goodbyes, I drove my father and brother back to our apartment over the gym. We entered the building, which had been quickly closed for the day, and there, still on the floor where he'd fallen, was Sean's blood —a dark red smear from someone's hasty attempt to clean it after we'd left with the ambulance.

"Oh, God," my father said, his voice shaking. "Someone should have cleaned that up."

"I'll take care of it," I said quietly.

Of course, Sean had been the *de facto* janitor for the gym so it would have been his job, if he hadn't been the victim. I helped my father inside, one arm under his, trying to avoid the blood. I took him up the stairs to the apartment, then got him situated in the living room with a glass of Guinness.

Conor had gone to his bedroom, but my father needed a drink to wind down.

Then, before I began processing my own grief, I spent the next half hour cleaning the floor in the gym where my brother had fallen after being shot by an FBI Special Agent during my uncle's arrest on a RICO warrant.

THE NEXT DAY, the gym opened at the usual time and life went on, as it does in any business after a tragedy. Luckily, my cousin John was the day manager. He arrived the next morning and so I was able to spend time with my dad and Conor, planning the funeral and memorial.

Conversation gradually turned to the events of the previous day. Donny was now in federal custody and would be charged eventually.

"When you live by the sword, you die by the sword. Isn't that what Donny always said?" Connor glanced between the two of us.

"Donny's small potatoes," I said, shaking my head. "Getting him means nothing. It's got to be someone ratting him out."

My father was a mess. He turned to me and said, "I need you," his voice haggard. "I can't do this on my own anymore. My ticker," he said and patted his chest. "I can't take the stress. Donny did most of the managing so I only looked over receipts. You went to business school. You know more about running a business that the rest of us put together. It's logical for you to take over, Hunter."

I sighed and closed my eyes, coming to terms with the reality of the situation. He was right. I *was* the logical choice to take over now that Donny was in custody and Sean was dead.

"I have a year to go on my contract," I said. It was true. I'd signed on for a five-year stint in the Marines and I loved my job.

"I know you never wanted to get involved with the family, but I need you. You were always the one who was going to manage things."

He looked at me, his expression pleading. "I'm not good with managing things. You know that."

Of course I knew he wasn't a manager. He was a boxer. He owned a gym, and he could count money, but where he really excelled was in teaching new boxers how to fight, picking out the good ones, the ones with potential, and training them up to top fighting shape.

That had been his strongest skill all his life; the success of the gym and fitness clubs had been due solely to Donny's greater management skills.

Like Sean before him, my dad had too many knockouts when he was young and foolish. Too many concussions. As a result, organizational issues were not his thing. Business was not his thing. He didn't run anything in terms of the business—that was Donny's purview. Now that he'd had a couple of heart attacks, my father merely hung around the gym, talking to the regulars, offering tips to the new fighters on how to improve. He locked up the receipts every night for his second wife Cathy, who did the books, and he opened the place every morning. He was more of a coach than a manager.

"We need you, Hunter," he said, leaning in and putting his arm on my shoulder. "I need you. I can't do this on my own."

I sighed. "I should be able to get an honorable discharge on compassionate grounds," I replied, recognizing his inability to cope. "

My father reached out and squeezed my arm. "Thank you. You don't know what a relief it is.

"I'll call this afternoon."

OF COURSE, my CO was upset that I'd be leaving. I was scheduled to start a new course soon and they'd have to scramble to find someone to replace me, but they could. I was good but I wasn't irreplaceable. There were a dozen or so other hopefuls they could consider for the job of selecting new officer candidates. I was just the best.

With reluctance, my CO called me back and said he'd set the process in motion. I should have my honorable discharge on compassionate grounds in a week—before my leave was over. I'd have to return to Quantico to pick up my belongings and sign papers, but other than that, I could stay in Boston and start running the businesses.

Not only did we have Saint Brothers Gym and Boxing Emporium, we also had several franchise locations of Saint Brothers Fitness across the eastern seaboard. I had to keep in touch with each franchisee and make sure they were reporting their business data and keeping up with expectations.

The next few days were busy and, at the same time, somber, as we planned for Sean's funeral and memorial at the graveside. In the meantime, we learned more details surrounding my uncle's arrest and charges. I spoke with John about him, and we had a family dinner with my father, Conor, and John, plus Donny's two other sons, where we discussed Donny's case and what his lawyer had said about his chances of getting released.

"He's not getting out," John said. "I spoke with his lawyer. They got him cold and no judge is going to let him out pending trial. The new hotshot DA has been salivating for the chance to get my dad on a RICO charge since he couldn't get him on anything local."

The new hotshot DA...

I had to smile grimly about that.

Spencer Grant, Graham Parker's bastard of a stepfather, had finally brought my uncle down. He couldn't get Donny himself but he had been able to pull together enough of a case to tempt the Feds. There was nothing any of us could do except fill in where Donny used to be—running the business and keeping the mafia at bay. That meant doing exactly what I had always wanted to avoid. Getting my hands dirty with family business.

Still, I had no other choice now that Donny was in federal custody and Sean was dead.

The first thing on my agenda was getting revenge.

CHAPTER 14

CELIA

"YOU'LL BE happy to know I finally got that bastard Donny Saint," Spencer said to me when I went over to the house to see my mother.

"What?" I said, frowning. "You arrested Hunter's Uncle Donny?"

"Not me personally, but the Feds."

I had no interest in speaking with Spencer. I'd thought he would be out of the house when I went over, but there he was in all his glory. He must have known I was coming over for a visit with my mom and wanted to gloat.

"Didn't you listen to the news today?" he asked, following me through the house.

"I've been busy."

"Turn on the TV," he said when I got to the living room. "You'll hear. I'm so glad you cut that boy out of your life back then. His family's trouble, but maybe with Donny Saint in federal custody, they'll be less of a threat."

"Threat to whom?" I asked, not really getting what he was talking about. "Who was he a threat to? He was a boxing promoter and runs a couple of nightclubs. "

"He's a thug. His whole family is a bunch of thugs. I provided some nice juicy tidbits of evidence that will help put him away for, oh, maybe a decade or more."

I switched on the television and turned to a local news channel. I'd been ensconced in my dorm studying for mid-term exams and hadn't been paying much attention to the news, so I had no idea what he was talking about.

There were a couple of talking heads and a picture of the gym on screen, so I turned up the volume.

"...report of a shooting at a local landmark, Saints Gym and Boxing Emporium, yesterday during an FBI operation to arrest Donald James Saint on a federal RICO warrant."

"What?"

My mouth fell open as I listened to the reporter describe the shooting of Sean, Hunter's older brother, after he had attacked one of the Special Agents there to arrest Donny. He'd been taken to Mass General but was not expected to survive, according to the family's lawyer, who spoke to the reporter outside the hospital.

"The Saint family is well-known for its historic boxing club. They've trained dozens of boxing stars over the decades since the gym was founded by Colm Saint in the early part of the twentieth century..."

"Oh my God..." I sat down hard on the coffee table across from the television and watched open-mouthed.

"Pretty amazing," Spencer said, a smile on his face.

"They shot *Sean?*"

"Oh, yeah, the brother. He assaulted an FBI Special Agent and was shot three times. He died sometime this morning."

"They killed Sean?" The fact filtered through my shock, making my pulse race. "Sean's *dead?*"

"Yeah, he kicked it during the night."

"Oh my God," I said, covering my mouth, tears filling my eyes.

I had known Sean Saint for half my life—or at least, I had seen him around the gym when I was growing up. "He was just the janitor. Why did they shoot him?"

"He assaulted a federal agent. The agent felt threatened and was in his rights to shoot him. The agent says he thought Sean was trying to take his weapon." Spencer shrugged like he didn't care one way or the other. Like Sean's death was an incidental part of the big event of arresting Donny Saint.

Of course, Spencer would feel that way. All he cared about was getting back at Donny Saint. He had a grudge against Donny over some failed case from years ago. That was the source of all the enmity between our two families all this time.

I hated Spencer.

Hated him.

"I don't know why you're so upset," Spencer said, his voice dismissive. "It's not like you're big friends with them anymore. At least I hope not, if you have any sense."

"Oh, God, poor Hunter..." I said, shaking my head sadly, not caring what Spencer thought. My heart broke for Hunter. I couldn't imagine how he must have felt. "He'll have to come to Boston for the funeral. Who knows where he is? The last I heard, he was deployed to Iraq."

"No, no, Hunter was there at the time," Spencer said, like he relished the fact. "He's on leave from the Marines for a couple of weeks."

I covered my mouth in shock. "He was there?" I said, turning to Spencer, scarcely able to process it. "He *saw* Sean being shot?"

Spencer shrugged. "So was Conor. The whole damn family saw it. I would have liked the FBI to take them all in, but they only had incriminating evidence on Donny's involvement with the Romanov family. He was a nice catch, though." Spencer stood there, his hands on his hips, like he had scored some huge victory. "The whole lot of them could be shot, for all I care. Sean worked for the Romanov family, breaking arms and legs. I showed you the evidence."

"He's a human being," I protested, disgusted that Spencer was so callous. "He *was* a human being," I said, correcting myself. Sean was dead...

"He's one less thug to deal with," Spencer scoffed. "He was a low-life thug, Celia. He broke people's bones when they failed to pay their protection money or loan shark interest."

"I can't believe he's dead," I said, my eyes filling with tears. I turned back to the television and watched stock footage of the gym, the old façade of the building with the original sign, reminiscent of another era. Early twentieth-century architecture. A newer sign had been placed beneath it featuring a muscle-bound boxer with his dukes up.

"Deader than a doornail," Spencer said, his hands on his hips, watching the television coverage. He glanced at me and saw my tears. "What are you all teary about? Sean Saint worked for the Russian mafia. You know that. My God, has everything I've shown you and told you about that family been a total waste of time?"

I didn't say anything more. Instead I sat and stared at the television screen, wiping my eyes while I listened to the talking heads go on about organized crime in Boston and how the Saint family was at the center of an investigation into their ties to the Romanov family.

I knew it all. Spencer had shown me information over the past couple of years on the Saints and their ties to the mob in Boston and New York. It made me thankful that Hunter had pulled himself out of the family business and joined the Marines. It made up for losing him as a friend, as a lover. Hunter was smart. He was good. He didn't want to be part of the family's business precisely because he knew he'd get pulled in.

I hoped this didn't change things.

I wanted to call Hunter up and say how sorry I was to hear about Sean's death. How horrible for him to see Sean shot, to have to make the decision to take him off life support.

I shivered and wrapped my arms around myself, suddenly cold.

"You're going to have to face facts. If you want to follow my foot-steps and be a prosecutor, you have to let your head guide you, not your heart," Spencer said, giving me a disapproving scowl.

I didn't respond. As far as I was concerned, Spencer was out of my life. I only showed up now and then to see my mother. Spencer tried to talk to me when I was there, prodding me to see how I was doing, what my grades were (great, thankyouverymuch) and whether I was seeing anyone at the time (nothankyouverymuch). I usually planned my visits for a time when he'd be at work so I wouldn't have to bump into him. For some reason, he was off work that day so I couldn't avoid him, but I decided I'd only stick around to say hi to mom and then leave.

"Aren't you staying for some tea?" she asked when I pulled on my sweater, planning to leave as quickly as possible. "We usually have a nice cup of tea when you come over."

"Not today," I said and grabbed my bag from the sofa. "I have things to do. I just popped by to check on how you're doing."

I bent down and gave her a kiss on the cheek. She seemed upset but I had no interest in staying and putting up with Spencer's nastiness and gloating over Donny Saint's arrest and Sean's death. I needed to talk to Graham and see what he knew, if he even knew anything. He and Hunter had never been friends again after that weekend when Hunter and I got together.

I slipped on my shoes and felt Spencer's disapproval from across the room. I opened the door but turned back to catch my mom's eye.

"I'll come back another day," I said.

She nodded. "Soon, " she said. "I miss you. You've been so busy lately and we barely see you here for a meal or visit."

She knew I didn't get along well with Spencer, but always held out hope that I'd come by and eat a meal with them. I never said much to her about him, but she must have known I planned to come by when he was out on purpose.

I took a bus back to the dorm, my mind totally occupied with thoughts of Hunter and of Sean's death, a pang of regret in my heart that everything had gone so wrong with Hunter and our family. Between Hunter and Graham. Most of all, between Hunter and me.

When we first got together, I had been ecstatic. Then, Spencer had intervened—once again—and ruined things. He forced both Graham and me to cut Hunter out of our lives.

How Hunter must hate us all.

· · ·

I ARRIVED BACK at my dorm room and threw my bag on the tiny two-seater sofa and myself on my bed. I lay there for an hour, numb, wild images passing through my mind of the FBI arriving at Saints Gym and arresting Donny Spencer, Sean trying to protect him and being shot, Hunter kneeling beside his body...

It was horrifying.

I clicked on the television and watched the news for a while, but then my cell dinged. I removed it from my bag and read the message from Amy.

AMY: OMG Celia!!! Did you watch the news? Sean Saint is dead...

I texted back, biting my cheek to stop my tears from starting once more.

CELIA: Yeah, I was at my mom's when Spencer told me the news. He actually gloated. He's hated the Saints for years.

AMY: Poor Hunter...

CELIA: I know. I feel sick.

There was a pause and I waited for her to reply.

AMY: I'm between classes. Want to come and meet me and have coffee?

CELIA: Don't really feel like it. I've got a mid-term to study for. Besides, what I really need is a drink.

AMY: Tonight. We'll go to the pub and drown our sorrows.

CELIA: Sounds like a plan.

AMY: I'll drop by after I finish class this afternoon. We can have supper and then go to the pub.

CELIA: See you then.

I turned off my cell and lay back on my bed, switching channels on the television to watch the coverage of the shooting. On one channel, I caught a glimpse of Hunter as the family left the hospital. A small gaggle of reporters followed them to a black SUV, throwing out questions, none of which were answered.

"Mr. Saint, do you have anything to say about the death of your son Sean?"

"Mr. Saint, the FBI reports that Sean Saint attacked a federal agent. Do you have any comment?"

Hunter looked haggard, his face even paler than normal, his brow furrowed. He was dressed in a black leather jacket, jeans, and a black t-shirt. He looked good but really upset—of course. I watched him open the door for his father, helping the older man in, adjusting the tank of portable oxygen, then close the door. Hunter said nothing, just got in the back seat on the other side of his father. The camera focused in on the car window, but it was darkened, and all you could see was a faint outline of Hunter's face, his square jaw, a few days' worth of stubble on his chin.

My heart squeezed to see him again and regret threatened to make me cry. He was good. He wasn't like the rest of his family. Maybe I could believe he had helped Sean on a job one time, but I knew Hunter after the alleged attack took place. He did not want to be part of his family or the mob.

He didn't.

I finally turned off the television when I felt such despair that I crawled under my covers to hide from the world.

A part of me reasoned that if I hadn't obeyed Spencer back when Hunter and I had been together, if I had continued to see him, maybe something worse would have happened—although I couldn't imagine anything worse than Sean being killed in front of Hunter.

Whatever might have happened, I would have lost my place in the dorm, and Spencer would have been on an even bigger witch hunt.

I took out my cell and called Graham, but the call went to voice mail so I left a message.

"Did you hear about Sean Saint? He was killed by the FBI when they arrested his uncle Donny. Give me a call."

I ended the call and then snuggled down into my covers, closing my eyes, trying to shove thoughts of the whole mess from my mind. I couldn't imagine studying at that moment. In fact, I couldn't imagine doing anything other than crying.

So I did.

LATER, Amy arrived and knocked on my door. The room was dark; I'd fallen asleep for an hour so I was groggy and a bit disoriented when I heard her. I crawled out from under the covers and walked to the door to let her in.

"There you are," she said and hugged me immediately. She pulled me over to the sofa and plopped down beside me. As usual, she knew just what to do to pull me out of my funk. "So tell me," she said and I recounted what Spencer had told me and what I had seen on the news. We sat and commiserated about my failed romance with Hunter, and the tragedy that had befallen the Saint family with Donny's arrest and Sean's death.

"Poor Hunter," Amy said. "He must be destroyed by it. Imagine watching Graham being shot right before your eyes."

"I can't."

"Will you send a condolence letter?"

"I don't know if I should. I'm sure Hunter would burn it. He must hate me and hate all of us, especially because it was Spencer who sicced the FBI on Donny..."

"Still, you should show him that you care."

I shrugged, not sure whether it would be appreciated.

We went to the cafeteria for a quick dinner, but I wasn't hungry and just picked at my salad. Then we did what I really wanted: We went for a drink or four.

The pub was just a few blocks away from campus and I wanted to drown my sorrows in margaritas. We did a shot of tequila to start, then sat at the bar and drank down three margaritas in a row. By the end of the night, I was hammered. I was glad we took a taxi home, because I couldn't walk straight and felt like I might throw up.

"I'll never find another guy like Hunter," I said in my inebriated state. "There's no one like him. Not one guy I've met since him has measured up. In any way," I said, raising my eyebrows suggestively at Amy as we tumbled out of the taxi and made our way into the dormitory building.

"You were really in love with him," she said, nodding. "I could tell. He was all you talked about."

"He was so nice. So smart..." I said, remembering how we used to talk about things like astronomy. Then I smiled. "He was *sooo* good in bed." I groaned out loud, remembering how well he knew his way around a woman's body.

"He's definitely a hunk," she said, as she practically carried me into my room.

"He's an Adonis," I replied, correcting her. "He looks so good, even with his hair so short. I've watched the report over and over."

"You recorded the newscast?"

I nodded. "I did." I went to my television and turned it on, then selected my recordings. The video of Hunter leading his father to the SUV after they left the hospital had been replayed on the news over and over and I'd found the wherewithal to record it before I finally flopped into my bed earlier that day.

Amy and I stood in front of the television and watched Hunter lead his father to the SUV three times in a row.

"He's gorgeous."

"He is," I replied, my throat all choked up at seeing him again while in my drunken state. I replayed the tape again and again, watching as he helped his father into the vehicle. How he scowled at the press and got inside the back seat. How the cameras tried to catch sight of him through the darkened window.

"Are you going to go to the funeral?"

I lay down on my bed and replayed the video once more. "I could never," I said, my voice quavering with emotion. "I'd be afraid he'd run me out of the church."

"He wouldn't," she said and sat on the bed beside me. "He'd be grateful that you came to pay your respects."

"I was so mean to him, pretending I found someone better."

"He was a player, Celia. He could always find someone willing. You said so yourself."

"I know, but the way I ended things was so cold…"

"You had no choice. Spencer—"

I held up my hand. "I don't want to talk about it anymore. I think I need to sleep."

She nodded and stood up to get her bag. "I'll talk to you tomorrow. We'll have a late breakfast."

I waved at her when she left and then lay back down, closing my eyes against the spinning of the room.

"Oh, God."

Then my cell rang. I grabbed it out of my bag and saw that it was Graham.

"Graham," I said, my emotions once more overwhelming me.

"I know," he said, his voice sounding tired. "I saw the news. Then Spencer called to crow about getting Hunter's uncle. Can you believe that bastard?"

"Yes," I said and rubbed my eyes. "I feel so bad."

"I do, too. I wish..."

"Me too," I said. I knew what Graham wished. Like me, he wished we'd gone against Spencer and remained friends with Hunter. "I wish I'd never listened to Spencer. I wish some mobster would shoot him."

"Don't say that, Celia," Graham admonished, but of course I was drunk and sad and wouldn't listen to reason. "You don't want him murdered by the mob."

"I do," I said. "He's a bastard. He was happy that Sean was killed. He said he wished the whole family would be shot. He's a monster." I bit my cheek to keep from sobbing out loud.

"Are you okay?" he asked. "You sound bad."

"I'm drunk, okay?" I said and then knocked myself on the head. I didn't need a lecture on drinking from Graham. "Amy and I went out for a few drinks to drown my sorrows."

"You should watch how much you drink, Celia. Remember what happened to Dad."

Of course, he would remind me that alcoholism was what killed our father. An alcoholic got into a car despite being drunk and drove down the wrong side of the freeway, killing my father and disabling my mother.

"Don't remind me."

"I feel like I have to."

"Even you get drunk now and then," I said defensively. "I deserve to now and then, too, and this is as good a reason as any."

"Just take it easy. Pretty soon, you'll get control over your inheritance and can tell Spencer to fuck off. We'll invest it and make even more off it and you'll be set up for when you graduate. Spencer will never have any power over us again."

I nodded. When I turned twenty-four, Spencer would no longer be the executor of my father's will. I'd be free from him. No more manipulation. I could write him out of my life. If only my mother hadn't married him and given him power of attorney when she had gotten so sick...

"I have to go to sleep," I said finally and we said our goodbyes.

I lay in the darkened room and thought about everything. All my regrets, starting with my father's death, Spencer's domination, my treatment of Hunter, and now, Sean's death and how hurt and filled with grief Hunter must be.

Despite all the alcohol, sleep was a long time coming.

CHAPTER 15

Hunter

THE FUNERAL WAS HELD on the following Thursday, and was well-attended by the local Irish Catholic community. During Mass, I noted a few faces in the pews I hadn't seen before—beady-eyed pale men with high Slavic cheekbones.

Russians.

Thugs from the Romanov family. I hated them.

I'd have to deal with them sooner or later. John was advising me on what protection money we had to pay and how money was laundered through illegal betting on the fights. It was small potatoes, compared to the Romanov family, whose tentacles spread all through the eastern US, in the docks, in fights, in drugs and prostitution.

It was enough to get a RICO charge against my uncle, but I suspected that was done as some kind of favor to Spencer, the new DA, rather than because my uncle was such a big prize.

This whole mess was what I had wanted to escape when I'd joined the Marines. Now here I was, being advised on how to get along in this corrupt world I'd always hated.

· · ·

THE NIGHT BEFORE, we'd held a real Irish wake for Sean at my uncle's club, although we didn't prop Sean's body in his coffin in the corner, which my father said had been common back in Ireland. Instead, we created a small shrine with a big picture of Sean, taken when he was still boxing. It was a photo of him standing in the ring after winning a bout, the referee holding his hand high, his face beatific. How he had loved boxing and MMA.

We toasted Sean, talked about the past, and shared our memories of him as a boy, then as a fighter, and finally as a man.

I had always looked up to Sean. He was my big brother who had shown me the ropes both in and out of the boxing ring. He had such a good disposition, and despite his traumatic brain injury he had been cheerful, always laughing and putting his arm around my shoulder.

Now, I was the big brother. I was the oldest Saint of my generation. John was younger than me, Conor younger still. My female cousins weren't involved in the business in any way, so I knew it was all down to me. In the coming weeks, my father would be looking to me to help him adjust to not having either Donny or Sean to help with the business. In the first few distraught hours after the shooting and Sean's death, I'd thought I might escape being drawn back into the business, but I'd been wrong. Finally, I acknowledged that my father needed me. I had to sacrifice what I wanted for him and for Conor.

I had to man up.

AFTER THE MASS, we took Sean's coffin to the local Catholic cemetery for burial. The priest led a small service at the graveside, and our closest family and friends stood around under the shade of an old oak tree, and we said our goodbyes to Sean.

There wasn't a dry eye in the place when my cousin John's youngest daughter Colleen played an Irish song on her fiddle, *Down by the Sally Gardens*. Based on a poem written by William Butler Yeats, it was Sean's favorite piece, and one he used to request when the family got together and listened to Irish music.

Then they lowered his casket into the freshly-dug grave and we took turns with the spade, shoveling dirt onto it.

After I finished my turn, I stood back and watched while John did his. My eye was caught by a woman about thirty feet away from our small group of family and close friends. She stood a few rows down in the shade beneath another tree. She had her hair up, and she wore a black dress and a pair of large sunglasses. I almost didn't recognize her. I thought she was just visiting some other grave, but there was something familiar about her. I glanced at her again and realized who it was.

Celia.

My heart squeezed to see her. I glanced around, wondering if Graham had come with her as well, but I didn't see him anywhere.

I was surprised to see her at the cemetery. I didn't think she'd care enough to show up and offer condolences. She'd never spoken to me again after that one night we spent together. She'd passed me over for Greg, who she must have thought had better prospects.

I frowned and glanced away, not wanting her to know I saw her.

I had nothing to say to her, nor did I want to hear her voice or listen to any condolences she might express about Sean's death.

When the ceremony was over, we left the graveside and made our way back to the limos that lined the narrow road through the cemetery. I slipped into the black limo behind the hearse and tried not to look around and see where Celia was, but failed, unable to resist checking to see if she was still there. I noted that she remained where she'd stood during the ceremony, and did not approach my family or friends to say anything. As we drove off, I saw her go to the grave and throw a single yellow rose onto the mound of earth.

That got me in the chest. I wished things had turned out differently for us.

Back then, I had the serious hots for Celia but had fought my lust for her. I'd thought she hated Spencer and would side with me and my family, but I was wrong. There was a reason I stayed single, not getting too deeply involved with any women. I knew how fickle they could be, telling you they loved you in one breath and then ending up with your best friend in the next.

I didn't need it.

Don't fall in love.

Don't get your hopes up too high.

Don't trust what people say. Watch what they do instead. Actions speak louder than words.

Celia proved that to me, and Graham proved that to me. I'd learned my lesson.

I MADE a trip back to Quantico when the paperwork came through for a hardship discharge. I was sad to be leaving before I'd be able to take a new group of hopeful officers through their paces, selecting the best of the best to join the Corps as Marine officers. I filled out the legal documents, presented statements from my father's doctors about his condition and prognosis, and had the paperwork about my brother's death sent to my CO.

One week and an hour of signing papers later, I was out.

I came back to Boston, back to my family's business. I was determined to find out who had ratted Donny out and get revenge. But to do that, I had to get really dirty.

In the meantime, I familiarized myself with my father's business while he recovered from Sean's death.

"It's not fair for a father to bury his son," he said to me one day while we sat in the office going over business receipts. "That's the worst thing a parent can imagine."

"I know, Dad," I said and leaned over to give him a squeeze, my arm around his shoulder. "It's hard to lose a big brother, too. I always looked up to Sean. You know that."

"I'm so glad you're out of the Marines," he said, his eyes wet. "I've been so afraid that you'd be killed over there in that mess. Every day while you were in a combat zone, I was afraid for you. Every phone call that came in, every time I saw a black sedan drive by the front of the building, I was afraid it was someone coming to tell me you were dead."

"I was lucky," I said, nodding. "I lost some men over there. My special operations unit was tight. We only went on operations that were planned down to the second. I was probably safer then than I will be now."

"None of us could have imagined Sean would do that," my father said, shaking his head and mopping his eyes with a handkerchief from his pocket. "I never would have thought he'd do something so rash."

I inhaled deeply, just as shocked and horrified that Sean had shown such bad judgement.

"Thank God you came back," he said emotionally. I stood up and put my arms around his shoulders while he tried to regain control over himself. "I'm so sorry, Hunter," he said between sobs. "I'm so sorry..."

"It's okay," I said softly. "I understand. I feel the same way."

It was going to take a while to get over what happened. With Donny in prison awaiting trial, and Sean dead and buried, it was just my dad and me running things, with the help of John, who managed the gym.

Conor would return to Vegas in another week or so, where he was training with one of the best amateur boxing organizations in the country. My father didn't want to see him go so soon, but Conor promised to come back at a moment's notice if anything changed, or if my father or I needed him to help with the business.

We wouldn't call on him for help. He had to make this go at the Olympics now, while he was in top form. The more he delayed, the harder it would be. I liked having him around, because he was a sweet kid and had a cheery disposition, even in the worst of times. But he had to try for the Olympics. I would never want to deny him that.

I agreed to run a security detail for my uncle's nightclubs, providing twenty-four-hour protection for their various locations. John relied on my expertise in that area, for Donny had been the one to run the clubs. So, not only would I be taking over the gym and franchises, I'd be taking over Donny's clubs. He had three, all in

Boston. I hadn't seen the books, or any of the details of the businesses, but I knew that once I did, I'd learn a lot more about my uncle's ties to the mob.

I leaned back in my chair and shook my head at my situation. For most of my life, I had done everything in my power to avoid my family's criminal ties. Now here I was, back in the middle of everything.

I hated it, but I had decided to work toward one goal.

Bring down the Romanov family, especially Sergei Romanov—the bastard who had his tentacles wrapped around my family, and who was ultimately responsible for my brother's death.

I was just biding my time until I had what I needed to take them down.

If I had my way, I'd set Sergei Romanov's empire on fire so I could watch it burn, just the way my grandfather had burned to death on a lonely road outside of Boston two dozen years ago when I was only six, just as I'd watched my brother get shot and die because of my family's inability to get out of Romanov's clutches.

They had tried, but the Romanovs' power was just too great, and both my father and uncle had failed.

I wouldn't.

CHAPTER 16

Hunter

THE PRETTY NURSE with tired blue eyes looked at me with skepticism when I arrived after visiting hours. I was determined to see Graham, so I turned on my charm, and leaned over the counter.

"I'm looking for Graham Parker's room."

"Are you immediate family?" she asked, her eyes moving over me questioningly.

I made a face of confusion. "What's immediate? I'm a cousin. I've been out of town and only just got back in." It was a lie but there was really no reason why I shouldn't be able to see him.

She shook her head and gave me an impatient look. "Visiting hours are over," she said, pointing to the sign on the wall. "Only immediate family can come in after hours."

"If I promise to just pop in for a minute? Pretty please?" I said, laying on the sad puppy eyes. I even held my hands up in mock prayer.

"Sixty seconds? I came all this way from the airport, and my taxi already left..."

She rolled her eyes and smiled reluctantly. "Okay, but only a minute. He's sleeping right now."

"I won't wake him. How is he?"

"He's stable, but his condition is still guarded."

"Okay," I said, nodding in understanding. "I'll just pop in quickly, just to see how he's doing."

She pointed down the hallway to Graham's room and I smiled.

"Thanks so much. I really appreciate this."

She smiled back and I felt her eyes on me as I walked down the hall to Graham's room. Being able to lay on the charm was a skill that I never let go to waste.

As I passed the rooms on my left and right, I realized how easy it would be for someone to get inside and hurt Graham. When Celia had texted me the last time, indicating Graham was in Mass General and it was a matter of life and death, I gave in and called the hospital to see what had happened.

A doctor had answered my questions when I'd said I was Graham's business partner and needed to know how long he'd be out of commission, giving him a story about a meeting regarding financing a new venture. The doc was reluctant to talk, but did acknowledge that Hunter had been beaten up pretty badly. I called over to Graham's office and spoke to Mark, who told me that the police had been by to question Graham and he'd insisted he was mugged in a back alley, but Mark let it slip he thought it was because Graham owed money to a loan shark.

That was my domain, so I called in a few markers and found out through the grapevine that Graham had been beaten up by one of the lower-level sharks in the Romanov universe.

Small-time hoods, but they were Russian and were always trying to make a name for themselves by how nasty they could be. I'd found that out only too well since I took over Donny's side of the business. It filtered down to me that Graham had failed to pay back the interest on a loan on time and they'd roughed him up to give him an incentive to pay up.

Given the lax security on the ward, I knew that if I didn't pay Graham's debt, he could easily be killed.

I'd seen a lot in my time in Iraq and Afghanistan, but when I saw Graham, even I was shocked. His face was bruised, his eyes swollen tight, his lip cut and stitched, his head wrapped in bandages. His leg and arm were in casts and he looked deathly pale.

Despite everything, I couldn't hate him.

I clenched my fists, wanting to pummel whoever did this to him.

It was clear he'd been beaten almost to death. I stood beside his bed for a few moments and watched him sleep. I didn't plan on waking him up. I truly didn't want him to know I'd been there, but I'd had to check on him myself after getting Celia's texts. She'd been increasingly distraught and so I thought I had better check it out myself.

Satisfied that he was alive, I left the room and smiled at the nurse on my way out of the ward.

I didn't text Celia.

I didn't want to deal with her.

Seeing her at the funeral almost a year earlier had sent me into a funk that lasted a week, where I'd spent my nights in an alcohol-induced haze, regretting everything, resenting that I had to give up my life and return to Boston. I didn't plan on repeating that mistake.

THE NEXT DAY, I spent time on the phone trying to get more info on what had happened to Graham. I called Pete Barnes, a cop in Boston PD who was friends with Donny and asked about the case.

"What can you tell me? How are the cops doing on finding the suspects?"

Barnes took in a breath. "Let me get the file."

I heard him flip through some papers on his desk. "We have a vehicle make and model, as well as a partial license plate given by the business partner. We know they're Russians, but nothing more."

"Who found him?"

"According to the police report, his partner found him in the back alley. Apparently, he'd met with some shady looking men in his office. There was shouting, from what our witnesses tell us. Then he went outside and got into a van with one of the men who had a Russian accent. He was gone for an hour. The partner found him in the back alley, unconscious and badly beaten badly, less than an hour later. Major Crimes interviewed Graham briefly yesterday, but he couldn't tell them anything specific about his assailants. Get this. Whoever did it carved '7 Days' on his chest."

"Holy shit." An image of Graham's bloody chest popped into my mind's eye. "Russian-sounding shady guys, you say?" I asked, wanting to know how close they were to finding the suspects. "I may know a few of those type of shady guys."

"I'm sure you do," Barnes said with a chuckle. "They're not even close to questioning anyone."

"I'll let my contacts know."

"Give them my regards," Barnes said. "Maybe you and I can have a drink after work sometime."

"Sounds good. Call me any time," I said and ended the call.

Then I called Misha Rabinov, one of the lower-level thugs I had cultivated in the Romanov family. The man had a taste for pretty blonde college students, so I made sure to invite several I knew to the club whenever he was there.

"I'm wondering about an old enemy of mine and whether he might have been given a visit lately about outstanding bills."

"Got a name? I can run it and see what I come up with."

"Graham Parker," I said. "Investment banker type. Runs an investment business in Boston."

"I'll let you know. Hey," Misha said, his voice expectant. "Any chance of partying at the Venue tonight? I got a bonus for my amazing skills and feel like living it up."

"I'd be glad to have you," I said, smiling to myself. "You can fill me in on what you find out about Parker. We can have a few drinks."

"Deal," Misha said and ended the call.

I sat back and wondered what his investigation would bring up. I was sure he'd be able to find out who was involved. It wasn't like these wise guys were trained in counterespionage. They loved to brag about their exploits. Gain points on each other about how close to death they'd brought some poor bastard who was in debt to their boss and behind on payments. It was a badge of honor.

LATER THAT NIGHT, I finished up at the gym and went to my apartment for a shower and to get ready for the evening at the Venue. I didn't relish spending it with Misha, but he was a useful idiot. I stood in front of the mirror and pulled on my shirt, buttoning it up while I contemplated the evening. I usually spent my weekends at one of my uncle's clubs, overseeing the place to make sure everything was running smoothly. Tonight, it was the Venue. Next weekend, it would be another one of the three clubs for which I was now responsible.

When I was finished dressing in a fresh white shirt, dark suit, and tie, I ran my hand through my hair, which was in dire need of a cut, and considered my face.

I looked as tired as I felt.

Running my uncle's and father's empire, such as it was, took all my time. I'd had a real life back when I was in the Marines. I had downtime, I had privacy in my place in Quantico, and I could always take leave and decompress for a week or so.

Now, I had no time off ever. I was always on call. It was me people came to when there was a problem, big or small, and there were small problems every single day that needed my attention. On top of that, I was busy working to get close to the Romanovs, actively recruiting several members of his family to be my 'friends.' They were loyal to Romanov but they always needed extra money or women and were willing to cheat around the edges to get them.

I found it for them. It was the easiest way to get in with a group of lowlifes. Appeal to their pocketbooks and dicks.

Tonight, I'd call in a marker and I'd return a favor. I'd invited a few pretty blonde hangers-on to the club, and I knew they'd keep my good buddy Misha happy. I'd have a bit of fun as well with one of the blondes, a girl who called herself Lila—who knew what her real name was. I didn't care.

So even on a Saturday night, even when I was playing, I was always working.

That was my new life. I didn't have time to think too deeply about what I'd become. Instead, I straightened my tie and left my apartment, ready to face the night.

I ARRIVED at the club around seven and did my usual walk-through to see how everything was going. The office manager was finalizing the lunch receipts from the restaurant, and the floor manager for the night was checking out the bar to make sure it was stocked and ready to go.

I sat in the office for a while and read over emails, trying to focus on the job at hand, but my mind kept going over my texts from Celia, and what I'd learned from Barnes about Graham.

I hoped I'd know tonight who beat him up and why. Then maybe I'd text Celia and let her know I'd pay off Graham's debt. Her texts had become increasingly frantic. I didn't want her to worry too much, but I wasn't going to call her. I didn't want to hear her voice or see her face again.

That part of my life was over.

AFTER MISHA ARRIVED and I had introduced him to Lila and her friend —whose name I couldn't remember—we sat in the back of the club and had a drink. After a suitable amount of time had passed, I leaned forward and asked Misha the question that had been on my mind all day.

"Any news on the wise guys who roughed up that enemy of mine?" I asked, expecting my quid pro quo.

"Yeah," he said and leaned forward as well, talking in a low voice so nobody could overhear our discussion. Beside me on the sofa, the two girls were busy admiring each other's manicures.

"His name's Stepan," Misha said. "He's real low-life muscle for Victor Romanov, Sergei's younger brother. I heard he fucked up some investment banker type who works downtown over an unpaid debt. His crew works for the Romanovs. They take care of any late payments on outstanding bills, if you know what I mean," Misha said, wagging his eyebrows.

"That's the one," I said. "Thanks."

He nodded and leaned back, picking up his drink and enjoying my hospitality.

Now I knew who had done the deed, and I knew who to pay off. I was set. I could take care of business and pay off Graham's debt—at least, that was the plan. I'd pay off Victor Romanov and then I'd swing by wherever Stepan hung out and give him a taste of my fist.

I'd never have to see Graham or Celia again.

A COUPLE of hours after Misha arrived and we'd had a few drinks, Kirk, one of my bodyguards, came up to where Misha and I were sitting at the back of the club's large open dance floor and bar to let me know I had a visitor.

He leaned over, blocking off his mouth so the others couldn't hear what he was saying.

"There's this woman who claims she knows you," he said, jerking his head to the side. "She said her name was Celia. She said you'd know her and that she's here to talk to you about her brother."

It was then that I saw her.

"Crap," I said, only half under my breath.

She looked... *fantastic.*

Stunning.

She wore a red dress that showed all her best womanly attributes —curves that could make a man weak in the knees, long dark hair like silk, a generous mouth painted red and eminently kissable. Her pretty face made you think about seeing it in the morning after a long night of fucking her brains out.

I remembered my mouth on her, her mouth on me. My body responded immediately, my pulse increasing, a low-level ache starting in my balls that told me I needed to fuck her and soon.

Yeah, she still had that effect on me. It surprised me how strongly I reacted to seeing her despite everything that had happened between us and our families.

I wanted her. *Badly*.

After all these years, I still wanted to possess her completely. The need I felt for her was completely primal. I was like some kind of caveman seeing my woman and wanting to haul her away into my cave and keep her to myself.

There I was, sitting beside the two blonde babes who were Misha's and mine for the night, and all I could think of in that moment was that my blonde, Lila, was a pale substitute for Celia.

When I saw Celia, I couldn't help but think that she was going to screw everything up. Not only would she make me want her all over again, but she might make a scene and talk about Graham in front of Misha. I wanted him to think I was a tough sonofabitch who didn't let anything upset me.

I had to send her away.

"Tell her I'm busy. Tell her to call Amanda at the gym if she has any business to discuss."

Kirk returned to where Celia stood with my other bodyguard, Phil. I could tell she wasn't happy with my message.

Then, much to everyone's surprise, she slipped around Kirk and Phil.

"Hunter!"

Before she could get to me, Phil had her in his arms, stopping her a few feet from where we sat.

"Sorry, Mr. Saint," Phil said, Celia's arms in his.

"Jesus Christ," I muttered. I stood and buttoned my suit jacket before leaning down to Lila.

"Excuse me for a moment," I said, trying my best to sound impatient. "I have a matter to attend to."

I went to where Phil held Celia, controlling my emotions with a few deep breaths.

"Hunter, I need to talk to you," Celia said, her eyes searching out mine. "It's about Graham."

I sighed heavily and theatrically. "What makes you think I care about anything to do with you and your family?"

"Graham asked me to come and speak with you," she said. "Can we go somewhere private?"

"Graham thinks he can send you to me like some kind of peace offering?" I replied, playing dumb for the moment. "I'm not biting. Now, I'm busy." I motioned to Phil. "Take her outside."

"Hunter, please!" Celia said, her voice breaking, tears in her eyes. "Graham's in the hospital. I need to talk to you in private."

I met her gaze, finally, and had to decide what to do. I wanted to avoid her at all costs. She was dangerous to me. She could distract me from my mission, and that wasn't going to happen.

I realized she wouldn't let this go until I spoke with her, so I gestured to Phil.

"Let her go." Then I headed for the rear door that led to the offices. "Follow me."

I led her past the kitchen and down the hallway to the business office.

"Hunter, I'm sorry to bother you but—"

I held out my hand to stop her from talking and went into the darkened office. She hesitated just outside, like she was afraid to come in with me.

"For God's sake, come inside," I said and returned to her, pulling her in.

She stood there, staring into my eyes, and I could see how close to the edge she was. I wondered if it was as hard for her, us being this close, as it was for me.

Then the rational part of my brain cut in and I realized.

No.

She was the one who threw me over. I was the one who had wanted it to continue.

"Quit with the tears," I said, sounding as impatient as possible. "I'm not moved by tears. I don't care if Graham's dying. Why would I care? My brother died right in front of my fucking eyes, Celia, or did you forget that little fact?"

"I could never forget," she said, her voice breaking. "I'm so sorry..."

She covered her face with her hands and cried in front of me. I tried to not respond, tried to not pull her into my arms and comfort her the way I wanted. Gradually, she regained control over herself.

"Graham borrowed money from a loan shark to pay back my inheritance, which he lost on a bad investment. He thought he could turn it around and pay me back and the loan shark, but he couldn't and they beat him up," she said quietly. "They broke his nose, his jaw, and his leg, and punched out his teeth. He has internal injuries and a serious concussion; he'll be in rehab for weeks. They carved '7 Days' on his chest with a knife and said if he didn't pay the money back by Wednesday night, they'll kill him, then come after me for his insurance money."

"Oh yeah?" I said and tapped my foot, not looking at her. I knew that if I saw real pain in her eyes, I'd be toast. "That's what happens when you invest money you can't afford to lose. I thought Graham was smarter than that. I guess not."

"Look, I didn't want to come to you," she said, "but Graham insisted that you were the only one who could help."

That hurt. "Yeah," I said with a rueful laugh. "It must have been hard for you to come to me and ask for help. You couldn't get me out of your life fast enough. Funny, but I thought there was something special between us. I guess I was a wrong."

"Hunter, it wasn't like that," she said. "I wish you could understand..."

I didn't say anything in response. Of course, she'd deny that she threw me away. She had to, if she wanted my help with Graham.

I wasn't buying it.

"Who does he owe money to?" I asked finally, although I already knew.

"Some guy named Stepan. That's all I know."

"Stepan, huh?" I said and smiled grimly. "You don't mess with the Russians. They mean business."

Actually, based on what I'd heard about him, Stepan had gone easy on Graham. He was a nasty piece of shit, as mafia pieces of shit went, and was known for taking delight in inflicting maximum pain. He'd delivered a serious beating on Graham but he hadn't tortured the man, which was Stepan's forte.

"I know the Russians. If you don't give them the money by Wednesday, Graham will be dead. You can count on that."

I turned to leave. I'd already decided I'd pay off Graham's fucking debt and save his fucking life, despite everything. But I was going to make Celia sweat it out a bit longer.

It was small of me. I should have comforted her and told her, "Of course I'll pay off your fucking traitorous bastard of a brother's debt," but I didn't.

She followed me to the door. "You're just going to let them kill Graham?"

I turned to her, enjoying the look of surprise and horror on her beautiful face.

"Tell me, Celia, why should I help?"

She came to my side, her eyes imploring.

"Because you and Graham were best friends all your life. From the time you were in middle school and all through college. You were going to go into business together..."

"You might think that would count for something," I said softly. "You might think that would mean he stood by me when I needed him. Instead, he went into business with someone else. He did nothing to stop Spencer from going after my uncle. Sean *died*, Celia," I said, losing it. "Sean's dead because of Spencer. Maybe if Graham dies, Spencer will know how it feels to lose someone."

I turned and walked away. Before I escaped her completely, she once again called out in a weepy voice.

"Yes, he died because of Spencer. Not because of Graham! You *know* Spencer," she said and came to my side, grabbed my arm. "You know what he was like with us. With me. There was nothing either of us could do."

I pulled my arm away.

"Graham should have thought about the cost before he went to the Russians. He should have come to *me* if he needed money."

"How could he? He knew you blamed him for what happened to Sean."

"I don't blame him," I said quietly. "But he turned his back on me when I wanted to go into business with him. *You* threw me away like I was a bad apple when there were so many other fresh shiny ones to eat."

"I didn't do that."

The, to my utter surprise, she got down on her knees. She actually got down on her fucking knees and begged, her hands folded as if in prayer. She looked up into my eyes and pleaded for my help.

"Will you help Graham?"

I took in a breath, surprised at how my body still responded to her, especially with her on her knees like that. The callous part of me couldn't help but think of her on her knees before me, sucking my dick. At that moment, a plan began to develop in my mind.

"Tell me why I should, Celia. What do I get out of this?"

Of course, I knew exactly what I wanted to get out of it. I wanted *her*.

I wanted her to be my fuck toy. My plaything. I wanted to be able to order her onto her knees and she'd comply, opening her mouth wide to accept my dick.

I stared her down, waiting, my hands on my hips.

"I'll do anything you want, Hunter," she said, her voice breaking. "Anything. Name it and I'll do it."

I shook my head. "What can you do for me that I can't get from any number of other women?" I asked, enjoying the way she looked as she knelt at my feet. "Women who'd enjoy it, and not hate every minute."

"Anything," she said once more, tears spilling out of her eyes and down her cheeks.

In truth, I would have been willing to pay off Graham's debt and not collect anything in return, but at that moment, I wanted her to suffer.

"I'll pay the debt," I said. "As for your offer, I'll consider my options. How much does he owe?"

I already knew, but I wanted her to have to say it, confess it all.

"A hundred and forty thousand."

I whistled, trying to imply it was big money, but it was pocket change.

"That's a lot of high-priced call girl services, Celia." I eyed her, amused now at my cunning plan. "At five hundred an hour, that works out to..." I said and smiled, "three hundred hours of being my fuck toy."

Her eyes widened and I'm sure I heard her intake of breath—in surprise or horror, I didn't know.

"Are you really going to hate fuck me in payment?" she asked, defiant to the end.

I liked that fire in her. She was willing to come to me and ask for help even though she knew I was now in deep with the mafia.

I respected her balls.

I bit my bottom lip. "Hate fucks are pretty good, Celia. You should know. Isn't that what you did to me?"

"That was never what happened between us," she protested, and I almost believed her. "Why would you even think that? "

"Graham told me." I met her eyes. "He told me you wanted Greg, not me, but I was easier. As soon as you got Greg, you threw me away like trash."

"No, *no*," she said. "That's not true. I never—"

"Stop," I said and chopped my hand down. "It doesn't matter anyway so no more lies." I walked down the hall. "I'll contact Stepan and pay the debt. As for you," I said opening the door that led back to the club. "I'll think about what I want from you, if anything. But you better make it worth my while."

Celia went through the door, wiping her eyes, and I passed her on the way back to the sofas where Misha and the girls sat. I stopped before I got to the dais and turned to face her.

"You should go home, Celia. Your makeup's all messed up and I'm sure one of your frat boys is waiting for you. We'll be in touch. You can count on that."

Then I went back up to the sofas where Lila and Misha were waiting. I bent down and kissed Lila on the mouth.

Celia left the club and I was determined to never see her again. I wouldn't collect on the debt Graham owed me. But then I thought of what Stepan had done to Graham. I thought about how Celia had been on her knees in front of me, begging.

I turned to Misha. "Do you feel like helping me out, teaching someone a lesson? Get a bit of boxing time in? There's someone who needs my special touch."

"What's his name?" Misha said, intrigued, and always up for some roughing up.

"Stepan."

"You serious? " he said and frowned. "You want to rough up Stepan? He's a nasty piece of work."

"He hurt someone close to me," I said and shrugged, as if it were normal for me to beat up those who crossed me. "I want payback."

He made a face. "He's a psycho. I hope you're in good with Romanov, cause he's one of Victor's boys."

"Close enough," I said. "I'll visit Victor and make sure things are okay between us before I do anything."

"Seriously," Misha said and made a face of fear. "You do not want to piss Victor off. Most guys who're muscle for Romanov do it out of loyalty. Stepan? He chooses jobs because he actually likes hurting people. Gets off on it."

"He fucked up that old friend of mine really bad," I said. "I want to pay him a visit. Do you know where he hangs?"

"I thought he was an enemy," Misha said, frowning.

"We were once friends," I said, trying to shrug it off.

"He hangs out at Martinov's by the docks. Listen, Stepan's pretty-low level. If you have something to offer Victor in return, he might not be too mad, but don't piss Victor off, man. I'm tellin' you."

"What's Stepan's last name?"

Misha shook his head. "Andreov. But really, Hunter. You don't want to mess with him unless Victor's a friend."

I waved him off. "Don't worry. Victor's a friend. Besides, I have to pay off a debt is all."

"Okay, but seriously. Don't piss him off."

"I'll set things up. When I call you, I want you ready to come with me."

He nodded but looked a bit hesitant. I ordered him another drink on my tab and then motioned to Lila's friend.

"Go over and be extra friendly with my good friend Misha," I said. She'd know what that meant.

Misha smiled and leaned back, already forgetting his concerns about my little plan to get some payback with Stepan. Hell no, I wouldn't piss Victor off. I'd pay Graham's bill. Then, I'd take that Stepan worm aside and break his fucking nose. With Victor's permission. I'd fuck him up, just as badly as he'd fucked Graham up. Victor would understand. With these thugs and criminals, you had to get down to their level and show them you could keep up or they wouldn't respect you. I planned on showing Victor that I could keep up.

Hell, I could do even better.

CHAPTER 17

CELIA

I WAITED.

I waited for Hunter to call me and tell me what he expected from me.

Nothing—not for a day, then two. I felt nervous that perhaps Hunter had backed out and soon, the Romanov family thugs would come for Graham, where he lay unprotected in the hospital neurology ward.

Each night I went to bed wondering if someone would go to the hospital to kill him—or come to the dorm to threaten me. Finally, on the night before the payment was due, I got a text from Hunter with two words:

HUNTER: It's done.

That was it.

Hunter had paid the debt off and so we were safe.

I heaved a sigh of relief—at least I wouldn't have to worry about Graham being murdered in his sleep. I sent him a text back right away.

CELIA: Thank you so much.

He didn't reply and so I didn't pursue the matter any further. Maybe he wasn't going to try to collect what I owed him. Maybe he had been joking that he expected me to be his fuck toy. I had no idea.

As for Graham, he was recovering—slowly. He still faced a long recovery. He'd had a brief setback when he got an infection and his fever soared, but they gave him IV antibiotics and in a few days, he was better.

I called my mom finally, once Hunter paid off the debt and Graham was out of danger—at least as far as being killed by the mafia. I would have called right away if Hunter hadn't come through. I didn't want to interrupt their cruise unless I had to.

"Celia! Why didn't you call me right away?" my mother cried when she heard Graham had been mugged. "We would have come right home."

"You don't need to come home, mom. Graham's out of danger now. If anything had changed, I would have called you, but Graham didn't want me to call you in the middle of the night and scare you. He's fine —really."

"When can I talk to him?" she asked, and I could hear the fear in her voice fading. "I want to hear his voice and know for myself that he's okay. What did they do to him? Do the police have the suspect?"

Then Spencer grabbed the phone from her and came on the line. "What the hell happened?"

I had to retell Spencer the whole story. I made it sound as if it happened only a couple of days earlier instead of a week. It was a lie but it was necessary. They didn't need to know how bad Graham had been. Graham was out of danger now. It was now all up to his physio-therapists as to how long it took him to get back to normal life.

"Celia, I don't approve of you waiting before calling us. For God's sake—what if Graham died?"

"He didn't die, and I didn't want to call you and have mom worry. Graham's fine. He's recovering on the neurology ward so they can watch him and then he'll go to rehab."

"Rehab? Why is he going to rehab?"

"They broke his leg and arm and jaw. His jaw is wired," I said and cringed, thinking about the white lies I was telling, downplaying how bad his head injury really was.

"We're on our way home," Spencer said, his voice firm.

"You only have three days left on the cruise," I said. "Graham doesn't want you to come home early. I'll go to see him and get him to call you. He'll say what I'm saying. Don't come home now. Stay on the cruise."

Finally, Spencer agreed that they would wait and talk to Graham before deciding. I was glad; I did not want them to come back so soon —not until we had things all figured out. Most of all, I hated the thought of telling them Graham had lost both of our inheritances. That would make Spencer furious and would really upset my mom.

I didn't want to face that any sooner than I had to. The past few days had been traumatic enough.

For the previous few days, images had haunted me from various mafia movies of some thug in a long black overcoat entering the hospital late at night and sneaking in, covering Graham's face with a pillow and smothering the life out of him.

At least now I no longer had to worry about that.

All I had to worry about now was when Hunter would contact me to tell me what he expected of me in return.

I waited. And waited some more.

Nothing.

Over the next few days, I spent time alternating between the hospital, my classrooms and my dorm, trying to study for exams while I tended to my brother and worried about how I'd pay for my dorm the next month. I signed myself up for twice as many shifts at the pub, but it meant that I'd be swamped with work—school and job plus Graham.

I wanted to speak with Hunter and thank him for paying off Graham's debt, and ask him what he wanted in return, but I was afraid.

I was afraid to contact him first. He'd suggested that my debt to him meant I'd be his fuck toy for three hundred hours.

That both titillated me and scared me.

Titillated me because sex with Hunter, even hate sex, sounded better than what I'd had recently—in other words, nothing.

Scared because he'd become notorious as the head of his family now that Sean was dead and he had taken over.

I always thought that if Hunter gained control of his family's business, he'd take it legitimate, and break all ties with organized crime, but I guess I was wrong. In the end, Spencer may have been right about the Saint family and about Hunter in particular.

Maybe the apple didn't fall far from the tree.

My only solace was in thinking that leaving the mafia's grip was harder than Hunter first imagined.

When I spoke to Graham about it, he seemed dismissive. "I guess we're seeing Hunter's true colors."

I didn't think so. I couldn't believe that Hunter was fine with carrying on with the way things were—the way that sent his uncle to federal prison for a decade and that got his brother killed. I had to think that Hunter was just having problems extricating the business from the grasp of the mafia, but his actions seemed the opposite of that.

He seemed to be in even more deeply. There was talk of Hunter spending time with members of the Romanov family—even the notorious head of the Romanovs, Sergei—the godfather who rarely spent time in Boston, preferring instead to spend his time on Martha's Vineyard.

I didn't go to the house anymore when Spencer was at home. There was no way I wanted to see him gloat when he told me of how close Hunter had become to the Romanov family—the very family Graham had gone to for a loan.

The very family that beat Graham so badly he almost had a permanent brain injury. He could have died if his partner Mark hadn't gone out into the alley for a smoke.

How could Hunter get in so close with them?

I just couldn't figure it out.

Hunter had changed. It hurt me to realize that, but in the end, I couldn't deny it.

FINALLY, a few days after Hunter paid off Graham's debt, I got a text from him.

HUNTER: You're coming to my place tonight. My driver will pick you up at ten.

That was it.

CELIA: Okay. Any specific instructions?

HUNTER: Don't be late.

I frowned and wished I could stick my tongue out at him.

CELIA: Yes, Sir.

There was a pause.

HUNTER: Oh, I like it. Maybe you should call me Sir all the time...

CELIA: Don't hold your breath.

Hunter wanted me at his place, and ten o'clock was late enough that I pretty much knew what he expected. He was seriously going to hate fuck me in repayment.

Part of me was disgusted. What kind of man expected someone to have sex with them as repayment of a debt?

Part of me—a part that hated myself—was aroused.

All day, I went around slightly wet and swollen at the thought that I'd be having sex with Hunter that night. I kicked myself mentally, wondering how I could sink so low. I wasn't some airhead bimbo. I was a Harvard law student. I was magna cum laude.

I was also indebted to a man who did business with the mafia.

What else could I expect from Hunter but this?

I silently cursed Graham for getting me into this mess. Now that I felt Graham was well enough, I allowed myself to feel some anger toward him. But most of all, I wanted to try to distract myself from thinking about how excited I was about going to Hunter's apartment and having sex with him. It had been months—*months*—since I'd been with a guy, and that experience had been completely unfulfilling.

The way I was feeling suggested that hate sex with Hunter might be better than anything I'd experienced since the first time I had been with him five years earlier.

I HAD A BATH AT EIGHT, washed my hair, brushed and flossed my teeth, and reapplied a bit of makeup—just some mascara and gloss—and blow-dried my hair so that it was long and straight.

Then I went to my closet and considered what I'd wear. Should I get all fixed up? Wear something pretty? Something sexy?

I chewed my bottom lip and couldn't decide.

Finally, instead of something sexy or pretty, I pulled on my boyfriend jeans, a t-shirt with a cat wearing Harry Potter glasses on the front, and my Doc Martens. I wiped off my lip gloss and pulled my hair back into a ponytail.

I wasn't going to present myself as a piece of meat for Hunter to eat. If he didn't like it, he could send me home and find one of the pretty blonde bimbos he appeared to prefer.

About thirty minutes before I left, I got a text.

HUNTER: Bring your toothbrush.

I shook my head. He expected me to stay the night?

CELIA: I have class early in the morning.

HUNTER: My driver will take you to class.

I frowned and texted him back, angered that he was being so crass.

CELIA: You're really going to get your pound of flesh.

HUNTER: Three hundred hours, Celia. That's a lot of flesh I get to pound. James will be on the street at 10 so be ready. I'll be waiting.

I wanted to text back *I HATE YOU* or *YOU'RE A SCUMBAG* but I didn't, deciding that I wouldn't give him the pleasure of seeing me upset.

Besides, his reference to 'pounding flesh' made my own flesh throb just a bit too eagerly for my own comfort.

Did he know he'd have that effect on me? Or did he think he'd be punishing me for what he thought was my betrayal?

I decided I'd tell him the truth—that back when I'd told him I didn't want to see him again, it was because Spencer had threatened me and showed me those police photos and the police file on him and Sean. Maybe if he knew I didn't really betray him—not really and not voluntarily—he'd feel differently about me and not make me be his sex toy.

I was determined to do just that. I'd confess that I had made it all up about Greg.

In truth, I thought Greg was a blowhard. A male slut. I wanted Hunter, not Greg, but I'd felt I had no choice. I felt I was doing the noble thing by making Hunter think I didn't really want him.

He left Boston and went away and that was a good thing. Unfortunately, it all fell apart when my bastard of a stepfather got his uncle arrested and his brother killed.

I knew Hunter would never forgive me for that, even if I had nothing to do with it.

I WAITED on the street outside the dorm building, my nightgown tucked away in my bag along with my toothbrush, and wondered what would happen.

When a black SUV drove up and parked on the street, I tried to swallow back my anxiety.

"Ms. Parker?" the middle-aged driver said when he saw me, tipping his driver's cap. "I'm James. Mr. Saint's driver."

"Yes," I said and forced a smile. "Hello."

James got out of the vehicle and came to the rear passenger door, opening it for me. "Please get in."

I slipped into the dark interior and fastened my seatbelt, my heart rate increasing as I imagined what lay ahead for me at Hunter's apartment.

We drove in silence through the streets of Cambridge to South Boston and the Burlington – a building with a lot of high priced apartments. The car drove into an underground parking area, and we parked in a slot close to the elevator.

James got out and opened my door, then escorted me upstairs, using a security card to get me into the building and up to the top floor.

When the elevator reached the twenty-first floor, I entered a narrow hallway that led to an ostentatious double door. Hunter must have the entire penthouse floor to himself.

While I waited for James to open the door, I thought how surprising it was that Hunter was living here instead of at the gym with his father. But I supposed that with his money and with moving up in the world of crime, he wanted to live the lifestyle.

It made me feel sad that he'd changed so much. What happened to the honorable Marine Corps officer who went off to defend America from foreign enemies? What happened to the man who wanted to take his family's business clean?

I couldn't accept that this was the same Hunter I used to know. That Hunter would never make me prostitute myself to pay off a debt that wasn't mine in the first place—but it seemed Hunter was no different from any other criminal out there after all.

Power corrupted, and Hunter was now the head of his family. The power he now had must have changed him into someone I didn't recognize, despite how much he looked like his old self, the young man I'd known five years ago, before all this happened.

We entered the quiet, dim apartment and I waited while James turned on some lights.

"Isn't Hunter—er, Mr. Saint here?" I asked.

"No," James said. "He asked me to bring you here and to tell you he'd be by later. He's caught up with some business associate and won't be back for a while. You're supposed to make yourself at home. There's food in the fridge and a big soaker tub in the master bathroom."

"Thanks," I said and stood in the entryway, a bit overwhelmed by the opulence of the place. It was gilded and appointed with the best materials—marble, dark wood, what looked like gold inlay in the furniture. Mirrors and crystal chandelier in the entry. Ceiling-to-floor windows overlooking the waterfront.

It was breathtaking.

James led me through the apartment, pointing out the living room, dining room, and then the professional kitchen with everything a chef could want. Down a narrow hall was a huge master bedroom with a massive four-poster king-sized bed, and an equally impressive master suite.

"This is your room," James said and opened the door to a smaller bedroom with another four-poster bed. "You can use this bathroom if you want." He pointed to a full bathroom across the hall.

"Thank you," I said, and stood there wondering what to do next.

"I'll be going now," James said. "I'm still on duty tomorrow morning so I'll take you to Harvard for your early class."

"Okay," I said, my cheeks hot, wondering whether James knew why I was staying the night. "Am I supposed to tip you?" I asked, my cheeks red.

"No, no," he said and laughed softly. "I'm very well-paid, and on staff. But thanks for the sentiment."

"Sorry, I didn't know…"

He shook his head. "No worries."

I walked James to the door. He turned to me before he left. "Mr. Saint doesn't usually allow guests to stay overnight. You must be special."

"We're old friends. I've known him pretty much all my life."

He nodded. "I figured as much." He smiled briefly and left me in the huge penthouse apartment.

Then I was alone, waiting for Hunter to come and do whatever it was he planned to do with me.

Pound my flesh. Get his pound of flesh. Was I really going to go through with this?

I'd never pimped myself out before, and doing so left this hollow feeling in the pit of my stomach. If we fucked, I knew it would be cheap and it would be empty. Sure, I had a low level of arousal at the prospect of being with Hunter despite everything, but part of me hated myself for it and another part hated Hunter for being willing to use me like that.

Why would he even want to? He could have sex with any number of pretty young things. He was rich, gorgeous, and powerful in the city. He'd have his pick.

Why bother with someone who you hated?

Was a hate fuck as good as he suggested?

I didn't hate him. In fact, I liked him too much. Even after these past five years, I still wanted him. Even though he had become some tough guy. I tried to tell myself that loyalty to his father had made him do the one thing he never wanted to do. I'd always thought he was noble, but the fact that he would take advantage of my misfortune for something as base as sex made me question that.

I remembered what my mother had told me soon after Hunter returned to Boston after Sean's death.

"Spencer says Hunter's just as bad as everyone else in his family. He's already in the pocket of the Romanov family. Not even six months after he took over and he's as corrupt as the others."

"I can't believe it," I said, my heart squeezing at the thought that Hunter had become one of the bad guys.

"You have to believe it, Celia," my mother said, her eyes heavy from her medication. "Spencer says it's in his genes."

"That's bullshit," I said, furious that Spencer was talking Hunter down—even now. "It was also in his genes to go to Harvard to do an MBA and graduate at the top of his class. It was in his genes to become a Marine officer and do two tours of duty in war zones. It's not in your genes to be a criminal. It's circumstances."

If I told myself that enough times, I might believe it. In the end, it was a choice. Hunter had made a choice to come back, and to get dirty when he did.

Whatever his reasons, I knew Hunter was dirty now. He was in deep. How would that have changed him in the intervening years since that one night we were together—the last night I considered myself his friend?

I PACED THE APARTMENT, walking from one room to the next, examining things, trying to get a sense of who Hunter was and who he'd become over the past five years. Everything in the place seemed picked out by a designer.

The decorations and furniture were nice but none of it seemed personal. His clothes were all neatly hung and folded in his huge walk-in closet. His kitchen was perfectly stocked, and all the dishes were done and neatly stacked in the cupboards.

Hundreds of books filled the shelves in the library, where his desk sat in front of a ceiling-to-floor window overlooking the bay. None of them looked like they'd been read. His desk was immaculate, but empty.

There was nothing there that said "Hunter." Pens and paperclips, blank paper, steno pads, thumbtacks—all of it neat, like some housekeeper had been there and straightened everything out.

The faint scent of a masculine cologne permeated the apartment—not strong, just enough to make me think of him.

There were no family photos, nothing personal.

This wasn't his home. Not his real home. It was an apartment, complete with everything he'd need, but I had the sense he didn't really live here.

When the front doorknob turned, I practically jumped out of my skin from nerves.

Hunter had arrived.

He entered the apartment and right away, I could see that he'd been in a fight. His cheek was bloody and his hands were, too, his knuckles red and bleeding.

"Can you help me with this?" he asked, trying to shrug off his jacket. I went over to where he stood beside the front closet and helped him remove his jacket, gingerly slipping it off each hand.

"What happened?" I asked, frowning as I hung up his jacket in the front closet. "You were in a fight."

"Good deduction," Hunter said, deadpan. "Can you do a bit of nursing for me? There's a first aid kit in the main bathroom under the sink."

"Sure," I said, surprised at the turn of events. Hunter had been in a fight before coming to the apartment to hate fuck me?

I was surprised but said nothing, attributing it to his new lifestyle of heading a family with mafia ties. I retrieved the first aid kit from the well-appointed bathroom, which was all done up with white marble and brass fixtures, the towels thick and plush, beautiful photographs of the ocean on the walls. I took the kit back to the kitchen where Hunter sat at the island on a stool, trying to unbutton his cuffs.

"Can you?" he asked, holding out one bloodied hand.

I put the first aid kit down on the granite countertop and took his hand in mine, unbuttoning the cuff as he asked. Then, he gave me his other hand, all the time watching me intently. I felt his gaze on me, and I wondered whether he was already thinking of how he wanted me. On my knees, like I'd been when I begged for his help? On the bed? On the floor?

I had no idea but even trying to imagine where and how aroused me, in spite of myself.

"Help me with this?" he asked and pointed to the front of his shirt. I nodded and began to unbutton it. He was still looking at me intently. "I see you went all out with your clothes and makeup trying to impress me," he said, his voice flat.

"I—I..." I stuttered, "I didn't know what to expect."

He said nothing, but I felt his gaze on my face while I finished unbuttoning his shirt. Was he going to have me undress him completely?

I pulled it gently over each hand, revealing his torso in all its naked glory.

And it was glorious. While he'd been a mafia thug for a year since returning from Virginia, he'd also apparently kept in top shape, with bulging biceps and a washboard abdomen. Once more, I noticed his tribal tattoo and remembered running my hands all over it that night we were together.

I saw a bruise on his rib, and another on his other side along with a huge abrasion.

"Why were you fighting? I thought you were a finance and management type, not some kind of enforcer."

"I'm a man of many talents, Celia," he said and bit his bottom lip.

It made me want to kiss his mouth, so I glanced away.

"Who did this to you?" I asked, unable to stop myself.

"This?" he said and shrugged. "This is nothing. You should see the other guy."

"You beat someone up?"

"Yeah," Hunter replied, amusement in his voice. "Just a bad guy. Name's Stepan. You might know of him."

My eyes widened at that. "You beat up Stepan? *The* Stepan who beat up Graham?"

"The very one." He said, his blue eyes hooded. "There are some photos on my cell in my pocket."

I shook my head. "You fought some guy and took pictures?" My mouth was open, wide. "I don't want to see them."

"Indulge me. Get my phone for me."

I sighed and checked in his inside jacket pocket, which had been thrown onto the back of a chair. I took out his cell and handed it to him. He unlocked it and opened his image folder, then scrolled through some images. Finally, he held one up for me.

I glanced at it carefully, afraid of what I'd see.

Sure enough, it was the face of a man I didn't know but who looked very much like Graham had when I'd first seen him in the ER —eyes black and swollen shut, nose bloody.

"You did that?"

He glanced back at it and nodded, saying nothing for a moment. Then he took in a deep breath.

"Yes," he said and turned off his cell, placing the phone on the counter. "I gave him what he gave Graham. A good beating. He's in the hospital now. I called the ambulance before I left the back alley behind his apartment."

A shock went through me. He beat up Stepan? Left him in the back alley?

That's what Stepan had done to Graham. It was then that I realized how dangerous Hunter had become. He was willing to exact revenge against Graham's attacker. An eye for an eye...

"Isn't that a big risk? Won't his boss come after you? I thought he was a Russian. You said you don't mess with the Russians..."

Hunter glanced at me and shook his head. "I don't mess with the Russians," he said, his voice sounding tired. "I had Victor's permission. We're good buddies now, Celia. Didn't you know that? I thought for sure Spencer would have filled you in on all the gory details."

I said nothing in reply. I did know it, only too well. Spencer relished the chance to tell me all about Hunter. He reminded me every chance he got.

I looked at Hunter's cheek. "You've got a cut there," I said. It was open and oozing blood. It wasn't too serious but it needed attention. "You might need stitches."

"Nah, it's nothing. You can fix it." Hunter shrugged like having me administer to his cuts was a normal thing. "There are some steristrips in the kit. I've had worse than this. No need for stitches."

"Whatever you say," I replied and removed a bottle of peroxide and some cotton swabs. Then, I proceeded to tend to Hunter's cut cheek, and the abrasions on his knuckles. It wasn't what I had thought would happen to me that night—nursing an injured Hunter.

"So, Stepan's boss just said okay? Beat my guy up?" I asked as I wiped peroxide on his cheek to clean up the blood.

He shrugged. "He was fine with it. He and my uncle go back a long way. He was pretty generous—especially after I paid off Graham's debt."

I felt my cheeks heat at that. "Thank you," I said softly. "I can't thank you enough."

"Oh yes you can. I expect a lot of thank yous from you, Celia. A *lot*."

My face grew even hotter at that. "You're really going to make me have sex with you in repayment?"

"That's a rhetorical question, right?" he replied with the smallest quirk of his mouth, obviously enjoying himself at my expense.

Then he frowned. "I haven't decided what I expect from you, or what I'm going to make you do in repayment," he said, his voice suddenly thick, deep. "The jury is still out, counsellor. You'll find out. Don't worry about it."

"Then why am I here?" I asked. I met his eyes, and felt a surge of desire race through my body. God, he was still so damn gorgeous. His blue, blue eyes, thick eyelashes. Dark hair, now long and tucked behind his ears. Chiseled jaw with just the right amount of scruff. And his buff body so close to mine...

I tore my eyes away and continued to work on his cut, applying the steristrips and pulling the edges of the wound together with them so that the bleeding stopped.

"There," I said and stood back, admiring my work. "It looks pretty good."

Hunter nodded and held up his knuckles. "Maybe just some peroxide on these."

I complied and wiped each knuckle off, his hand in mine, our heads bent close together. When I finished, I glanced up and our faces were only inches apart.

He reached up and pulled me closer, kissing me, and I let him, kissing him back without a thought.

The kiss was warm, but brief. He pulled away, his eyes moving over my face. He brushed a strand of hair from my cheek and then shook his head.

"I need a drink," he said, his voice husky. "There's some whisky in the bar over there," he said, pointing to a credenza at the side of the dining area. "Pour us each a drink and join me in the living room."

I nodded, surprised that he stopped but I was, for all intents and purposes, his for the night. He was calling the shots. I left the kitchen and went over to the credenza, opening the cupboard to find crystal glasses and a bottle of George Dickel, a good whisky I recognized from circulars we received at the pub.

"George Dickel?" I said while I examined the bottle. "You buy the high-end stuff now."

"It was a gift from a sponsor," Hunter replied. Then he came up behind me while I poured an ounce or so into each glass. In fact, he stood right behind me, so close I could feel his body heat, almost touching me but not quite. He lifted a strand of my hair and sniffed it, and then leaned in, pulling my hair to one side, smelling my hair and neck. It sent a shiver through my body.

He pressed his body against mine, his hands on either side of the credenza, trapping me against it. There was no doubt in my mind that he was aroused. I felt his hardness against my butt, his breath warm on my neck. I closed my eyes, unable to deny my desire for him. My body warmed, my flesh swelling, already wet.

His hand slipped around my body to caress my belly, my hip, while he breathed in deeply, his nose beneath my ear.

Just when I was going to turn around in his arms, he inexplicably pulled back and left me, taking a glass and walking down the hallway.

"I'm going to have a shower," he said, his voice deep. "You can go and sit on the sofa. I'll be right out."

"You shouldn't get the steristrips wet," I said.

"Don't worry about me."

I nodded, wondering what would happen next. I took my glass of whisky and did as he ordered, sitting on the sofa, which faced a huge panoramic view of Boston's city lights. Hunter was going to have a shower? He'd probably want to have sex afterward, and I squirmed a bit on the sofa, trying to get comfortable. I was a little breathless as I waited for him to return, needing a drink to relax me. I drank down my glass of whisky and then tiptoed back to the credenza to refill it.

I needed the liquid courage.

Finally, about ten minutes later, Hunter returned, wearing only a large white towel wrapped around his waist, his nice bulge visible underneath it. As if he were used to parading around half naked in front of women, Hunter refilled his glass of whisky and sauntered over to the sofa, plopping down beside me. He turned to me and eyed me up and down, his expression unreadable.

"Let's toast," he said and held out his glass of whisky.

I picked up mine in response.

"To revenge," he said.

"To revenge," I replied, and together, we shot back the whisky. I was completely surprised that he was being so undemanding. When would he make his move?

When would he order me onto my knees or to lie back on his bed?

Why wasn't he making me fuck him right then and there?

He leaned closer to me, burying his face in my neck, once again breathing in deeply like he couldn't get enough of my perfume. He pressed closer and I lay back on the sofa until my head rested on the arm. He leaned over me, his arms on either side of my body, and stared down at me, his eyes intense.

I closed my eyes and waited for him to—to do whatever he would. Whatever he wanted, I was ready. Part of me blanked my mind, resigning myself to whatever he wanted. The other part was giddy, almost dizzy with desire for him, wanting to fuck him, the sooner the better.

Then he sighed and rose, standing in front of me. I glanced up at him, my eyes moving over his body, over his bulge, and up over his amazing abs to his beautiful if slightly injured face.

"In the morning, I'll need a hot bath," he said and lifted up one arm, grimacing a bit. I saw his bruise and realized he was right. He'd have an even bigger bruise in the morning. "Then, I like my coffee and eggs. Fried eggs with bacon. There's food in the fridge. I'm sure you can find your way around a kitchen."

"I have a class early in the morning," I said, slightly insulted that he was going to make me be his cook.

"Nine o'clock," he replied. "I checked. I get up at seven so we're fine. My driver will take you to Harvard when I'm done with you. You'll have enough time to change your clothes, get your books. Whatever you need."

When he was done with me... Was he going to bed now? He wasn't going to make me fuck him now?

He was going to make me stay the night, fix him a bath and breakfast, and then fuck me in the morning? After his bath or before?

My mind was whirling with questions and possibilities. I was shocked that Hunter hadn't ordered me onto my knees to deliver a blow job.

In fact, part of me was disappointed that he hadn't. At least then I'd know what to expect.

"Then I want you back here tomorrow night at ten."

"I can't stay here every night," I said, frowning. "I have a job. In fact, I'm on the schedule for double shifts and tomorrow night, I'm working late."

He frowned. "Why are you working? I thought Spencer promised you wouldn't have to work if you threw me over. Wasn't that your thirty pieces of silver?"

My mouth fell open. "Who told you that?"

Of course, it was true. Spencer had promised me that. How Hunter must hate my guts...

"Graham told me. So, my question remains, why are you working?"

"I told you, Graham lost my inheritance. I can't pay for my dorm at Harvard."

"Oh, yeah... that's right. He lost the entire fucking inheritance? How much was it? Half a million?"

I nodded. "The interest was paying my room and board."

He stood there, his hands on his hips, considering. "Tell you what," he said, his eyes narrow. "I'll pay your room and board. But I want you here every night that I'm not working. You'll stay the night. You'll do whatever I ask. *Whatever* I ask." He raised his eyebrows suggestively. "In the morning, you'll make my coffee and breakfast, run my bath, and then you'll go to your classes. Rinse. Repeat. I think repaying your debt this way might be a pretty good deal. Sound fair?"

"For how long?" I asked, swallowing back my nerves at the 'whatever' comment.

"Well, let's see... Eleven hours a night, three hundred hours to work off just on the interest alone. If we add in the room and board, which is..."

"Fourteen thousand," I said.

"Fourteen thousand, that makes one hundred sixty-four thousand—"

"A hundred fifty-four," I said. "Graham already paid off ten thousand."

"I stand corrected," Hunter said, his hand on his chin. "So, that comes out to about four weeks of work. If I paid off your entire inheritance? That would be..." He paused and mimed calculating. "A lot of days, Celia." He smiled.

"I said anything," I replied. "I meant it."

"Good. Just so we know where we stand."

He stood there looking at me, and I didn't know what to do or say in response. I felt relieved that he'd pay back my inheritance. In truth, being paid five hundred dollars an hour was way more than I could make in a week at the pub as a bartender, even with twice the number of shifts. It was a deal, I realized, except that I was pimping myself out like some call girl.

"Is five hundred an hour cheap or expensive?" I asked, my eyes filling with tears.

"Cheap," he said, his face expressionless. "But consider yourself lucky. It's usually a thousand an hour with the really top-of-the-line girls." He glanced at me, his eyes moving up and down over my body. "You'll have to work a little harder if you want to compete with them."

"I don't want to compete," I replied, wanting to stand up for myself. "I just want to get what I'm worth." Of course, that made me feel even worse, and I had to bite my cheek to stop more tears.

He nodded. "I think you're getting a fair deal. Look at it this way. If I hadn't paid off Graham's debt, Graham would be dead now, and Stepan and his boys would be after you for your inheritance—with interest. You'd probably owe him three hundred thousand instead of one-fifty. You'd still have no money. You'd have to work two jobs to afford your room and board at Harvard. You'd probably be so tired, your grades would fall. You'd lose your tuition scholarship. Then you'd really be in trouble. You'd be working for beans at a job seven days a week just to scrape by. This way, you get your inheritance back, you get to stay at Harvard, and keep up your grades. That sounds pretty sweet. There are probably thousands of people who would jump at the chance to have your little ethical problem."

Then he turned and left me alone, going down the hall to his room and closing the door.

I sat there for a few minutes, wondering if he'd come back and order me onto my knees or something, shove his dick down my throat—I could imagine all kinds of acts he might make me do, some of them making me a bit achy inside.

But nothing.

He didn't come back.

After about ten minutes of sitting in front of the television, I went down the hallway and stood outside his bedroom. I checked under the door and realized he'd turned off his bedroom light.

He'd gone to bed.

Totally surprised by now, I went to the bathroom across from my own bedroom and brushed my teeth once more to get the taste of whisky out of my mouth, then went to my own room and changed into my nightgown.

Finally, I climbed under the bedcovers, amazed at the turn of events that had led to me being in Hunter's apartment, in a separate bed, wondering when we'd actually fuck and what he'd make me do.

THE NIGHT PASSED SLOWLY. I didn't sleep well, being in a strange huge bed all alone in a strange room. I woke up several times, wondering what Hunter had planned for the morning. I slept in fits and starts, and finally, woke up at six, jumping up and slipping into the bathroom for a pee. I glanced at myself in the mirror.

Call girl. Not even a high-class call girl.

I turned on the shower and stepped inside, wishing I had the foresight to bring a fresh pair of underwear, but whatever. I'd stop off at my dorm on the way to class.

I finished washing and stepped out into the steam-filled bathroom, grabbing a huge fluffy towel, which I wrapped around my body. I brushed my hair and then my teeth, and considered myself in the mirror.

Hunter knocked at the bathroom door.

"Yes?" I said hesitantly.

"You're up already," he said, his voice sounding amused. "Eager beaver."

I frowned, not sure whether he meant the double entendre. "I had a terrible night's sleep."

"That's too bad. As for me, I slept like a baby."

I had started to put my clothes back on when he jiggled the doorknob. "Come on out. I need a bath."

"I'm getting dressed."

"Don't bother," he replied. "I'll just end up undressing you. Although that might be fun…"

I put down my bra and stopped dressing. Then, I wrapped the towel around myself again, frowning. I opened the door a crack and saw Hunter standing there in his black boxer briefs. Steam billowed out of the door.

"You're really going to go through with this, aren't you?"

His eyes narrowed. "You thought I was joking?"

I frowned. "I thought you were more honorable than that."

"I'm not."

I took in a deep breath and opened the door fully, leaving the bathroom with my clothes on the floor.

"What do you want me to do first?" I said, not meeting his gaze, because I knew he'd be grinning. "Shall I get on my knees? You must have liked that the other day. Maybe on all fours? Or on my back?"

I couldn't keep the hurt out of my voice, despite the fact that even making those suggestions made me wet, my body betraying my mind.

"I was thinking of a bath. Nice and warm to help with these," he said and when I glanced up at him, I saw the bruises he pointed to. They looked nasty and must have hurt. "Some of those bath salts would be good. Then, I want breakfast and coffee."

My cheeks heated and I said nothing. Instead, I marched to his bedroom, past his huge four-poster bed, and into the huge ensuite bathroom with its soaker tub. I bent down and started the bath, feeling the water to make sure it was nice and warm but not too hot. There was an unopened jar of bath salts beside the tub, with a scoop attached. The scent was some tropical flower.

Hunter entered the bathroom and watched me while I worked.

"You really want this in your bath?"

He stepped closer and picked the jar up. "The decorator said bath salts were good for sore muscles. What the fuck is freesia anyway?"

"It's a flower."

"Whatever. Do you like it?"

"What does it matter if I like it?"

He shrugged, half a grin on his mouth. "You're going to get in, too."

"I just had a shower."

"You need to wash my... back. The tub's too big for you to do it from outside."

I glanced around and saw a long wood-handled scrub brush with a loofah on the end, meant to wash a person's back.

Score!

I grabbed it. "I can use this." I smiled back at him.

He took it from me and broke it in half, handing the two pieces to me. "Not anymore."

"I can't believe you just did that," I said, frowning.

"I did," he said, his smile brilliant.

"You're enjoying this."

"Not as much as I'm going to enjoy it, soon enough. Put the bath salts in if you like them. Or not. I'll leave that up to you."

I frowned and examined the jar. I opened the lid, and took a whiff of the scent. It was nice. I put a scoop in and watched as the bath water became foamy, bubbles appearing on the surface.

The two of us stood there, watching, and then he stood closer, right behind me. The water level rose to about half full.

"Get in," he said, his voice soft. "I'll be right behind you."

I swallowed back my nerves, noting that my body was ready, my groin achy with desire even when my mind was busy fighting him.

I dropped my towel and quickly stepped in, not looking back when he pulled down his boxer briefs and stepped in behind me. I steadfastly refused to look at his body, which I knew would be beautiful. I remembered how beautiful—hard and lean, but buff, his skin fair and unblemished. Most of all, I didn't want to look at his face, because I'd see amusement there. He liked having me at his disposal. Under his control.

The truth was that I liked it a bit too much for my own good.

I sank below the waterline so he couldn't see my breasts, and watched as he sank down as well. I couldn't help but notice his erection, which was as big and thick as I remembered. Seeing his arousal sent a throb through my core and I imagined impaling myself on him and how good it would feel, especially since I was starting to feel a deep ache in my body. It had been too long since I'd felt a man inside me.

He turned off the water and then leaned back across from me, his legs spreading and slipping on either side of me at the other end of the huge tub. I heard him sigh in pleasure as he sank deeper, his head resting on the edge of the tub. He closed his eyes for a moment and we sat there in silence, the *drip drip drip* of the tap and the bubbles breaking around us the only sounds.

He cracked one eye open and looked at me. "Come over here," he said, his voice throaty. "Lie on top of me."

I hesitated. I could resist, or I could shut off my brain and just let my body take over. It was clear my body wanted him, even if I hated this arrangement I'd gotten myself into.

Then I realized something. I'd *always* wanted Hunter. I *still* wanted Hunter. Having sex with Hunter was not going to be unpleasant. In fact, I expected it would be very pleasant indeed.

He seemed like he wanted to play with me. He wanted to tease me. He wasn't going to just wham-bam-thank-you-ma'am. He wanted to fuck. Even if this wasn't going to be as good and as memorable as the first time he fucked me, it wouldn't feel anything like work.

I took in a deep breath and crawled over to him, my body floating above his, my face just inches from his. I lay there, above him, my legs between his knees, my hands on the side of the tub beside his shoulders.

God, he was beautiful. His face, despite the cut and butterfly sutures on his cheek, was beautiful, his eyes so light blue against his thick dark lashes. He breathed in deeply, his nostrils flaring, and licked his lips—his full sensuous lips.

"Kiss me," he ordered.

I bit my bottom lip, unable not to resist just a bit. "I thought prosti-
tutes didn't kiss their johns."

I raised my eyebrows at him expectantly.

"You're no prostitute and I'm no john," he replied and then he
reached one hand behind my head and pulled me to him, my lips
meeting his in a kiss that sent a jolt of lust through me from my chest
right to my clit, my core aching to feel him fill me up completely. My
mouth opened when his did, and he groaned when his tongue
touched mine. He pulled me closer, the water splashing around us, his
hands slipping down my back to grab a buttock and pull me against
his groin.

His erection was hard against my belly and I longed to rub
myself against it, to feel it push inside of me, spreading me,
filling me.

"Oh, God," I said when our kiss ended. I hadn't intended to let him
know how aroused I was, but it slipped out despite of my attempts to
control myself.

He pulled back and met my eyes, his half-lidded. "That's what I
want to hear."

We lay like that, his legs trapping my body against his, his erection
jutting into my groin, my arms around his shoulders, both of us
panting with arousal.

"Don't you want me to wash you?" I asked lightly, trying to look
coquettish.

His eyes narrowed. "Good idea." Then he pushed me back to my
place across from him. He got on his knees and crawled over so that
he was between my thighs. Of course, his big, thick, beautiful cock
was right at eye level. He leaned his hands against the wall behind me
and looked down. I glanced up and met his gaze. His longish hair fell
into his eyes, his cheeks were flushed, and his lips were parted. At that
moment, he was so gorgeous and so dominant, I felt breathless
beneath him.

I knew what he wanted. In front of my face, his dick throbbed, the
head wet.

"Suck me," he ordered but he didn't need to say anything. I would have on my own, because I'd loved the way he responded that night so long ago when I took him in my mouth that first time.

I leaned forward and licked the head, lapping around the crown, then took the head in my mouth, making sure to glance up and meet his eyes when I did.

"Oh, fuck," he whispered, and bit his lip. "Suck me, Celia."

I did, one hand grasping his shaft, while I worked my tongue under the head and around the crown once more. Then I took him in deeper—as deep as I could before gagging on him, he was so big and thick. He pulled back and I started a smooth rhythm, taking him in deep and then pulling off with a loud wet pop while my hand stroked his shaft.

I squeezed him, pulling out some moisture, then licked the head and he groaned to watch me taste him. Before I could take him in deep once more, he stopped me and stood up, lifting me up with him.

"Enough," he said and stood up, towering over me. He reached down, and I took his hand and stood up as well. He helped me out of the tub and onto the mat, where the two of us dripped for a moment. I reached for a towel but he grabbed my arm and led me out of the bathroom and over to his huge bed. He gripped me under my arms and lifted me up onto the bed, and I turned and crawled up, turning to lie on my back. He crawled up behind me and spread my thighs with his hands, kneeling there, staring down at me, possession clear in his eyes.

I was his at that moment. Completely his to do with as he wanted. I'd be his for weeks—maybe a full year—and he could do whatever he wanted, every night of the week if he wanted.

I liked that idea far too much for my own good.

That knowledge did something to me, my pulse rapid, my body throbbing with lust. I wanted him to push his big thick cock into me and fuck me until I came, but he had other plans. First, he lay completely on top of me, his weight almost crushing me, but it was a comforting weight. I slipped my legs around his hips, wanting to feel his hard cock against my clit, and rub against it wantonly.

He kissed me again, sucking my tongue into his mouth, devouring me with his kiss as I kissed him back hungrily. Our wet bodies pressed against each other, the pressure in all the right places making me even more aroused. He broke the kiss and began licking and kissing my skin—my neck, my collar bone, then down to one breast, which he squeezed. I glanced down to see my breast in his hand, my nipple hard. He licked it, ran his tongue all around the areola, and then took it between his lips and sucked, his tongue pulling at it so that shocks of lust coursed through my body right to my clit.

"Oh, God," I moaned, my eyes closing.

"Watch me," he said in a throaty voice.

I opened my eyes and watched as he moved from one nipple to the other, squeezing my breasts together and lapping his tongue across them, nipping them with his teeth just enough to make me gasp, but without pain.

"Now I'm going to eat you, Celia. I've been thinking about eating you ever since I saw you in the club. I'm going to eat you until you scream my name."

His expression was so intense that I knew he intended to do just that. He moved down my body, lower, his face over my belly, kissing a trail down to my mound. Then he pressed my thighs completely open, his gaze on my pussy.

I ached to feel his mouth on me, his fingers in me, his cock in me. Anything to relieve the arousal I felt. He spread my lips and then glanced up, meeting my gaze. He licked me deliberately, not taking his eyes off mine, wanting me to watch him. I gasped to feel his tongue on my clit, soft and warm and wet against my aching flesh. He kept licking me, running his tongue all around my clit, and then down to the opening to my body. My whole pussy throbbed with need and I knew it wouldn't be long before I came if he kept that up.

Which he did.

He slipped a finger inside me, and I remembered that night five years earlier when he had done the same—the first time I'd felt a man touch me that way. He slipped two fingers inside, stroking up exactly the right way. When he clamped his mouth over my clit and sucked me into his mouth, I groaned out loud, not caring what I sounded like.

He sucked and stroked me, and soon I felt the familiar sensation as my orgasm approached. The lust made me breathless, my core tightening as pleasure spread through me.

"Oh, God, Hunter..." I cried out as my orgasm crested. He kept his mouth on me, sucking me so intently. I tried to stop him because it was too much, but he only slowed the motion of his tongue. I shuddered beneath him, gasping from the sensations that rocked through my body.

My response was so intense it startled me. When he finally removed his mouth from me, I collapsed back, covering my eyes with a hand.

I felt embarrassed that he could make me respond that way. Someone who I knew hated me. Someone to whom I hadn't spoken more than a few dozen words in five years.

But I'd gone months without a lover and clearly, all my solo masturbatory sessions hadn't been enough to keep me fulfilled.

I needed a man. Hunter had proven that to me more clearly than anything else could have.

"That was fast, " he said and when I opened my eyes, he was grinning up at me, his face still above my pussy, his fingers still deep inside me. "A little needy, are you, Celia?"

I couldn't help but clench around his fingers when he licked me slowly once more.

"Oh, God," I gasped, his tongue sending new shivers through me.

"You're ready for more," he said and pulled out his fingers. "Nice and wet. I'll give you more. I'll give you this," he said and knelt between my thighs, his thick hard shaft in his hand. Precum dripped from the head. He crawled on top of me, his knees on either side of my chest and leaned his hands against the wall so that his cock was positioned over my face.

"Suck me again," he ordered. I opened my mouth and stuck out my tongue to receive him, licking the precum from the tip, tasting him. I took the head in my mouth once more and sucked while he gripped the shaft, feeding me his cock slowly. "That's nice."

He thrust slowly in my mouth and I did my best to keep my teeth from the head, sucking him when he thrust, releasing when he pulled out. His body was taut above me, his muscles all tense. I wondered if he'd come in my mouth but he pulled off completely. I licked my lips, waiting for what he wanted next.

"I'm going to fuck you until you come on my cock, Celia," he said, his voice low, sexy.

I knew he would, and I knew *I* would, because sucking him, tasting him, watching him feed me his cock had aroused me once more. I needed to come again, and knew I would if he filled me up and fucked me.

He leaned over to the bedside table and removed a condom, unwrapped it, and unrolled it over his erection. Then he crawled lower on the bed and lifted my hips so that one thigh was on either side of his hips. He leaned over me while he knelt like that and pressed the head of his cock against my clit, rubbing the head all over my slit. I could feel how wet I was, the head of his cock sliding easily up and down my flesh, around my clit and then down again to the entrance to my body.

I closed my eyes and let the sensations wash over me as he built me back up again with his cock. One hand grabbed one of my breasts, squeezing, his thumb circling the nipple until it was hard. He leaned down for a moment and sucked each nipple, biting each one gently before licking them to soothe them.

"You're so fucking beautiful," he murmured as he rose and watched while he rubbed his cock against my clit. "I'm going to fuck you hard."

When he pressed the head of his cock against the opening to my body, I gasped, needing him to fill me up, almost desperate to feel him stretch me open wide.

"Do you want me, Celia?" he asked, poised at the opening, his thumb circling my clit in lazy strokes that drove me wild with need.

"Yes," I managed, barely able to speak.

"What do you want me to do, Celia?" he asked. "Say it."

I licked my lips. "Fuck me," I whispered.

"Louder," he said.

"Fuck me," I said more forcefully. I remembered him playing with me like that years ago, wanting me to beg. "Please," I added and he smiled.

"Why should I?" he asked, not satisfied with just my begging. "Why should I fuck you and make you come, Celia? Tell me."

"Because I need it," I replied, and it was true. I needed to feel his cock inside of me. All the way.

"You need it, do you? How long has it been since you had a cock inside you?"

He kept pressing gently at my opening, kept stroking my clit.

"Eight months."

He frowned at that. "Eight months? *Fuck*," he said, his voice incredulous. "How can you survive so long without sex? Jesus..."

I licked my lips, pushing my hips up, not wanting to talk about my lack of love life. "Fuck me please, Hunter."

"God," he said, his gaze moving over me. "Why don't you have someone fucking you every night? If you were mine..."

Then he pushed into me entirely, his hands gripping my hips, and it felt so good, I groaned out loud, my eyes closed. He positioned me so that he could thrust while still stroking my clit, and soon, with very few thrusts, my body went over the edge once more and I began to spasm, my core tightening, my flesh clenching around his thick hard cock.

"Oh God, oh God," I cried out as I came, the sensation of pleasure so intense I felt momentarily blinded by it. He thrust even harder at that, and soon, when I cracked open my eyes and peeked at him through my eyelashes, I saw he was close as well, eyes half-closed but watching his cock sliding in and out of me, his face red, neck muscles and shoulders tense, jaw clenched.

"Fuck, oh, fuck," he groaned, thrusting hard and deep, ejaculating with each thrust. When he finally collapsed on top of me and lay still, I could still feel his cock spasm inside of me.

I wrapped my arms around him, and together we breathed deeply as we both recovered.

It felt completely strange and, at the same time, completely right to be lying like that, in Hunter's arms, his cock still deep inside me. It felt like no time had passed since that first night—except, of course, so much had happened.

So much bad had happened between us, to each of us, since then...

After a few moments, he rose and removed the condom from his cock, still semi-erect, then tied it off and tossed it in a trash can beside the bed. He crawled off the bed and grabbed his boxer briefs, pulling them on quickly.

Then he turned and left me lying there while he went to the ensuite bathroom.

I frowned. I heard him take a piss, then decided I had better get up myself. I went into the bathroom and found my towel, then stopped beside him, wondering what I should do next.

"Bacon and eggs," he said and pointed at the door. "I like my toast light with butter. Oh, and fresh-squeezed juice. There's a juicer in the cupboard by the refrigerator."

"Yes, Sir," I said tartly, feeling suddenly like what I was—a servant. A sex servant. A sex worker, who doubled as a cook and whatever else Hunter wanted.

There was no moment of post-coital intimacy between us. It was like I'd just made his bed or cleaned his room. He leaned close to the mirror and examined his cut, touching the butterfly bandages where one had come a bit loose from the steam.

He saw me still standing there, and turned to me.

"You don't want to be late for class, Celia. Chop-chop."

I stomped out of the bathroom and went to my own bedroom, my body feeling well-used after two shattering orgasms and his big thick cock pounding into me, but my feelings were hurt. I felt empty as I pulled on my clothes. I brushed my hair back and stared at my face in the mirror.

"You're a prostitute," I said to my reflection. "So much for your fancy Harvard degree..."

I MADE HIM BREAKFAST, frying bacon and eggs in a pan I found in a cupboard, and he finally showed up to eat, dressed in an impeccable black suit with a pale blue shirt and black tie that set off his eyes.

I placed his plate of food down, along with a glass of fresh orange juice and coffee. Barely a word passed between us the entire time. He sat at the island and read the paper while he ate, his focus on the financial section. For my part, I ate some eggs and toast, and drank some coffee.

Finally, he glanced at his very expensive watch and eyed me. "Gotta go. James should be downstairs for you in about thirty minutes."

He folded up his paper and left it on the island, then went to the closet by the front entrance to slip on his shoes. He adjusted his tie in the mirror beside the door and then left, not even looking back.

I sat there in mute incomprehension.

He felt nothing. While I was all mixed up inside, aroused and upset, feeling sick about everything but enjoying it anyway, he acted like nothing happened out of the ordinary.

I left the kitchen and plopped onto the sofa, staring out the window at the bay, a sense of emptiness making me feel like crying. I glanced around the apartment. In truth, it wasn't a bad job, as jobs went. Sleep in a huge four-poster bed, fuck the lord of the manor and orgasm twice. Make breakfast, and then go to class.

Hunter had become a mafia money man. He owned me—at least, for as long as it took to pay off my debt. I'd become his call girl.

I sighed and went to the bedroom to make the bed before I left for class.

One night down, one hundred and ninety-nine nights to go...

CHAPTER 18

Hunter

RUNNING the clubs and gym were child's play for me—a piece of cake.

I could run them in my fucking sleep.

Figuring out what to do with Celia? That was a bit more of a challenge, and was precisely why it occupied an even larger share of my hungry mind's attention.

I stood by the huge multi-paned window on the third floor of the warehouse I owned by the waterfront and waited for George to arrive. While I waited, I contemplated recent events.

Paying off Celia's and Graham's debt had been a success. I met with Victor Romanov and had a real heart-to-heart with him about my old friend's money problems and what I wanted to do. Victor apologized that Stepan had beaten up Graham, but protested that he had no idea Graham was my friend. He agreed that Stepan should have done more research into who Graham was and come to me when there were problems with the payment. He agreed with me that Stepan could take a beating so I could exact punishment for the oversight. Stepan was a psychopath who loved to torture, and he could always use a reminder of who was boss.

Victor was boss. I was his new friend, fast becoming a very good friend, and now considered the head of my family, which held sway in the world of gangsters and thugs.

My approach to Victor was well-planned and successfully executed. My first drill sergeant in the Marines—the one who had said I would go far one day if I put my mind to it—would be proud of the efficiency with which I arranged a meeting with the mafia boss and got my way with him.

"Who is this fellow to you?" Victor asked as we sat in a booth in his restaurant. Several big-muscled thugs stood around us, watching for any threats to Victor, who was second in command in the Romanov family in Boston.

"He's an old friend," I said. "He and I were supposed to go into business once upon a time but things didn't work out. He made a bad investment, lost his sister's inheritance, and then couldn't pay the interest. I'm paying it for him out of loyalty and friendship. He couldn't pay the debt, and neither could his little sister."

"That's big of you," he said, eyeing me over his plate of food. "I like a man who's loyal to friends and family. Very big of you to look after his little sister's debt. Isn't his father the current DA?"

I nodded. "Stepfather. A man doesn't choose his mother's second husband," I said, defending Graham, even though Graham had chosen Spencer over me. I hoped to distract his attention away from Celia.

"He doesn't," Victor said and took a drink. "Your friend needs a new investment advisor. Maybe he should have gone into business with you. You've made some smart moves since you took over for Donny. I've been watching you."

I nodded. "Thank you. I have a mind for money."

"My kind of man," Victor said and held up his glass of vodka. We toasted each other and I shot back the vodka, enjoying it as it burned down my throat.

"Was this the pretty little thing that came to the club the other night and made a scene?"

I frowned. How did Victor know?

Then I kicked myself mentally. Of course Victor would know. *Misha...*

"Yes, that was Celia," I replied, hoping to shrug her off like she was nothing to me. I didn't want Victor to think he could use her to get leverage over me.

We finished our drinks and I left as quickly as I could, hoping he wouldn't ask any more questions about Celia. I didn't want him interested in her.

The whole business gave me a great deal of satisfaction. Only a few weeks earlier, I'd been wondering how I could get in deeper with Victor and his brother. Now, thanks to Graham's foolhardy investing scheme, I'd found a way in. On his part, Victor probably thought he finally had something to use to reel me in under his control. I was using him to get closer to Sergei, my real target. What better way to ingratiate yourself with a mafia type than to be in debt to them and pay it off on time and with interest?

I left with a promise to come to his restaurant some night for a special family dinner. That was a good sign—if Victor invited me to one of their big family meals, I'd get to meet Sergei, my eventual target.

I heaved a sigh of relief as I left the restaurant. I didn't want Victor to know how much Celia still meant to me. Even if she had thrown me over for Greg, I didn't want anything to happen to her.

I wasn't obsessed with her, but I thought about her a lot. The idea of having her completely under my control was keeping me in a state of semi-arousal.

As Sun Tzu wrote thousands of years ago, if you know the enemy as you knew yourself, you need not fear the result of a hundred battles.

I knew myself and I knew what was happening, but I had it under control.

I'd indulge myself in Celia, enjoy her body, use it for my own pleasure, and then I'd lose interest in her the way I lost interest in every other woman I'd been with.

As I walked down the block to my car, I couldn't remember the last time I'd felt this way about a woman. I never struggled much to have whatever woman I wanted and had never obsessed over those that got away. There weren't many women worthy of much obsessing.

Celia was the exception. She was worthy. She was also proving to be a real challenge but I was always up for a challenge. Hell, lately, I was always up, sporting a semi-hard-on at the prospect of seeing her at night. But my little visit to Victor worried me. He seemed too interested in her for my own good. That was the thing about gangsters. They were always thinking of ways to get more money out of you.

I planned on visiting Celia's dorm later in the day to install some bugs so she'd be safe when she was away from me.

I didn't want to have to hire a bodyguard for her, because that wouldn't work on campus, but I could install a hidden camera and mic so her room could be monitored.

As for Celia, she had been nicely responsive to me the previous night. She couldn't deny her body's response to me.

But I wanted more than just reluctant obedience.

I wanted her willing compliance. I had to use different tactics to win her over than what I'd used on the usual women I'd seduced and bedded.

I wanted Celia to willingly spread her quivering thighs for me.

Sure, she'd obeyed me when I ordered her to suck and fuck me. She'd even had two orgasms under my tongue and with my cock deep inside of her. But I wanted complete surrender. I wanted her to come to me, to *ask* me to fuck her.

The question was—how?

The real skill would be in making her surrender feel less like a loss than allowing what she had wanted to happen all along. I'd have to make it so that she felt she'd won.

That would take a lot of skill.

She'd reach a point when giving in would be appealing, better than remaining in her safe little dorm.

She'd come to me and put her arms around me, kiss me, ask me to fuck her. Tell me that she needed me.

That would be victory.

A sweet, sweet victory.

I intended to savor every moment of my victory when it came. I was certain it would.

I ARRIVED at the warehouse I owned on the waterfront and went up to the third-floor apartment where I'd set up an office. Several of my security staff were there, waiting for my orders. As for me, I was waiting for my best friend from Afghanistan to arrive—a merc who worked with the US Marines and who was now freelance. He was scheduled to fly in that afternoon and I looked forward to having him with me while I planned my revenge against the Romanov family.

Raucous laughter from the guys brought me back to the present. A pile of money from the weekend's fights at the gym was two feet tall and twice as wide. The mob loved to launder their dirty money through the fights. Two of the guys played with it, fanning their faces with the wads of cash, smelling the money, throwing the wads at each other like the little boys they really were, so impressed with a bunch of paper.

Despite being an investment adviser and stockbroker by training, I didn't get this fetish with actual paper money. For me, it was nothing more than a bargaining chip, a weapon in my war against those who had destroyed my family.

The guys saw it as bottles of booze, dope, women, flashy clothes, and nice cars.

For me, money became a means for vengeance. The more of it I had, the more respect among the mob I gained, the more ins I had with the dirty cops, and the politicians. The more power I had, the more freedom I had to exact revenge.

Luckily, it also gave me a way into Celia's life, and between her milky white thighs.

There was also a way to Celia's heart. Although I could order her to fuck me, suck my dick, that wasn't what I really wanted. I wanted her to wrap her thighs willingly around my neck, around my waist.

Willingly. Not because she had to.

Then, when she did, I'd leave her the way she'd left me.

NOISE outside the warehouse dragged my attention away from pleasantly erotic thoughts of Celia's milky white thighs to a black SUV on the street below—Georgi, whom we jokingly called Yorgi after the movie *Triple X*, and who now went by just George.

He'd been my right-hand man in Afghanistan. Tough but affectionate, with smarts enough to be able to admit he just didn't know something, George was loyal to a fault. Together, we'd worked the towns and villages in Afghanistan, stalking al Qaeda, paying off tribal leaders to ensure the negotiations for the pipeline from the Caspian went through without a hitch.

I smiled when I saw his salt-and-pepper brush cut, a legacy of his years working with Marines. After months of us each going our own separate paths, seeing George was one of the few moments of genuine pleasure I'd felt in a long time.

I rubbed my hands together with glee and went to the elevator to wait and ambush him once the doors opened.

One of my men emerged first, carrying George's luggage, and I was unable to hold myself back, almost jumping on George as I threw his arms around him. For his part, George dropped a briefcase and embraced me, clapping me on the back.

"Come in, come in, you old bastard." I led George through the door into the third floor. "Welcome to your new home."

George followed me inside and looked around the empty space.

"I'm staying here?" he asked in his thick Russian accent.

"This is your new home. All of it."

He went up to the pile of money on the table. "What's this for?" He picked up a wad of cash. "Do you expect me to make bed out of this? Stack into table and couch?"

"No," I said, leaning back against the table, crossing my arms. "It's called mon-ey. M–O–N–E–Y. You exchange it for commodities on a market. I want you to go right out and furnish the place to your tastes.

Use whatever you need. I want an office up here with a full security system, cameras inside and outside. Whatever you need to provide security."

George nodded and glanced around the empty space. Finally, he turned back to me.

"Where is Donny? Didn't his lawyers get him out of custody?"

I shook my head. "No luck so far."

"I am surprised you didn't spring him," George said and dropped the wad of money back on the pile.

"You're joking, right?"

"You could pull off. How many times we capture bad guys and take them to safe house? It would be great mission. Real challenge. Can you imagine? Getting into his cell and getting him out?"

"Donny'll be fine." I didn't add that I was glad he was out of the way, or that I blamed him for my brother's death.

"How is your dad?"

I shrugged, a hollow feeling in the pit of my stomach. "Not so good. His heart is bad, plus he has COPD. Losing Sean hit him hard."

George nodded and then sighed, glancing at the pile of money. He took another wad and flipped through it. "First thing I need is bed. Nice big bed fit for sultan. I have been sleeping in flea-bite motels for weeks."

"Ah," I said and put my arm around him and walked him to the door. "The sultan needs a bed fit for his station in life. Will you be requiring a harem? You know, to restore you to your former magnificent self?"

"First things first. I want to buy bed. For past two weeks, I eat nothing but chicken fry steak, tacos, and grits down in South. I want big Russian dinner. Tonight, I want to sleep for twelve hours straight. Then we talk pretty little things."

"Your wish is one of my men's commands. Speaking of pretty little things, I have myself a nice one." I licked my lips. "I'm going over to her place later today to check it out while she's at class. Wanna come and snoop with me?"

"Why you snooping? Can't you just go over?"

I shook my head. "No. This one's still wild. I'm..." I tilted my head to one side. "I have her milky white thighs, George, but I want her pink little beating heart. She's a pretty little bird, very small and very timid. She'll take some time to," I said and grinned at George, "tame to hand."

"Who is this pretty little bird?"

"Graham's little sister."

George made a face. "His little sister?" he pursed his lips. "The one that got away?"

"The very one," I said, for George had been my confessor during my time in Afghanistan.

I hadn't told him about my plans to have Celia as my personal fuck toy.

"George, she's the sweetest piece of ass I've had in years."

George shook his head. "If you were anyone else, I would say you are crazy."

"Oh, I'm probably insane, but when you see her, you'll understand." The elevator doors opened and I ushered George inside. "And now, my dear man, you go out and buy yourself a bed. I have a job to do, but when I get back, we'll get you some borscht, or whatever the hell it is you Russians eat."

RICHARDSON, my current tech expert, came with me to Celia's dorm while George scoured the local furniture stores for an appropriate sultan's bed. We had some fake order papers and a story about checking the cable and internet service. While I snooped, Richardson installed hidden cameras and bugs. I was worried about Celia, now that she was known to Victor.

Victor had been digging around trying to understand why I'd pay off so much of her debt—of Graham's debt. I didn't want to give him too much reason to be interested in her, but I also wanted her to be safe. She needed protection when she wasn't with me. The bugs and video would make sure George could watch over her when I was busy. Hell, I could connect to her feed anytime I wanted on my smartphone but George would be the one I trusted to take care of her.

"You don't trust this lady friend?" Richardson said as he installed a camera in the room, overlooking the forlorn bed with its rumpled sheets.

"Trust has nothing to do with this," I said, irritated that the man would think of questioning my motives. "This is purely for security purposes. And none of your goddamned business."

"Sorry. Just trying to make conversation."

My pulse was raised; my stomach had that butterfly feeling that accompanied arousal. I had Celia's body at my disposal, but I wanted more. I wanted her mind and heart. I sorted through the items on top of her old dresser looking for hints about her as a person. A selection of hand and body lotions, hair clips, a jar filled with pennies and small change. Pictures of an older woman stuck in the frame of the mirror, middle-aged, with dark hair and dark eyes—her mother. A woman I'd barely met because she spent her time in her bedroom, tripped out on pain killers.

Beside the window sat a telescope. Still attached to the case on the table beside it was a gift sticker taped to the black fabric, although the sides of the sticker were curling.

To Celia on Your 8th Birthday
Love, Dad

The year her father had been killed in the accident that would eventually bring Spencer into her life...

A telescope she'd had all her life. It explained her love of astronomy.

I was almost overwhelmed by the scent that seemed to permeate the apartment. It reminded me of the warm spring evenings I'd spent on leave in Virginia when the scent of cherry blossoms drenched the air.

I sat at her desk and checked out her MacBook. It was open and there was no password so I started snooping into her files. Dozens of

PDF documents—all of them journal articles on this or that aspect of law or contracts. Papers she'd written in university. Nothing revealing.

I opened a bottom drawer and rustled through files and papers. Beneath it all, several notebooks filled with lecture notes from her classes. Again, nothing revealing.

But then—a goldmine.

The fucking mother lode.

A diary.

I opened it and flipped through the pages. Written in a tiny hand, with tight script, was the outpouring of Celia's mind dating back a few years. She wasn't a prodigious writer, skipping months at a time, but here, in the two hundred odd pages, were her private thoughts.

I had to take it. I'd read it quickly and return it and she'd be none the wiser.

I wanted to see what she'd written about me, if anything, and about any men she'd been with. I felt almost breathless as I turned the pages, guilt almost overwhelming my curiosity. On page seventy-three, she wrote about Christmas at home with her mother.

Nothing too uncommon—her mother asking her about boyfriends, about any interesting law students or lawyers she might date, and Celia's frustration that her mother thought only of her romantic life and never once complimented her on being in law school.

I wanted to sit down right now and read the rest, but it could wait till later. I slipped the small book into a pocket in my jacket and turned to her computer. I opened Safari, checking out her browsing history only to find that most of the links were to her webmail account, which I couldn't get into, and to her YouTube account and an assortment of funny cat videos and comic ones of fat men dancing in tutus.

I checked out her pictures and saw dozens of various people, girls her own age, her family—her father. Giant redwoods. The coast of California.

I logged off the computer and turned to the rest of the tiny dorm room. The devices Richardson was installing were state of the art. No one would detect them unless they had the right technology, and most likely Celia wouldn't. You'd have to be in the CIA to trace the little beauties Richardson was installing.

"How long are you going to be?" I watched as Richardson used the existing architecture of the closet to hide the tiny recorder/transmitter. It resembled the other tiny black holes in the wood where nails had been hammered. Richardson even had a little mini vacuum to suck up the wood dust and plaster he had carved out for the device. It was undetectable. It would piggyback onto the building's internet and transmit images to the warehouse through a series of satellite hookups and remote servers using wireless technology.

"Almost done. Just need to clean up and we're through."

I nodded, glancing around the room. When Celia returned to her apartment for the occasional night off, I'd have access to her 24/7. I could watch her sleep, I could watch her eat, I could watch her working at her desk.

I was a peeping Tom, yes, but one of the highest order. And all of it done for her security.

If I told myself that enough times, I might actually believe it.

IT WAS SO DAMN good to see George again.

I reserved the entire dining room of a local Russian restaurant in Boston's old downtown district for the evening so I didn't have to worry about other diners. It was one of the few run by a family of Russian immigrants not controlled by Sergei Romanov, so of course, I wanted to use it. I didn't want Sergei's people to get too close a look at George. He was my secret weapon and would help me understand and get revenge against the Russian underworld.

We sat at a round booth in the back so we could see the entrance and enjoyed course after course of Russian food specially prepared for George. While we ate, a waiter hovered in the background, watching as the meal progressed, a white cloth folded over his arm.

Potatoes, cabbage, and smoked sturgeon.

Solyanka, a Slavic chowder thick with smoked meats and olives.

Elk dumplings brought in by air express, direct from St. Petersburg.

A half-dozen shots of vodka and toasts to our health, to friendship, to success—to women.

I felt the warmth of the liquor, the food and the company seep into my bones and I finally relaxed, a real smile on my face.

"This sweet little sister of yours," George said, and I could tell from his expression—lips pursed, brow furrowed—that George was trying to broach the subject very carefully. "Do you like her?"

"Do I like her?" I frowned. "Do I *like* her?" I said nothing for a moment, trying to gauge why George had asked. "I don't know if I fucking like her. I'm fucking her. Why?"

George popped another dumpling in his mouth and chewed for a moment, the expression of concern remaining on his face. "I know you don't want me to say, but if you get too close to her," he said and gestured to me with his knife, "Victor and then Sergei will take interest in her. Once you get close to them, they want to know all your business. They want to know your weak spots. They exploit those weak spots."

"That's why you're here," I said. "I need your advice on how to deal with the Russians."

"If you like her, let her go."

I said nothing in reply. I usually gave George a lot of license. He could say what he pleased, because I needed good advice from someone I trusted, and I trusted George without reservation, having put my life in the Russian's hands many times in the past.

George drank some wine. "If you like her," he repeated once again, "leave her alone. In Russian *vory v zakone*, we do not involve our women—not ones we love. They cannot become bargaining chips."

"She's not 'my woman.'"

"Lie to me, but tell yourself truth." He let that stand for a moment. "If you like her, let her go."

I didn't say anything. He was right, of course. I should just never see her again.

"Come on," I said and waved him off. "I can protect her."

"If you need someone in your bed, pick someone who doesn't matter to you. They will become target."

"George, I know about the risks. I know how to manage risks."

"Of course. I was just reminding." George swirled his glass of wine. "You can't find someone else while you go on your mission for revenge? Or," he said and leaned forward, nodding as he looked at me, thrusting his wine glass at me, "are you in love with her?"

I frowned. "I'm not in love."

I rubbed the delicate etching along the edge of my crystal wine glass and thought about George's question.

I decided that, no, I wasn't in love with her. I wanted her. I wanted to make her want me and offer herself to me.

That was all.

George said nothing, but he gave me a look, his eyebrows raised.

"I'm *not* in love," I repeated.

He shrugged. "If you really like her," he said again. "If you love her, let her go unless you are prepared to own her. Remember Powell's rule in Iraq."

"The Pottery Barn Rule," I said, frowning. I knew where George was going and I didn't like it.

"Exactly. If you break, you own. If you put her in danger, if you break her life," he said and sat back, "you own her. If you don't like? If she is just pretty fuck, then so what? Collateral damage. Who gives fuck if they take her, torture her, kill her?" George glanced at me, his eyes hooded. "And they will, if they ever want to punish you, black-mail you."

"I know that." I didn't like the way this conversation was turning. Tension rose in my body, and I felt a need to throw something, kick something.

"Mixing business and pleasure?" George shook his head. "Not good idea. Keep separate. Hunter, you can have any pretty little bit of pussy you want with that big pile of money in the warehouse."

"She owes me."

"Well, I say no more," he said and clapped me on the back. "I can see there is no talking with you. Just something to think about."

"I don't want to think right now," I said and thrust my shot glass forward. "Fuck thinking. More vodka."

I WALKED arm-in-arm with George into the third-floor loft and laughed when I saw the bed standing in the corner by the makeshift bathroom that, even now, plumbers and tillers were finishing, working late the previous night for almost triple time. "Yeah, that's a sultan's bed all right, you ostentatious son of a bitch."

"Why not have best if you have such big pile of money?"

"Have a good sleep. I'm going to do a little light reading." I pulled out the diary and flashed it at George.

"What is?"

"Her diary."

"What?" George made a face. "You are reading diary now?" He shook his head.

I flipped through the pages. "I found it at her apartment today when we were installing the bugs. Now I get to know all her little secrets."

"Let me see." George held out his hand.

I passed it to him, watching as George opened it and turned a few pages. As he read, George rubbed his chin, where a serious six-o'clock shadow was forming. "Oh, yes?" He raised his eyebrows. "Really?" He turned away from me, shielding the diary from my view.

I followed him, trying to get the diary back. "I'll take that now, thanks."

George eluded me, always keeping a step ahead, turning the page and reading carefully, his expression one of fascination. "Ho, ho. Celia. You little minx."

"Give it to me," I said, half-smiling, but also half-wanting to pop George a good one.

George turned another page, moving his lips as he read, his eyes wide. "Oh my God."

I grabbed the diary from George, ensuring I had it still opened to the same page.

March 21

Today I got a video camera! I spent all afternoon learning how to use it so I could connect it to my telescope to take time-lapse photographs of the Milky Way...

The rest was just more of the same, with Celia recording the intricate details of the camera's various settings and capabilities.

"You bastard." I couldn't help but smile as George roared with laughter, holding his stomach as he did.

"What you think you find?" George said, wiping his eyes. "Confessions of nymphomania?"

"Well," I said, nodding. "That'd be a bonus, but no, I thought I might discover the essence of Celia so I could better... know her."

"In biblical sense?"

"I already did that." I closed the diary and stuffed it back in my pocket. "Come on, George, you remember the old adage that you have to know your enemy as you know yourself if you want to be successful in battle."

"Celia is enemy now?"

I put my arm around George's shoulder and squeezed. "You know what I mean."

I glanced over at the office space we had hastily set up, using some office dividers, a couple of desks and computers. Richardson sat at a desk and worked on a computer. I stood behind him. "How's the system working?"

"Great," he said and leaned back, rubbing his eyes. "She's in the bathroom."

"What?"

"She returned home while you were out. I called, but you didn't answer."

"Damn." I took out my cell phone and turned it back on. I hadn't wanted to be interrupted while George and I enjoyed our meal, but I also hadn't thought Celia would be returning to her dorm so soon.

On the split screen, two images—live video feed from her apartment. On one side, the fish-eye camera showed the tiny living room from the vantage point of the main doorway. To the right, her bedroom. To the left, a metal desk. Flanking the main window, a small love seat and arm chair. A tiny television on a table beside the love seat. The telescope in the alcove of the bay window itself.

"When did she get back?"

"Around four o'clock."

"What's she been doing?"

Richardson pointed to the screen. "Nothing much. Sitting at her desk, reading textbooks."

Sure enough, when I bent down to check out the video feed, I saw her sitting at her desk, her back to the camera, reading and taking notes.

She was wearing a long white robe of some sort, slippers on her feet. She sat on the chair with one foot tucked under her.

"What's she listening to? Can you turn up the volume?"

Richardson handed me the earphones so I could listen in. Something folksy that I didn't recognize.

"You're recording this somewhere?"

"Yep. You can access it on your own computer. I've sent you the link to the archives. Once you've watched it, you can delete it or save it."

"You can't really see her well," I said to George. "But come here."

George came to my side and looked at the monitor. "She looks delicate."

"A delicacy."

George shook his head. "So now, you read her diary, you watch her every move in dorm room..." George patted me on the back. "Poor girl. I feel sorry for her."

"Hey, she asked for my help. She said she'd do anything."

"She didn't want this, I think."

"Yeah, well, I didn't want a lot of things. Shit happens." Irritation with George built in me. As fond as I was of him, I didn't need the man's subtle innuendo. "She needs to be protected. Her stupid brother got her into trouble and now I have to clean up his mess and make sure she's safe."

The three of us watched as Celia disappeared from view. I had no idea what she was doing, but then she emerged in only her bra and panties.

"That's more than enough," I said. "You don't need to watch this."

Richardson smiled and clicked off the feed.

"Well," I said turning to George, taking the diary out again, holding it up. "I'm going to my apartment to do some... reconnaissance."

"Poor girl," George said, shaking his head, a grudging smile on his face. "She won't know what hit her."

"Oh, she'll know." I walked to the door, inexplicable anger filling me. When I got there, I turned and watched George for a moment as the man went over to the bed and ran his hand over the luxurious cover.

Finally, I softened just a bit. "George," I said. "It's good to have you here."

"Is good to be here." George nodded. "Is pretty little bird coming to you for fun tonight?"

"Of course," I said and smiled. "I have a big debt to collect."

George shrugged and grinned back. "Good night."

I DIDN'T KNOW what I expected when I started to read Celia's diary, but I learned pretty damn fast that she led a very mundane existence.

Chronicled in the pages of her diary, which dated from a year and a half earlier, was her daily existence in her last year of pre-law.

I felt a bit breathless as I read, a touch of arousal mixed with a smidgen of guilt, but I justified it as intel that would help me carry out an operation with the greatest efficiency and chance of success. Well, it was a good rationalization. I was just fucking curious.

I searched page after page for some reference to a sex life, but was sorely disappointed. The closest I came to finding evidence that she was an actual woman was a disturbing account of her dealings with a fellow pre-law student, Steve, whom she called simply "The Creep."

Seems the guy wouldn't take no for an answer, and pursued her despite her repeated rejections.

"The Creep's been pestering me again to go out with him. He's such a slimebucket," she wrote on one page. *"He walks around with this air of superiority, as if he's God's gift to women. I can barely stand to even look at him. He's so slick, he's so suave. Flattering, complimenting. He's a snake. The other female students giggle when he pays them attention because he's so good looking, and even Nan and Dana eat it up. Dana said she thought he probably had a big dick by the way his pants fit.*

"I told her he was a big dickhead."

That made me laugh out loud.

"God—are they potential law students or high school cheerleaders? Don't they recognize him for what he is? He's always breathing down my neck like a vampire waiting to bite. He's an empty bag of wind. Full of himself. I wouldn't go out with him on a date if he was the last man on Earth."

I turned the pages to see if the saga of Steve the Narcissist Creep Dickhead continued. For pages, she wrote about her application to Harvard law, her advisor, problems with the process of getting accepted. She even had a list of to-dos for the next week and month.

Finally, another entry about The Creep.

"The Creep's been at it again. I finally got so fed up, I told him I was a lesbian. He thought I was lying and asked me who my girlfriend was. I told him her name was Amy and that she had green eyes and that we slept together every night and that I was more than satisfied with my private life. Of all the nerve, he suggested that he liked to watch women together and he wouldn't mind if we didn't. But he's stopped pestering me, even though now, when he sees me coming, he sticks his tongue out and makes a rude gesture with it. Creep. I was afraid I was going to have a stalker situation going on. Jesus, even if I was desperate for it, I'd rather use a dildo over him any day."

Celia used a dildo?

I almost laughed at her little lie about her best friend, but then she had to mention a dildo and my mirth evaporated.

Did this mean she had a dildo or had used one or would think of using one? The idea of her playing with herself, inserting a dildo, making herself come with it . . . the heat of lust spread through me until I thought my fucking head might explode. Images filled my mind, causing an immediate ache in my groin, my semi-erect dick now thickening as I contemplated all the possibilities.

Oh, God, that was it.

I closed the diary and leaned back on my bed, my erection straining against my pants. I glanced at my watch. It was now just after five o'clock. I took out my cell phone and texted her number.

HUNTER: I want you at the apartment at 10 sharp. I have something for you.

Then, I went downstairs to the gym and tried to keep my mind busy so I wouldn't think too much about Celia.

I LEFT the gym at nine and flopped in front of the flat screen, eager for Celia to arrive. At quarter to ten, I checked my watch once more and then my cell, wondering why James hadn't texted me to let me know he was on his way.

Finally, my cell dinged, indicating an incoming message.

JAMES: Sorry, we were in an accident downtown on our way over. The car was totaled, but we're okay. Chris was following us and offered to take her to your place. She should be there in about ten.

Chris? Who the fuck was Chris?

HUNTER: I don't know any Chris.

There was a pregnant pause.

JAMES: He said you told him to follow me, to make sure she got there okay. He showed me his ID and it looked legit.

I didn't respond, sitting back, alarmed now that someone had picked up Celia and I had no idea who he was.

I called John and asked him if he knew anyone named Chris.

"Chris?" he said and I could hear the confusion in his voice. "I don't know anyone named Chris. Certainly not anyone on our staff."

"I thought as much." I hung up and closed my eyes as I considered what to do.

Then, my cell dinged. It was a text from, of all people, Victor Romanov.

VICTOR: My driver Christian ran into your little sister friend down-town after her car was in an accident. She's here with us right now, having a cup of tea. Maybe you want to drop by and have a drink with us.

Victor had her. He'd figured out that she mattered to me. He was showing me how easy it would be to pick her up and take her anywhere he wanted.

HUNTER: Thanks for that. I'll be right down to pick her up. I appreciate your help.

Then I left the apartment and made my way through the streets of Boston to Victor Romanov's restaurant.

Fucking hell... Victor Romanov had already outflanked me and the war had only just begun.

CHAPTER 19

CELIA

I PUT on my coat and scarf and rushed down the stairs to the street where Hunter's driver waited. I'd received his text less than ten minutes earlier and had been wondering whether he'd call me that night or ignore me.

The streets around my dorm were empty, the streetlights casting shadows along the roads. I got into the SUV and said hello to James. He nodded his head and touched the brim of his cap, but said nothing else as we drove off.

The late October air was crisp and I pulled my scarf more closely around my face to keep the chill off my neck. We drove through mostly deserted streets and I imagined James was taking back streets to avoid the heavier traffic on the main roads.

Out of nowhere, a car sped through a red light and hit us, knocking the car sideways and forcing it into the middle of the inter-section. Seconds later, another car skidded to a stop. The car hit us at a funny angle and I hit my head on the side window, pain searing through my head.

In a few seconds, both James and I came to our senses. The impact had knocked his hat off but he seemed unscathed, although the front of the car had received considerable damage. Steam hissed from under the hood, and the right turn signal clicked in a steady rhythm.

"You okay?" James asked, craning his head to see me.

"I think so," I said but felt my forehead. "I think I hit my head."

He nodded and worked away at his seatbelt. "Let's get out of the vehicle."

I unfastened my own belt and struggled to open the door. James got out and pulled on it. A tall man got out of the car beside us, helping James open the door.

"Are you okay?" the man asked when I got out. "You have a scrape on your forehead."

I reached up and felt. There was no cut, but it was sore. "It's a scratch."

"You should come with me," he said. "I'll take you to Mr. Saint's apartment."

James frowned at the man. "Who are you?"

"Chris," the man said. "Mr. Saint asked me to follow. I'm a tail." He shrugged guiltily. "He wanted extra protection for her."

"Do you have ID?"

He pulled out an ID from his jacket pocket. "Saints Gym" was printed on the front with the gym's logo.

"Okay, but maybe she should go to the hospital and be checked out."

"Sure," Chris said. "I can take her to Mass General once I talk to Mr. Saint."

"Okay," James said and turned to me. "Maybe you should go with him. I have to wait for the police."

I didn't know what to think. In truth, I didn't want to wait around for the police and ambulance to arrive. I felt fine other than the bump on my head.

"Whatever you think," I said.

I followed Chris to his vehicle, which looked identical to the vehicle James was driving. I got in the passenger side and Chris got in the driver's seat and we drove off.

"Are we going to Hunter's—I mean, Mr. Saint's apartment first?" I asked, watching the streets fly by.

"I'll take you," he said and that was it. Nothing more.

We finally arrived at a building in downtown Boston, not the apartment where Hunter lived. I thought maybe Hunter wasn't yet at the apartment. I checked my watch, but it said it was already ten.

"Why are we here?" I asked. "Aren't we going to the apartment?"

"We're going here," he said and opened my door. "I'll take you."

I followed him, wondering at the sudden change in venue.

"Hunter's here?"

Chris said nothing, just opened the door for me. I went through and he led the way from the front entrance past a row of doors which I assumed led to offices. Finally, we arrived at a room at the back. He opened the door and waved me inside.

I entered to find an elegant office with dark wood paneling and a huge desk in front of the large picture window. Behind it sat a man with short dark hair combed back, a well-trimmed goatee, and an impeccable suit. He had a laptop open in front of him and glanced up when I walked inside. Behind him, the lights of the harbor sparkled against a black sky.

"Ms. Parker, please to come in," the man said, his accent thick, Slavic-sounding. Russian?

Oh, God...

I immediately thought of Stepan and entered the room with hesitation. Chris came in behind me and closed the door. He stood there, his hands folded, and glanced up at the ceiling.

"Have a seat," the man said and pointed to the chair across from him.

I sat across from him and glanced around. "Where's Hunter?"

The man shrugged. "I expect he'll be here in a few moments. Excuse me. I didn't introduce myself. I'm Ivan. A business associate of Stepan, whom I understand you already know."

That sent a shock through me. The man who called himself Chris was not a tail approved by Hunter. He was a tail for the Russians.

I swallowed hard, my heart rate increasing. Ivan leaned across the desk and held out his hand. I took it with reluctance and we shook.

"I don't know him," I said, my voice wavering with fear, "but my brother had some business with him, I understand. I'm Celia."

"Yes, I know," Ivan said and sat back. "We had financial dealings with your brother—Graham is his name."

"Yes, that's right." I felt heat rise in my cheeks. "You work with Stepan? You invest with my brother's company?"

"He invested with us," Ivan said. "We just completed a business contract with Mr. Saint's help."

I nodded. I knew what he was referring to. "Why am I here?"

"My driver saw that your car was in an accident and wanted to help. He saw you and called me, and I suggested that he pick you up, bring you here. I've contacted Mr. Saint. He'll be by to collect you."

"Thank you," I said and smiled, but smiling was the very last thing I felt like doing. There wasn't enough time between the accident and his offer of help for Chris to have called Ivan and for Ivan to have called Hunter. That could only mean he'd been following us. Or perhaps, they had caused the crash, hoping to pick me up in the process. Knowing what I did about the Russian mafia, I wouldn't put it past them. "You could have taken me directly to Mr. Saint's apartment," I said, wanting to argue with him despite my predicament.

"I could have, but this way, I get to meet the reason why Mr. Saint —Hunter—would pay off your brother's debt."

"He paid it off because he and Graham were friends all their lives. Not because of me. I'm nothing to him."

Ivan smiled like he found what I said amusing. "When I see you, I think otherwise. But come," he said and stood, walking around the desk to where I sat. "You need a drink after that accident. Luckily, my club is next door."

He went to the door. Chris opened it and I followed him down another hallway, out the back of the building, into the dark alley with only a single light shining over the loading dock, and into yet another door. I felt nervous, but what could I do? Run for it? If Hunter was really on his way to pick me up, I wanted to be there when he came for me.

We entered a long hallway and then a large kitchen area, with sinks and counters where several young men stood chopping vegetables. There was a dishwasher and a young man in white pushing dishes through, the room filled with steam. We went through the kitchen area where the cooks were busy frying and sautéing and steaming food of various kinds. It smelled wonderful and my stomach growled a bit in response.

Ivan stopped and we watched while the prep guys chopped and the chefs cooked.

"Good Russian food," Ivan said. He picked up a knife and examined it, running his finger briefly along the end. He grimaced and looked at his finger.

"Sharp knives," he said and smiled at me.

Was he threatening me?

Was he trying to scare me?

If so, it was working. He was a Russian—and a friend of Stepan. Maybe a brother or cousin. Or even just another hood in Stepan's little sphere of influence.

Whoever he was, he was sending me a clear message.

He put the knife down and led me into a large dining room with opulent décor and a long elegant bar appointed in brass and crystal. In the back was a room that could see the rest of the dining room but was partially hidden for added privacy. The table was huge, with probably twenty or more chairs, and was set with silverware and glasses, bowls of flowers every couple of place settings. Overhead was a huge crystal chandelier with twinkling lights that resembled flames.

"Have a seat. We wait for your boyfriend to come."

"He's not my boyfriend."

"My little birds tell me otherwise."

"We've known each other half our lives," I protested, shrugging it off. "He was worried about me. That's all. I'm not his girlfriend."

"We shall see," Ivan said, nodding his head slowly, his eyes narrow.

We sat and Ivan took out his phone after it chimed. He spoke into it in Russian, his voice soft. He didn't raise his voice the entire time, but I could tell he was giving orders. His brow was furrowed at some of the answers he received. Finally, he ended the call and slipped the cell back into his pocket.

"So," he said and folded his hands on the table. "Tell me about Celia Parker. I understand you are first-year law student at Harvard. Very impressive."

Before I could answer, Ivan's cell chimed again. He took it out and examined a text.

"Ah," he said and slipped his phone back in his jacket. "As I thought. Hunter is here already. He didn't waste any time getting down to collect his possession."

"I'm not his possession—"

Ivan held up his hand. "His speed in getting here tells me that you are a very prized possession." He smiled like he'd won a bet. "If you meant nothing to him, he would simply let me take you home. Instead, he comes right away, dropping everything." He shook his head slowly, side to side, like he was surprised. "Hunter must be in love."

"He's not in love. We're just old friends. Actually, more like old enemies. If you knew anything about my family, you'd know that."

"Yes, your family," Ivan said and leaned forward, his eyes bright. "Your stepfather, Spencer Grant, has quite the history with Hunter's family. He was the one who helped get a RICO warrant against Hunter's uncle. Poor Sean Saint. Sick in the brain. Lost control."

Then, Ivan mimed getting shot in the head with a gun, his finger pointing at his temple.

"Shame. How mad must Hunter be at your family? And yet, he comes to get you as soon as he finds out you're with me? I think maybe, just maybe, he likes you in spite of everything. No?"

I turned my head away from his too-piercing gaze, those ice blue eyes cold and amused at my predicament.

"You're wrong. Hunter hates me."

"I don't think so."

At that moment, there was a commotion from the back of the restaurant and the door burst open. There stood Hunter, dressed in a black leather jacket and jeans, a black turtleneck sweater underneath. He had a gun in his hand. Two other men followed him. I recognized them from the restaurant the other night—his bodyguards. I'd never seen him so angry.

CHAPTER 20

Hunter

Jesus fucking Christ.

"Where the fuck was backup?"

"You didn't assign backup," Celia's bodyguard James replied.

I kept my voice calm, but I could feel my muscles tighten. "There's no way this was an accident. Whoever he is, he must have been trailing her. He may have even caused the accident just to get hold of her." I rubbed my forehead. "They probably took her into their territory."

"He said he'd take her to you."

"Yeah, but I have no one on staff with that name."

I threw my burner cell phone across the room. It hit the brick wall and shattered with a satisfying crack, the battery and pieces of the plastic body flying across the polished hardwood.

I grabbed my personal cell phone from my office and took the elevator to the underground parking. I hopped into one of the SUVs and squealed out the exit, driving to Stepan's neighbourhood.

I drove along the streets of one of Boston's older neighbourhoods where Stepan's brother's restaurant was located. I pulled over and sat for a moment, rubbing my head, trying to think ahead, plan my attack.

I dialled George. "Stepan's older brother's got her."

"Oh, no," George said, his voice low. "That was quick. What do you want me to do? Is there someone I can call?"

"No, let me call. I want action."

I entered the number of a contact I had in Stepan's family as I drove back to the warehouse, my blood cold in my veins, the fury at bay for now, but it was just under my skin, ready to burst out.

After a few moments of negotiation with him and promises of an ample reward, I said goodbye and called George back.

"They have her at the family restaurant on the waterfront. I need a full assault team organized in fifteen minutes. At least five men, with everything we'll need to take the location. I'm going there now and will set up a couple of blocks away. Meet me there."

I sped through the back streets, not needing to attract the attention of Boston's finest on my way. As I drove, fury bubbled up inside me, and I slammed my hand against the steering wheel.

"Goddammit."

I drove toward the restaurant Stepan's family owned. When I arrived and parked, I noticed the sentries on each street corner, standing in dark doorways.

George exited a vehicle and walked up to my SUV, hopping in the passenger side.

"Has the team arrived?"

"Not yet. Just relax, Hunter. He has probably just brought her in to scare you."

"I'm scared." I'd been such a fool to let Celia get under my skin. "By all rights, I should let him keep her, George."

"It would be best," George said and nodded. "What is so special about her? There are other prettier birds, far easier to tame, I think. This one will just give you trouble."

I frowned. "That's what you think? That's your advice?"

"Is not advice. Does not matter what I think—is what is best for you. I just offer one side for you to consider. Is maybe harder choice, but cleaner all around. Will show them how nothing matters to you—certainly not little bird."

I ground my fist into my temple. "I have to get her back. Everything you said is true, but it doesn't matter."

He squeezed my arm. "She will be fine."

I shook my head, my fists clenched. "She could already be dead."

"No, no," George said, shaking his head. "Ivan knows that would mean all-out war. You are Victor's friend. You had his consent to beat up Stepan. She is probably fine."

"She can't stay in her apartment any longer. She's coming to live at the safe house."

"To stay with you?"

"She'll have to stay with me so I can protect her. You'll be providing security."

George nodded.

"If anything happens to her…" I exhaled, trying to get control over myself. "I knew it was a mistake to help her. I knew she was trouble the minute I laid eyes on her again."

George shrugged. "Then let him do what he wants with her if you feel she is too much trouble. He takes care of problem for you."

I said nothing. There was no way I would abandon Celia.

"You can still call off operation," George said softly.

I shook my head even more firmly. I couldn't respond, so I just picked up my weapon and waited for the signal that my crew had arrived.

Once they had, all my thoughts turned to executing the operation. I exited the vehicle, grabbed my weapon, and in full battle rattle, I signalled to my men to take up pre-determined positions around the four-block-wide perimeter surrounding the warehouse before moving in on my signal. One had already scoped out the area, checking for sentries, and had let us know where the men were located.

We moved in, knocking out the guard inside the warehouse so I could slip inside and check out what was happening before I ordered the team in.

The warehouse was filled floor to ceiling with row upon row of furniture—couches, chairs, tables, and beds. I entered the kitchen and two of my men followed, holding their guns up, urging the cooks and prep people to be quiet.

I went through the building to the restaurant and saw Celia sitting with Ivan. Her face was pale and she looked so fragile. It made my once-ice-cold blood almost boil. Ivan had gone too fucking far. Undaunted by my presence, Ivan pulled out a switchblade and proceeded to clean his nails with it. That was a clear signal that he would harm Celia if he and I didn't come to some agreement.

By all rights, I should have let Ivan do whatever he wanted with Celia. By rescuing her, I was reinforcing how important she was to me. I had to go over the top, send a message that could not be mistaken.

Mess with me and you will suffer.

My response had to be all out of proportion. I had to turn it into a matter of pure dominance.

You harm my possessions, you will pay.

Big time.

Standing on the top of the heap invited every jerk with ambition to try to climb up and knock you off. I understood I had to show Stepan and Victor that I would not allow even a single step up on the edges of the heap.

WHEN I STEPPED into the dining room, Ivan stood up and held out his palms. Celia stood as well, her face pale, but her eyes told me she was relieved to see me.

"Slow," Ivan said and held out his hand. "There is no need for weapons. I'm merely returning your property."

I moved closer, my gun now held down at my side. I went to Celia and ran my thumb over her cheek where she must have hit her head in the crash. A bruise was starting, the tissue red and abraded.

"Are you okay? Do you need to go to the ER?"

She shook her head and stepped back, glancing at Ivan, who was smiling.

Ivan nodded. "You see what I mean, pretty girl?"

"You're wrong."

"You're wrong, what?" I asked, but Celia didn't reply. She kept staring at me, her gaze intense. Finally, I turned to Ivan, and pointed the gun at his head.

"Stop!" Celia said and tried to grab my arm. "He didn't hurt me."

I said and did nothing, but kept my gun pointed at Ivan.

"If you or any of your Russian thugs are ever within one hundred feet of her, I'll kill you."

I lowered my gun and grabbed her arm. On his part, Ivan smiled like he found my threat amusing.

"Just trying to do a good deed," Ivan said, chuckling. "What thanks do I get? A gun pointed at my head…"

"You're lucky that's all I did," I replied and pulled Celia past my two men, who remained behind, their weapons still drawn. We went back through the restaurant, past white-faced cooks who knew enough to stand back from their counters and grills, their activities halted. My other two other men stood guard, watching them. Finally, we left through the back exit into my SUV, which was idling, the rear passenger door open. A driver stood beside it, his hand on the door at the ready.

"Get in," I said softly. I helped her in and then started to fasten her seat belt.

She pushed my hand away. "I can do it."

I lifted my head and met her eyes. I said nothing, watching while she fastened the belt and sat back.

I got in beside her and the driver took off, tires squealing as we left the back alley and merged onto one of Boston's busy downtown streets.

"Where to?" the driver asked.

I said nothing for a moment, my finger tapping on my cell.

"I have to get back to my dorm," Celia said. "I have to study—"

"The safe house," I replied.

"What?" Celia said in protest.

I held up my hand. "Don't say a word."

"Hunter!" Celia was clearly upset. "Our agreement doesn't extend to my ordinary life. I need to go home."

I leaned closer and put my hand behind her head, turning her face so she had to meet my gaze.

"This isn't ordinary life anymore, Celia. *That* was a message sent from Stepan's brother to me," I said, trying hard to keep my voice calm. "You're in danger in case you didn't get the message. Taking you was a threat that he could harm you at any time if he wanted. Do you understand?"

She blinked several times, but didn't respond, nodding her head.

I let go and leaned back for a moment, calming myself. Then, I texted the guard at the safe house, and we drove the rest of the way in silence.

While we drove, I considered my circumstances. I wasn't going to let some Russian Goodfella mobster-wannabe take away a toy I was planning on playing with—and playing with real fucking soon.

CHAPTER 21

CELIA

WE ARRIVED at a warehouse on the other side of the waterfront, the vehicles screeching to a halt in the back alley. I followed Hunter out of the vehicle and into the rear door to the building, which appeared to be an empty furniture store.

We took a freight elevator to the top floor and emerged into a wide sparsely decorated space. A large bed stood in one corner – four-poster with a thick gold and burgundy damask coverlet and several matching throw pillows. In another corner was a small office of sorts with a few desks and some computer monitors separated off from the rest of the room by some office space dividers. An older man with a grey brush cut sat in front of one of the screens. He turned to us when we approached.

"Leave us," Hunter said to the man, who merely nodded without a word. He grabbed a messenger bag off the desk and left out the door we entered.

When we were alone, Hunter grabbed my hand and pulled me

over to the bed, pushing me back onto it, his gaze fixed on me. He leaned over me, forcing me back onto the bed beneath him.

"Don't say a word," he said, his face inches from mine, his voice low and husky. He pulled off my jacket and then tore at my blouse, removing it roughly, then unfastened my bra. "Take off your clothes," he ordered and I complied, my hands shaking.

When I was completely naked, he lay on top of me, grabbing my hands and holding them over my head.

"I'm going to fuck you. *Now.*"

He unbuckled his pants, unzipped and, without undressing at all, pulled out his erection, which was thick and hard. He leaned back over me, pressing against me so that I could feel his length between the lips of my sex. He held my hands in his once more, his mouth almost touching mine, but not quite, and he stared into my eyes. I was barely able to breathe, my pulse rapid, a mix of fear and desire battling inside me.

Then he kissed me, his kiss almost desperate, his mouth devouring mine like he couldn't get enough. The kiss went on and on, and despite everything, I responded, my body unable to resist his weight on top of me, his cock pressing against my clit. When he broke the kiss, he entered me fully, right to the hilt, exhaling as he did, his eyes closing.

No condom.

"Nice and wet. Nice and tight," he whispered. He reached down, spreading the lips of my sex, feeling the hard nub of my clit with his fingers. I tried not to respond, but couldn't help but gasp at the feel of his fingers on my flesh. "Nice and hard. Almost ready to burst."

He grabbed one foot in each hand and lifted my legs so that my heels rested on his shoulders, and started to thrust inside me, his hands pulling my hips toward him with each thrust. I watched him from beneath my lashes as his gaze moved over my body, from my face to my breasts and down to watch himself fucking me.

Then he leaned down further, cupping my breasts, his finger and thumb squeezing each nipple briefly. He supported his weight on his hands so that his face was above mine, my legs now spread wide. I closed my eyes.

"Don't close your eyes," he said. "Look at me."

I did, staring into his face, his expression one of lust and determination. Because of his position, with each deep thrust his pubic bone rubbed against me and the sensations built inside me even though I'd thought I wouldn't get enough direct stimulation. I bore down with each of his thrusts, squeezing my muscles, trying to increase the pressure when his body met mine. I gritted my teeth with the effort to increase the sensations.

Finally, when his pace quickened, it was enough and I felt an incredible wave of pleasure start deep inside of me, causing my muscles to tense then contract, my body arching as my orgasm began. I couldn't hold back a groan of pleasure, my eyes closing despite my best efforts, my body spasming around him as he thrust even more rapidly inside of me.

When his thrusts became erratic, his climax began, his lips by my ear, grunting with each thrust as he ejaculated.

When he was finished, he lay on top of me for a moment, his face beside mine, his mouth by my ear, his breathing rapid.

"You're staying here now," Hunter said, his voice low. "James will drive you to class and wait for you in the parking lot. You'll come here right after your classes are over for the day. If I'm not here, George will be. He'll protect you."

I nodded, unable to argue. I felt as scared of Ivan, Victor and his thugs as Hunter seemed to want me to be.

"I want you ready for me whenever I need you. Any time of the day, any day of the week."

I didn't nod or reply. What could I say? From the way my body responded to him with barely any preliminaries, I'd have no problem being ready for him.

He rose and tucked himself in, zipped up, and fastened his belt.

Then he turned and left the apartment.

I rolled onto my side, my body vibrating from the experience. I didn't know what to think of the night and what had happened to me, or what Hunter had done and how he'd responded.

I only knew one thing: I was his now.

He *owned* me in more ways than one.

END OF PART TWO

BAD BOY SOLDIER

THE BAD BOY SERIES: BOOK THREE

COPYRIGHT 2017 S. E. LUND

PREFACE

"He who fights with monsters should be careful lest he thereby become a monster."

Friedrich Nietzsche

CHAPTER 22

ONE YEAR earlier

Hunter

LOSING Sean was harder than anything I'd been through. He was my older brother and the one I always looked up to. One day he was in my life and I took him for granted. The next, he was dead and I realized I'd never see him again.

At first, the pain felt like it would never end.

Sean's dead... He's dead...

I felt as though a dark shroud covered me and was going to smother me with despair.

But the sun rose the next day like it had the day before. Life went on despite everything. My pain didn't matter to the universe.

A month passed. Then two. We began to find our way back to some kind of new normal without Sean around, cleaning the gym in his slow deliberate way and making us smile with his wit. My Uncle

Donny was still in custody awaiting trial on several racketeering charges.

We all began to emerge from that darkness. My father began to spend more time with the new fighters who came to train at the gym. Donny's boys—my cousins—talked less and less about their father's case and more about the usual material—which fights they bet on, which women they were fucking, and other mundane topics.

As for me, I felt almost normal being back in Boston. I spent weekends at the cottage, lying in the sun and drinking myself to sleep at night.

Donny wasn't there to take the helm, so I ran the business, gradually assuming management of Donny's properties and the work my father couldn't handle. Since I was no longer in the service and had fallen out of my usual routine of rigorous training to keep in top shape for special operations forces, I lost the hard cut of my muscles and top fitness levels from when I was in the service. My hair grew out of the trademark Marine whitewalls I'd worn for the past four years.

ONE AFTERNOON, when Conor had some time off from his rigorous fight schedule, he was back in Boston showing a new gym member the ropes while Dad and I looked on. I watched as Conor landed a soft punch on the flabby young man's abdomen. Not hard. Just enough to make him pay attention.

"Keep your guard up," Conor said, pushing the young man's gloved hands up higher. "Like this." Then Conor demonstrated how to guard his face and the flabby young man followed suit.

My father turned to me. "Why are you slumming around? I thought you were in meetings all day."

I shrugged. "Meeting's cancelled for the afternoon so I thought I'd come down and visit my favorite old man." I put my arm around his shoulder and squeezed affectionately. Since Sean's death, I found myself spending more time with my dad, showing him more affection that was perhaps my usual. Losing Sean made me realize how quickly everything could go wrong. I didn't want to waste any more time not showing him or Conor how I felt.

My father grimaced at that, no doubt thinking about my stepfather down in Florida, who married my mother after they divorced.

"Your *only* old man. He's no father," he said, and I knew exactly what he meant. He had an intense dislike of my stepfather and liked to show it as often as possible.

"He's all right, Dad," I said, thinking of the man my mother had chosen to marry after she and my father divorced a dozen years earlier. "He's a lightweight, unlike you. Mom knows she could never find another you. He's the best substitute."

"Yeah, right. Tell me about it."

My father found someone new almost right away—in fact, I suspect his girlfriend and now second wife, Cathy, had been waiting in the wings. None of us boys had known about her, but a few months after the divorce was final, he brought her home for dinner one night and she never left. That was that.

"Since you're free and easy, how about taking the bank deposit down for Cath?" he suggested and turned to me. "She's got a bitch of a cold and would rather go up to bed. I could take it, but I've got a meeting about the fight on Saturday."

"Sure," I said, having made the deposit dozens of times over the years, before I stopped working for my dad and joined the Marines.

"Are you coming to the fight?" he asked, his expression hopeful. "We'd love to see you."

I shrugged, not sure I would. I'd stopped fighting when my mom and dad divorced and I went to live with her for a few years. Her new husband was a lawyer who had tried to get me to focus on academics instead of sports for a change. Still, Conor would be fighting, and I knew it would please my dad if I was there.

"Sure," I said and smiled at him when I saw how pleased he was. "I'll come for Conor's fight."

"Bring a date." He punched my arm playfully. "It's about time you started to get serious about someone."

"I'm doing fine," I said, waving him off.

"Seriously, Hunter. Don't get too used to being a bachelor. You should find someone before you get too old and ugly."

"Hey, old man, watch yourself." I held up my fists in mock anger. "I can still take you."

We sparred playfully for a moment, and then I gave him a quick hug. "I'm currently single, so I'll be coming alone, although I might bring Juice along."

'Juice' was Justin Thomas, a friend from high school who used to fight at my dad's gym and who now worked for us as a driver. Juice didn't break arms or legs—maybe a nose or two in a bar fight, but nothing pro.

"I'll go talk to Cath and take the deposit."

"Great," he said and turned back to watch Conor and the new member. "See you and Juice Saturday."

I went to the back of the gym and popped my head in the office, where my stepmother sat at a desk, tallying up the previous day's receipts. When she saw me, she smiled and took off her reading glasses.

"Hunter," she said and stood, opening her arms. "I thought you were in meetings with your finance friends all afternoon. Your father will be so pleased. I know he wanted to talk to you about the fight on Saturday..."

"I already spoke to him," I said and gave her a warm hug.

"You should bring a girl," she said and narrowed her eyes. "Are you going steady with anyone?"

"Don't you start on me, too," I said, my hands on my hips. "Besides, we don't 'go steady' anymore. We 'see' each other." I leaned in to kiss her cheek.

"Don't kiss me," she said and held a hand up over her mouth. "I have a nasty cold."

"I won't," I said and pulled back. When she sat back down, I took the chair beside her desk. "You know I'm swamped with the business, but I'm coming on Saturday."

"Oh, good. Conor will be happy to have you there. Moral support and all."

I nodded. "Dad asked me to do the deposit for you."

"I'm almost done," she said and grabbed a handful of cash and a deposit slip, as well as several rolls of change. She stuffed them into the battered leather zip bag that was used for the deposit.

"I better go," I said and picked up the deposit bag. "See you on Saturday."

"Are you going to mass on Sunday?" she called out and frowned at me over her glasses.

"Always," I said, but it was a bald-faced lie. I stopped going to mass years earlier.

"Good boy," she said and blew me a kiss. Then she turned back to the computer and I left, deposit bag in hand.

I drove the few blocks to the bank and parked across the street, then picked up the bank deposit bag. Although it was rush hour, the bank was on a quiet side street a few blocks off Boylston. Barely any cars drove by as I stood on the street corner, waiting for the light to change. Then a white van drove up and screeched to a halt outside the bank. A man jumped out, assault weapon in hand. When I saw him he entered the bank, he pulled a balaclava over his head. Another man got out and stood sentry at the door, his face uncovered. He was dressed in a generic security guard uniform in blue and grey, and held a hand on the weapon on his utility belt, at the ready in case anyone confronted him. He'd try to look as inconspicuous as possible, but would discourage any potential bank customer from entry. I knew the drill. A driver remained in the vehicle, the van's engine idling, at the ready for the getaway.

I thought I'd put my old MMA training and the skills I'd developed in special operations behind me, but at that moment, I realized they'd come in handy despite the fact I was no longer a Marine. Knowing what was about to go down, I tossed the deposit back into the car on the floor, then took out my phone and dialed 911.

"What's your emergency?"

"You got a 10-60 in progress," I said, using the code for a bank robbery. "First National off Boylston. One armed man just entered the building. One armed sentry dressed in a generic security guard outfit is outside. A driver in a white van is parked in front of the bank in the getaway vehicle."

"Are you a cop?" the operator asked, sounding surprised that I seemed so calm.

"No, former Marine," I replied. I was used to this kind of situation from two tours of duty in Afghanistan and Iraq.

"Please do not intervene," the operator said, her voice firm. "Civilians should remain away from the scene and let police take over. Units are being dispatched."

"Ten-four," I said and hung up before she could take my name and details. I ignored her order to stand down, determined to use my skills for something good. I was licensed to carry a concealed weapon, and had both tactical training and special operations training. I was going to see what I could do to stop this thing, or at least disable their ability to escape the scene. I crossed the street against the light, dodging the few cars that drove down the street. I casually walked up beside the van and when the wide-eyed driver saw me, he opened his mouth and his body stiffened, but I hit him once and then twice before he could call out, knocking him out cold. Then, I reached in over top of him and turned off the vehicle, taking the keys and the weapon on the seat beside him with me.

I ducked down, peering over the hood to see if the sentry saw what happened. He was busy glancing the other direction, so it was my time to act. I checked inside to see if there were any others, and saw that the van was empty. Then, I walked to the bank's entrance, a smile on my face so the sentry thought I was just a customer. When he finally saw me coming, he stood at attention like he was a real guard.

"Bank's closed," he said, jerking his thumb to the door, thinking I was a civilian coming in to do my business.

I kept moving until I was right in front of him.

He frowned and straightened to stand even taller, trying to look more authoritative. "I said the bank's closed, asshole."

When I didn't stop, he pulled out his weapon and pointed it at me, trying to intimidate me into standing down, but I didn't comply.

He grimaced. I was definitely not part of the plan. "Stop or I'll have to arrest you."

First I kicked his hand away, which sent his weapon flying. Next, I took him out with a quick punch to the jaw that he didn't expect or see coming. A lifetime of boxing and mixed martial arts helped.

Startled by the sheer speed of my attack, he was unable to defend himself. When he straightened back up, I hit him directly in the throat and he fell to his knees, his hands around his throat. I honestly hoped I hadn't killed him.

While he choked and gasped for air, I retrieved his weapon from where it had fallen from the ground and removed his two-way from his belt so he couldn't alert his partner inside to my presence. Then, I went inside.

I entered the bank without anyone noticing, slipping inside while keeping low, and went to my knees, surveying the scene to get my bearings. As I watched, the thug got the attention of the bank customers by shouting and waving his weapon in the air.

"Get down, get the fuck down!"

In response, several customers and tellers screamed and ducked, falling to the floor like dominoes knocked over by some malevolent force. Seizing my opportunity, I slipped further inside the bank and hid behind a column, keeping the gunman in my sights.

I crept along the line of tables where people filled out their deposit slips, watching for an opportunity to intervene. Maybe it was foolish of me to do so, but these thugs were amateurs. I'd seen worse on the streets of Afghanistan—men who knew what they were doing and why, and would let nothing get in their way.

The robber corralled the customers into one corner of the bank and forced one of the tellers to take his burlap bag and empty the tills, dumping wads of money into the bag. He kept waving his weapon towards the cowering bank customers, and from where I crouched, I could tell he was an amateur. He needed at least one more man to really take control of the bank. As it was, he was trying to do two jobs at once, and was doing neither very well.

While he had his back to me, I crouched behind a desk, watching, waiting to make my move. He grabbed the bag of money and walked backwards, his weapon still pointed at the customers and employees huddling against one wall. When he turned to run, I easily jumped him, knocking him to the floor. We struggled, but I had the upper hand due to the element of surprise. I wrestled his weapon free and threw it skidding across the floor. Taller and heavier than him, I easily grabbed him, pinning his arms behind his back, pointing my gun to his head, the tip pressing against his temple.

"Quit fighting or I'll fucking take off the side of your head, " I hissed into his ear. He stiffened in response, perhaps thinking he could still fight his way out of it. "I've already alerted the police," I said, my voice low but loud enough for them all to hear. "By my count, they'll be driving up in about two minutes, if not sooner."

"Where's Johnson?" the thug said, his voice sounding surprised.

"Your sentry's incapacitated," I replied. My gun was pressed to his head and when he moved, I pressed it a bit harder. "Your driver as well. Now, I'm going to restrain you until the police arrive. You'll be cooling your heels in lockup in no time. Put your hands in front of you."

When he hesitated, I pressed the gun more firmly into the side of his head. "I killed worse scum than you in Iraq," I said menacingly. "I have no qualms killing you in self-defense."

He remained on his stomach, and dutifully stretched his arms out in front of him. Then, I tucked my sidearm back into my holster and removed my belt. I pulled his hands behind his back and fastened them using the belt.

"Who the fuck are you?" he asked as I finished looping the belt around his wrists. "I didn't hear of any undercover cops working this bank."

"I'm not an undercover cop. I'm just some lucky former special ops motherfucker you idiots didn't expect. Let's just say this was my lucky day and your very unlucky one."

I glanced around. "Which one of you is the bank manager?" I asked, checking the people who were cowering on the floor.

A tall slim man wearing a slate grey suit and blue tie stood up from where he crouched.

"I'm the manager," he said hesitantly. "George McCall."

"I need something to tie his feet," I said and pointed to his belt. "Care to make a donation?"

He nodded in understanding. "I think we have duct tape," he said and turned to one of the tellers. She nodded and ran to the back of the bank, returning with a roll in her hand.

"I remembered we had a roll in the supply room." She handed it to me and I smiled at her.

"Thanks," I said and gave the roll to McCall. "Can you?"

He nodded and proceeded to wrap his ankles together. Once we had him restrained, I went outside. The sentry had recovered and was gone. I kicked myself mentally. I should have dragged him inside but at least I had a good look at him. The guy in the van was gone as well, so I went back into the bank, wishing I had been able to restrain them all.

I checked with the other customers to make sure they were all okay.

"The police will be here any second," I said, trying to calm them. When I got back to the bank manager, he extended his hand for a shake.

"What's your name? Are you an off-duty cop?" McCall asked.

"Nope," I said as I took his hand. "Just a citizen with some training."

"We're lucky to have you here," he said, not willing to let go of my hand. "The police will thank you."

I didn't offer my name, and he didn't press, turning to his staff to check them out, go over the procedure for a robbery.

I called 911 once more to let them know the robbery had been stopped.

"The men who did this are in custody?" the operator asked.

"Two got away on foot, and the other is currently in my custody."

We all sat down on the floor, our hands behind our heads, and waited. Less than a minute later, members of a SWAT team entered the building, their weapons drawn, and took control of the premises.

Once they realized everything was under control, the members of the team relaxed visibly. I was sitting with the bank manager and his head teller, waiting for them to question us, but they seemed prepared to merely hold us there until the detectives from Boston PD entered.

Within five minutes, several men in dark suits approached us and while I watched, police began escorting customers into corners to speak with them about what happened.

One black-suited man came to us, his dark hair short, his glasses thick-rimmed. He looked me over suspiciously and then turned to McCall.

"I'm Sergeant Mahoney of the Boston Major Crimes Unit. I'll be the officer in charge. Who are you?" he asked, turning to McCall, who stood beside me.

"I'm the bank manager, George McCall," he replied and extended his hand. "Glad to see you and your crew."

"Which one of you called this in?"

McCall turned to me, his hand on my shoulder. "This young man," he said and squeezed. "He saved the day."

Mahoney eyed me suspiciously. "So you're the hero," he said, eyeing me up and down, trying to place me. "You took them all down?"

I nodded. "I did."

"What's your name? You cop or military?" he said, extending his hand.

"Hunter Saint." We shook hands, his grip firm, his glance discerning. "Former Marine. Special Operations Forces."

When he heard my name, he didn't show any recognition and I wondered whether he was merely a good actor, or really didn't recognize my last name. Saint was not a common name in Boston, and given the recent arrest of my uncle and death of my brother, I was surprised he didn't say more.

He nodded thoughtfully, his eyes narrowed. "So, you thought you'd be a hero and stop a bank robbery in progress?" He shook his head. "You got balls, but not much brains."

The head bank teller turned away to hide her smile.

"Pardon me," Mahoney said, noticing her response. "Let me rephrase that: You got more guts than brains. You could have been killed or worse, got these citizens killed."

I shrugged. "I didn't. They weren't."

He turned to McCall. "We have to question you and your customers, take their statements. You'll have to close the bank so we can do our investigation."

"I know the procedure," the manager said, his voice weary. He turned to me before he left. "I appreciate what you've done and your service, whatever they say. And whoever you are," he said. I didn't miss the emphasis on his last words.

We shook hands and I smiled. "Thanks."

Another detective escorted the two of them to the manager's office. I was left standing with Mahoney.

"As for you, Mr. Saint," he said and turned to me, "you're coming with us to the precinct."

"You can't take my statement and let me go like the rest of the bank customers?"

"You were more than just a customer," he replied. "With your training and experience, you have tactical intel you could share with us on this crew. It might help us figure out who they work for. We think they're responsible for a string of armed robberies in Boston over the past month."

I sighed, resigned to the fact I'd have to spend time at the precinct.

"No good deed goes unpunished," I said sarcastically.

"Tell me about it," the detective replied, his tone matching mine. "I'll be the one working late at night to wrap up the paperwork on this."

"That's why they pay you the big bucks," I quipped.

He laughed and that was the first crack in his façade.

Then he spoke into a cell turning away so I couldn't hear what he said. He listened to the response and then turned back.

"Let's go."

"Okay," I said. "I need to make a call first." I pointed to my cell and he nodded.

"Make it fast."

I stood off to the side of the room and called the gym. Cath answered, her voice nasally from her cold. "Hey, Hunter. What's up?"

"I'm going to be late getting back to the gym," I said, watching as the cops queued up the bank customers in front of a desk so they could interview them.

"Is there something wrong?"

"The bank was robbed while I was here," I said. "They want to take statements. I'm fine but I'll be late getting back. Oh, and the bank's closed so I'll have to use the night deposit."

"As long as you're fine," she said. "I'll tell your father."

"I'm fine. No worse for the wear."

I ended the call and turned back to Mahoney, who was speaking with another detective.

He came over to me, smiling wryly. "So, my partner pointed out that you're the nephew of Donny Saint. I didn't get it when you said your name."

"That's right," I said. "You're not from Boston, I take it."

"Recent transfer from Queens, New York." He nodded. "My condolences about your brother."

I frowned, surprised that a police detective would offer condolences on the death of Sean. I'd expected to be treated with derision once they found out who I was.

"Thanks," I said, trying to be gracious, unsure if he really meant it.

"I just want to say that Boston PD wasn't involved in your uncle's case or what happened. That was all the feds."

"I understand," I said.

Mahoney spoke briefly with another detective and then turned back to me.

"This is Detective Brand," he said and Brand extended his hand for a shake. He had a pasty complexion, thinning hair, and a belly that suggested he liked donuts more than an exercise bike.

We shook and then Mahoney gestured for me to follow them. We left the bank and walked to a black sedan waiting at the curb.

When we got to the sedan, Mahoney held open the door to the back seat.

"If you don't mind," he said and motioned inside.

We drove off through the streets of downtown Boston and I had a few moments to think about the attack and what I'd say.

Before we arrived at the precinct, Mahoney's cell rang and he answered while we were stopped at a red light.

"Yeah, he's here with me."

A pause.

"Are you sure?"

Another pause.

"Okay, we're on our way."

He ended his call and glanced at me in the rear view mirror.

"It's your lucky day," Mahoney said, his voice slightly amused. "Seems your name lit up the system and the big boss called. Chief of Police wants to see you in his office."

I shrugged. "I'm at your disposal." I didn't relishing being interrogated by the chief of Boston PD about my actions in the bank but resigned myself to the fact that my day wouldn't be my own.

CHAPTER 23

Hunter

I SAID NO MORE during the drive to the precinct and Mahoney and Brand seemed uninclined to make small talk.

Within fifteen minutes, we arrived and I was ushered into a small interrogation room with no windows but with a big and very obvious two-way mirror across from where I sat. I smiled and waved, then sat back and waited.

Mahoney said I was there to meet the Chief of Police himself, so why I was put in an interrogation room was a question I hoped would be answered sooner rather than later. I'd seen the Chief on television before during press conferences, so I knew what to expect. Short and pug-faced, Barlow was a bulldog of a man with a presence so strong that conversations hushed when he walked into the room.

Time passed, and I began to be impatient. I checked my watch, which indicated I'd been waiting for twenty minutes.

"Hello?" I said into the mirror. "I have a life to live."

There was no response. Finally, after another fifteen minutes, the door opened and Mahoney stuck his head inside.

"Sorry to make you wait. We had to do some checking first before we could do the interview. You can come with me."

I stood and followed Mahoney down the hall to a big corner office on the first floor. I entered the office, which was all glass and chrome.

Chief Barlow sat behind a big mahogany desk. A man in an FBI blue and yellow jacket leaned against the wall, his hands in his pockets.

"This is Chief Barlow," Mahoney said, pointing to the Chief.

I leaned over the desk when Barlow stood and extended his hand. We shook.

"Glad to meet you," I said, although I didn't mean it. Usually, I'd be on the side of police because of my time in the military and my hatred of organized crime. Now, however, I was still recovering from watching one shoot my brother and wasn't all that predisposed to being friendly or compliant. It was probably foolish of me, but Sean's death was still too close to have overcome it. Not yet.

"The pleasure's all mine," he said and turned to the other man, who now stood up straight. "This is Special Agent Gladwell. He's with the FBI's Transnational Organized Crime program."

I recognized him from an appearance on television talking about links to organized crime in the Balkans or Russia and efforts to stop their crime spree in Massachusetts. Tall and lean with an eagle-eyed look to him, he was in top fighting shape.

To my surprise, he extended his hand for a shake. I shook it, but didn't smile when he said hello.

"Please," Chief Barlow said and motioned to a chair in front of his desk. "Have a seat."

I sat in the chair directly across from his desk. Behind me, the two detectives left the room so that there were only the three of us remaining.

Chief Barlow turned to his credenza and poured some amber liquid I assumed was whiskey into three tumblers. Agent Gladwell turned his down, but I accepted the glass Barlow offered.

"That's Old Number 8, George Dickel Tennessee sipping whiskey," he said and nodded to his glass. "Drink it down. You'll need it after your morning."

We both took a sip and I sighed as the whiskey burned down my throat.

"Sorry to keep you waiting," he said finally. "We wanted to check out the security video feed we recovered from the bank and from a store across the street first to verify your actions relating to the robbery. You can understand."

I shrugged, knowing exactly what he meant. Because of my family's background, they wanted to see whether I was part of the heist or had truly tried to stop it.

"Tell me what happened," he said. "Tell me everything. From the start. When you're done, Special Agent Gladwell here wants to talk to you about the FBI's case against the Romanov family, who we think was involved in the robbery. I want to hear what you have to say first. You should know that we already have the video feed from the cameras and were able to ID you from our database."

I leaned back in my chair and nodded. I recounted the events of the morning, from the time I entered the bank to the end, explaining that I'd decided to use my skills as a former special operator to disrupt the robbery.

They listened without comment.

"You called in the hit and stopped it," Barlow said, smiling at me over his glass when he took a sip. "But we don't want it to get out who you are."

"I understand. Neither do I."

"Stopping bank robberies isn't the usual MO for your family," Gladwell said from where he remained leaning against the wall behind Barlow, his face showing no emotion. "Why did you do it?"

"Because I could," I said. "It's very simple. I have skills. I used them. That's really all there is to it."

"So, I take it you know we're suspicious about your role in all this, given your uncle's history?" he asked. "We know he has ties with the Romanov family."

"His ties are tenuous at best."

"We know your family's history and your past. Your father and uncle both had dealings with the Romanovs before, " he said.

"Not me."

"Your uncle's part owner of your father's gym, and the two of them are business partners, so the gym's not clean. The money's dirty —or should I say, gets cleaned through the gym, the fights, and the clubs."

"My uncle was just a financial backer of fights," I said, although I knew he did more than that. But it was small potatoes compared to the Romanov crime family. "He runs a few dance clubs. We have nothing to do with the Romanov business, so you're wrong."

"I know your father's trying hard to seem clean," Gladwell said and made a face. "What are your personal connections to the Romanov family? What you did today could be seen as your family trying to show them who has control over that sector of Boston."

I laughed at that. "My father's a former boxer, a gym owner, and a promoter. He has nothing to do with the mafia and certainly isn't interested in the bank robbery business, so you're on the wrong track. We're not criminals."

Gladwell nodded. "Your uncle being in federal custody puts lie to that claim."

"Innocent until proven guilty."

He shrugged. "The suspects we have in custody are low-level grunts in the Romanov empire. You should know that if the Romanov family discovers it was you at the bank, you've probably gotten your family in whole lot of trouble with them. Consider this a warning. There may be repercussions. You should have just left things the way they were."

"Warning received and acknowledged."

"You should have let us handle things," the Chief said. "As it was, our units arrived just moments after you entered the bank and set up, waiting for the SWAT team to arrive. I admire your bravery but we could have handled it."

"I handled it."

"You shouldn't have," Gladwell said. "The Romanovs don't play around. They skin their enemies alive and smother them with their own skin."

"The Romanovs are a bunch of thugs."

Gladwell seemed surprised at my comment, his only change in expression since our interview began.

"They are, but don't be too smug. What you did was heroic but stupid. If they figure out it was you, they'll now be on you and your family."

"Too late at this point," I said and downed the rest of the whiskey. "I did what I was trained to do—respond. They could have killed people."

Barlow smiled but said nothing.

"When they come to your father's gym and mess him up in revenge for the botched robbery, you'll be singing a different tune."

I shrugged but, of course, I knew there might be blowback. "I've got ample security in place."

"Look," Gladwell said, standing up straight. "The reason I'm here is because we want to use you. You're a soldier by training. You have special operations experience. We want you to work for us. We've been watching you for a while, and we want you to keep us informed of what you hear and what, if anything, happens in your family business that is at all connected to the Romanovs."

"You want me to help you take down the Romanov family?"

"Yes," Gladwell said. "You're the perfect man in the perfect position. We understand that you're head of your family now, even if your father's still alive. You could insinuate yourself with the Romanovs and then once you get enough evidence, you can help bring them down. I imagine you'd be happy to do that, considering that your brother's dead because of them."

"He's dead because of one of your men," I replied, my body tensing.

"He's dead because he overreacted. The new DA's been dying to take down your uncle for a decade or more. He finally got some good intel and that's what led to your uncle being served with a RICO warrant. One of the Romanov boys provided a bit of evidence to help take Donny down."

I frowned. "What?"

"Yes," Gladwell said. "The DA has a confidential informant in the Romanov family who helped us take your uncle down. I figure if you help us take the Romanovs down, it's payback. That seems to be the only way to get mafia types to cooperate. Petty turf wars and jealousy lead to mutually assured destruction. Usually that prevents people from turning on each other, but there is no honor among thieves, despite the old saying to the contrary."

I sighed, realizing that he was right. I had potentially endangered my family, which was the very last thing I intended. I considered Gladwell's offer seriously. I had nothing against the FBI—usually. They were that thin line between order and chaos in a free society.

I had something against one FBI agent in particular—the one who killed my brother. Still, I wanted to protect my father and brothers from any negative consequences of my actions, so I really had no choice.

"What do you want me to do?"

"Romanov's an arrogant son of a bitch. He thinks he's smarter than everyone."

"That he does."

"He thinks he can do whatever he likes in this city and I suspect he'll welcome you into the fold if you approach him personally."

"I don't know if I want to get in too close to him."

"You have background in security. You could provide security for their operations in return for them laying off your family's business."

I considered.

"Your uncle Donny had a love-hate relationship with the Romanovs. They knew it but they used him anyway. You could go to them and offer your services, say you want to go after the DA for arresting Donny and for Sean's death. If you could get them to start planning a hit against the DA, we could use that to take Sergei down."

"I was going to try to keep as far as I could from the Romanovs," I replied—but, of course, I was already planning how to get revenge. "What are you thinking I should do?"

"Make the offer of services. Use it to get in closer. They'll understand your wanting revenge against the DA. In the meantime, we'll coordinate with the local police to put some protection in place for your father and brother just in case anyone outed you, but then we want you to get in close to your uncle's old contacts in the family."

I considered. "I'm willing to do whatever it takes to break ties between my family and organized crime. And if the Romanovs were involved in my uncle's arrest, then all the better."

"We want you to go undercover."

"I have no clandestine training."

"We have an excellent training program," he said firmly.

I shrugged.

"Besides, you won't really need the full training. Maybe a couple of weeks, tops."

"It's hard to be away for a couple of weeks," I replied. "What's involved?"

"Basic clandestine techniques so you know how to handle yourself. What we really want you to do is befriend your uncle's contacts in the Romanov family. Find out what's going on," he said. "Look, you're a soldier. One of the best. Special operations forces. We know you wanted your family out of organized crime. We want you to find out what you can about Sergei Romanov's plans. Anything in particular so we can get some real evidence on them. We could just take him out, but we want his entire organization. We can't get it unless we get inside his organization. You're a fortuitous part of the plan. We'll send you in and you'll give him to us."

I sighed and took a sip. "I gave up operations when I left the Marines. Besides, everyone knows that I don't approve of my family ties to the mafia. I'll have to convince them that I had a change of heart."

Gladwell shook his head.

"You can pull a Michael Corleone and pretend you want to protect your father and need his help. You can say you want revenge against the DA."

"My uncle is small potatoes," I said, still angry at Spencer Grant for going after him, causing all the trouble and heartbreak in my family.

"The DA and FBI should have gone after the Romanov family, not someone small like my uncle."

"Whatever," Gladwell said. "That's the past. This is now. I want you to befriend Victor Romanov. See what you can get out of him. We know your uncle always wanted you to join the family business after you returned from Afghanistan. You could play up that angle."

"I'm a businessman," I said, fighting it a bit longer, although I had already decided to take their offer. "I'm not an undercover FBI agent."

"Oh, you won't be an actual agent," he said and chuckled. "You'll get training and be part of an off-the-books program that isn't directly tied to the FBI or any government agency. We don't want to get *our* hands dirty, but we need people who can roll around in the dirt with the animals."

"Thanks," I said, frowning at the way they described my uncle. "I like my job. I'm not the least bit interested in trying to get in deeper with my uncle's business." I finished my drink and placed the empty glass on the desk.

"Your choice," Gladwell said. "I understand your younger brother is currently linked to several questionable people in Las Vegas. We may or may not have evidence that he's been involved in some illegal activities."

I glanced up at him. "Are you threatening me?"

"I'm only making suggestions."

I sighed. I wanted my family to be safe and certainly didn't want them to be in danger because of my actions at the bank.

"I need to think about it."

"I'll wait for your answer. You have exactly five minutes. You either sign this offer for operations training or you and your family are on your own and your baby brother may be taking a trip to the local lock-up."

"What about rules of engagement? If I have to get down with the dogs, I might have to get dirty. What can I do to protect myself? Prove myself to them?"

"Wide open," Gladwell said. "But you have to have pretty good reason if you use lethal force. Of course, if you get caught, we may have to pick you up, put you in jail for a few days or weeks, just to make it look legit. I'm sure as a Marine you've been through hell and back. If anyone can take it, you can."

I nodded.

Of course, I said yes. It wasn't just that I wanted to protect Conor and my father. It was that I wanted revenge.

I wanted to make Spencer pay for his role in bringing my uncle in on trumped-up charges. Sure, he was dirty, but in the greater scheme of things, my uncle was a flea on a gorilla's ass compared to the Romanovs.

I signed his paper and stood, recognizing that the meeting was over by the way Barlow opened a new file and said nothing else.

I left and went back to the gym, wondering if I'd made the right decision. I felt it was my only choice. I was a soldier. Despite my MBA, it was in the military that I felt at home. Taking down the Romanov family with the approval of the FBI and with police support?

How could I say no?

I WENT to Langley for a couple of weeks of intensive training, emerging relatively unscathed. After the two-week training period was up, I had a few more bruises from the physical training and a lot more respect for the rigorous training clandestine operatives underwent.

I returned to Boston, tired but ready to move forward with the next phase of my performance as a Romanov insider.

"I'm glad you're back," my father said the first night I returned and we were sitting around the table in our kitchen. I'd made a quick meal of steak and potatoes with a side of green salad, and was happy to sit down with him. He looked tired, his breathing a bit faster than I'd like. I took his hand.

"How are you? You look exhausted. I'm sorry I went away when I did. I should have stayed."

"No, no," he said and waved me off. "We all went through hell these past months. Everyone deals with their grief in different ways. I'm just glad you're back."

I smiled at him and then attacked my steak. My dad had to rely on Mike for the past two weeks while I was gone and neither of them had much of a head for business, so I had a lot of work to do catching up with the books. All the while, I wondered when I'd get called in to talk to Gladwell about the plan.

A week passed and then another. My life seemed to get back in order, with days spent in the office, talking to suppliers and match organizers for the fights, plus dealing with franchisees, making sure they were keeping up with reporting requirements.

On the personal side, I hadn't had any action since I returned to Boston, having said goodbye to a woman I'd had an on-again off-again arrangement with in Quantico. She was going through a divorce and didn't have a lot of time for a relationship, so we met a couple of times a week and fucked, then said goodbye. Nothing more.

Every night, when I finally crawled into bed after closing the gym and club, I lay awake and wondered when things would get going with the Romanovs. My mind kept returning unbidden to the grave-side service and catching sight of Celia Franklin.

How a woman could still hold my interest years after one night of sex I'd never know, but she did. There was something about Celia that I couldn't get out of my mind. I always thought she was the kind of woman I could make an exception for regarding serious relationships, but I'd been so damn wrong. How she could go from so sweet and passionate and fun and intelligent to being a cold-hearted bitch who'd used me and then thrown me away when Greg finally asked her out blew me away. I'd been hurt before by a woman, and I expected I would again, if I let my guard down.

So I had many frustrated bouts of masturbation to get me through the week, and always, my mind's eye returned to lovely Celia lying beneath me, her thighs spread wide for me to see her, her eyes half-closed in pleasure, her mouth open, licking her lips... I imagined ramming into her tight pussy, into her willing mouth—and more.

It was unsatisfactory but it was all I had until I found a new fuck buddy.

FINALLY, the day came for me to meet with Gladwell and learn more about my mission. I knocked on the door to his office and waited.

"Come," he said. I opened the door and entered, standing in front of his desk to wait for his orders.

"Sit," he said finally, pointing to the chair. I sat and waited some more.

"I hear you did a pretty decent job in your training," he said without looking up at me.

"I survived," I said.

"Good," he said and finally took off his reading glasses and glanced up at me. "We're going to let you loose. We expect you to try to reconnect with your uncle's old contacts in the Romanov family, get deeper into his organization."

"I'll do it," I said, having already heard from my father that several thugs with Russian accents had been by asking about me, wondering if I was going to be their contact now that Donny was in federal custody. "I've been quite vocal about my objection to my uncle's ties to racketeering and money laundering for drug money so I'll have to use Spencer as the excuse to get in and roll around in the dirt with them."

Gladwell smirked. "Victor Romanov is pretty arrogant and might be only too glad to have you at his side. We'll see what he does. Don't worry," he said and put his glasses back on. "He'll think you've finally come around. At the least, he'll understand your desire to get revenge for your family. Even he could understand that."

I nodded. "I hope so."

Gladwell shook his head. "He's smart," he said, "and has been good to your uncle, but he's hell on his enemies. Don't become an enemy."

"Isn't that precisely what I'll be doing?" I asked.

"Don't let him find out," Gladwell said simply. "We won't out you. We want to keep you involved for as long as we can so there'll be no leaks on our side. Keep your own mouth shut about your mission and you'll be okay as well. Don't tell your father or anyone in your family what you're doing. Don't tell your girlfriend."

"Don't worry. I understand the need for secrecy."

As my handler in the FBI and I planned, I met with Victor Romanov, one of Donny's business associates in the Romanov family, and made the offer to provide security for their businesses in exchange for them leaving our family alone. I set up a security detail for them so they could guard their properties on the waterfront against rival families muscling into their territory or attacking any of their family members.

We were finally free of any financial debt to Romanov. No more protection money. It was one small victory in my larger war to take the family business legit. Better to provide a legitimate service than break the law by paying protection money. I could protect our businesses myself.

I hired a few retired Marines I knew, who were quite happy to take on light duties on a part-time basis. Standing around and watching streets for suspicious vehicles and taking names at the door to the business was child's play for them.

Despite it all going well, I had a bad feeling in my gut. What was I getting myself into? All my life I had done everything I could to keep out of the "family business." Now, I'd be immersing myself in it. I had to shut my mind off. I couldn't stop thinking about being bait for a mafia boss.

What I knew about bait, from fishing with my grandfather when I was a young boy, was this: In the process of catching a fish, bait got eaten.

CHAPTER 24

Present Day

Celia

James took me to my dorm room and together, we boxed up my few possessions so I could move in to the safe house. Amy poked her head into the room while James and I were busy.

"What's up?" she asked, frowning when she saw James. "Who are you?"

James was wearing his sober blue suit and looked official. He stood up from the box he was taping shut.

"I'm James," he said and smiled. "A friend."

Amy turned to me, her eyes wide. I stood up from my own box and exhaled, wondering how I'd explain things. I brushed the hair from my face and shrugged.

"James is a friend," I said, hoping she'd believe me. "He's helping me move some stuff."

"Where?" she said, not letting up. "You never said anything about moving. What happened?"

I glanced at James, who returned to his box. "I'm moving in with Hunter," I said lightly. Then I returned to packing my own box, hoping to avoid too much of a long explanation.

"What?"

Of course, I was foolish to think I could get away without a complete debrief.

"Hunter?" she said when I continued packing, her mouth open wide. "*The* Hunter? As in Hunter Saint?"

"The very one," I replied, wishing she'd just get the hint and leave.

"And you were going to tell me when?"

I stood up again, exasperated. "Look, I'm sorry, but some stuff happened and I haven't had time to talk to you."

"Your best friend? You didn't have time to talk to me about moving out and moving in with Hunter Saint? You've never heard of a thing called texting? Your fingers broken or something?"

"Amy, I'm sorry, but can I talk to you later about all this?" I made a helpless face, shrugging my shoulders. "I promise I'll explain everything. And I'm not really moving out permanently. It's just temporary, okay?"

She frowned and glanced between me and James, who I could tell was trying to look inconspicuous.

"You're okay, though, right?" she asked and came over to me, her hand on my arm. "There's nothing wrong? You're not in any danger?"

I shook my head. "I'm fine. Things have happened and, well, I can't say anything right now." I tilted my head to the side, gesturing to James. "I wanted to talk to you about it, but I couldn't. I promise I'll tell you later tonight, okay?" I made a face of regret.

"If you say so," she said, and I could hear the hesitation in her voice. "As long as you're really okay…"

"I am. I'm *fine*," I replied.

"Okay," she said and glanced around. "Do you need any help?"

I shook my head, wanting her to leave so I didn't have to explain who James was. "No," I said and glanced around. "We're pretty much done."

"Where are you staying?" she asked. "At the gym? Does Hunter still live there?"

"No," I said and handed the box to James. "At one of Hunter's other properties."

"Where?" she asked, her expression hopeful. "I'll come and visit you."

I shrugged and made a face. "I can't tell you."

She frowned. "Why not?"

"Security reasons?" I said and cringed. "I can't tell you anything more than that."

"What?" she said and glanced between James and me again. "You are in danger, right? Something to do with Hunter's family business?"

"No, I'm not in any real danger. Hunter has a lot of security, for obvious reasons," I said, wishing she would stop questioning every-thing, but I knew it was because she was worried about me. "I'm fine," I said. "Really."

"This is about the bad guys who beat up Graham, right?"

"Yes," I said, exasperated, deciding to satisfy her. "This is about that. But you can't say anything about it to anyone, especially not Spencer if he comes by."

"Are they back from Europe? I thought they weren't back for a while."

"Not yet, but in case he comes by or anyone comes by asking about me. Tell them I moved out and you don't know where I am."

"All right, Ms. Mysterious. I won't tell anyone. But I don't like this whole clandestine business. You should be telling me. I'm the best friend, remember?"

"You are," I said and went to her, hugging her.

She squeezed me and then pulled back. "Text me later tonight, okay? Promise?"

I nodded. "Promise."

Then, with clear reluctance, she left, closing the door to my apart-ment behind her.

"I'm sorry about that," I said to James. "She's my best friend and has been for years. She's just worried about me."

"Completely understandable." James picked up a box and went to the door. "I'll take these out to the vehicle."

"I'll help," I said and together, we packed the SUV with the few boxes of my things, clothes, computer, books. Lots of books. The apartment was now empty except for my furniture.

When we were done, I stood at the door and glanced around the apartment. Hunter would pay off my room and board, but I wasn't going to live there for my own safety. Finally, I closed the door, feeling sad that a part of my life was gone—the 'independent me' part of my life. The girl who had finally escaped Spencer's tyranny and was living free and on her own. Now, I'd be some gangster's fuck toy, living in his safe house for my own protection and for his ease of use.

I hated that the idea of being his to use excited me, but it *was* Hunter.

The man I'd been fantasizing about half my life.

AFTER WE UNLOADED the boxes back at the safe house, I went to class. James drove me to the building, waited for the class to finish, and then took me to the hospital so I could drop in and check on Graham, but he was gone to physio and wouldn't be back for an hour. I decided to go see him later and left him a note on a sticky I had in my book bag. Then James drove me back to the warehouse.

I went inside to find that there were construction guys on site, busy installing drywall and another crew working on a bathroom. Now that I had the time, I could explore the loft a bit more.

A new kitchen sat at the far end of the space, with an island and a bank of cupboards facing the floor-to-ceiling windows overlooking the bay. It was high-end, the fixtures and cupboards top of the line. A huge marble-top island contained a sink and professional stove and the fridge was so big you could practically store a dead body in it.

George was there, working in a small office near the entry. He came over when he saw me.

"Hello, Miss Celia," he said with a smile. "Your classes finished for the day?"

I nodded. "This is all new," I said and glanced around.

"Yes," he said. "Boss wanted to make comfortable. Is going to be very secure when everything finished. Thick walls. Steel doors. Security cameras on perimeter. No one will be able to get near building without us knowing. You will be safe here."

Then he pointed to a small alcove where James was busy stacking the boxes from my dorm room.

"I buy you desk so you can work," George said. "I hope you like."

I went over and ran my hand along the modular desk. It had a hutch with cupboards and drawers and was in a dark cherry wood. It was expensive. Much more so than anything I'd ever owned before.

"It's a lot better than my desk at the dorm," I said with a laugh, thinking of the rickety old student desk I'd left.

George smiled at me again. "If you need anything, just ask. I am your keeper while Hunter is away."

I nodded. "Thanks."

Then I began unpacking my boxes and getting my computer set up, resigned to my new reality.

After I finished organizing my books and files, I glanced around. Several workers were finishing a new bathroom, installing a tub and sink. They were working fast, and before the end of the afternoon, the walls to the bathroom had gone up and drywall was in place, the sections taped and mudded. It wasn't the best environment for studying, and I finally gave up and sat on the sofa and watched television for a while.

Different contractors came in that evening, putting down flooring in the bathroom and cleaning up. George came over to me and pointed at the bathroom.

"Is yours to use," he said, apparently pleased with it. "I pick best fixtures and colors. I hope you like."

I looked inside. It was ostentatious, with gilded faucets, marble countertops, and granite tiles on the two-person shower. A fantastic tub. All of it looked out over the bay.

"Blinds are inside windows," George said and pressed a switch that closed the blinds, blocking out the light. He opened them again. "You can put things in," he said and opened the vanity mirror. "I bring towels and soaps." He went to a bag beside the bathroom and sure enough, there were thick plush towels and bars of soap.

"It's very nice."

He smiled, pleased with the bathroom.

"Are you staying here, too?" I asked, noticing the small military cot beside his bank of security cameras in his office.

"When Hunter isn't here, twenty-four seven," he said and nodded. "You don't have to worry. You're safe here with us."

"Who are you to Hunter?" I asked, curious about the man and his relationship to Hunter.

"We work together in Afghanistan. We trust each other," he said. "He save my life many times. He is good man, Celia."

"Good men don't get messed up with the mafia," I said, unable to bite my tongue. For all I knew, George might be in the Russian mob.

"Sometimes good men do bad things for greater good," George said and shrugged. "I know Hunter for several years. He is best, very honorable. Hero."

I didn't say anything else, because there was no sense arguing with someone who was obviously a good friend and employee.

I used to think Hunter was a good man, but he seemed to be quite happy to get down and dirty with the Russian mob, being just as bad as they were—beating people up like Stepan, partying with them at his clubs, doing business with them. He was on a first-name basis with Stepan and his ilk. From what I understood, Hunter was still running fights at the gym and there would be illegal betting involved, and who knew what else.

While I had no love for the thug Hunter had beat up and was glad he was paying for what he'd done to Graham, I believed in law and order, not vigilante justice. By beating Stepan up, Hunter had reduced himself to Stepan's level. That was the only conclusion you could draw from what he did. I remembered a quote from my philosophy class on Nietzsche and quoted it, not expecting George to know it.

"He who fights with monsters should be careful lest he thereby become a monster."

George made a face, pursing his lips. "And if you gaze long into abyss, abyss will also gaze into you." Then he smiled.

"You know Nietzsche," I said, pleasantly surprised.

"I am old," he said with a laugh. "I spend many hours in desert waiting for fight to start. Books get you through long waits." He shook his head. "Hunter is not monster."

"So you say." I forced a smile, starting to feel a grudging admiration for George. I wasn't going to argue with him about how much of a monster Hunter had become. He obviously thought very highly of Hunter.

I glanced around the large space. "I unpacked my things," I said with a sigh. "If I'm going to be here for the duration, I might as well get comfortable."

"Hunter will protect you," George said, nodding. "Until all blows over."

"All what blows over?" I asked, genuinely curious.

"This problem with Romanovs. Once they are gone, you will be safe."

"Gone where?" I frowned. Was Hunter planning to kill the Romanovs?

He shrugged. "Prison? Back to Russia?" Then he ran a finger across his neck and raised his eyebrows. I knew what that meant...

I shuddered. "I hope Hunter won't kill anyone."

"He is soldier," George said. "He fights for what he loves. Friends, family. Country. He is honorable man."

"You keep saying that, but if he's involved with the mafia, that's not honorable."

"Fight fire with fire." George shrugged once more like he was help-less. "We shall see."

Then he left me alone to wonder what he meant.

CHAPTER 25

CELIA

I SPENT the next few hours in the small seating area, watching television and intermittently reading my journal articles for the next day's class. George spent his time in his cubbyhole office. The sun went down and the space was cast into mostly darkness, except for a few lights in each of our two places. George sat and watched his video feeds, and I watched him, wondering when Hunter would show up and what he would make me do to earn my keep.

Scrub his back?

Cook him supper?

Finally, after eight, my stomach started to growl and I got up to look in the refrigerator to see if there was something I could eat. While I was checking out the jar of pickles, Hunter entered the apartment with two bags of takeout food in his hands.

"Dinner is served," he said, holding the bags up high.

George went over to him and took the bags, checking out the receipts. "You got any Russian food?"

"That bag," Hunter said and pointed to one of the two. "Although it

285

may be Ukrainian or Romanian or something." Then, he caught my eye. "I hope you like ribs."

"I'll eat pretty much anything at this point," I said. "The only thing in the refrigerator is some pickles."

Hunter nodded. "We can get groceries tomorrow if you want. I'm sure George would love to cook you some good food from St. Peters-burg. What do you say, George?"

"I would love," George said and carried the bags to the kitchen, where he proceeded to prepare the meal for us, taking out plates and cutlery, and organizing the containers of food. He seemed to take on an avuncular role with Hunter, like he was Hunter's batboy. Hunter seemed used to it, and even relished it.

Hunter came over to me and looked me up and down. "How are you?" he asked, his voice soft. He ran his fingers over my bruised cheek. "Do you need anything? Pain killers?"

"Tylenol's good enough," I said, shaking my head.

"How about something to drink?"

"Sure," I said and sighed. "What do you have?"

"I can get you anything. George prefers vodka but I seem to recall that you like tequila."

"Tequila's good," I said. "Do you have salt and limes?"

"That bad?" he asked, smiling softly. "I'm sorry about all this," he said and looked around the apartment. "It's my fault. I knew better, but I have this weakness for you."

"Weakness?" I said, surprised at his choice of words. "Seems to me like you're the one in the position of strength here, seeing as you paid off my debts and I owe you hours and hours of," I said and hesitated, not really wanting to put it into words. I glanced at George, who was humming to himself at the sink. "Payback," I said quietly.

"Oh, I'm pretty sure the weakness is all on my side." Then he lifted a strand of my hair, his gaze moving over my face and lower. Then, to my utter surprise, he bent down and kissed me.

I startled a bit, not expecting it, but he persisted, his lips pressing against mine. He slipped one hand behind my head and held me there as if he thought I'd try to escape. In truth, a thrill went through me at his sudden show of desire and affection and his words about being weak towards me.

It was the opposite of how I thought he would act and feel.

If anything, it was always me who wanted him—me who couldn't resist him. Of course, he thought I had used him, discarding him when Greg came along...

"We should talk," I said, deciding to reveal the truth of what had happened five years earlier when I'd cut things off between us.

"We can talk later," he said with a sigh. "I'm hungry and tired and want a nice warm bath."

He raised his eyebrows at that, and I knew what my evening was going to be like. My body responded immediately at the prospect of sex with Hunter. I was so damn weak... But I also wanted to see Graham.

"I wanted to go see my brother after supper," I said, clearing my throat, which had suddenly choked up.

He frowned. "That isn't exactly in my plans for tonight."

"He's injured and all alone except for his co-worker. I stopped by this afternoon, but he was in physio, so..." I shrugged, trying to look like it was out of my control.

He inhaled and turned away, sitting at the island, taking a plate. Obviously, he didn't want his plans to be interrupted, but I had a life. Graham needed family.

We ate our meal together, and it took some time before Hunter warmed up again. As I watched, George brought him out, teasing him, reminiscing about their shared past. I could see by the way Hunter and George talked and joked with each other that there was a great deal of respect and mutual affection between them.

"You two knew each other in Afghanistan?" I asked, wanting to hear some stories and encourage Hunter to be in a better mood.

"We met when George here joined our Special Operations Forces unit on a rescue," Hunter said, smiling at George affectionately. "A convoy of supplies was attacked and two civilian contractors were abducted and kept in a compound in the tribal areas. We joined up with him and a few other mercs to take them back."

George nodded slowly, regarding Hunter with a critical eye. "That was first mission together," George said. "I didn't know what to think of pretty boy Marine lieutenant. All shiny and new. First operation. I give him hard time at first. He showed me he was good enough."

"Just good enough?" Hunter said with a mock tone of affront. He cuffed George playfully, reaching out across the island where we sat eating. "You sang my praises to high heaven that night in the bar back at our FOB."

"Vodka always makes things look better."

"I didn't think you could drink while on deployment in the Persian Gulf," I said, frowning.

"General Order number 1A prohibits consumption of alcohol while in Iraq, Afghanistan, or Kuwait," Hunter said as if he'd memorized the regulation. "We still drank. Private contractors drank and we spent a lot of time with private contractors. Especially old Russian veterans. You can't separate Russians from their vodka and expect to win a war."

George laughed and nodded. "Is true." Then, he threw back another ounce of vodka. "To your health."

We replied and I took a shot. Later, the talk died down and the three of us sat staring at our empty glasses. George stood up and stretched.

"Well, I clean up and then I think I go downstairs," he said and grabbed his half-empty bottle of Stolichnaya.

"Don't worry about cleaning up. James will take Celia to the hospital for a quick visit, and I'll take care of things while she's away, but then I'm staying for the night," Hunter said, his voice low. "You can go downstairs if you want."

"I will," George said and he laid his hand on Hunter's shoulder. "I be back tomorrow morning bright and early."

"Don't bother," Hunter said. "I'm sleeping in tomorrow. I'll call you when I need you back here."

George nodded, glancing over at me. "Have good night," he said. "Remember what I told you." Then he left us sitting at the island.

Before he was out the door, Hunter turned to me, frowning. "What did George tell you? Only good things, I hope…"

"Yes," I said, not knowing what else to say.

Hunter got on his cell and called James, asking him to pull the car around the back so I could go to the hospital. Then, he escorted me to the door, helping me on with my coat.

"Don't stay too long," he said as he stood behind me, adjusting my collar. He leaned closer, pressing his body against mine, his face in my hair. I heard him inhale deeply. "I'm an impatient man."

"I won't take too long," I replied, a thrill going through my body at the sound of desire in his voice.

Then I left and took the service elevator to the loading dock where James waited, the rear passenger door open.

I HAD a nice visit with Graham, and got an update on how his physio was going, how long he might have to stay in rehab.

He was now on the rehab ward and was getting help from occupational therapists with looking after himself, doing basic things like going to the toilet himself and brushing his teeth.

Everything was hard for him, and I felt sick watching how much his independence had been reduced. The doctor said he would be like that for weeks until they could get him walking again when the cast was off his leg and the broken bone had healed.

"I talked to Mom," he said and then filled me in on his call with her. "They'll be home tomorrow," he said and handed me his cell, which was open to an email from Spencer.

"I was enjoying his absence," I said ruefully. "I hope Mom had a good time."

"She sounded good," Graham said. "Refreshed. The trip was on her bucket list, so she's really happy they went."

I checked my watch. "Well, I have to go," I said and leaned over to kiss Graham's cheek and give his good arm a squeeze. "I'll be back tomorrow for another visit."

"Bring your lunch or stay and have dinner with me," he said hopefully. "I get pretty damn lonely."

"I will," I said.

I left him, walking through the maze of hallways to the front entrance where James waited with the SUV. As we drove through the darkened streets of Boston, I stared numbly out the window at the passing city lights, wondering what Hunter would make me do to service his needs.

I hated myself for being so aroused at the thought of servicing his needs...

ONCE BACK AT the safe house, I entered the apartment and removed my coat. Hunter was sprawling on one of the sofas watching news, remote in hand.

I went over to the kitchen, feeling suddenly awkward, and saw that, as he promised, Hunter had removed our glasses and plates and had put them into the dishwasher. I stood at the island counter and watched the city lights outside the huge window, wondering what Hunter would do and when he would make his move.

"There you are," Hunter said and came into the kitchen. He stood directly behind me, his body touching mine. There was no doubt what he had in mind when he corralled me against the counter, one arm on either side of me.

He pulled my hair to one side and kissed my neck, his lips warm against my skin. He moved his mouth higher, pressing it against my jaw and then my cheek when I turned my head to the side. His hands gripped my shoulders, pulling me against him so I could feel his erection pressing against my butt.

My body responded but my mind was surprisingly resistant. I could have just melted into his arms, because there was no doubt I was aroused. For some reason—maybe having to do with self-esteem—I couldn't allow myself to just go along with him. I couldn't allow myself to respond even though I could feel my flesh throb in response to his touch.

I stiffened, turning my head the other way, running the water in the island sink and making a show of washing a pot off before sliding beside Hunter and placing it in the dishwasher.

Hunter didn't say anything, but he did stand back a few feet and watched me. I kept up the façade of cleaning up and he watched.

"So that's how it's going to be, is it?" he said, his voice low.

"Isn't this my job?" I said a bit too tartly. "I clean up, run your bath, wash your back, take care of your needs? You own me, after all."

When he didn't respond, I turned to see his expression and found him leaning against the counter, his arms crossed. He was wearing a black cashmere sweater with a V-neck, the fabric molding to his body, showing his very well-developed muscles, his wide bulky shoulders and his bulging biceps. His black jeans hung low on his narrow hips, a thick black belt with a big buckle over a nicely bulging package. He was watching me from under a frown, his head bowed, his blue blue eyes intense, his longish hair falling on his cheeks in a very sexy way.

What was wrong with me? Why was I resisting?

The man was gorgeous. He was also clearly not happy with my lack of response to him.

"What?" I said, seeing his disapproving expression. "You're not happy that I'm cleaning your kitchen? You want me down on my knees?"

He glanced away and I saw a muscle twitch in his too-square jaw, which was covered with just the right amount of scruff.

Damn him! Why did I still want him so much despite everything?

"You know what?" he said finally, his voice sounding weary. "Fuck it." He left the kitchen area and started walking to the door. I kicked myself mentally. I didn't necessarily want him to leave, but I also didn't want this arrangement to keep on the way it was.

Then he turned suddenly and came back, pressing me against the island before I could respond. He kissed me, one hand behind my head so I couldn't escape. The kiss was passionate, rough, his mouth devouring mine, his tongue finding mine. With the other hand, he squeezed my breast, his thumb unerringly finding my nipple through the fabric of my t-shirt.

I couldn't deny that my body responded immediately to his kiss and his touch. When I finally kissed him back, giving in instead of fighting, he stopped and pulled away, leaving me almost panting with desire.

"I don't need this," he said, his hands on his hips. "I don't force women and I don't enjoy hesitation. So, we're done until you come to me. Willingly."

Then he turned and left me alone, my heart racing, my body aching with desire. I watched in silence as he grabbed his leather jacket from the back of a chair beside the door and left, slamming the door behind him.

I should have admitted that I wanted him as much as he wanted me—probably more—but my pride prevented me.

I couldn't get around the fact that he owned me financially. Sure, he'd saved my brother's life, paid of his debts, and protected me when the mob became too interested in me. He'd paid off my tuition and the lost inheritance.

But I wanted more.

The truth was that I couldn't be happy being his fuck toy no matter how much I enjoyed it.

I *did* enjoy it. He'd proven that multiple times.

But I wasn't just some Boston wiseguy's fuck toy.

Until he understood that, we'd have to be enemies. So, instead giving Hunter a bath, washing his back, and then having sex with him, I sat alone on the sofa, my arms crossed. In truth, I wanted things to work out with him, but not like this. Not with me beholden to him, doing things because I had to rather than because I had chosen to. He was right. Sex had to be chosen freely or it was rape. At the least, it was prostitution.

I was better than that.

I waited for a few moments, wondering if he'd come back, but he didn't, so I got up and did a bit of tidying to try to distract myself. When I came to look at the seating area for more dishes, I saw the bank of video cameras and decided to check and see if George was returning to be my babysitter. Honestly, at that moment, I preferred his company. He was nice, friendly, and besides, I wanted to pump him for more information about Hunter.

I sat at the desk where I remembered George sitting and checked out the feed. On one screen, I saw the exterior of the building. A lone car drove down the street, but otherwise the neighborhood was deserted. On another screen, I saw the rear loading dock and back alley between the two buildings. Then, I noticed a small screen to the left and saw...

I saw my own apartment at the dorm.

What?

Hunter had a hidden camera in my apartment? There were two angles—one showing my bedroom, the wide-eye camera catching the bed itself and the closet area and window. The other showed the living room, doorway, and door to the tiny kitchenette.

Hunter had been spying on me at the dorm?

My pulse raced. What a bastard...

I couldn't believe it.

He'd been freaking spying on me, watching me sleep? Did he see me get dressed and undressed every day? Worse, was *George* watching me?

For how long?

It had to be recent...

Just then, when my pulse was racing and I was fuming in anger, my face red, the door to the apartment opened and George entered. He saw me sitting at his place and frowned.

I stood up quickly, feeling guilty that I'd been snooping, and yet fully justified and incensed that I'd discovered they'd been watching me on hidden cameras.

"I can't believe that you and Hunter have been spying on me," I said, stepping out of the way when he entered the small office space. "I thought Hunter was above being a voyeur."

George bent down and clicked off the screen and then stood up straight. "We do it for your protection only. Not as voyeur."

"But I got dressed and undressed in my room."

George shrugged and sat at his chair. "I don't watch. Only make sure you are okay. Hunter was very worried about your safety. He put in cameras to make sure Stepan and his guys don't come for you. Hurt you."

I frowned. Of course, he was right that I was in danger from Stepan and his mob goons, but to put in a camera...

"Why not just have a tail on me or something?" I asked, trying to come up with some excuse. "No bodyguards?"

"Bodyguards not work at dorm. Tail is already in place but it takes three men to do one tail, Celia."

"I still don't like it," I said. "I don't like being spied on. It's an invasion of privacy. Couldn't you just have one camera watching my door?"

"Is better this way. Someone could break into window..."

"That sounds like an excuse," I replied, my hands on my hips.

"It was only for few nights," George said, exhaling in frustration. "Now, you are here. Much safer."

I glanced around the space. "Are there cameras hidden here as well? So Hunter can watch my every move?"

"No need for cameras," George said, his voice sounding tired. "I watch. I protect."

"Well, I don't like it."

I stomped away to the seating area and plopped down on the small sofa, upset that not only had I been surveilled, I was now a prisoner. And Hunter was going to ignore me until I came to him and asked for him to fuck me.

Like I was going to ask him to fuck me.

Not likely...

I checked my watch. It was almost nine o'clock. I had early class the next day and so I clicked on the widescreen and surfed the channels, looking for something to watch to pass the time until I was tired enough to sleep. I laughed to myself when I saw what was on AMC.

Goodfellas.

The story of my life...

CHAPTER 26

Hunter

LATER THAT NIGHT, I received a message from George.

RUSKIE5: Celia found video feed from dorm. She is not happy. Maybe you should come by. Talk to her.

Damn.

I knew she'd be mad if she discovered I'd had her dorm bugged and a hidden camera installed, but I also knew she'd never believe me when I told her it was for her own safety.

I should have gone right over and confronted her, explained things, but I decided to let it ride. She'd get over it.

Or she wouldn't. I was going to avoid the safe house as much as possible, visiting only when Celia was away. Until she came to me and asked me to fuck her, she could spend her time alone if that was what she wanted.

I was through with trying to seduce her and fed up with her resistance. I thought she wanted me. I thought, by the way her body responded to me when we had sex, that she enjoyed being with me. She orgasmed. Easily.

I'd figured I was giving her an excuse to do what she really wanted anyway, but I was wrong.

She didn't really want it. Not really.

So, that was it for me. I didn't have to coax women to fuck me. They did so because they wanted it.

That was my bottom line.

I figured if I left her alone for a while, she'd come to her senses and just fuck me the way I thought she really wanted. Instead, I felt a sense of gloom, because I'd grown used to being able to drop in and see her whenever I wanted. I enjoyed fucking her just a little too much for my own good.

I wanted her to want me back just as much.

As to the debt? Fuck it. I did it out of loyalty to Graham, despite how badly he'd betrayed me. I didn't want anything to happen to him despite what he did to me.

Finally, I did it because I *could*.

I arrived at the safe house a few days later to talk to George before I went out of town.

"How does she seem?" I asked, keeping my voice as neutral as possible, despite the fact I felt less and less certain about my decision to force the issue between us.

"She is fine," George said, misinterpreting my intent, of course. I didn't want her to be fine. I wanted her to feel lonely and upset and missing out on my company.

"What does she do all day when she's not at class?"

"She is very studious," George replied, nodding to himself. "Reads books and papers all the time. Writes on computer. No need to worry. She is not lonely. Too busy."

"Huh," I replied, trying hard not to show my frustration.

Of course, I could have found release in the company of one of the club regulars. Lila was always willing and able, but I couldn't take her vapid conversation and her focus on the way things looked. How rich I was, how much respect the thugs from the Romanov family showed me...

The truth was that I wanted Celia.

Later that day, I met my handler down by the docks south of the city, behind an old warehouse that had seen better days. I parked the SUV and turned off the engine, sitting with my cell, checking my texts to see if he was still on his way.

About five minutes later, Millar arrived, pulling up beside me, his window beside mine. I rolled down my window and he nodded, his dark glasses hiding his eyes from view.

I didn't like that. I wanted to look in someone's eyes when I spoke to them to see if I could detect falsehood.

"You shouldn't have roughed up Stepan," Millar said. "His family's lawyer is pushing for an arrest. Can you believe it? The nerve of these thugs."

I shook my head. "That's the biggest joke of all."

"Well, it puts us in a very tough position. Since you've been named and we have video that puts you there, if we don't arrest you then too much focus could come down on us. You should have kept your nose clean."

"Look," I said, my fists clenched. "You gave me wide open rules of engagement. If I did nothing, none of them would respect me. If you really want me to get next to Sergei Romanov, I have to fit in. They have to believe I'm in this for real, and not a plant."

"This is my operation," Millar said, his voice firm. "I'm the one who developed the plan. I'm the one who changes it. Got that?"

"Hey," I said, holding up my hands in submission. "I'm doing my job. You want me to get close to Sergei. I can't do that unless he thinks I'm legit. A real wiseguy would have beaten up Stepan. That's the way they work."

"The way the cops work is when they have a suspect, they make an arrest."

I exhaled. Of course, it would look suspicious if they had direct evidence of me beating Stepan to a pulp and didn't even bring me in.

"What do you want to do?"

"We need to arrest you." Millar said. "We can pick you up or you could turn yourself in. We'll put you in lockup for a few days, in a segregated unit, then you make bail, and when the case comes to trial, you can conveniently get off due to some technicality."

I gave him a dark look. "It's that easy, is it?"

"We have ways." Millar shrugged. "Sometimes, we have to cooperate with the bad guys to get the biggest bad guy there is."

"There's a slippery slope," I said ruefully. "Careful we aren't standing too close to the edge."

"I'm fine with my own morals," Millar said and glanced away. "I can live with myself and what our unit is doing. Can you?" He turned back to look at me pointedly.

"I sleep very well, thanks," I replied.

"What about Spencer Grant's stepdaughter? You fucking her or something?"

I glanced away, not happy that they were monitoring my every move. "We have a history."

"Are you using her to get revenge against Grant? You have to tell me these things."

"Grant is a sonofabitch who's had it in for me and my family for decades."

"Yeah, I know. He was all butthurt because your uncle got off years ago when he was Assistant DA. He's still gunning for you."

"Some people can't let the past go."

"So, *are* you using the stepdaughter to get back at Grant? Throw her in his face or something?"

"No," I said. "It's not like that. We go a long way back." Then, I tried to change the subject from Celia. "So did you find that information I asked you about?"

He sucked his teeth thoughtfully for a moment. "As a matter of fact, I heard that the Bureau's looking at Spencer Grant as part of an investigation into a sex ring operating in the DC area. Seems he developed a preference for young things when he first worked as Commonwealth's Attorney in Alexandria. There were rumors, but nothing stuck. A task force has a few leads and they're moving forward with the case."

"What?" I said and turned to him, a surge of adrenaline going through me. "He's a pedophile?"

"Apparently, he likes them pubescent and just illegal. There's some modelling agency that provides vulnerable young things from Eastern Europe, the old Soviet Union, who don't know what to expect when they get to the US. These creeps lavish these girls with booze and money and have their way with them. Get them gigs with the big agencies."

I frowned and wondered if he'd ever done anything to Celia. Then I shook my head mentally. Celia had been a virgin. He'd made her sign a chastity contract.

Maybe that was to protect him more than her…

"That fucking bastard," I said, anger coiling inside me. "He's been involved with trafficking young Russian girls?"

"Yeah," he replied. "He's just slimy enough to have slipped out of reach."

"What a fucking hypocrite. He's condemned my family all this time because of our ties to the Russian mob, and he's using them for his own perversions? He's all kinds of evil," I said, remembering how he'd hurt Celia and Graham when they were kids. "I'd like to take him down, too. Believe me. Seeing him in prison would be the cherry on top of the Sergei Romanov ice cream sundae."

"One mission at a time," Millar said. "We need you on the Romanovs. That's your world."

"Grant's stepdaughter is an old friend. He was a bastard to those two kids, beating them both. What a psychopath."

"He's a real case, if what the task force thinks happened is true. Like I say, they're building a case against him."

I nodded. "What do you want from me?"

"I want you to lie low for a week or so until the stuff with Stepan settles down. Can you take a vacation or something? When you get back, we could make a show of picking you up, bring you down to the station, then have you released on bail."

"I could go to Quantico for a week, but it's really inconvenient." Then I thought I could kill two birds with one stone—get out of town and investigate what I could about Spencer and his time in Alexandria chasing after pretty little Eastern European girls who thought they were coming to the USA to become rich and famous...

"We either pick you up now or later, but it would be best to let things die down a bit before we take you in, get everything in place. It would be good to have you stay in lockup for a while. Make your bones with the Russians, so to speak."

"I'd rather not, but I survived Hell Week, so I think I can survive a week in lockup."

"I'll see what I can arrange."

Then, we parted, Millar driving off in one direction and me in the other.

As MILLAR SUGGESTED, I left Boston for a week, spending time in Alexandria. If I had to lay low, I wanted to achieve something during my off time, and that something was to track down intel on Spencer Grant and the possibility he was a fucking pedophile pervert who trafficked in Russian immigrant girls. The thought he might have harmed Celia in some way made my blood boil and I could think of nothing else.

While in Alexandria, I called on contacts I had in Virginia, tracing Spencer's past before he'd met Celia's mother and moved in with them. I tapped a private eye friend, asking him to do some snooping into Spencer's background for me. Bill O'Donnell had worked for DC police in their cyber-crimes unit and was now retired, but had a PI business on the side. An aging man with a big potbelly and a shaved head, he had an easy smile and laugh.

I liked him the first time I met him years earlier.

"What can you tell me about these kinds of scum?" I asked when we met at a bar in Alexandria.

"What can I tell you? Too much, most of it will make you puke your guts out. Often, pedophiles belong to ultra-secret networks that operate on the dark web. They're difficult to infiltrate, but this modelling gig is almost too easy. It makes everything above board, look legit. They appear to be just a group of men helping to fund a modelling agency looking for new talent. If you want to dig up dirt on a suspect, I'll have to have more to go on than just a name."

"The current DA in Boston," I said and nodded when I saw his expression of surprise.

"Seriously?"

"Yep. There's an ongoing FBI case, but it's stalled. He has a lot of power, as you can imagine."

"No shit," he replied and stared off in the distance.

"Dig up as much dirt as you can on Spencer Grant as fast as you can. I can pay you handsomely."

"That's always an incentive."

TWENTY-FOUR HOURS LATER, as I sat at a hotel in Alexandria, doing my own research on Spencer's past, Bill called me with some usable intel.

"I got some stuff for you," he said. "We should meet somewhere private."

I agreed and we met later that evening at an Irish pub in DC.

"So, what have you got for me?" I asked, impatient to get to the good stuff. I took a long pull on my glass of Guinness and waited while Bill did the same.

"Spencer was quite the big religious leader in Alexandria when he was living there, and was known as a pious man among his colleagues," Bill said, licking the foam off his lip. "It took some digging, but there was an incident in his past that I found alarming. He'd gone through a messy divorce and his ex made an allegation that he was abusing their daughter, but then, when the court date was scheduled, she withdrew the charge and nothing more was said. Typical of these kinds of cases."

"Let me guess: the allegation was true but he threatened to ruin her if she went through with it."

"Something like that," Bill replied, raising his eyebrows.

Bill finished filling me in on his findings, taking out a reporter's notepad and flipping through pages.

"Grant still owns a few properties in Virginia, including a cabin near Chesapeake Beach. The address was linked to some chat logs of staff at the modelling agency."

"That sounds very suspicious. You got an address?" I asked. Bill nodded and wrote it down on a sheet of paper, ripping it out and handing it to me.

"You shouldn't go there alone," Bill said. "No vigilante stuff, Hunter."

"Don't worry about me."

We finished our beers and I drove back to my hotel room, deciding to take a drive out there the next day, check it out. I wasn't above a little breaking and entering to see what I might dig up that could incriminate Spencer.

THE VIRGINIA COAST in October was wet and cold. I knew my way around the locale and felt comfortable driving the streets. I retraced a few of my old visits to the area, even went to stand and stare at one of the battleships in the harbor.

My life had been good before Sean's death, before I took over the business, and I wished now that I could go back to it, back to the days when I was in the Marines, getting ready to teach the incoming officer selection course. But I couldn't.

This was my life now, for better or worse. I had to make the most of it.

I pulled into a narrow back road that ran beside Spencer's property, trying to remain invisible to anyone who might be in the cabin. I didn't think Spencer would be there. It was off-season so the cabin should have been empty. From where I parked, I could just see the house and the circular driveway in front. It resembled a log cabin, with rustic cedar and a stone fireplace. Totally innocuous, in other words.

I wondered, as I sat in the rental car and debated whether to break in, if Celia and I would have become a couple had Greg not come along.

While I mused on Celia and her possible likes and dislikes in men, I was surprised to see a car drive up the lane. I was glad I'd had the forethought to park on a different street out of sight but with the cabin in my line of vision. One of the cabin doors opened and a tall, gangly young girl left and walked to the waiting car, whose engine was still running.

Who was she?

Then I saw her face straight on before she got in the back seat, and I got a sick feeling in my gut.

Her long fair hair was a mess, her makeup was a smeared, there was lipstick on her cheek, black streaks under her eyes.

She was no more than twelve or thirteen by her height and physical development, but the makeup was sickeningly adult. The car drove off and I was just about to follow it when a man appeared at the cabin door, wrapping a scarf around his neck before striking off on foot. He must have parked somewhere else and walked to the cabin.

I got out of my car, pulled up my own collar against the wind, and followed him.

The man entered a narrow walkway that skirted the coast a few hundred feet ahead of me. I sped up and bumped into him, knocking him in an attempt to intimidate him, put him off balance.

"How do you live with yourself?" I said in a hushed voice, my disgust with him and his type making me feel that violence was the only solution.

He stopped and turned to face me, his response showing he was alert, but not expecting to be followed.

"Who the fuck are you?"

I grabbed his arm when he tried to run. "Who do you think I am?"

He shook his head, his eyes wide. "I don't know." He looked me up and down, sizing me up. "Are you one of Franklin's men? I paid up."

"No," I said, making a mental note to check all Spencer's contacts for a Franklin.

"Then who are you?"

I reached into his pocket and grabbed his keys, his wallet, and his cell. He tried to wrestle with me, but I was a few inches taller and a few dozen pounds heavier.

"Go," I said and shoved him.

"Give those back," he replied, reaching for the wallet and cell, trying to take them from me.

I withdrew my sidearm and pointed it at him. "Leave before I shoot your sorry ass," I said and backed away. "Be prepared."

He frowned. "For what?"

But by the paleness to his face, I could tell he knew what I meant. He'd better prepare himself for being arrested when I turned the bastard in.

"Go, *now*," I said waving my gun at him. "Or I may lose my temper and shoot you, you perverted fuck."

He turned and hustled down the walkway, disappearing into the trees where the walkway met the forest. I watched for a moment and then turned back, running along the pathway back to the cabin. I tucked the phone and wallet into my jacket pocket and did a recon of the cabin, looking for a point of entry.

Before I did anything, I slipped on a pair of latex gloves. No need to leave my fingerprints all over everywhere. Then, I used the handy little device George had given me that jammed the radio frequency used in any alarm system, enabling me to open a window and slip inside undetected. Your average neighborhood thug didn't have access to sweet tech like I had.

The living room looked completely normal, except for a dozen empty bottles of beer, and ashtrays filled with cigarette butts. A distinct scent of weed hung over the room.

I took my time, examining everything. Then, I opened the door to the basement and walked down the stairs, my heart in my throat as I went. I knew that if there was anything incriminating, it would be located down here, where the air was cool and damp.

When I got to the bottom of the stairs, I felt sick to my stomach.

Video cameras set up on tripods.

They were making child porn. Inside a dark room was a bed against one wall and video equipment, a camera on a tripod, an assortment of other cameras on a table against another wall. Restraints of many kinds—leather straps and chains, belts and whips —were laid out on a table. Whoever owned this cabin was not only into abusing children sexually, he was a sadist who enjoyed their pain and fear.

I felt the blood freeze in my veins as I examined the sadistic pedophile's paraphernalia, my anger making my muscles tense. This stuff between consenting adults I had no problems with, but against children?

Had the worm been this bad, this developed in his sick perversion, when he'd lived with Celia? He'd hit her, he'd hit Graham, but had he spared Celia this hell?

I could only hope so.

I couldn't imagine Celia as a little eleven- or twelve-year-old girl, tied up and abused.

It was impossible.

I checked around, looking for a stash of pornography, magazines, photographs, or films in the room that Spencer and his pedophile associates used as a trophy room, but there was nothing.

Then I found it.

Inside the closet, at the back, behind a box of clothes, was a locked cupboard. That was surely where the goods were kept. I easily broke the lock and checked inside, where I found row upon row of cassettes, old reel-to-reel tapes, and newer CDs. Boxes filled with Polaroids of young girls just pubescent, their eyes blank, their faces pale, some with makeup on, red smears on their lips, bodies in obscene poses that made sense only when assumed by adult women.

I felt my guts roil, my gorge rise, as I sorted through them, looking for Celia among the faces—for the black hair and chocolate-brown eyes. Spencer and his group of perverts were meticulous, documenting each child, the name, age and a little comment on each. One depicted a little girl doing something little girls shouldn't even know about, let alone perform on an adult. The label read, "Penny. 8."

There was nothing in the box showing Celia—thank God. Perhaps these predated Spencer's time with her. They were older, taken in the 80s, the color fading.

I started sorting through the cassettes, reading dates and labels. I sat on the edge of the bed and held the tapes in my hand, considering whether to watch then or not. If I did, I'd be witness to horror I knew I could probably not forget, but I wanted to see him and know he deserved to die. I'd know, beyond a shadow of a doubt, that killing him was completely just. I knew that already, but I needed to see what the worm did so I could look him in the eye and exact a confession, forcing Spencer to admit to his crimes.

When I killed Spencer, and I *would* kill him, I'd make him say the words.

I slipped a tape into the VCR and watched it. On it, the most devastating scenes I could imagine for a little girl—any little girl. As I watched, I thought about Celia and about our encounters when she was a teen. Was Spencer doing this kind of thing to her back then?

It made me ill to even consider it.

I'd seen and done shit that would make most people's skin crawl. I'd been in firefights where I'd blown off the heads of enemy fighters; I'd been in the aftermath of car bombings, seeing body parts strewn around the road, bodies burnt beyond recognition.

I'd never seen anything like this.

The men I killed were all enemies—soldiers or insurgents. They were terrorists. They were adults, they were hardened, they knew what was going to happen, they had been prepared for it.

When I made them bleed, the blood was justified. When I made them cry out in pain, inflicting the pain was legitimate.

The only response to witnessing a video like this was to kill the man. Death was the only justice possible. All that kept me from losing complete control were thoughts of killing him in as slow and deliberate and painful a way as possible.

Witnessing the anonymous child's abuse made me feel a need to purge myself through violence. I could kill the man today, when I returned to Boston. That would give me immediate satisfaction.

However, I wanted to do it right. I wanted to do it legally. On top of that, I wanted to make sure all his perverted associates went down with him.

In public.

I put the tapes back into the cupboard and then left the basement, left the cabin through the window, and went to my car.

Before I reached it, I stopped and bent over, emptying the contents of my stomach on the leaf-strewn forest floor.

I STOPPED on a side street in downtown Alexandria and called Millar on my burner, using a secure line he'd given me for when I needed to contact him.

"I'm coming back early," I said, a feeling of exhaustion hitting me now that the adrenaline had burned off.

"What's up?"

"I've been snooping around Alexandria, and found something. I think your boys need to check out Grant's old property in Chesapeake Beach. He or his fellow perverts are using it as a fun house. There's material there that could put him and his associates away."

"You broke into his property?"

"I saw a young girl leave and then an older man. I stopped him and got his name and cell. You better have someone go there quick before he alerts Grant and they go and clean the place out."

"What's the address?"

I gave him the address and I heard him flip through a file.

"We haven't got a warrant to do a search."

"You better get one, and quick. I'm ready to go kill the bastard myself," I said, remembering the images I'd seen.

"Don't do that," Millar said, his voice firm. "It won't do anyone any good to have you in jail for murder for real."

"Don't worry," I said. "I got control of myself. I'll leave the rest up to you, but I'm warning you. If nothing happens because of this, I can't promise anything."

"I'll call my contacts in Alexandria and get to the cabin as soon as we can. As for you, lie low until I have things in place. Then we'll take you in."

"I'm coming back to Boston," I said, impatient to return and see things through.

"I can't talk you into staying there for another few days? Things aren't in place yet to bring you in."

"I'll stay quiet. I don't like being away when things are going to go down."

"Okay, but lay low."

I ended the call. What I really wanted to do was go and find Spencer and choke the man to death, but I'd leave justice to the justice system. Only if it failed would I take matters into my own hands.

I RETURNED to Boston and went right to the warehouse. I slumped in a chair beside George, who sat in front of a computer, reading the newspaper.

He put down his paper and turned to me, his reading glasses perched at the end of his nose. "How are you? Back so soon? I thought you were staying for a week."

I rubbed my eyes, not able to put how I was feeling in words.

"It was bad?" George asked, frowning at me.

"Yeah, it was bad," I said finally, leaning my head back, closing my eyes. "Worse than I expected. But thanks for this nifty little piece of technology."

I handed him back the radio jammer and he slipped it into a drawer in his desk.

"Glad it was of use. Tell me what happened."

"Celia's stepfather," I said and shook my head. "I found evidence at his old cabin. He's going down."

"Is good, no?"

"Yeah, but I don't know what, if anything, he did to her."

"Talk to her. See what she says."

"This isn't something you just ask a person," I said and rubbed my forehead. "'Hey, did your stepfather sexually abuse you when you were eleven?'"

George nodded. "Is delicate personal matter. You have thought through this whole business with her being your little bit of pussy? "

"I've thought a lot about it," I said. "Now, given what I've seen, I'm rethinking it. If there is any possibility that she was abused..."

George shrugged. "Is your decision."

"You think I should let her go?"

"I think nothing. You are good man, Hunter. You do wrong things for right reasons."

I gripped the armrests of my chair and exhaled. "I should have let her be. Paid the debt and let her alone. Now, I've got her in trouble. She's in Victor's sights."

"You have to protect her if nothing else."

"I will," I said, resting a hand on George's shoulder. "The Pottery Barn rule applies here. Graham got her in trouble. I got her in even more by becoming personally involved with her. I have to look after her."

"You will," George said, nodding.

I would. Even if she didn't want anything to do with me, I would protect her.

CHAPTER 27

CELIA

My WEEK without Hunter was strangely lonely, despite the fact that Spencer and my mom returned from their European cruise and we visited the hospital together. My mom wanted me to spend more time with her now that she was back, but I begged off, claiming that I was too busy with law school and wouldn't be able to see her very much, given that I wanted to spend time each day with Graham.

"Come and have dinner with us," my mom pleaded one afternoon when we'd all been at the hospital visiting Graham. "It's been so long since we spent time as a family…"

I shook my head, feeling Spencer's gaze on me. "Can't do it. I have so much material to read before tomorrow. Some other time."

"You're okay?" Spencer asked me, frowning. "You have everything you need?"

I forced a smile. "I'm doing really well, thanks," I said, hoping like hell that he didn't check in at my dorm to find that I'd moved out.

Every day, I went to class and was a good little law student. Now that Hunter wasn't visiting and there were apparently no prospects for him doing so, I was able to keep up with my reading and asked pertinent questions in seminar.

Every evening, after I visited with Graham, I ate my meals alone while George sat in his little cubbyhole of an office, eating his. He didn't seem to want any company and although I was lonely, I didn't want to invite him, not really knowing what to say.

Finally, about eight days after I'd first arrived, Hunter returned to the safe house without any notice. Late one morning, after I'd returned from early class, he entered the floor and spoke quietly to George, who glanced over at me and then nodded. They talked for a moment and then George gathered up his backpack and left the apartment. Then, Hunter came right over to me, his eyes intense. The look on his face sent a shiver down my spine.

"We have to talk." He pulled me over to the seating area.

"We do." I resisted, standing my ground. "You've been spying on me."

He turned to face me, his expression guarded, as if he expected me to say something about it and was prepared.

"Only for your own good," Hunter said. "Only because you're in Victor Romanov's sights due to Graham and the fact that I paid off his debt. You don't know these people, Celia. I do."

"So you don't deny you were spying on me? A camera in my bedroom? Hunter, that's low even for you."

"Even for me," he said and shook his head, his hands on his hips. He looked up at me. "I did it to protect you"

"How does that protect me?"

"In case someone broke in, or forced you into the apartment. It wasn't me watching. It was George. He just monitored the video feed to make sure you were okay. It's moot now, anyway," Hunter said, his voice impatient. "I thought you understood that you're in danger. I'm trying to protect you. The cameras were a way to protect you."

I said nothing, because I knew he was right. It still irked me.

"Listen, I know you're upset, but there are more important things to discuss," he said and took my arm softly, pulling me into the seating area. "Have a seat."

I sat dutifully and waited while he paced in front of the sofa.

Finally, he sat on the coffee table in front of me, resting his elbows on his knees, his eyes on me, his expression serious.

"What is it?" I asked finally, wondering why he seemed so agitated.

"Did Spencer ever abuse you? Sexually, I mean?"

I frowned, totally shocked by his question.

Had Spencer sexually abused me? I took in a deep breath and wondered why Hunter was asking me that question, of all the questions he could ask.

"Why do you want to know?" I replied, my mind going back to my past with Spencer and all the nastiness.

"You didn't answer. Did he ever sexually abuse you? I know it's a hard thing to talk about, but I need to know."

"Why do you need to know? What do you mean, sexual abuse?" I asked, stalling for time. "He abused me by any definition of the word. He beat me, he slapped me. As punishment, he made me stand naked in cold showers and used to scrub my skin with a really rough sponge. Sometimes, he scrubbed so hard that my skin bruised." I thought back to those times when he punished me for some transgression. "He found me and a couple of neighborhood kids getting undressed together, you now, playing doctor. He told me I was a sinner and he had to cleanse me of my sins. But he never actually touched me in a sexual way, if that's what you mean."

Hunter took in a deep breath. "The fact that he even had you naked in the shower is sexual abuse," Hunter said. "Even if he didn't touch you."

"He touched me," I said. "He held onto me and when I fought, he grabbed me until I stopped fighting and stood still so he could scrub me down."

I sighed, the memory of those times making me choke up.

"I'm sorry I had to ask you that. It's bad enough that he beat you and abused you emotionally."

I shrugged, lifting one shoulder. "I had never thought of those punishments as sexual in nature. They always seemed to be about humiliating me, and making me hurt. Punishing me for doing anything that might be sexual in nature."

"They were sexual," Hunter said. "Even if he didn't touch you in any place that's usually defined as sexual."

"Why are we talking about this?" I asked, frustrated and embarrassed. "Unless you tell me why, I'm not saying anything else."

"Let's just say I heard some things. I was told some things. I'm doing a bit of sleuthing to find out more. That's really all I can say without getting in trouble."

I thought back to Spencer and his punishments. "He hated me right from the start," I said, my voice breaking. "He never hid it."

"Did you talk to your mom about him? Did she know the things he did?"

I frowned. "My mom was too drugged out to see. She was always in the bedroom sleeping, or on the couch snoozing. She was happy to have Spencer there to discipline us because she couldn't do anything. When I complained, she just told us to be obedient if we wanted Spencer to treat us nicely."

"Did he ever do anything else you can think of that might be sexual? Did he ever expose himself to you? Did he ever show you pornography?"

I frowned. "No," I said. "Nothing like that. He was so uptight about sex, I thought he was a real prude about it. When my friends came over for sleepovers, he was pretty standoffish. I don't think I ever saw him naked. He barely even wore a bathing suit when we were on vacation—not that we went very often anyway, because of my mother."

He nodded. "She's been pretty sick all this time," he said softly.

"She sleeps most of the time unless she's watching television or reading. There's nothing the doctors can do for her pain. She has a pain pump and is pretty much an invalid."

Hunter sighed and leaned back, running his hand through his hair.

"Why are you asking all this?"

He shrugged and glanced away. "I wondered if he was abusive sexually as well as physically and emotionally abusive. Creeps like him often are." He stared at his knuckles, which were now healing up from the beating he administered to Stepan. "Guys like Spencer take advantage of their power over children. It's an easy step into taking advantage sexually so I was concerned." He glanced up like he was trying to see if I believed him.

"You *know* something," I said, getting this sense from him that he was fishing because he had something on Spencer. "Tell me."

Hunter shook his head. "I can't, but he's a piece of work."

"I already know that," I said ruefully. "Graham and I know that all too well, but you must know something if you're asking me questions about him."

"If I do, I can't say what. I'm really sorry about all of it," Hunter said, his voice soft, his eyes soft as well. "You and Graham... you both suffered so much all those years. It must have been hell."

I lifted a shoulder. It was hell, but it was normal for us when Spencer took over.

"I rebelled, and Graham tried to be the good older brother and protect me, but it only got him in more trouble. Spencer doesn't like his authority to be questioned."

"I guess that's why he wants to be the authority. What a fucking bastard."

"That he is." I sighed. "So, why is it that the first thing you ask when you come back after being away for a week is a question about Spencer?"

"I just know things," Hunter said. "I'll tell you when I can. It's about his past, before he met your mother. When he lived in Alexandria. That's really all I can say."

"All right," I said and leaned back, watching him. He seemed preoccupied.

Then, he stood up and shoved his hands into his jeans pockets. "Well, that's really all I wanted to ask you other than how Graham's doing."

I took in a breath and exhaled. "Pretty well, all things considered. He's going to be in rehab for a few weeks. Then physiotherapy for a while. He's really thankful that you paid off his debts, and wants you to know he'll try to pay you back when he's back on his feet."

Hunter nodded. "Tell him not to worry about it. If and when he can pay me back, that's fine. Tell him to get better. That's all I care about."

I looked at him closely, trying to see if he really meant it or was just going through the motions. "That's nice of you, Hunter. I know he's really relieved that he didn't have to go to Spencer. Not that Spencer could have paid off the debt, but you know what I mean."

Hunter nodded. He glanced around and sighed. "I better go. George will be with you tonight. If you need anything, he can help you."

"Thanks," I said, but of course, I didn't really feel all that happy having to be a prisoner of the safe house.

Hunter turned and left the apartment, closing the door behind him. I felt strange after he left, knowing there was something going on that Hunter couldn't tell me.

It was about Spencer's past in Alexandria. That was all I knew.

LATER THAT AFTERNOON, I asked George if he could take me to see my mother. I was concerned about her, and wanted to see her and make sure she was all right. I didn't relish the thought of seeing Spencer, especially after the strange discussion Hunter and I'd had earlier, but I had this vague sense of doom hovering over me.

James drove me to my mom's house in Cambridge and I went inside, using my key to enter. When I got there, the house was quiet. I usually called before I came over but that afternoon I hadn't, hoping that Spencer would still be at work. When I walked into the cool dark interior, I was surprised at how quiet it was. The drapes were drawn and the lights were all off. I walked through the house, checking the living room first to see if she was on the sofa, but she wasn't so I went to her bedroom.

Inside, she was lying on her side under the covers, her back to the door.

"Mom?" I said softly, not wanting to wake her if she was deeply asleep.

When she didn't answer, I went to the side of her bed and saw that her bottle of pills was open, next to a glass of water. The pills had spilled out onto the night table.

Alarmed, I sat on the side of the bed and shook her, worried now that she may have taken too much. She didn't respond.

"Mom? Wake up," I said. She opened her eyes, blinking and my heart rate slowed a bit. She wasn't too drugged up if she was able to blink.

"Sweetie," she said and tried to roll over, but she made a face and I had to help her. "I didn't know you were coming over. How nice to see you."

"You spilled your pills," I said and picked up the few stray ones that were on the floor. "The bottle must have fallen over."

"Oh, I'm sorry, dear," she said. "I'm so clumsy." She kept her eyes closed and lay on her back, a slight smile on her face. "I'm glad you're here. I missed you and Graham when I was away."

"We missed you, Mom," I said and leaned over and kissed her. Then, I adjusted the blankets and glanced around. "Did you have lunch?"

She didn't open her eyes. "Lunch?" she said, dreamily. "What time is it?"

"It's four," I said, frowning. "Didn't you have lunch yet?"

"I don't remember," she replied. "I remember eating breakfast this morning. Is it really four o'clock? I needed some more pain pills and must have fallen asleep. Is Spencer here?"

"I didn't see his car in the drive, but I didn't check the garage. I'll go see."

I left my mom on the bed and went down the hall to the stairs, taking them to Spencer's basement room where he had his office. I knocked on the door and pushed it open, only to find Spencer hunched over a laptop, earphones in. When he saw me at the door, I could tell he was shocked and quickly closed the laptop.

"Celia," he said, pulling the earbuds out. "What are you doing here? Why didn't you call first before you came over?"

"Have you given my mom anything for lunch?"

He made a face, his back straightening. "She wasn't hungry," he replied and I could see the anger start. It started in his body, and then made its way to his face, his mouth turned down, his lips thin. "I know how to look after your mother."

"Her pills were spilled onto the floor," I said, unable to keep the disgust from my voice. "She hasn't eaten since breakfast. Don't you know she has to eat when she takes those pills? You've been told enough times that she needs to keep her calories up."

"Don't you talk to me like that," he said and came over to where I stood by the door. "This is my office. You shouldn't just come in without my permission. I have classified material here." He covered up some files on his desk.

"Are you hiding something?" I said saucily, unable to hold myself back. "Surfing kiddie porn sites?"

He slapped me, his move so fast I barely saw it coming.

"You little bitch," he growled and then his hands went around my neck. I grabbed his hands, fighting with him, my anger now so great that I was not going to let him hurt me again. I kicked his shins and tried to elbow him but he was bigger and stronger.

"Stop," I managed, despite how tightly he held my throat. "You're choking me."

He said nothing, his face a mask of hatred.

"Stop!" I screamed, and kept kicking him, my heart racing from adrenaline.

"Spencer!" my mother said, and it was only her voice that stopped him from choking me to death. "What are you doing?"

He let go of me immediately and I pulled away, my hands on my throat, coughing to get air.

My mother leaned against the wall, and I knew it must have taken almost all her strength to come down the stairs. While I tried to recover, Spencer muscled past me and took her into his arms, one arm under hers for support.

"Why were you two fighting? " she asked and started to slide down the wall. "Why can't the two of you get along?"

I frowned. Did she not realize that Spencer was choking me?

"Now look what you've done," Spencer growled at me. "You've upset your mother. Come, dear," he said to her, his voice all soft. "Let me help you back into bed. You must be hungry."

"Why were you two fighting?" she asked again as he led her back up the stairs.

"We weren't fighting, dear," Spencer said. "I was showing her some self-defense moves they teach all the new female recruits with the police department."

"Liar!" I said and went to her side. "Mom, let me take you to Aunt Diane's place, You should stay with her."

"Why would she want to do that?" Spencer said, frowning at me. "She's my wife. She stays with me."

"I'll just stay here," my mother said when Spencer got her to her bed, her voice so tired she sounded as if she was going to fall asleep while she was still speaking. She rolled onto her side and that was it.

"You're a monster," I said to Spencer when he left the bedroom. I followed him into the hallway. "I could charge you with assault."

"Go ahead and try," he replied. "I've told the police about you. How you steal from your mother. How you take her money and never visit. Who do you think they're going to believe, you or me?"

"You bastard," I said, barely able to speak. I stormed out of the house, tears in my eyes, determined to talk to someone about my mother's safety.

I couldn't go to Graham. He was still learning how to walk again and use his left hand to do things, because his right arm was in a cast. He couldn't talk well because his jaw was wired.

Would the cops really not believe me?

When I got to the car, James was waiting by the door.

"Are you all right?" he asked when he saw my tears.

"Let's go," I said.

He closed the door behind me and got inside, driving off. "Back to the warehouse?"

I nodded, not able to speak.

My life had fallen into pure shit.

WHEN WE ARRIVED BACK at the safe house, I practically ran into the building, taking the freight elevator up, hoping that Hunter wasn't there so I didn't have to talk to him. When I got to the top floor, I entered the hallway and then tried the door. It opened and George was standing there, waiting for me.

"You all right, Celia?" he asked, his expression full of concern. He must have seen my face on the security cameras and knew I'd been crying.

"Oh, I'm fine, George, really," I said, wiping my eyes and cheeks. "Just my bastard of a stepfather is all. Nothing I haven't dealt with a hundred times before." I forced a smile and tried to walk past him, but he stopped me.

"Your neck," he said and pointed.

I felt my neck, which was sore and realized I must have a bruise there from Spencer's hands. "It's nothing," I said, not wanting a fuss to be made. "I'm going to have a bath."

"You sure?" George said. "Is big bruise. Did your stepfather do to you?"

I nodded. "We had a fight," I said, and went to the washroom, waving George off. "Like a thousand others. I'm fine."

I turned back to see George before I closed the door. He was frowning. "Really, George," I said, smiling once more even though I felt like crying. "I'm fine. Don't tell Hunter, whatever you do."

He shook his head like he thought I was being foolish, but I didn't need any fuss made. I would call my Aunt Diane and tell her I wanted my mom to have a day nurse or something to watch over her. She was too doped up. I was afraid she'd overdose. But first, I wanted to soak in the bath and recover from my run-in with Spencer.

The monster.

CHAPTER 28

CELIA

I SOAKED IN THE BATH, enjoying the same scented bath salts I had used for Hunter's bath that night. He must have had them brought over from his apartment. I wondered whether he had done it to bother me or if he had really enjoyed the scent—and the bath itself.

I didn't know what to think about Hunter.

He seemed like he cared—some of the time—by showing concern for my welfare, protecting me, providing security for me. At the same time, the fact he was spying on me gave me a bad feeling, like he was tipping over into stalker territory. Yes, he was an expert in security, and I knew he provided security for the Romanov family, but still, it was creepy having him—or George—watching me 24/7, even if it somewhat comforted me to know they could respond immediately if anything threatened me.

I guess I was just confused about how to feel.

Most of all, I was confused about this relationship with Hunter. He'd sworn off trying to force me to pleasure him. I was glad, but once again, I was also somewhat disappointed. I still had a great deal of desire for Hunter. That wouldn't change, even if he did horrible things. He would still cause my body to respond with only a touch or a glance. But he wasn't the honorable man I'd known him to be.

I finished my bath and got out of the tub. After brushing my hair out, I stared at my reflection in the mirror. Red marks were clearly visible on my neck where Spencer had choked me. On my cheek where he slapped me. Would he have killed me if my mother hadn't stumbled down the stairs to find us? Or would I have been able to successfully fight him off? I'd managed to kick him a few good times while he was choking me, but it hadn't seemed to faze him at all. He really was like a madman with his hands around my neck.

I had to do something about it, and get my mother out of there. I had to call my Aunt Diane and ask her to help. Graham was unable to do anything. I didn't want to talk to Hunter about it for fear he might go ballistic.

I wrapped a towel around myself and went to the bedroom area to get ready for bed before Hunter returned—if he returned. I suspected he wouldn't, given his promise to stop demanding sex from me.

Of course, while I was searching through my clothes, he marched into the apartment and went right over to where George was sitting in the corner office.

Great. George was certain to tell Hunter about my injuries, such as they were.

I grabbed my nightgown and robe and tried to rush back to the bathroom, but Hunter came over and stopped me before I could close the bathroom door.

"Let me see," he said, taking hold of my arm and preventing me from slipping inside the bathroom. "What did that sonofabitch do to you?"

I stopped and stood there, my clothes draped over my arm, a towel around my body, and let him examine me. There was no use fighting. Hunter was taller and stronger than me.

"We got into an argument," I said. "I may have told him he was a fucking bastard."

Hunter touched my neck, shaking his head slowly while he examined the marks Spencer left there.

"That fucking bastard," he said, his voice low, menacing. "I'll kill him."

"Don't do anything stupid, Hunter," I said, fearful that he'd rush out and beat Spencer up. As much as that might personally make me happy, I didn't want Hunter to get into trouble over what happened. "Remember who he is. He's the DA. No one is going to believe it. He told me he'd already talked trash about me to the police. They think I'm a thief who's stealing money from my mother."

"He told you that?"

I nodded, tears springing to my eyes now that I had time to process that fact. "Yes. Who do you think they'll believe—Spencer or me?"

Then I covered my eyes with a hand and cried. I didn't care anymore that Hunter could see me crying like a baby. It hurt that Spencer hated me so much that he would lie about me like that.

Why did Spencer's opinion of me still matter so much? He'd always been such a bastard to me... In the beginning, when he first started seeing my mother, he was so nice to us—to Graham and me. I had no idea what I did to change that, but once he moved in, after mom got back from the hospital, he changed.

He started policing us like he was our own father. Our own father had just died and I was not willing to let Spencer order me around.

Graham tried to get along with Spencer, but I would not let him tell me what to do. I spent a lot of time in time-out or grounded because I refused when he ordered me around.

It had been years and years of anger and rebellion on my part.

Hunter took me in his arms, holding me against his body while I cried. His tenderness made me cry even harder, for it was the first real affection anyone had shown me for a long time. In fact, it was the first time in months anyone other than Amy had hugged me.

"It's okay, it's okay," he murmured, his face in my hair. He squeezed me more tightly and I let loose, crying harder than before. Finally, I began to regain control over myself, wiping my eyes and face with a hand.

"I'm sorry." I tried to hide my face from him because I knew my eyes would be red and swollen. Even at that moment, I didn't want Hunter to see me ugly-cry. I didn't have much pride remaining, given my debt to him, but I had some.

"Shh, shh," he whispered. "From the looks of those bruises, he could have killed you, Celia. He could have killed you."

"He didn't," I said, thinking of how his hands had felt around my neck. "Luckily, my mother was awake enough to come downstairs to his lair and save me. But he threatened me. There's nothing I can do but try to get her out of there. I'm worried about her, Hunter. I'm afraid he might hurt her."

"I don't blame you," he said softly. "We could put her into a safe house somewhere. Get her 24/7 nursing care."

I glanced up at him finally, surprised that he offered. "You'd do that?"

He shook his head. "Of course I would," he said, and I could hear the emotion in his voice. "She's your mother and Graham's mother. You two were my only friends for all those years..."

Then he kissed me, the kiss tender. It surprised me, given his earlier declaration that he wouldn't touch me again and if anything was going to happen between us, it would be me asking, not him taking.

I didn't kiss him back, but neither did I pull away. Finally, he broke the kiss and wiped tears off my cheeks with a thumb.

"Will you be okay?" he asked. "I have to go somewhere. Take care of some business. George will be here with you."

"I'll be fine," I said and forced a smile. Then, I frowned, wondering what business he had to take care of at that time of night. "Where are you going?"

Hunter turned to me when he got to the door. "I've got some business, that's all. Don't worry about me. George," he said and turned to George. "Can I speak with you downstairs?"

George nodded and gave me a smile. "I be right back, Celia."

I nodded and watched as the two of them left the apartment, for another floor. I hadn't yet had a chance to explore the building and so I had no idea what else was in the building, but I assumed Hunter owned the entire place.

I went to the bathroom and changed, then crawled into my bed to nurse my wounds. I lay in the late afternoon dimness, the only light coming from the monitors in George's office space and a hanging light over the island in the kitchen.

I wondered what Hunter was doing and where he was going, but I had been so upset over what happened to me and how Spencer treated me that I quickly fell asleep.

CHAPTER 29

Hunter

"I'M GOING to kill the bastard."

George gave me a look of exasperation and shook his head. "I know you want, but would not be best thing. How can you help Celia if you are in jail? Think for moment. What can you do to keep her safe and get him justice?"

I paced the empty warehouse floor and considered. "I'll talk to my handler in the FBI, and see what they have for evidence. What I saw in Alexandria should count for something. Even if he wasn't directly involved, the fact that he still owns that building should mean he gets charged with owning a business that was used for child prostitution or something. Plus, there's the tapes. That's evidence of, at a minimum, production of child pornography. My handler will know."

George nodded, apparently satisfied that I wasn't going to go off half-cocked and kill Spencer in a rage. My blood was much cooler after talking to George. But I would go to Spencer and deliver a beating. I would punch him in the face and make him regret that he hurt Celia earlier that night.

No one could blame me for that. I had pretty much carte blanche in terms of rules of engagement with the enemy—my handler in the FBI said as much. I could do what I needed to fit in with the Romanovs and they'd only make a show of punishing me if I got caught.

I accepted that risk. I was willing to sacrifice my life for my fellow Marines if needed over in Iraq and Afghanistan. I figured stopping Spencer and his fellow worms would be worth the risk. I'd do what had to be done for the greater good, even if it meant I spent some time in solitary confinement to make it look like I was a real thug.

"You go back upstairs," I said to George.

"Where you going?"

"I'm going over there to punch his face in," I replied. "He deserves at least that much attention from me, even if I can't kill him outright."

"That could be dangerous, Hunter," George said and I could hear in his voice that he didn't like the idea. "Don't lose control."

"I won't. He's a worm. He'll crumple at the first blow, believe me. I know his type."

I went to the stairwell to take the stairs to the street. "Watch out for Celia. If anyone shows up at the warehouse for any reason, don't let them in without contacting me first."

"Who you think would come here? Who knows about?" George asked, frowning.

"No one," I said. "Just the crew and my handler."

"Okay," George said and nodded. "I watch Celia. She was very upset. You should come back, not leave her alone for whole night."

"I'll be back."

I ARRIVED at the house where Celia's mother and Spencer lived, parking a half block away and walking quietly up to the house and around the back to what I expected would be a rear entrance. I was right—there was a sliding screen door leading off to a patio. The yard was fenced, and I expected that if Spencer decided to run, I could catch him before he was able to get out the back gate. I checked out the fence, to see any other escape routes, and then I went back around to the front door and rang the doorbell.

There was no answer, so I rang it again.

Finally, I saw the outline of a figure through the frosted glass pane in the door and realized someone was peering out the eyehole.

"What do you want?" came a male voice. Spencer.

"I need to talk to you about Celia," I said.

"What's the problem with her?" he asked, not opening the door.

"I don't want to talk on the front porch. Let me in. It's private."

"You really think I'm that stupid?" Spencer replied, laughing. "Go away, little boy."

"She's been badly hurt," I said, trying to sound really upset. "She wanted me to talk to you."

"Get lost before I call the police. You're not here about Celia. You should know one of my staff is here. My assistant, Stuart. He's a witness."

"No, you're right," I said, stalling for time. "I'm not here about Celia. I have something you might want to see," I said, trying to think what I could do to get him to open the door. Then it came to me. "I got it at the cabin in Alexandria. You know, the one near the bay?"

"What cabin?" he said, but now his voice wavered. "I don't own a cabin in Alexandria."

"Oh, really?" I said. "That's funny, because I saw the property title and it's clearly in your name. I have a tape here that I found there. In the room in the basement? In a locked cupboard? You might want to see this. Your assistant might want to see it was well. In fact, your entire office might want to see it."

I reached to my jacket and patted my pocket meaningfully, as if I really had something in it.

When he didn't respond, I smiled. I heard him talking to someone, his voice hushed and soon, the door opened and a pasty-faced young man came out, slipping on a jacket.

"Stuart, I presume?" I said, smiling coldly.

"Yes," he said. "I know you're here and I know who you are, in case anything happens to Mr. Grant."

"Go home," I said and turned back to the door, which was closed once more, but I suspected that Spencer would be so curious about what I had, so worried about what it could be, that he'd let me in. I was counting on it.

Once Stuart left, his car backing down the driveway and driving off down the street, I turned back to the door.

"You can send me away, but I thought you and I could negotiate about this tape. We could find a mutual price. If not, I can always take it to the police."

Good, that would make him open the door. He'd think I was just a thug wanting to extort money from him instead of a thug wanting to beat his face to a pulp.

He opened the door and I pushed inside, knocking into him in the process before closing the door behind me. The force sent Spencer sprawling onto his back.

"What the fuck?" he said, struggling up to his feet. "What did you do that for? I let you in." He frowned, adjusting his clothing. "Show me the tape."

"You think I'm that stupid?" I said, and then I ploughed him one with a right hook that struck squarely on the chin. It knocked him back three steps and he ran into the back of the sofa, holding his hands up in protection—and maybe supplication—but I didn't let that stop me.

"This is for Celia," I said and punched him again, striking him in the gut. He grabbed his stomach and bent over. Then, I hit him in the nose. By now, he was cowering, blood pouring out of his nose, which I assumed I had broken. "And this," I said, holding up a fist, "this is for all the little girls you hurt."

Then I punched him one last time. That punch sent him back over the sofa and he crashed onto the floor. I stood and watched, my heart pounding in my chest. I hoped I hadn't killed him, but I couldn't be sure. I usually knew my limit in a fight, but I was still furious about Celia. About Sean. About Donny. About everything that he had ever done to Graham and Celia and everyone he hurt all those years...

I went over to where he lay and turned him over. He was conscious and held up his hands over his face.

"No, please!" he cried, blubbering like a baby. "Don't kill me."

I saw Celia's mom standing in the doorway, or should I say leaning there. She looked like a corpse, her skin grey, her hair a mess. She was dressed in a long nightgown and robe, slippers on her feet.

"What are you doing?" she whispered, seemingly unable to raise her voice up enough to really speak.

"I was just meting out justice," I said and gave Spencer a kick in the ribs. Not hard enough to injure him seriously, but hard enough to hurt. "He's lucky I didn't kill him outright. He deserves it."

Then I went over to her, because she looked like she might fall over. "You should pack up your things and come with me."

"Who are you?" she asked. "I'm going to call the police."

"I'm Hunter," I said, surprised she didn't recognize me, but I'd been *persona non grata* for years. "Celia may have spoken to you about me before. I was Graham's friend. Celia's staying with me at my apartment. I'm protecting her. She wants you to come and get away from Spencer."

She frowned and backed away. "Spencer told me about you. You're with the mafia."

"There's a lot you don't know," I said, frustrated that she believed all Spencer's lies. "Celia's staying with me. Call her if you want. I can wait."

"I'm not coming with you," she said, shaking her head, her eyes wide.

I shrugged and went to the door, deciding to leave. Before I left, I turned to her. She was over beside Spencer, who had rolled over and was grimacing.

"I'm calling the police right now," she said and grabbed a portable phone off its stand.

"Don't call," Spencer said, holding his hand up to her. "I'll deal with this. You go back to bed."

She put the phone down and waited while Spencer stood up, a hand to his bloody nose.

That was how I left him, going to his sick and drug-addicted wife for comfort, who was herself barely able to stand up. I didn't want to leave her there, but there was only so much you could do to help some people. They had to choose their own hell. She hadn't chosen hers—it had been thrust on her when her husband was killed in a car crash and she was disabled by chronic pain. Spencer had been right there, waiting to take over and she was probably happy to have a man look after her.

I walked down the street to my car, knowing that Spencer wouldn't be calling the police about the assault. He thought I had a tape of him molesting little girls, and would probably pack a bag and leave for Malaysia if he was smart. We'd see how smart he really was or if he was stupid enough to think he could talk or bluster or abuse his way out of the mess he was in.

I had a feeling I should prepare a room at the warehouse for Celia's mother, and soon. I knew Spencer's type. He was a coward, full of bravado when standing behind his desk or when in control over a child, but when faced with the reality of his crimes, he'd run.

It would be up to Celia—with my help—to clean up the mess he left behind.

I COOLED DOWN CONSIDERABLY on my way back to the warehouse. As I drove, I thought about what I would do, and how I would approach turning Spencer in.

Given the evidence of child prostitution I found at the cabin in Alexandria, I knew something would stick to Spencer.

He'd be arrested and charged with making child pornography at a minimum based on the tapes I found and collected—and who knew what else there was in that cabin. I had told my handler about it, and he promised to send a team out to collect evidence but it would take a while to get a warrant for search and seizure of evidence. I wasn't sure if the place would be wiped clean by then, but before I'd left that day, I had taken some evidence with me that I could use for leverage if I needed it.

The FBI worked at its own pace on cases, so I had to let things go and let them take care of what needed to be done to bring the guilty parties to justice.

BY THE TIME I got back to the warehouse, I was almost calm. I parked the vehicle at the rear of the building, checking in with the sentry who was responsible for the alleyway, and then sat in silence for a moment, thinking of what I'd do next. What was my move with Celia? Seeing her with wounds on her neck had almost made me homicidal. I knew she mattered more to me than just an easy fuck. That much was clear now. I tried to keep a distance from her, tried to treat her like a mere fuck toy, but that had obviously failed.

I wanted her.

I wanted her to be mine and not just to pay back a debt. Not just obeying my orders.

I wanted her to want me back just as much as I wanted her.

I was in deep.

CHAPTER 30

Hunter

I TOOK the freight elevator up to the third-floor apartment and let myself in. George was in his office space, watching the video feed of the building and surrounding area. He was already packing up when I arrived at the desk, expecting that I'd be staying the night.

"I go downstairs and sleep," he said, nodding when he saw me.

"I hope the bed downstairs is comfortable enough for a sultan," I said. "I feel bad that you were forced out of this space. I initially intended it for you."

He shrugged and made a face. "I am old soldier. I am used to hard living. This is vacation compared to some places I have slept."

"Thanks," I said and clapped him on the back. "Is she asleep?"

George nodded. "She went right to bed, and I have heard no peeps out of her."

"I'll call you tomorrow when I need you."

Then he left me with Celia and I watched the video feed as he took the elevator and went to the first-floor apartment that had been hastily furnished for his use when I was at the apartment. It wasn't nearly as nice as the top floor, but as George said, it would do. We were both solders, and had slept in the worst places possible—on dusty back roads in Afghanistan and Iraq, beneath oily and greasy armored vehicles, in holes we'd dug in the ground.

A soft bed in a warehouse was like heaven in comparison.

I removed my shoes and walked as quietly as possible to the bed and watched Celia, wondering if she was awake or was really sleeping. Her breathing was slow and deep so I assumed she was truly asleep.

I left her there and went to the bathroom, stripping off my clothes for a shower. I needed to wash off the day's sweat and dust, and most of all to wash off the sick feeling I had from dealing with Spencer.

Then I went to the kitchen, with only a towel wrapped around my waist, and had a long drink of orange juice. I needed something stronger but didn't want to drink. I didn't want to lose control. I'd have to be completely in control of myself if I was to successfully deal with Celia and her issues.

I grabbed a bottle of water out of the refrigerator and then switched off the extra lights, leaving only a single light on in George's office. Finally, I went to the bed where Celia was sleeping and stood in silence for a few moments, watching her, listening to her breathing to see if she was awake. She seemed to be sleeping so I slipped off my towel and slid under the covers and into the bed beside her. She didn't wake up, so I lay there quietly on my side facing her back, and tried to go to sleep.

Of course, lying naked in bed with her beside me had only one possible conclusion—a raging hard-on. I wanted to slip closer to her and pull her against me, wake her up for a nice long fuck, but that was my man-brain talking, and not my neo-cortex. She'd had a very bad day, week, and probably life since her father died and Spencer moved in. The last thing she needed was some horndog man pestering her when she really needed understanding and patience.

So I decided to let things wait until she came to me. I'd be patient. I knew she'd been through hell, with Graham's attack and everything that happened after. So, instead of trying to wake her up and arouse her enough that she'd want to have sex, I decided to try to sleep. I sighed, nestled down into the pillow, and tried to blank my mind of anything to do with Celia's delicious body—a body that I had come to know much more intimately over the past while, and instead thought about my next move with Spencer and with Victor and Sergei Romanov.

After what felt like an hour, I turned over and lay on my back, my erection having died a natural death after focusing on business rather than pleasure. I was almost asleep when Celia turned over, the sheets rustling. I kept my eyes closed and tried not to respond, but I heard her sharp intake of breath and knew she'd awoken to find me in bed beside her.

Now what would she do?

We lay there in silence for a moment, and I thought she might pretend to be asleep, probably hoping not to wake me.

Then to my surprise, she spoke, her soft voice almost a whisper. "Are you awake?"

I turned over to face her, but kept the space between us. I could barely see her face in the darkness, but could just make out the curve of her cheek, and a brief glint of light in her eyes.

"Yes," I said, keeping my voice low. "Sorry I woke you. I tried to be as quiet as I could."

"I hope you didn't do anything rash."

I smiled. "Me? Do something rash? I'm insulted."

I caught her smile even in the dim room, and a surge of something went through me.

"I mean, rash like killing my bastard of a stepfather."

I shook my head. "No, I didn't kill him, but I did give him a beating."

"Hunter!" she said, her voice shocked. "You beat him?" She rose up and turned on the light beside the bed. She looked deliciously seductive in the low light from the tiny lamp, her hair mussed, her eyes sleepy.

"He's fine. Maybe a broken nose, but nothing he didn't deserve. I should have sent him to the hospital, considering everything he's done." I held out my hand, and saw that the knuckles were scraped pretty badly. "I think I injured myself in the bargain."

She reached out and took my hand, holding it up in front of her face. "Oh, God, Hunter..."

Then, she kissed my knuckles.

She actually kissed my injured hand.

She turned my hand over and kissed my palm and then looked in my eyes.

"Thank you," she whispered.

"For what?" I replied, my throat constricting.

"For everything," she said. Then, she crawled over to my side of the bed and pushed me onto my back, lying on top of me, her mouth finding mine.

I didn't fight.

Why would I fight the one thing I had wanted for most of the past five years?

Celia.

Her body on top of mine made me instantly hard as a rock. I wrapped my arms around her and pulled her tightly against me, grinding my hips up so she knew how much I wanted her.

How much I needed her.

We kissed, our mouths devouring each other, her fingers gripping my hair like she needed me desperately.

Then she sat up and pulled her nightgown off to reveal her beautiful curves, full and rounded breasts, her nipples hardening in the cool air. I couldn't help but reach up and cup them with my hands, admiring their heavy fullness, my thumbs and fingers tweaking her nipples. I sat up and took one into my mouth, sucking firmly, the nub hardening against my tongue. In response, she moaned and arched her back, her eyes closing.

"Oh, God, I need you," she whispered. When I lay back, she leaned down and kissed me once more. "Fuck me, Hunter."

I didn't make her say please.

Instead, I did everything I could to please her. It should have been me begging her, because no matter how much I tried to deny it to myself, I wanted her. I'd always wanted her.

With every woman I'd been with since that first night with her, back before I joined the Marines, I'd compared them to Celia. None could measure up.

She needed me. She'd been through so much shit, with Graham being beat up, with the loan shark threats, the loss of her inheritance, and Spencer's abuse, she needed pleasure to blank her mind of all of it.

I was happy to provide her with it. I may not have been her first, or even twentieth, choice when it came to a lover, but I'd do.

I rolled her over onto her back and kissed her deeply, my hand roaming over her body, from one lush breast to her softly rounded hip, to the lips of her sex, which I parted with my fingers to find her hard little clit. She moaned into my mouth when I stroked it, opening her thighs to accommodate my hand. I pressed more deeply, pushing my fingers inside to stroke her and felt her body clench around me.

"So hot," I whispered in her ear. "So wet for me."

She pressed her hips up, hungry for sensation. I didn't deny her.

I kissed a trail down her jaw to her collar bone and lower, claiming one nipple while I thumbed her clit, circling it slowly. I moved lower, licking my way down her belly to her pussy. I glanced up, enjoying the sight of her body arching with each stroke of her g-spot, her body trembling with lust.

"I'm going to eat you," I said, smiling as she gripped the sheets in her fists, pressing her hips up to meet my hand. "I'm going to make you come with my tongue."

She licked her lips but said nothing, her eyes closed, her focus entirely on my fingers. Then I licked her clit while I kept my fingers inside of her, stroking inside her with two fingers while I stroked her clit with my tongue.

"Oh, God," she gasped, and it wasn't long before I felt her body clenching around my fingers as her orgasm began, her body shuddering. When she reached down and tried to pull my head away, I knew she'd had enough of my tongue and fingers.

I pulled away, letting her recover a bit.

Usually, I'd make her suck me for a while, warm me up even more, but this time, I didn't. I was already harder than rock and dripping. I wouldn't wait. I couldn't wait.

"Are you safe?" I asked, because I didn't have a condom on me.

"Yes," she said. "I'm on the pill. Are you safe?"

I nodded. "I've been tested."

Then, I pushed inside of her silky wetness, the sensation so amazing, my eyes almost rolled back into my head.

"Oh, God, you're so wet, so tight," I said, unable to help myself. I stroked inside of her, pleasuring myself while I watched her body beneath me, her breasts jiggling in the most delicious way. Her eyes were half-lidded, her face flushed from her orgasm, and I thought at that moment that she was the most beautiful creature I'd ever seen.

I wanted to make her orgasm again, so as hard and ready as I was, I delayed, pulling out and stroking the head of my cock over her clit once more. She closed her eyes in response and I knew she could come again when she thrust up to meet me each time I did. I fucked her like that for a while, two or three thrusts inside of her, then two or three against her clit, and soon, she was focused once more, her body tensing.

"Come for me," I growled, my own orgasm nearing.

She met me thrust for thrust, her eyes open and focused on mine and then she did come, her eyes closing, her body tightening around my cock, her head thrown back.

"Oh, oh, oh..."

That did it for me and I rammed into her, pounding into her tightness as she clenched around me, the white-hot pleasure surging through my body as I ejaculated again and again...

I fell on top of her, breathing hard, my face pressed into her neck as I recovered.

"Fuck," I said, my cock still pulsing, the pleasure still intense. Then, I relaxed completely, my arms beside her face, watching her recover. I kissed her finally, my desire slaked for now, but I knew even at that moment that I'd want her again and again so I could watch her pleasure, feel her body clenching around my cock, her body shuddering in ecstasy…

So much for my plans to use her and make her serve *my* needs.

IT TOOK QUITE a while before Celia fell asleep. For the first hour, she tossed and turned, flipping first on her side facing me and then her back, with a pillow over her face, then to her side facing the room. Finally, she fell asleep facing the bathroom, her back to me. I could tell by the sound of her breathing, slow and even.

I took the opportunity to get up and go to the can and wash up. Being around her had its pleasures and frustrations, one of which was always being semi-hard at the prospect of fucking her. I decided I'd get George up to watch Celia while I went out for a run along the waterfront to burn off some of my excess energy.

I took out my cell after I finished washing up. "Come up and stay with her for a while," I said, trying like hell to keep my voice low so I didn't wake her. "I need to go out and get some fresh air."

"Be right up."

I sat in George's small office space with my eyes closed, and waited, wondering what would happen now that Spencer knew I had dirt on him and could destroy his life if I chose. Would he come after me, threaten me, or try to get the evidence and destroy it? Would he run?

When George entered the apartment, I stood and stretched. Usually, sex made me sleepy, but tonight, after seeing what Spencer did to Celia, after punching him out, and after fucking her, I had too much energy.

George peered at me when he arrived. "Are you OK?"

"Yeah, I'm fine. I need to go for a run or I'll never sleep."

George stood beside the door while I tied my runners and shook his head. "I don't like you going out by yourself."

"I have to," I said and waved him off. "I'll be fine. I'll go out the back."

I did, taking the exit next to the alley and then a parking lot on the other side of the street, walking around the building in the pitch black to the boardwalk. The wind had died down, and now, nearing midnight, I inhaled the moist cool air and started running.

After about fifteen minutes, I had to stop, my heart rate too high. I sat on a bench along the boardwalk, catching my breath, staring straight up at the clear sky overhead. A wind had picked up blew through the bare trees, the rustle of the few remaining leaves the only sound in the night. The city of Boston had over a half million people living within its boundaries, and the Greater Boston area was home to over four million. There was enough ambient light even here along the bay so that the stars were dim.

I picked out the location of a star Celia had shown me that night more than five years earlier. I still remembered it, and almost everything from that night and the nights after, before she told me thanks but she'd found someone better. Graham had told me that she thought I wasn't in her league despite my family's wealth. That she would prefer someone not embroiled in organized crime, considering the fact she wanted to go into criminal law and be a prosecutor like her father before her. That Spencer had bought her off, ensuring she didn't have to work if she never saw me again. She chose Grey and she chose money over me.

I breathed in deeply, trying not to think of that. Even now, even after everything, it still hurt.

My pulse had slowed considerably and now I just sat there, shivering despite the heat from my run. I thought that if she came to me, wanted me, asked me to fuck her, I'd be satisfied. I thought I'd feel like I had won something—validation.

I didn't.

I covered my eyes. God, I wanted her.

CHAPTER 31

CELIA

I WOKE ALONE, and turned over, reaching out to feel how warm the bed was so I had some idea of how long Hunter had been gone. The bed was cold, so I knew he must have left soon after we had sex.

I didn't know what to think of things at that moment, my emotions all confused and my gut slightly sick with worry and at the same time, excited that what was happening between us felt like more than just servicing Hunter's needs.

I didn't want to be merely an easy way for him to get off. I wanted to be the one he turned to because he wanted and needed me.

Me...

His shell was tough, though, and it was hard to read him. I figured that tough shell was from years fighting and taking body blows, and then his time in the military. You had to be exceptionally tough to be a Marine and to go into Special Operations Forces, no matter what branch of the military you were in.

Those soldiers were the elite of the elite, tough in mind and body.

Hunter was tough, but was he hard to the core?

That's what I didn't know.

It felt as if he was softening towards me. The fact he got so upset after seeing my bruises suggested that he felt more for me than he let on. I was more than just a fuck toy, like he said I was. It seemed personal to him because he cared about me as more than just a convenient receptacle for his dick.

I didn't want to hope too much. That way lay disappointment and heartbreak.

So, instead of hoping too much that Hunter had changed, and now actually felt some semblance of affection for me besides enjoying my body, I turned over and tried to go back to sleep. Of course, that was a hopeless venture. Now, my mind was working overtime wondering how Spencer was and what my mother thought of Hunter showing up and punching Spencer's lights out.

I wished I could have witnessed Hunter punching Spencer. It would have felt like payback and like justice for all those times Spencer had hit me or Graham. I didn't really want Hunter to become one of those men who beat people up without thought, but he was trained as a fighter and a soldier. I had to accept that part of him. As long as I saw the other part, the tender part that touched my bruises and felt rage that I had been hurt, I could accept it.

Even though it was only six, I got up instead of lying in bed for another hour with my eyes wide open, and went to the bathroom to have a shower and get ready for the day. When I was done, I dressed and tried to make myself somewhat presentable. Then I went to the kitchen where I found a pot of fresh coffee and a note from George that he was downstairs and there were fresh eggs in the fridge.

I smiled and took them out, and fixed myself some scrambled eggs, toast, and orange juice to go along with my coffee. Then I sat at the island and ate, reading over a copy of the morning paper, and wondering where Hunter was this early in the morning, and why he hadn't stayed with me.

After about an hour, the door opened and George came in. He smiled when he saw me and came over to the island, peering over my shoulder at the paper.

"How you doing, Celia? Did you have good sleep?"

"Yes," I said, smiling at him, unable to resist liking him despite the fact he was a Russian and, perhaps, a thug at heart. "I woke up early and couldn't get back to sleep. Where's Hunter?"

George shrugged. "He went out for run and then went to gym to do some work. Couldn't sleep. He said he would be back later. You have class today?"

I nodded, and thought about my schedule. "At ten. But I'd like to stop by the hospital before, if I could, to see how my brother is doing. Would that be okay? Is James available?"

George nodded. "Of course. I call. You tell me when you're ready and I tell him."

"Thanks," I said. "Before you go," I said, feeling like I wanted to talk some more to George about Hunter, "tell me more about how you met Hunter. I know it was in the military in Afghanistan, and that you were a mercenary who worked with his unit, but how did you two become friends?"

George stopped and pursed his lips in thought. "When you fight with a man, side by side, risking life, you become blood brothers," he said and glanced at me.

"Do you have a family?"

"Me? No. I am old soldier who can't go home and sit quietly. Have war in blood. I meet Hunter. We do rescue for resupply convoys attacked by enemy. We spent time together when we both have leave. We become good friends. I trust him. He trust me."

I didn't really understand the military hierarchy, or what role mercenaries had in the war, so I nodded and let it go.

"He is good man, Celia," George said.

"You've said that before. If he's such a good man, why is he back involved with the family business? He's working directly for the Romanov family."

"He is doing legitimate security work for Romanovs. No mafia stuff."

I nodded. "It surprised me he was willing to quit the Marines," I replied. "He always talked about getting the family business out of organized crime."

"He is doing best he can," George said, his tone a bit impatient, like he resented me even questioning Hunter. I brushed it off. If George was at all involved with the Russians, he would be defensive.

"I hope so," I said. "Thanks for the fresh eggs," I didn't want him to be mad at me so I decided to drop it.

"Is no problem," he said and waved me off. "I go do work now. You let me know when is time to go."

"I will."

I watched as George got himself a cup of coffee and then went to his little office space with the bank of video screens. After I cleaned up my dishes, I went to my own little office and sorted through my files to find the articles I needed to read before class and then tucked them away into my book bag.

I went to George. "I'm ready now," I said, checking my watch. It was almost eight. "I'll stay with Graham for an hour and then after my first class, maybe I can swing by the dorm and see if my friend Amy is there. She has class with me after. We could go together."

"Sure thing," George said and picked up his cell. "I call James. You can go right down to loading dock. He will be waiting."

"Thanks, George," I said. "See you later."

He nodded and spoke into the phone. I lugged my book bag and threw on my jacket before taking the service elevator to the main floor. I walked through the empty floor to the loading dock and sure enough, when I opened the rear exit, James and the black SUV were both waiting for me.

I could get used to having a driver.

WHEN I GOT to the hospital, Graham was sitting up in his bed, sipping a bottle of Ensure.

"Is that breakfast?" I asked, horrified, putting my book bag down and giving him a kiss on the cheek.

He nodded and raised his eyebrows. "It will be until I get this jaw unwired. At least it's chocolate fudge."

"Chocolate fudge for breakfast?" I replied, making a face. "That would make me puke."

"You always liked eggs and toast for breakfast," Graham said and smiled. "When Dad used to take us out for brunch after mass, you used to have eggs and sausages and I always had pancakes."

"Mutt and Jeff," I said with a smile, remembering what our father—our real father—used to call us. I always looked up to my big brother, and always wanted to be with him and do things with him. He let me tag along most of the time when he was still young enough not to worry about his reputation with his friends. It endeared him to me in a way that could never be erased, even if he got me into all this trouble because of his bad business deals.

"How are you?" he asked. "You have a bruise on your neck. Not Spencer again?"

I reached up and felt my sore neck, rubbing it gently. "I gave him an earful. He didn't like it. Don't worry," I said with a laugh. "Hunter punched his lights out, apparently."

"Hunter fought Spencer?" Graham said, his eyes wide. He glanced away. "I always thought that of the three of us, Hunter would be the one to get into a fist fight with Spencer. He's the only one with the balls to face up to him. Hunter hated Spencer even before all this happened. Even before Sean died."

"I know," I said and remembered kissing Hunter's bruised and scraped knuckles the previous night and how that had turned into so much more. What would Graham think if he knew what was happening between us? He would be livid, no doubt about it.

"I'm staying at Hunter's safe house."

Graham frowned. "What?"

"After Hunter beat up Stepan, Stepan's cousin picked me up and took me to his restaurant to make a show of force to Hunter. Hunter came and rescued me, with weapons drawn. He said I was at risk and so I'm staying at this big old warehouse with 24/7 security guards and an old Russian mercenary who is providing personal security for me."

"What the fuck, Celia?" Graham said through gritted teeth. He put down his bottle of Ensure and frowned. "When did all this happen?"

"Just this week. I guess Stepan's cousin saw me with Hunter at the club and thought I could be used as leverage. These mobsters seem to be always looking at how they can get one up on each other."

Graham lay back and sighed, glancing out the window. "I'm sorry I did all this to you. It's my fault," he said and turned back. I could see real pain in his eyes.

"There's nothing we can do about it now. This will all blow over soon," I said, remembering what Hunter told me. "Hunter paid off your debt, and he's giving me back my inheritance."

"What?" Graham's eyes widened. "The entire thing?"

I nodded. "Yes. Every penny."

Graham lay back and stared at the ceiling. Then, he turned to face me. "What does he expect in return?"

I shrugged, not certain I wanted to confess just yet. "He's doing it out of loyalty to you and me."

"Just out of loyalty?" His eyes narrowed.

"What else? He hates our family, but he still feels some loyalty to us because of his friendship with you."

That seemed to appease him for the moment so I didn't say any more. I didn't want him to think I was prostituting myself in repayment of his debt. That would infuriate him and make him feel even worse. I wanted him to recover, and if he was really upset and if he hated himself for what he did, that might not be good for his health.

"I don't like the idea of you staying at his safe house, or whatever it is," Graham said. "If he forces you to do anything against your will..."

So Graham's mind went immediately to where Hunter's had...

"I'm not doing anything against my will," I said, my voice firm. "I'm my own person, Graham. You know that."

"Only too well," he said and sighed.

We talked for a while about his physiotherapy, and the second surgery he'd have to have done on his arm because of a problem with the way it was healing. After about an hour, I stood up.

"Well, I better go. My driver will be waiting and I want to stop by and pick up Amy."

"You have a driver?"

"He's on Hunter's staff."

Graham sighed. "I'm sorry that all this happened."

"Don't mention it," I said and kissed him on the forehead, stroking his hair back. "What's done is done. I'm fine. I'm going to class now, and then I'll go by and see Mom."

"Tell her not to worry about coming up to see me," Graham said when I picked up my book bag and started to leave. "I know how hard it is for her to get out."

"I will," I said and waved at him. "I'll stop by later tonight."

"Okay," he said and I turned and left him, feeling a little catch in my throat to see him still so incapacitated. It would be a few weeks before he could go home, so I'd have to be the go-between for my mother, who would be unable to spend much time in the hospital, visiting. I had been surprised she'd gone on the cruise, but it had been on her bucket list. Since they had a special room on the ship for disabled people, she and Spencer had gone as her birthday gift and to celebrate fifteen years of being together.

I'd hated those fifteen years. Fifteen of the worst years of my and Graham's lives. When my father died and my mother turned to Spencer to take over, my own happiness disappeared and Graham and I took comfort in each other's company.

I wished my father and mother had never gone on that trip down to New York City. If they had delayed for even an hour, things—my life—would have turned out completely different.

One bad decision and that was it. That was all it took to change a life.

I knew that now with such clarity that I weighed every decision I had to make as if it might change everything in an instant. One false move and that was it. Game over. I didn't always live up to my goal of thinking twice, looking before I leapt, but I tried.

. . .

349

I WENT TO CLASS, barely able to concentrate on the material. I was looking forward to seeing Amy for our next class so James drove me over to the dorm. I knocked on Amy's door and she opened, peering around the door at me like she was afraid.

"Celia!" she said, her mouth opening. "You're here. I didn't think you'd come today."

"Why not?" I asked as I entered her tiny apartment, a few doors down from my own dorm room.

"Haven't you been listening to the news?"

I frowned and sat down on the sofa across from her flat screen TV. On the screen was a breaking news report showing a wooded area by the bay somewhere along the coast outside Alexandria, Virginia.

"What's this?" I asked, glancing at her face, which was white.

"I was just going to call you again," she said and sat down beside me, one of her arms going around my shoulder. "Spencer's dead."

My eyes flew open and I gasped out loud. "What?"

"I tried to call you a few minutes ago but you didn't answer. I texted you as well."

I removed my phone and stared at it. The battery had died in the night and I didn't think of charging it.

"Oh, my God, my battery died." I showed it to her. Then I turned back to the television. Amy increased the volume so we could listen. "Spencer's dead?"

Of course, my mind went immediately to Hunter. He'd left me in the night and had punched Spencer out the previous day.

Had he killed Spencer?

If he didn't kill Spencer yesterday before he came to me, he could have killed him in the night after he left me...

"Oh, my God," I said as I watched the video footage, taken from a helicopter which was hovering above a path along the bay by Alexandria, Virginia. I remembered that Spencer used to live there, had worked there after he graduated from law school.

According to the news report, his body had been found in a copse of trees by the path. He'd been shot. That was all the news reporter said.

Spencer was shot... He hadn't been beaten to death—so at least that much was true. Hunter hadn't beaten him to death by accident the previous day.

What was Spencer doing in Alexandria? Why had he gone there late at night?

More importantly, where was my mother?

"Give me your phone," I said and reached for it when she grabbed it from the coffee table. "I have to call my mom."

I dialed my mom's cell, and the call went to voice mail right away. I glanced at Amy, panic rising in me. "She's not answering."

I listened to the message and then spoke. "Mom, call me right away and let me know you're okay!"

I didn't know what else to do so I called my Auntie Diane, who lived in New Bedford. She answered right away.

"Hi, Auntie," I said, my heart pounding in my chest. "Have you spoken with my mother?"

"No," she said and I could hear the panic in her voice. "I've been calling her ever since I heard on the news that Spencer was murdered. I've called the police and they're on their way to the house to check."

"Oh, my God," I said. "I can't believe it."

"What was he doing in Alexandria?" she asked, sounding confused. "He hasn't been there for fifteen years."

"I have no idea."

Of course, I had some idea. Hunter had told me he found out something about Spencer from when he lived in Alexandria. He'd asked me questions about whether Spencer had ever sexually abused me, so I had assumed Spencer had done something bad there—child pornography?

I watched in silence as the news report showed a picture of Spencer from stock footage they must have had from cases in which Spencer had been the DA or Assistant DA. They also showed a photo of our family, with Spencer and my mother, Graham and me. It was probably one of the only photos taken of us and it was one I hated because Spencer had his hands on my shoulder. I was frowning.

I wondered who had given them that photo, then remembered that the local paper had done a spread about Spencer when he became Assistant DA back when he and my mother were first together. I'd hated him back then. I hated him now.

He was dead. I couldn't get in touch with my mother.

I called Hunter's number, and listened as the line rang and rang. Finally, it went to voice mail.

"Hunter, it's me, Celia. Have you heard the news? Spencer's dead and I can't get a hold of my mother. Call me right away."

Where was Hunter?

"I don't know what to do," I said, glancing at Amy.

"You can't go to class," she replied.

"Should I call Graham? He should know."

"Do you want to go to your mom's house?"

I nodded and stood up. "James will take me. Come with me," I said and grabbed her hand. "I don't want to go through this alone."

"Let's go."

WHEN WE REACHED THE CAR, James was standing there, waiting. "What's the matter?" he asked when he saw me. "Your face is white as a ghost."

"Can you take me to my mother's place? My stepfather's dead. I need to see if she's okay and she's not answering the phone."

"Sure," he said and opened the door. "You should call Hunter."

"I tried, but there's no answer."

"Call George," he said and I nodded, getting in the rear passenger side. Amy got in the other side and we drove off.

I dialed Hunter's number once more but there was still no answer and it went to voice mail again.

"Hunter, please, call me when you get this."

Then, I dialed George's number. He answered on the second ring.

"George," I said, my mind a blur. "Is Hunter there? He's not answering his phone."

"No, he is not. I haven't talked for several hours."

"When you talk to him, tell him to call me right away."

"What is wrong?"

I took in a deep breath. "My stepfather's dead," I said and closed my eyes.

"Oh, I am sorry," George said, his voice sounding shocked. "Was not Hunter."

"Are you sure?" I said, feeling very bad about the prospect that Hunter may have killed Spencer. "He hated Spencer. He blames Spencer for his brother's death."

"No," George said, his voice a little more certain. "I know. He didn't kill."

"Then where is he?"

"I don't know. He will call soon. Don't worry."

"Tell him to call me," I said and then hung up.

I wasn't sad that Spencer was dead—just shocked and fearful that Hunter had killed him. Fearful that I couldn't get in touch with my mother. Had whoever killed Spencer killed her as well?

Amy took my hand and together, we watched out the windows in silence as the streets of Boston passed by.

END OF BOOK THREE

BAD BOY SAVIOR

THE BAD BOY SERIES: BOOK FOUR

PREFACE

"Let your plans be dark and impenetrable as night, and when you move, fall like a thunderbolt."

Sun Tzu, The Art of War

CHAPTER 32

Hunter

Two months earlier...

Sergei Romanov lived in a bedroom community outside of Boston, tucked in a large acreage with high stone walls and exceptionally tight security.

A driveway led to the front entrance to the mansion, and on each side of the door stood security personnel armed to the teeth. They were better protected than some of the SWAT teams I'd seen in the past, so Sergei meant business. He knew he was in constant danger and made sure nothing and no one got to him that he hadn't already approved.

I stopped my SUV at the guard gate and spoke into a speaker. A small camera watched the entrance, deciding whether to admit me.

"Hunter Saint to see Mr. Romanov."

"I know who you are," came a tired voice with a thick Russian accent. "Please drive in and stop where the guards are waiting."

I nodded at the camera and when the metal doors swung open, I drove through, coming to a halt once my vehicle was fully inside. Three guards with assault weapons stood just to the left. One other guard circled my car with a German shepherd on a leash, the dog no doubt sniffing for explosives or other contraband. Another guard walked around my vehicle with a small mirror on a long pole, checking for bombs under the vehicle chassis.

Once they were sure my car contained nothing untoward, an armed guard wearing sunglasses, bearded and looking like former Spec Ops, leaned in my open side window.

"Please to turn over weapons," he said, gesturing with his chin. "Not allowed on property."

I nodded and removed my sidearm, handing it to him. I kept another in my glove compartment, just in case. "I'm going to lean over and take my other pistol from the glove compartment."

He nodded, watching me closely. I retrieved the Glock and handed it to the guard as well. He took both and then motioned me forward.

Unarmed, and impressed with the security at Sergei's compound, I drove to the front entrance where the other two guards stood, hands on their weapons, barrels pointing to the ground.

Thankfully, they were familiar with security and wouldn't be likely to accidentally shoot anyone. Say what you would about Sergei – he was professional. His security team appeared more suited to a head of state than a hood, but he was a Russian hood, and a big one at that.

I got out of the vehicle and handed the keys to the guard who met me at the stairs. He nodded, and let me pass. The final guard – one of six – motioned me through the door.

Talk about ostentatious...

I grew up with wealth, but nothing even close to this. All my father's and uncle's wealth went right back into the business, and we lived a comfortable but hardly glaringly wealthy lifestyle.

This – this was beyond the pale.

Gilded fixtures, marble floors and walls, dark woods, plush Persian carpets, old Masters-looking paintings on the walls: Sergei was one wealthy Russian.

A well-dressed young man with a goatee and moustache came to meet me. I assumed it was Sergei's secretary or admin person.

"Mr. Romanov is busy. Please to come in and wait in here," he said, ushering me into a small sitting room. Like the entrance, it was plush and resembled something out of Catherine the Great's Russia, not Cambridge, Massachusetts. I roamed the room while I waited, examining the paintings on the dark paneled walls, the huge fireplace of polished oak and stone, the large floor-to-ceiling windows. After about ten minutes, I sat on an ornate couch and took out my cell, wanting to amuse myself with local news while I waited.

Was Sergei making me wait because he could? Or was he truly busy?

Finally, I heard a commotion in the entrance outside my sitting room and saw Sergei himself with four other men, all dressed in expensive business suits. They spoke in Russian amongst themselves, laughing softly at something Sergei said, and then left. At that, Sergei turned and came into the sitting room.

I stood and he extended a hand. "Hunter," he said and we shook. "My apologies for making you wait. A business meeting scheduled before yours went over the allotted time. Please, follow me."

"No problem," I replied. "I was enjoying the art on your walls. They look several hundred years old. Not that I know anything about art."

"You're right. They're by artists from pre-Revolution Russia. I hated the art after the Revolution. Too political for my tastes. This shows the Russian countryside and life before everything went to hell."

I followed him back to a large bright office space, which was in stark contrast to the other room. In front of a huge floor-to-ceiling multi-paned window sat an ornate oak desk. Sergei went behind it and pointed to a plush chair directly in front of the desk.

I waited for him to sit before I took my own seat. He folded his hands on the desk and watched me for a moment.

"So, my spies tell me you want revenge against the DA and the FBI for the death of your brother and the arrest and imprisonment of your uncle."

I was surprised that he got right to the meat of the issue.

"In a nutshell."

He nodded. "I can completely understand that. Your uncle was treated most terribly. Your brother Sean – what a tragedy. Certainly, that demands restitution and vengeance. It would be a simple matter of executing the FBI agent who killed him. I understand that it was an impulsive move on his part, rather than something planned. Your brother's impulse control was not as good as it could be due to his years of boxing and many concussions?"

"That's right," I said. "But I'm more interested in getting revenge against the DA for trumping up the charges against my uncle. Donny was small potatoes but Grant has had it in for my family for years. He finally found enough dirt to bring a RICO charge or three."

"It's unfortunate. Grant is persistent, if nothing else. But he's also a very small man with a small vision. He wanted revenge for perceived slights by your family, as I understand it. You and his daughter are in love? You are like the Montagues and the Capulets."

I caught the reference to *Romeo and Juliet*. And of course, to his reference to Celia.

"She's just an old friend," I said, trying to downplay how much Celia meant to me.

Sergei nodded, making a face like he believed me and understood she was inconsequential, but we both knew she wasn't. Besides my brother and father, she was everything to me.

I didn't like that these gangsters knew about Celia, but that barn door had been left open long ago and there was nothing I could do to retroactively shut it short of sending Celia away with a new identity. I didn't want to consider that – not yet, at least. I wanted her with me. There was this huge selfish part of me that was too strong and overpowered the more honorable part of me, which should have thought first about protecting her.

I should have sent her away immediately, getting the FBI to give her a new identity as soon as the Romanovs showed an interest in her.

But I didn't. I hoped I wouldn't live to regret that decision, and if I was going to be selfish and keep her in Boston for myself, I'd have to do everything I could to protect her.

"So, what is it you want from me today?" Sergei said. "Why did you ask for this meeting?"

"I want to provide security for your properties. As you may know, I was in the military and did several tours of duty in Afghanistan and Iraq. I have several years of experience providing security for private business in Iraq. I want to get out of the gym business and into security. You have a lot of properties in Boston, around the waterfront. I'd like to bid on the contracts. Get my foot in the door, so to speak."

Sergei made a face and shrugged. "I already have signed contracts with a security company. Tell me why I should use you instead?"

"I wouldn't suggest you break any contracts, but for any new properties, I'd be really pleased to provide services. And when any contracts came up for renewal, I'd like to bid on them."

"Fair enough. What would you do for me in return?"

I frowned, playing dumb. "I'd provide security, of course. Highly skilled operators who would be the best you could hire."

He gave an icy smile. "Like I say, I already have contracts in place. What else could you do for me?"

"What do you need me to do?"

He stood and walked around the desk, leaning against it so he was closer to me, his hands folded.

"I get shipments of… items, shall we say, that need to be warehoused for a time before being sold. You could store them for me. I understand you have several warehouses in the downtown area."

I knew immediately what he meant. He wanted me to store his contraband – most likely guns from Russia, if I knew Sergei Romanov. I'd get the charges if they were discovered by ATF. It was a layer of protection that many gangsters put in place, spreading out the risk.

"I could do that," I said. "What in particular did you have in mind for me to be storing? I'd like to know what I'm getting myself into."

"Very well," he said and went to the door. "Come with me and I'll show you. You might like some of my products for your security business."

We walked down a narrow hallway to a side door and into a large garage where several expensive vehicles were parked – a Porsche, a Mercedes, and a Bentley. The man liked his vehicles. There were about two dozen wooden crates stacked against one wall. A guard stood beside them and nodded when he saw Sergei.

"Open one," he said to the guard.

The guard complied, using a crowbar to pry open a box. Inside was straw and about a dozen weapons. Sniper rifles. I was familiar with them, having trained on them while working for special forces.

"Nice," I said and stepped closer.

Sergei removed one from the crate and handed it to me. A Dragunov sniper rifle used by the Russian military. I checked it out, examining the weapon with keen interest.

"They're beauties," Sergei said as I tested the weapon's weight.

"Very nice," I replied.

"You should take," he said, smiling like he enjoyed seeing me hold one. "I'll sell you them at a good price."

"Why would I need sniper rifles?" I asked, attaching a sight he handed me. "I use semi-automatics in my security business."

"Every man needs at least one sniper. You never know when it might come in handy. Besides, is very good for practice."

I held the weapon and aimed at the far wall, checking the sight and feeling the trigger. The weapon was nice, but I preferred my .300 Win Mag – a weapon preferred by American snipers. I handed it back to him and he replaced it into the crate.

"What other weapons do you sell? I might be interested in something."

"We shall talk again, when I consider what we need. In the meantime, please accept this as a gift from me to you."

He removed a different rifle and scope from the crate, slipping them into a carrying case, and then handed it to me. I accepted. You don't question when a mobster gives you a gift – that much I knew.

I nodded and followed him back to the main entrance where one of his guards stood waiting.

"And now, if you'll excuse me, I have other business to attend to. We'll be in touch about the contracts and anything I need from you."

"Thanks for this," I said and held up the rifle bag.

"My pleasure," he said and waved a hand dismissively.

Then he turned and went back to his office.

I went to the front door and the guard opened it for me. Outside, my SUV stood at the ready, the engine idling. These Russians were on top of things. They'd no doubt checked every inch of my vehicle and probably planted a listening device or GPS tracking device somewhere. I'd have to check it out when I got back to the gym, use one of George's little sniffers to find them. I'd probably leave them in so Sergei could think he was tracking me. I could disable them, but I wanted to keep in Sergei's good graces.

He'd know I'd check for bugs, if I was even the least bit competent. How I handled it would tell him what he needed to know. I'd disable the bugs and then re-enable them, so he knew I was aware of them, but accepted them as part of doing business with him. I just wouldn't use that vehicle anymore for anything I didn't want Sergei to know.

It was a game of chess, this working with the FBI to get in deep with the Russian mob. Luckily, I was a natural at the game. But I couldn't afford to be too proud – as they say, pride goeth before a fall.

And I didn't plan on falling.

CHAPTER 33

CELIA

PRESENT DAY

WE ARRIVED at my mother's house. There were already satellite vehicles outside on the street, and several reporters standing together talking.

"What do I do?" I asked as we pulled up. "I don't want to talk to them."

"Let me escort you," James said from the front of the SUV. "I'll keep them from talking to you."

"My mother must be okay if they released Spencer's name," I said, hoping that my mother had somehow forgot to call me when the police contacted her about Spencer's body being found. But how could she forget? How could she not think of calling me right away as soon as she knew Spencer was dead?

James got out and opened the door to let Amy and me out, then he led us up the driveway to the house. A reporter must have recognized me – he came up to us, sticking his microphone into my face.

"Celia Parker? Can you tell us what you know about your stepfather's death?"

I turned away, and James stepped between me and the reporter. "Ms. Parker's not taking any questions. Please respect her privacy at this sensitive time."

We made it to the door without any other reporters arriving. I tried the door but it was locked. I entered the security code on the pad and the door opened, admitting us into the entrance.

Inside, two uniformed police officers sat in the living room with my mother. She was dressed in a robe and slippers – her usual garb – and looked haggard, her hair a mess, her skin grey.

"Mom," I cried out and ran to her. I sat on the sofa beside her, my arm around her shoulder. "Why didn't you call?"

"I tried," she said, her voice tired. "It said the cellular customer was out of range or something."

Then I realized she must have used my old cell. I was using a new one since I met Hunter.

"Tell me what happened," I said, turning to the two police officers.

"We're waiting for detectives to arrive," one of the cops said. "I'm Constable Roberts. This is Constable Franks. We came by to notify your mother of your stepfather's death and she asked us to stay until the detectives came by. They should be here soon."

I nodded. "You can leave us now, if you want. My friend and I will stay with my mother."

Roberts nodded and the two police officers stood and left us alone.

"Mom, what happened? What did they tell you about Spencer?"

She covered her face. "He was shot," she said, her voice wavering with emotion. "He's dead and has been for hours. He was at Chesapeake Beach for some reason, checking out one of his properties, I imagine. He left right after you and Hunter were here and he never came back. He must have been robbed but I don't know any details. They're still investigating."

My mother seemed unusually clear-headed. The shock of

THE BAD BOY SERIES COLLECTION

Spencer's murder must have pierced through her usual brain fog from the morphine.

"I'm so sorry, mom," I said, squeezing her arm, moving closer. Although I hated Spencer, I knew that my mother loved him. She'd be devastated to learn he was dead. After relying on him for years, she'd be afraid of who would look after her.

"I know you and Graham hated him, but he was my life after your father died."

"I know," I said, not wanting to talk about just how much I hated Spencer or how much Graham did as well. She already knew. It had been a sensitive matter between the three of us since she married Spencer. In Graham's and my minds, he was never our father. We made sure Spencer knew as much.

"Did anyone call Graham?"

My mom nodded. "We tried, but he must have been out of his room. I left a message for him to call me as soon as he got my message."

I called Graham right away, wanting to make sure he heard the news from us, rather than finding out on television that Spencer was dead.

I didn't feel at all sad or bad that Spencer was dead. In fact, there was a part of me that rejoiced. Finally, I could get my mother away from his clutches and get her more help.

While I waited for him to answer, I turned to my mother.

"Have you called Aunt Diane?"

She shook her head. "No," she said. "I didn't think..."

"You should call her. You'll need somewhere to stay. You can't stay alone—"

"Can't you stay with me?" she asked. "You could sleep in your old room."

I shook my head. "No, mom. I'm staying somewhere else. You should go stay with Aunt Diane. Get away from here. There are reporters, and trucks with satellite dishes. They won't leave you alone for a few days. We could sneak you out the back and take you there."

"If you think so."

Graham's phone went to voice mail, so I left a message for him to call me as soon as he could.

Then, I dialed my Aunt Diane's number. She answered on the second ring.

"Hi, Auntie," I said, my voice a bit emotional. "Have you heard the news?"

"No," she said, sounding confused. "What news? I've been in the darkroom all morning. What is it? Is your mom okay? Is Graham worse?"

"No, they're both okay. Spencer's dead. He was shot. That's all I know."

"Oh, thank God," she said and I was shocked to hear her say that. "I mean, I was worried that your mom overdosed or Graham had a complication. So, Spencer's dead? I have to tell you I'm not sad that the bastard is finally gone."

"My thoughts exactly," I said, glad to know that she felt the same way I did.

"God forgive me for saying that, but I hated that bastard right from the start. I tried to tell your mother to leave him but she was so unable to do anything to help herself."

"I know. Listen, speaking of which, can Mom come and stay with you for a few days until we can find some care for her? I can't stay here and she needs help."

"Why can't you stay with her, hun?"

I hesitated. How could I explain things? *There's a Russian mobster who thinks I'm juicy bait to ensnare my gangster lover...*

I couldn't tell her the whole truth.

"I can't tell you now, but I have good reasons."

She hesitated, but then I heard her sigh. "Of course she can come and stay with me. She's my sister. She can sleep in the spare bedroom."

"Good," I said. "Thank you. We'll bring her over after the detectives come and we can get her things together."

We said goodbye and then I turned to my mother, who sat watching me expectantly.

"You'll go and stay with Aunt Diane until we can get someone to come and stay with you."

She nodded. "I'm sorry about all this. I just don't know what to do..."

I put my arm around her and hugged her more tightly.

"Don't worry about anything," I said, kissing her cheek. "I'll make sure you're taken care of."

I glanced at Amy, who sat watching, an expression of sympathy in her eyes.

About ten minutes later, Graham finally called.

"He's dead?" Graham said, his voice shocked.

"Yes," I replied. "Shot twice. He was in Alexandria. That's all I know."

There was silence on the other line for a moment. "Well, I can't say I'm unhappy. I know mom will be devastated but really? I'm glad the bastard's dead."

"I know," I said, unable to disagree. "I'll come by later once I get mom settled at Aunt Diane's."

"Okay," he said and we ended the call.

TWO DETECTIVES ARRIVED about fifteen minutes later. The older man – balding, a paunch barely hidden by his suit jacket, his face red from exertion – introduced himself as Detective O'Grady and his partner as Detective Álvaro. I doubted either man could pass a fitness test, but hoped they were good investigators.

"We think your husband's death was foul play," he said, his elbows on his knees, leaning forward to look in her eyes. "Preliminary analysis suggests he was shot in the head with a high-powered rifle. Another bullet hit him in the chest. He died instantly and suffered no pain."

I grimaced. I watched enough CSI to know that a high-powered rifle was a sniper rifle. That suggested this was not some random murder, or even a robbery gone wrong. It didn't sound like an ex-military former MMA fighter gone nuts and beating him to death in anger. It was deliberate. Two shots? One in the head and one in the chest?

He'd been terminated.

"Is there anyone you can think of who might have had a personal grudge against your husband?" O'Grady asked, his voice calm.

"He was the DA and made a lot of enemies," my mother said. "I have no idea who might want to kill him but he was on the trail of some big Russian mobsters. They're known for being barbaric against their enemies. Spencer always knew he was a target, but he was usually so careful..."

My mother covered her eyes and wept for a moment. The rest of us were silent while she regained her composure.

"The murder took place in a relatively isolated part of Alexandria along the waterfront – a mostly residential part of the city and not much traffic. We've done a preliminary canvas of the area, but so far we have no witnesses and no suspects."

The detectives filled us in on what would happen next – a full autopsy to determine the exact time and cause of death and confirm ballistics, and then his body would be turned over to whatever funeral home we requested. O'Grady promised to keep in touch as the case progressed.

The detectives showed themselves out and then sat looking at each other.

"Are you okay to be going anywhere?" I asked. "We could stay here for a while if you want a shower or anything."

My mother shook her head. "I'm too sick," she said and I knew that she needed some of her morphine to fight the pain. She rustled through her bag and took out a pill for the breakthrough pain, swallowing it and lying back on the sofa.

Amy and I gathered up my mother's personal items – her meds, her makeup and toothbrush, as well as some clothes – and then we snuck her out the back way and into the waiting SUV. James had taken a circuitous route through the neighborhood to try to escape notice by the press, who were still outside the house on the street. Once she was in her seat and I'd fastened the belt for her, we drove to my Aunt Diane's house. Amy and James helped me get her inside, and we sat and had a cup of tea and talked about the whole business.

By the time my mom was lying on the bed in the spare bedroom, drowsy from the breakthrough does she'd taken to help manage her pain from all the activity. I was tired and ready for some food. I said goodbye to my aunt and the three of us left.

"Can we stop and get something to eat? Then can you take me to the hospital so I can see Graham? I told him I'd come by and see him tonight."

James nodded and we went for some McDonald's. I was so exhausted I could barely think. We dropped Amy off at the dorm with her bag of food and then James and I drove to the hospital. In the entire day, I hadn't received one text or call from Hunter. I was afraid of what I might hear when I did.

Had *he* killed Spencer?

We arrived at Mass Gen and I went in, finding Graham alone in his room. He was waiting for me, his expression almost gleeful.

"So, the old bastard's dead, is he?"

Graham's expression said it all. He didn't break down and cry. Neither did I, of course. I would have liked to high-five someone, but my fear that Hunter had killed Spencer stopped me from celebrating. How could Graham and I *not* be happy to hear Spencer had died? He'd been a bastard to us from the start.

I hated him.

Now he was gone and maybe, finally, my mother would get better.

"He's dead. Shot in the head and chest."

"Good, " Graham said. "Did Hunter killed him?"

I shook my head. "Why would you ask?"

Graham shrugged. "He's the logical suspect."

"I can't believe he'd killed Spencer." I said it, but doubt was starting to creep in. He'd said he wanted to kill Spencer. He had a motive – revenge against Spencer for the arrest of Donny and Sean's death.

Did he do it?

I felt slightly sick to my stomach, mostly due to my fear that if he had killed Spencer, I wouldn't see him again outside of prison for a long, long time.

I spend about half an hour with Graham and then, when I yawned for the fourth time, he waved at me.

"Go home," he said. "I'm tired and you're tired. We can talk tomorrow."

I gave him a kiss and then trudged out to the waiting SUV. We drove through the dark Boston streets to the safe house, and I was so exhausted I didn't even try to make polite conversation with James.

I felt sick as I trudged up the stairs to the building entrance and James keyed in the entry code.

When I got to the third floor, George was there to greet me.

"Where's Hunter? I've tried to get in touch with him all day. Have you talked to him?"

He shook his head quickly. "No. He has not answered my calls."

"Do you think something happened?" I asked, a surge of adrenaline flowing through me. "He always gets back to me quickly. I haven't received a text from him all day."

George held up his hands. "I'm sure is okay. Probably just had trouble with cell phone. Don't worry."

I plopped down in front of the television, feeling like a dark cloud was hanging over my head.

I couldn't get it out of my mind that Hunter had killed Spencer in a fit of rage. He'd been so mad when he saw my neck.

I ate my McDonald's, but by that time my stomach was a bit sick from worry. Now that I knew my mother was safe at Aunt Diane's, I had to start worrying about Hunter.

Why hadn't he called?

Where was he?

I WENT to bed after having a warm bath, thinking of the last time I'd spent with Hunter and how pleasurable it had been. I wanted him to open the door and poke his head in. I wanted to see that gleam in his eye.

Most of all, I wanted to know he was safe.

My stepfather was dead – murdered. My lover – such as he was – was missing and hadn't contacted me for more than twelve hours, which was so unlike him.

I went to bed, tossing and turning for several hours, worrying that something bad had happened and I'd find out the next morning that he'd been arrested. Abducted.

Or worse.

CHAPTER 34

CELIA

I WOKE in the middle of the night to sounds in the apartment, and a light flicking on over George's desk, where he sat hunched over his laptop. He was speaking into a microphone in Russian, his words sounding angry.

I sat up in bed and watched as George closed his laptop and came over to my bed.

"I hear from Hunter's lawyer. Hunter was taken in by police earlier in evening."

Adrenaline coursed through me once more and my heart pounded. "Do they think he killed Spencer?"

George nodded. "Yes. But I know he did not. He would not, Celia. That I know for true."

"He was really angry when he saw my neck," I said doubtfully. "He even said he wanted to kill Spencer."

George shrugged. "He says many things in anger, but he is soldier. Special Operations Forces. Hunter does not lose control."

"I hope you're right," I said and sighed. "At least we know he's alive. I was afraid someone killed him."

George nodded and rubbed his forehead. "He is alive. You go to sleep, now, Celia. You have had big shock. You need rest."

"I can't sleep," I said and wrapped my arms around my knees. "What time is it?" I glanced over to the bedside table and saw that it was three o'clock in the morning.

"When did they take him in? Has he been in custody all day?"

"I don't know. They arrest him in Alexandria. That's all I know."

Oh, God... Hunter was arrested in Alexandria? That's where Spencer was murdered. It had to mean only one thing – Hunter killed Spencer.

"Spencer was killed in Alexandria."

"Hunter is not killer, Celia."

I wrapped my arms around myself, feeling sick that Hunter might have killed Spencer because he saw my injuries. "I hope he's okay."

"He will be fine," George said, nodding. "He is strong. Tough. You'll see. Lawyer will get him out and he will be home soon."

I lay back down when George left and tried to sleep, but it was a losing venture. Finally, I took out my cell and checked my texts one more time.

There was nothing from Hunter, of course. It was too early to text Amy so I spent an hour searching on Google for news about Spencer. Much was made of the fact he was supposedly investigating the Russian mob. Political pundits talked about his work prosecuting thugs in the mafia.

A reporter claimed that someone identified as a 'close family friend' said Spencer was targeted by the mafia. Who was that? I had no idea who the 'close family friend' was.

Was that the case? Spencer had brought in Hunter's uncle and charged him with several offenses under RICO. The Irish mafia, the Russian mafia, the Italian mafia...

I hoped that Hunter hadn't gotten any more mixed up in it than he claimed – just providing security for them, legitimate work.

Finally, an hour before dawn, I got up and had a shower, deciding that since I couldn't to sleep, I might as well start my day. After drying off and dressing, I went to the kitchen to pour myself some juice and think about what to eat. The sun was just starting to rise on the horizon; its warm orange glow reflecting off the water in the bay. It was beautiful, and I could have appreciated it, if only I'd known what was going on with Hunter.

I couldn't stop thinking about him, wondering if he really had killed Spencer. I would never have thought it possible, but he was so angry...

I'd seen the results of his anger before in the broken and bruised skin on his knuckles after he beat up Stepan. He hated Spencer so much more than he did Stepan. What if he'd lost control? George didn't think it was possible, but Hunter hated Spencer was almost as I did.

I spent the early part of the morning reading over journal articles and trying to distract myself from thoughts of Hunter, wondering when he'd finally call. At about ten, I called over to my Aunt Diane's to see how my mother was doing.

"She slept like a baby," Aunt Diane said softly. "She seems oblivious, frankly. I think she needs to have her meds checked and maybe the levels adjusted. She's on a pretty high dose."

"I know," I said and chewed a fingernail, feeling guilty that I hadn't paid more attention to her over the past few years. "She becomes tolerant to the smaller doses, so they keep having to up the amount. I want her to cut back, but she says she can't tolerate the pain. What can you do?"

"She's a pain patient. For them, they're sometimes just as dependent on the thought of taking the drug as they are the drug itself. They structure their entire lives around the pain and it controls their every thought. She needs therapy, Celia."

I sighed. "I know. When this all settles down, we can talk with her, but she's resistant. Maybe now without Spencer around, we can get her to consider going into the hospital to get her meds adjusted."

"It's a deal. Once things are calmer, we'll have a family discussion.

Speaking of family, how's Graham doing? He must be going insane stuck in the hospital for his rehab."

"I saw him last night, but I feel guilty I haven't visited as much as I'd like. He's doing well enough, getting better."

"That's good," she said, her voice sympathetic. "You can't be expected to do everything."

"I'll go over this morning and see him."

"Okay, sweetheart," she said. "You give him my love and tell him I'll drop in to see him later today when I know your mom is sleeping."

As we ended the call, George came over to my office space.

"How are you, Miss Celia?"

"I hardly slept. Did you hear from Hunter yet?"

He shook his head. "His lawyer calls me. Hunter is fine but is probably not going to get out for few days. Preliminary hearing is tomorrow so he stays in jail until then."

"What's the charge?"

"First degree murder," George said, and made a face. "So no bail."

"Do they really think he killed Spencer?"

George shrugged. "They must, but I know Hunter. He didn't kill."

"I hope you're right," I said and finished packing my book bag. "Can you ask if James can take me to see my brother at the hospital? Then I have to go to class."

"Sure," George said and left me in my little cubbyhole of an office. I checked my email once more and found one from Hunter's lawyer, a Frank McNeal, with McNeal Crowe and Torrance, Attorneys at Law.

Ms. Franklin,

Hunter asked me to contact you on his behalf. He is currently remanded in custody at the county jail and will remain there until a grand jury is convened to determine if there is enough evidence to move forward with the case. If you have any questions, please feel free to contact me. If you would like to visit, I can arrange it but Hunter is only entitled to three visits a week and I know his father wants to visit as well. Let me know.

Yours truly,

F. J. McNeal, J.D.

.   .   .

I SENT him back an email immediately:

Dear Mr. McNeal,

Thank you for writing me. Please arrange a visit as soon as you can. Thank you.

Celia Franklin

I went over to George's office. "I got an email from Hunter's lawyer. He'll be in custody until a grand jury is convened to consider the evidence. I asked him to arrange a visit so I can see Hunter."

"Oh, that's good," George said, obviously upset. "Hunter will be happy to see you. I get James to take you."

"Thanks. I'll let you know when I go."

He nodded and opened the door for me. I made my way down the stairs to the main floor where James was waiting with the SUV.

CHAPTER 35

Hunter

WHILE I WATCHED the stars twinkling in the vast expanse of sky overhead, I got a text from Millar, my contact in the FBI.

MILLAR: You up?

HUNTER: Yes.

MILLAR: Can we meet? There's some movement on that matter you and I discussed earlier about Alexandria. My contact in the Crimes Against Children Unit called me and needs to talk with you.

HUNTER: At this time of night? Don't you FBI types sleep?

MILLAR: The task force never sleeps because these creeps come out at night.

HUNTER: Sure, I can meet you. Our usual place?

MILLAR: No. There's a warehouse down by the old docks. We can spend some time going over things. Meet me in thirty minutes.

I checked my watch. It was three o'clock in the morning. I had enough time to get to the gym, have a shower in the apartment, and make it to the waterfront in time to meet Millar if I hurried.

HUNTER: Okay. I'll be there as soon as possible.

I gathered up my things, and headed to the gym. I had a quick shower, needing the heat of the water to soothe my aching muscles. My hand stung in the water, but it felt good, the steam and heat invigorating me. I dried off and dressed, then took the SUV and drove to the waterfront, to the old docks that Millar mentioned. I saw the warehouse once I turned down a side street bordering the waterfront. It was an old hulk of a brick building, with dark windows that stared out over the bay like dead eyes.

A car was parked at the rear loading dock. I pulled up beside it and saw that it was Millar's sedan. Beside him sat another man wearing the usual FBI blue windbreaker with yellow lettering. He looked to be about forty, lean and sharp-eyed with a shaved head.

"Come inside," Millar said and gestured to the building.

I parked my SUV and got out of my vehicle, then went to where the two men were standing, waiting for me.

"This is Special Agent Cross of the Crimes Against Children Unit." Millar pointed to Cross and the two of us shook.

"Good to meet you," I said and met his eyes. "Glad you guys are going to look into this."

"They'll do more than look into it. They'll take the bastard down," Millar said.

I followed them up to the entrance and watched as Millar unlocked the door before ushering us inside.

"Is this an FBI office?" I asked, looking around at the bank of desks with a dozen computer stations.

"This is the task force's main office in Boston." Cross pointed to a corner office behind a wall of windows. I followed Millar inside and we sat around a large table. "We're coordinating with Alexandria."

Cross went over the case with me, detailing the evidence they had gathered on Spencer over the past six months. None of it was enough to bring charges—it was instead based on the testimony of our informants —so the FBI was happy to learn about the cabin and that it was being used as a place to make child porn as well as abuse children.

"The young girls are all immigrants from former Soviet Republics, like Georgia. They're lured here with promises of a job modelling and then they're abused, taken to parties where they're passed around the men with money. They're drugged, sometimes beaten if they don't cooperate; they're raped and given drugs to get them addicted and then they work for whatever drug they're hooked on. The conditions they live in are horrific."

It made my stomach tighten, remembering the young girl I'd seen come out of the cabin, her makeup smeared, her hair a mess. I wondered what hell she'd been through and what she had left behind back in whatever Eastern European state she'd come from, thinking she was heading for fame and fortune in America.

I hated the men who did this to her and to other young girls like her. I was sure Spencer would have done it to Celia if he could have, and wondered how hard it had been for him to refrain from abusing her sexually. Probably the reason he was so abusive to her physically and emotionally for all those years.

"I'm glad you're going to nail him," I said. "He's been a bastard to his step-kids for years. I'm totally shocked that he's been a pornographer involved in the human trafficking business. How did he get away with it for so long? I never would have believed it."

"Believe it. He's a sly one. He's kept himself squeaky clean since he moved to Boston but there were rumors of his past in Alexandria. We could never connect him, but we made the connection when he took down your uncle. He used intel from a confidential informant in the Romanov family. That led us to the Romanov's involvement in human trafficking and some online child porn websites. We figured we might be able to connect Grant to that part of the Romanov business. Now we can. The cabin was owned by one of his shell companies. It stayed under the radar for a while but we would have gotten to it sooner or later. It was on our list. You got to it first. How was that possible?"

Millar turned to Cross. "I told him about the case, and he went from there."

Cross nodded, eyeing me closely, like he was trying to figure me out.

"I'm trying to talk him into applying to be a Special Agent. Right now, he's working for us but off the books."

"We can use good experienced operators," Cross said. "Guys with military experience, especially special operations, are a bonus. Good luck if you apply. I'm sure your work with us will help."

"I hope so," I said, now even more convinced I'd like to join the FBI.

"Come and sit in the car with me for a minute," Millar said.

"Okay," I said, and hopped in beside him. "Thanks for letting me take part," I said. "Spencer's a sick fuck, and a bastard on top of it."

"You got that right," Millar responded.

"What happens now? When will you pick up Grant? What about the Jones guy I stopped outside the cabin? Have they arrested him?"

"And charged him with what? He was walking along a pathway. Until they have a case against Grant and have a link to him, he's an innocent man. In fact, you're more likely to be arrested than him, at least in the short term, for assault and robbery."

"I couldn't argue I was doing a citizen's arrest?" I said half-jokingly.

"Nope," he said. "Likely the only reason he didn't bring charges against you for assault and battery is that he's guilty as hell. Count yourself lucky."

I sighed and glanced around. "What's next?"

"We'll start our investigation, collect the evidence and then turn it over to the federal prosecutor. He'll decide whether to charge Grant or not based on the evidence and links to him."

I nodded, eager to get on with it. "I hope they get the bastard and put him away for a very long time."

"If he's smart, he'll leave the country—go to someplace where there's no extradition treaty with the US."

"He'd be leaving behind a real big career. But I can't see that he can recover from this."

Millar closed his file. "What's up with the Grant girl?"

Cross turned to me, his interest obviously piqued.

"Her name's Parker, not Grant," I said, slightly annoyed that he was asking about my personal life. "Nothing's up. She's a family friend. I'm protecting her because I'm friends with her brother."

"I heard you paid off his debts," Millar said.

"I did. Victor Romanov thought he could get to me through her. I'm putting her up in one of my properties."

"Whatever," Millar said, like he didn't believe me. Cops have a gut sense of things, and he probably knew I was lying through my teeth. She was a lot more to me than a family friend.

Millar checked his cell. "Well, we're in luck. They got the search warrant. I guess their judge isn't a fan of Grant. They've put a unit on it to watch in case anyone tries to go in and clean the place up. They'll be going in later today."

"That soon?"

Millar shrugged. "The sooner the better. I'm going to fly down later."

"Can I come along? I'd love to see it go down."

"Sure," he said, but shot me a look. "You're not part of any official team, Hunter. Remember – you're off the books. We need deniability but maybe I'll say that you're working with me and leave it at that. I have some leeway. You'll have to fly domestic on your nickel."

"Fine," I said, glad that I could go along and watch. I checked my cell and found a flight leaving just after lunch. "I could catch the two o'clock flight and be there by four."

"It's your decision. Now, when you get to Alexandria, I don't want you to come to the cabin right away. Let us do our work. Go get yourself a hotel room. Call me when you get in town. I'll be at my office in Washington. You got the number. You can show up about half an hour after I let you know we're in."

I nodded, my nerves all primed and ready, the way I used to be while waiting for action in Iraq or Afghanistan. Waiting was the hardest part when you were at war. The long hours of calm were deceptive. Suddenly, all hell would break loose and the bullets would be flying, explosions, fire, shouts and screams. Your adrenaline pumped like crazy but you stayed calm and just *acted*. No real fear. Just determination to act.

Stay frosty.

It was hard to stay frosty when what I really wanted to do was go to Spencer and plow his face in, but I had to. Couldn't lose control. That would help no one and accomplish nothing. The cops would go in and find the stuff I did and that would be that. I was sure that Spencer didn't have enough time to go to the cabin and clear it out, and besides, I'd alerted the cops right away about what I found and they'd have someone watching the cabin just in case.

"I'll get a hotel room and call you. I gotta get back to Boston as soon as I can. I got an empire to run," I said sarcastically.

"Yeah," Millar said. "Watch your six."

At that, we parted and I drove to my apartment and crashed for a few hours so I'd be fresh for the op at the cabin. I slept for about six hours, falling asleep almost as soon as my head hit the pillow. Once I woke, I had a quick shower, packed a bag, then went to the gym to make sure things were on track with the daily cash.

After I was finished looking over the books and receipts, I drove to the airport and purchased my ticket for flight to Washington, went through security, and sat in the United first class lounge and did some work on my laptop.

As I sat waiting for my flight, I thought about Celia and what was happening between us. When I first considered using Celia as my fuck toy to repay Graham's debt, I felt guilty. My mind went there immediately – I couldn't help it. Part of me thought I was a total asshole to use my money to take advantage of her but another part relished the idea. I tried to tell myself that it meant nothing – that *she* meant nothing to me besides a good, easy fuck – but even I knew that was a lie.

The fact was that Celia had always inhabited a part of my mind since that night she gave me her virginity, and I'd always felt a mix of desire for her and anger that she threw me over for Greg – and for Spencer's money.

Now, it felt like she was warming up to me. Our recent night together, when she came to me on her own, suggested that the walls between us were breaking down. That maybe she wanted me as a man, aside from being the one to pay back her brother's debt and protect her.

I was glad to be able to pay back Graham's debt. I was glad to be able to protect her. Most of all, I wanted her to want me.

As much as I wanted her.

CHAPTER 36

Hunter

THE FLIGHT WAS UNEVENTFUL, and I arrived in D.C. only fifteen minutes late due to a hold on the tarmac in Boston. I sat in an alcove in the lounge and called Millar at his D.C. FBI office, getting his admin person.

"Hunter Saint for Special Agent Millar."

An admin connected me and Millar came on the line.

"So, you're just in time," he said. In the background, I heard papers shuffling and muted conversation. "The team's getting ready and we'll be going out to the cabin in about thirty minutes. You can meet me there in an hour. I need time to get things set up before I want to bring you in."

"Will do."

"Oh, and Hunter? Keep it quiet that you're here and what we're doing. We don't want anyone to know we're going in. Gotta try to keep our advantage so no one goes in and removes the evidence."

"Don't worry. I understand the need for secrecy."

I hung up and felt invigorated now that something was going to happen. I was certain that investigators would find more than enough to arrest Spencer. There were tapes of him doing illegal stuff to barely pubescent girls. He was going down and for Spencer, all that was left was the crying. He was such a worm, I was sure he'd try to escape. Part of me hoped he'd run and get caught at the airport, trying to buy a one-way ticket to some third-world country where he wouldn't get shipped back to face charges in the US. I wanted to sit in the stands and watch his trial, see him cringe when they brought out evidence of his perversion. Knowing Spencer, he'd plead to some lesser charges and minimize the public exposure of his crimes.

Then, he'd go to jail and live out the rest of his miserable life in protective custody. Someone like Spencer would not do well in prison. He'd sent away too many bad guys for him to be safe. Besides, even criminals hated pedophiles.

I had a quick shower to revive myself, and considered calling Celia to let her know I was going to be out of town for a few days, but I didn't want to have to lie about what I was doing. I also didn't want to bother her, considering she'd probably be busy with her studies. Instead, I texted George, letting him know instead.

HUNTER: I'll be in Alexandria for a couple of days, checking out that matter I told you about. Stuff is going to go down soon and I want to be here to watch. Let Celia know I'm going to be away for a while and won't be in contact. How is she?

RUSKIE5: Celia is fine. She was studying all morning. She ask about you but I tell her you went to office to do some work.

HUNTER: Good. I'll let you know when I'm coming back.

RUSKIE5: Roger that.

I put my cell away and then waited, my eye on my watch and my mind on the cabin along the bay and what the FBI sex crimes team would find once they got there.

I hoped Spencer hadn't the chance to let people know to take out the trash. I hoped to be able to do that myself, or at least help. It would be a real shame if we went into the cabin and found it had been wiped clean.

. . .

I SHOWED up at the cabin on time, only to find a police barricade about half a block on either side of the location. A cop stood with his hands on his hips, guarding the perimeter.

"This area is closed to traffic," the cop said.

"Hunter Saint," I replied. "I'm meeting Special Agent Millar."

He spoke into the mike on his shoulder and waited for a response. He nodded and then gestured to the cabin.

"He's expecting you. Go ahead."

I ducked under the yellow police tape and made my way up the drive to the front door. It was open, and a blue-jacketed FBI Special Agent emerged with a box. I expected it was filled with tapes or other evidence.

He nodded to me and I went in the front entrance. Millar met me at the door and handed me some blue paper booties.

"Put these on. We don't want you to contaminate the crime scene. Don't touch anything."

I slipped the paper booties on and followed him to the basement. Down there, some forensic workers were dusting for prints and taking photos of the set up used to make videos. Another forensic worker was shining a fluorescent light on the sink in the tiny bathroom, no doubt looking for evidence of blood.

"We got a boatload of evidence," Millar said, standing in the center of the room, his hands on his hips. "We have you to thank, so thanks."

I glanced around, feeling satisfied that they'd be able to bring Spencer down with all the evidence he and his fellow perverts left behind.

"I'd love to be with you when you arrest him."

"We'll have to process this evidence and then make sure we have enough to take him in, but yeah. Since you tipped us off to this place, I'm sure I could arrange things so you could come along with the team. You like this kind of work?"

I shrugged. "Yeah," I said. "Not as messy as what I did as a Marine, but still fighting bad guys."

"If you need a reference, you got it."

. . .

I FOLLOWED Millar around and listened as he spoke to the various Special Agents about the crime scene and evidence they were collecting. Special Agent Cross appeared and we discussed the evidence they'd found. While I listened, I thought seriously about Millar's suggestion that I join the FBI. I could see myself doing this work – of that I was certain. I'd joined the Marines to fight for my country and to escape my family's business ties to the mafia and organized crime. Getting the short training at Quantico gave me insight into what an FBI agent did and I found it a natural fit with my training in the Marines.

About an hour into the investigation, Millar got a call and stood off to the side of the room, his hand over one ear. He spoke into the cell and then glanced up at me and the look on his face was one of concern. When he ended the call, he came over and put his hands in his pockets, eyeing me.

"Grant's body was just found," he said, watching me closely.

"What?" My jaw dropped at the news. "He's dead?"

Millar nodded and Cross came over, looking me over once before turning to Millar.

"You got the news?"

They both turned to me.

"I'm as shocked as you are," I said, knowing immediately that they probably suspected me.

"The coroner's just now determining the approximate time of death, but it's been hours."

"Where did they find him? How did he die?"

"According to the report I got, he died within the past eight hours. Shot in the head and chest."

"He was shot?" I shook my head, shocked at the development. "Two shots? That sounds like a hit job."

"It does," Millar replied, his eyes narrow. "With a high-performance rifle. Russian make. Left at the scene of the crime. They're pulling prints off it as we speak."

"Russian?" I said, shocked that Spencer would have been killed by a Russian weapon.

It was then that I remembered my meeting with Sergei Romanov. He'd had a shipment of Russian sniper rifles. I'd shot one.

He had given me one as a gift.

"It wasn't me," I said and held up my hands defensively. "I was with you early in the morning, and then I caught the flight to Washington."

"Coroner's working out an exact time of death," Millar said like he didn't believe me. "We should have it soon."

I frowned and wanted to text Celia right away to see how she was doing.

"I have to make a call," I said and held up my cell. "I'm close to Spencer Grant's kids."

"I'd rather you didn't," Millar said, holding up his hand.

"Why not?"

"Hunter, you have to know you're a suspect."

"What?" I said, glancing between the two. "Why am I a suspect?"

"Just don't call anyone right now. Not until we have more details."

"I'm close to his step daughter. I need to contact her."

"Hunter," Millar said, coming closer to me. "You're here under my authority. I'm asking you to hold off from contacting anyone until we have more information. That's all I can say."

I shrugged and decided to cooperate. He must know something if he wanted me not to contact anyone back in Boston.

LATER, after we'd gone through every part of the cabin, checking for hidden compartments where pornography might have been kept, which were common in places like this, Millar and I stood in the living room and discussed the next steps. The forensic team had finished their sweep of the house and were starting to pack up. My stomach growled and I needed some food.

"What's next? I mean, now that Grant's dead?"

Millar shrugged. "He had lots of accomplices. They'll haul all the evidence down to the forensic labs in DC and we'll meet with federal prosecutors."

"I was afraid someone would have cleaned up the premises after I stopped Jones."

"His secretary at the mortgage brokerage where he works said he was out of town on business. When we asked where, she said he'd gone to Hong Kong to meet some foreign clients."

"He must have been a busy bee getting new ID. I'm surprised he could get it and take a flight out of the US on such short notice. He must have gone right out and decided to escape."

"I don't blame him. Interestingly, we don't have an Extradition Treaty with Hong Kong so Mr. Jones is likely going to stay there indefinitely..."

"Smart move. But he didn't squeal to Grant about being caught. I wonder why."

I shook my head. "Who knows? Maybe he was the one who shot Spencer."

"Maybe," Millar said and shrugged.

We went outside and stood on the front step while one of the FBI Special Agents sealed the door.

"Well, we're going back to the office to process this stuff." Millar glanced at me. "It's going to be a late night."

Then his cell rang and he answered it.

"Okay," he said and glanced at me. Then he walked a few steps away and spoke quietly into his cell. He appeared to be arguing, but kept his voice low enough that I couldn't hear. Then, he turned to me, his expression dark.

"Bad news, Hunter. I just got a call from HQ. Officer, you have authority to place this man under arrest for the murder of Spencer Grant."

The cop glanced at Millar, a quizzical expression on his face like he didn't believe it.

Adrenaline jolted through me. "What?"

He motioned one of the nearby cops over and handed him the cell. The cop listened and nodded. "I got it. Will do."

After he handed the cell back to Millar, the cop turned to me.

"Do it," Millar said.

Finally, almost reluctantly, the cop took hold of my arm, pulling it behind my back, his cuffs already out and on one wrist. I felt like fighting but I knew that was stupid, so I cooperated, providing him with the other wrist so he could cuff me.

After the cop read me my rights, he led me to a waiting police squad car and opened the door.

"I'm not guilty, " I said to Millar, who had an expression of disgust on his face.

"We got a Russian sniper rifle with your prints on it at the scene of the crime that says otherwise."

"Do you really think I'd be stupid enough to leave the murder weapon at the scene of the crime? Do you think I wouldn't wipe the prints off? That rifle was a plant. If you want to know who killed Spencer Grant, it's Sergei Romanov. That was his rifle. He set me up."

"Well," Millar said and opened the back door of the police sedan. "We'll let the evidence tell us the story."

"If the evidence is faked," I said, glaring at him, "you shouldn't trust it. Come on, you know that."

Millar didn't answer. The cop shoved me into the rear seat, pushing my head down in the process. I sat in the back and fumed. There was no doubt that I was being framed for the murder of Spencer Grant. I'd been set up by Sergei Romanov. I thought back to my meeting with him months earlier. Had he been planning to kill Spencer all that time? Why?

I knew that Celia would be in shock and would have to be taking care of her mother now that Spencer was no longer there. She'd be frantic to know what had happened and where I was, but I couldn't call her.

Sergei must have learned about the investigation into Spencer's property and killed him to shut him up – which meant Sergei was involved in Spencer's little perversion.

I had threatened to kill Spencer. Publicly. I'd done so in front of his assistant the previous day. They had the murder weapon with my prints on it. Depending on when he was killed, they might have a timeline that worked to put me there when he was killed. I wasn't guilty, of course, but if the bulk of evidence made it look that way, given the nature of the crime – murder – I knew I'd be in custody until they either dropped the charges or the case went to trial.

I closed my eyes and tried to calm myself as the vehicle drove off – to where, I had no idea. To the local police department? To some FBI facility?

I tried to tell myself that the matter would be cleared up in a short time once they discovered the timelines didn't match up.

Were they making a show of arresting me? Millar had said they wanted to bring me in on the assault charge, but this seemed excessive. My mind tried to concoct several scenarios where arresting me was necessary for some other goal, but I had no idea what. I'd call my lawyer as soon as I had the chance, before they could interrogate me. I knew enough to keep my mouth shut and not talk to them without my lawyer present. Even for an innocent man, the cops could trip you up, put words in your mouth.

Whatever was going on, I kept repeating to myself that Spencer was dead.

He was dead – the man responsible for Sean's death. The bastard who'd put my small-potatoes uncle away in a federal prison. The creep who molested pretty little girls and abused Celia and Graham.

I'd deal with the current shit I was facing easily enough. The fact that Spencer was dead almost made me laugh, except it was hard to be happy when I thought about all the pain and suffering he'd caused in his perverted existence.

The fact he was dead was small comfort, considering. The fact that they had evidence pointing to me was a real source of concern, but one I was certain would be cleared up once they had the time of death and I was exonerated.

CHAPTER 37

CELIA

FOR THE NEXT TWENTY-FOUR HOURS, I felt totally lost. Hunter was in police custody charged with the murder of my stepfather. My mother was a mess and staying in my aunt's spare bedroom, unable to process the fact that Spencer was dead and she was now all alone. Graham was recovering in the rehab hospital, learning to walk again, learning to use his arm, still talking through gritted teeth due to his broken jaw.

I sent a text to my advisor, telling him that my stepfather had been murdered and I'd need some time off to process things and take care of family matters, but in truth, studying would have at least distracted me from my turmoil. He wrote back and told me it was fine – that I could take a week off, even two if I needed it. He'd contact my profs and ask them to send me any reading material and excuse me from assignments if necessary.

I was thankful I was on good terms with my advisor and that he supported me. I needed to be with my mom and brother as much as possible for the next few days until we got things figured out.

I sat at a table in my aunt's house and drank a cup of coffee, staring out the window, ticking off in my mind what I'd have to do over the next few days to keep things under control. I had to make sure my mom's meds were all up to date, and pick up a prescription that she needed. I wanted to take her to a new doctor and get her meds reviewed. Spencer may have encouraged her addiction to morphine to keep her sedated and out of his business, but I wouldn't allow that to continue. I wanted to see my mother improve and have some sort of life – whatever was possible, given the fact that her injury had never healed properly and she was now disabled due to chronic pain.

My cell dinged and I checked it.

AMY: How are you?

CELIA: I'm at my Aunt Diane's trying to figure out what to do.

AMY: Do you want me to come over and spend time with you? Whatever you need. Should I bring tequila?

I smiled, glad that I had as good a friend as Amy.

CELIA: No, it's all right. I'm here for a while, but then I'll go back to the warehouse. Hunter was arrested.

AMY: WHAT??? Did he kill Spencer? Not that I'm sad Spencer's dead but... They arrested Hunter?

CELIA: Yeah... He was furious when he saw my neck after Spencer choked me, but I can't believe Hunter would actually kill him. Hunter was an officer in the Marines. He's not the type to lose control and just murder someone...

AMY: Oh, God, I hope not. Have you talked to him?

CELIA: Nope. But his lawyer did send me an email. He's been charged and because it was murder, there'll be no bail. He'll be held at the jail until the grand jury decides whether to indict him.

AMY: Okay. Let me know if you need anything. Do you need me to contact your profs about class?

CELIA: Already did. My advisor contacted them for me and I'm on a leave of absence for a week or two if I need it.

AMY: When is the funeral? I suppose you have to arrange that. It must be hard for you to do it.

CELIA: I do. It's not like Graham can take over, and my mom is a mess.

Aunt Diane's already looking after mom. I'll have a quiet viewing and that's it. No funeral. No mass. Nothing. He was a bastard, Amy. He was being investigated for being part of a child prostitution ring. Who would go to his funeral anyway?

AMY: *He was? You never said...*

CELIA: *Yeah, Hunter told me.*

AMY: *What a huge fall from grace. To think he was the DA.*

CELIA: *I know. I can't imagine what will happen when that story gets out. There were already reporters at my mom's place. When they learn what he was being investigated for, it will be mayhem. UGH.*

AMY: *I know. I'll be there for you, sweets.*

CELIA: *Thanks. I'll talk to you later. Maybe we can have a beer or something. I'll need to get away from it all at some point.*

AMY: *Let me know. Bye.*

CELIA: *Bye. <3*

I watched my mom sleep on the sofa, her face pasty, her eyes puffy from crying. Only her breakthrough dose of morphine could take away her pain for a while, making her sleep through the afternoon and evening.

"Your poor mom," Aunt Diane said, sitting beside me on the sofa, her arm around me. "She must be so upset. I know none of us liked Spencer, but she loved him. He looked after her all this time. She must be so afraid."

"We'll look after her better," I said. "He didn't really take care of her. He let her become addicted to morphine and she's slept most of her life away since they've been together."

"I know that but your mom only knows her husband was murdered."

I sighed and watched my mother sleep, wondering when Hunter would get out of custody and when I'd see him again. I wanted to see him, to make sure he was all right. I needed to look in his eyes and have him tell me he had nothing to do with Spencer's death.

As much as I hated Spencer and was relieved that he was dead, I didn't want to think that Hunter had done it and would go to jail probably for decades to pay for it.

I was selfish like that. I wanted Hunter for myself.

I always had.

AFTER I PUT my mom to bed that night, tucking her in and kissing her cheek, I said goodbye to my Aunt Diane and went back to the warehouse with James.

"How are you doing?" he asked as we drove through the darkened streets.

"I'm exhausted. And I'm worried about Hunter."

"I know it looks bad, but I'm sure Hunter didn't do it. You'll see. They'll clear him when they'll discover that he didn't do it. Things will get back to normal."

"I hope so."

"I know so," James said. "I know Hunter as a man and as a soldier. He's honorable. He wouldn't kill Spencer no matter how angry he was. He'd want Spencer to get justice."

I nodded, but wasn't so sure.

Spencer was the cause of Sean's death. I knew anger had been brewing inside of Hunter because of that fact. He'd shown me his willingness to use violence to get revenge, and killing Spencer was just that next step up from almost beating a man to death. He'd done that twice since I'd been with him – first Stepan and then he'd beaten Spencer.

For all I knew, he'd gone back in anger and killed him.

There was nothing I could do about it, so I stopped worrying and closed my eyes.

When we got back to the warehouse, I went inside and took the stairs to the third-floor apartment where I expected George would be waiting. I was glad when I saw him, even though his face was haggard and his eyes were bleary. He stood when I entered and came right over to me.

"How are you, Ms. Celia?" He peered at me, checking me over. "You need sleep, I think. Hunter will be cleared and let out soon."

"I hope so."

George shook his head. "I know so."

"You really don't think he did it? I mean, really? Be honest with me."

"No," he said. "Hunter did not kill. He wanted to but didn't."

"You know that for sure?" I looked in his eyes, trying to see deception.

He put his hand over his heart. "I know Hunter. He did not do."

I sighed, still not sure myself, but if George thought he was innocent, I had to accept that. George knew Hunter as a man better than most of us.

THE NEXT DAY, I woke early and checked my email, but there was no update from Hunter's lawyer about the case, or a time for a visit. I drank a coffee after my shower and read over the local news. Spencer's death was still making headlines, and there was a line in the latest article about an arrest being made, but there was no name included. I wondered why they wouldn't mention Hunter's name, but perhaps they had some technical reason.

Whatever the case, Hunter was still in police custody and I had to take care of the arrangements for Spencer's viewing at the funeral home in case anyone wanted to come by and pay their respects. Interestingly, no one at the DA's office called to ask about a funeral. I suspected they must have known about the investigation into Spencer's past and the connection to a child prostitution ring back in Alexandria.

That made me wonder if Spencer hadn't been killed to shut him up. I felt a sense of justice that Spencer was dead. He'd been such a bastard to Graham and me all our lives with him. I felt no sadness at his death or the fact he'd been murdered.

But Hunter was still in custody. That made me nervous. The grand jury would be convening later in the week and I hoped that they would decide to let Hunter go. Why they would have arrested him in the first place I couldn't figure out. The prosecutor would bring evidence against Hunter to the grand jury and they would decide whether to indict him. If so, the case would go to trial. If not, he would be released.

Until then, Hunter would stay at the local jail.

I WENT to see Graham at the rehab hospital and we talked about the case and Hunter's arrest.

"Do you think he did it?" he asked me through gritted teeth.

I shook my head. "I don't really think so. I mean, he was angry at Spencer for hurting me, but he came back from the house and said Spencer was fine. That was the night before he was killed."

"Was Hunter with you?" Graham asked, his voice light.

"He was for part of the night. Then he went for a run and went back to the gym. He said he was going to Alexandria for some work, but that was in the afternoon. They found Spencer that afternoon."

"Sounds guilty as hell to me," Graham said. "They don't usually arrest innocent people."

"They do sometimes," I replied, remembering the stats I'd read from The Innocence Project, which investigates those falsely accused of murder and on death row. "The process is good, but not perfect. There are cases that slip through all the safeguards."

"But you said Spencer was in Alexandria and so was Hunter. Spencer was found dead in Alexandria. Sounds pretty damn suspicious to me."

"It does, but I don't believe it. I don't think Hunter was angry. He'd calmed down considerably when I saw him. He's not that kind of man, Graham. He was in the special operations forces. Those guys are cool as cucumbers. They don't go off on rampages."

"Some do," Graham said, his expression dark. "I could see Hunter killing Spencer because of Sean. He must still hate Spencer because of that. That alone is enough to make me suspicious. That's probably why he was arrested."

I sighed and leaned back in the uncomfortable hospital chair beside Graham's bed. The hospital was busy at that time of day, with visitors crowding into the rooms and nurses going in and out, helping the patients with their needs.

"How long will you be in here?" I asked, glancing around.

"Another week or so," Graham replied and adjusted his pillow. "I've got to be able to do certain things before they'll let me go home. We're working on it."

"Will you come to the memorial service?"

"When will it be?"

"On Monday afternoon."

"I doubt it. Not that I'd want to come anyway, even if I wasn't in here."

"Graham!" I made a face.

"Well, it's the truth. I'm happy he's dead. I'm ecstatic. Wasn't soon enough. Whoever killed him? I want to shake his hand – and if it was Hunter, I'd buy him a fucking drink."

I laughed nervously, sympathetic to him but feeling bad about it. "I feel the same way, except I don't want Hunter to go to jail."

"I'm just glad he's gone. If Hunter did it, that's his choice and his consequences. Whoever killed him, I really don't care. And I don't want to go and pretend I do."

"Come for Mom. She'll want to you go. I'm sure there'll be people there who have no idea what a bastard he is and it would look strange if either of us weren't there. You can go in a wheelchair."

He shrugged helplessly. "I'll see what I the nurses say. I can get a day pass and we can go together."

I checked my watch and saw that it was getting late. "I'm going back to the warehouse," I said. "I'll go over to Aunt Diane's for supper and spend time with Mom. We have to write up an obituary. How do you write an obituary for a man you hate with all your guts?"

"I'm glad it's you instead of me," Graham said, grinning through his wired jaw.

"We'll spring you and bring you to the service no matter what you want," I said with a laugh and then bent down and kissed him on the cheek. "Take it easy. I'll come and see you again tomorrow."

"Okay, sister," he said and met my eyes. "Thanks for coming by. Let me know if anything happens on the case."

"I will."

I LEFT the hospital and James took me to the dorm so I could see Amy. I'd gotten a text from her and wanted to spend some time with her before going to Aunt Diane's. When I arrived, I felt a pang of regret that I was no longer living in my room. Although I liked being with Hunter – when I was with him – I also liked my independence and being on my own. Amy was just down the hallway and we'd spent a lot of time together, so I missed the old connection we had. I missed sitting with her in the dining hall for our meals and spending time in each other's rooms, watching movies or Netflix, drinking beer.

I missed my old life – the one not filled with Russian mafia bosses, loan sharks, and gangsters. The one before Sean Saint was killed, before Graham lost all our inheritances, and before Hunter was in custody.

I wanted Hunter, but like this?

I FINALLY GOT an email from Hunter's lawyer about a time to meet Hunter. I'd go for the last visiting time of the day, from seven to eight forty-five in the evening. James agreed to take me, and I was nervous as we drove to Alexandria.

Hi, Celia -- Make sure you get there about an hour early. There are only so many rooms and if they're filled up, you won't be able to see him. Oh, and don't wear any jewelry or any t-shirts with political messages. They're strict about what visitors can wear.

I SENT him an email in reply that I'd be there an hour early, thanking him for letting me know about the whole process. Although I was in first year law, I had no idea how the real system worked on a day-to-day basis.

Since my visit was scheduled for seven, I made sure James dropped me off at the facility at five forty-five, just to be on the safe side. When I arrived, there were already people waiting in line in front of a metal detector. We were made to remove all outerwear and jewelry other than wedding rings and medical alert bracelets. Everything went into a lockers and we were then each given a key to our locker. After that, I had to fill out a visitor's form and wait while my ID was put through a computer search. I was then given a lanyard with a printed card with the floor and room number where I would go to meet Hunter. The other visitors seemed more familiar with everything and were ready, scribbling down their info on the visitor's forms and lining up to go through the metal detector. Once the clock struck six, we were shuttled through the detector and our hands stamped. After that, we went through a set of doors and had our stamped hands checked under a UV light. Finally, we took the elevator to our respective floors and then to a special room for visitors. It was tiny, with a desk, a metal stool, and a glass partition dividing the room in half. There were holes in the glass so you could supposedly hear the person you were visiting.

It was horrible.

After I was seated, the door opened and in walked Hunter, wearing a jumpsuit.

He looked haggard, his hair a mess, his skin pale.

He sat on the stool and faced me, smiling sadly.

"You came," he said, and I was shocked that he felt that way.

"Of course I came," I said, and leaned closer, because it was difficult to hear him. "How are you holding up?"

He shrugged. "I've been worse. Frankly, cells are better than some of the places I've slept."

I smiled, but I didn't know what else to say.

"Aren't you going to ask me if I did it?" he said, his eyebrows raised.

"Did you do it?"

"Do you think I did?"

I shook my head. "You were angry when you saw what he did."

"I was," he replied. "I wanted to kill him, but I didn't."

"Who did?"

"Sergei."

"You know that?"

He nodded. "Yeah, he set me up. I'll tell you all about it when I get out."

"When do you think that will happen?" I said and leaned closer. "I miss you."

He smiled softly. "I miss *you*. I feel like I just found you and now here I am."

"If you're innocent, they'll drop the charges."

He shook his head, his expression dark. "So trusting," he said. "I don't have the same faith in the justice system that you do. Not after what happened to Sean."

"If you didn't do it, they'll find evidence and let you go."

"Unless they want me for it. My family isn't exactly liked by the FBI or the local police. I thought they liked me, personally, but now I wonder..."

"Tell me what happened. Why were you in Alexandria?"

For the next hour and a half, Hunter told me about his trip to Alexandria. He explained about his meeting with the FBI's Child Sex Crimes unit about Spencer's ties to a child prostitution ring using Russian and Eastern European girls who were hoping to come to the USA and become models.

"They have to know you didn't kill him, Hunter. Why else would they work with you if they didn't trust you?"

He shrugged. "It all comes down to timing. My prints were on the weapon. If it was possible for me to have killed him because of his time of death, they'll indict me and I'll go to trial."

"So his time of death is important," I said, nodding in understanding.

"It depends on what the coroner finds. If there was any chance that I did it, I'm afraid I'm going down for it, even though I didn't do it. Sometimes, the police start down one line of investigation and can't see any other options."

"When will the coroner come out with his final decision on time of death?"

He folded his hands on the table. "Should be soon. I can only hope there's no overlap in time."

"Me, too." I leaned in closer. "I wish I could kiss you."

He smiled at that, his eyes soft. "Me, too. Believe me, if and when I get out, I'm going to be doing a lot more than kissing you. You owe me." Then he cracked a grin – that old familiar Hunter Saint grin that made my heart squeeze.

"I *do* owe you, don't I?" I smiled back, narrowing my eyes. "I have a lot of debt to pay off."

"You do."

We leaned closer, inches from each other with the glass between us. Then, just as we were staring into each other's eyes, there came a knock at the door to Hunter's room and it was time to leave.

"If you're still in here next week, I'll be back," I said, feeling a bit teary-eyed that I had to leave him.

"I hope I'm not still here next week, though. If I'm not, I'll either be transferred to prison to wait for trial or I'll be home in bed with you."

I kissed my fingers and blew him a kiss. Then a guard opened Hunter's door, impatient for him to leave the room. I stood, caught his eye one last time, and then he was gone.

OVER THE NEXT FEW DAYS, I divided my time between my classes, seeing Graham at the hospital and visiting my mom at Aunt Diane's. I asked George what he'd heard about Hunter and checked my mail in hopes that I'd receive another email from Hunter's lawyer, but there was nothing new.

The grand jury was coming up on Wednesday, almost a week since Hunter was taken in, due to the weekend. He was doing well enough in custody, according to George, who went to see him in the morning.

According to George, there was a very brief time of overlap when Hunter could have killed Spencer, although it was next to impossible given the location of the murder scene and where Hunter was at the time, so they were keeping him in custody, presenting the evidence to the grand jury to decide.

We finished the last of the plans for the memorial service, and wrote up obituaries for various papers. James agreed to pick Graham up, since he had a huge SUV.

It was held in a funeral home in town, and the casket was closed, given the nature of Spencer's death. From what the police told us, the bullet had gone through the front of his skull and exited out the back. He'd been shot in the chest as well, almost perfectly through his heart. Whoever did it was an expert marksman. He was dead in seconds.

Considering what Hunter had told me about his sordid past, I thought it wasn't good enough justice. I would have liked to have seen him publicly shamed and forced to face his crimes, standing trial and going to jail. That he died quickly, and probably without knowing what happened, was so unfair. The only good thing was that I would never have to see him again. Our last encounter could have killed me, if my mom hadn't come down and called him off.

You don't always get exactly what you want, but he was gone and that was almost good enough.

CHAPTER 38

CELIA

THE FUNERAL HOME WAS PACKED, every chair taken, with overflow in the room next to the one we chose. I'd had no idea how many colleagues and friends Spencer had. We ran out of printed handouts and our assistant from the funeral home had to quickly print off more. Luckily, they had a color printer in the office or there would have been a lot of people leaving without a memorial flyer. A few of Spencer's colleagues spoke – about his work as a ADA and then DA, how he was dedicated to fighting organized crime and bringing criminals to justice.

I had a hard time not laughing out loud when the colleague said that, because standing at the back while the eulogies were being read, wearing dark glasses, was Sergei Romanov himself. When I glanced back and caught sight of him, I had to do a double take. He caught me watching and removed his glasses, smiling at me.

That smile made me shiver.

I turned back to watch the Assistant DA while he finished his eulogy and felt a sense of doom. Hunter was in jail. I wasn't entirely sure Hunter wasn't guilty. I was still in danger because the Romanov brothers knew me and knew I was a way to get to Hunter.

After the memorial was over and we had shaken hands with those colleagues who wanted to give us their condolences, we packed up the wheelchair and drove to my Aunt Diane's for a small family gathering.

It was very small, just my mother – who was exhausted and immediately took her morphine and lay on the sofa – my Aunt Diane and her husband Mike, their kids, Graham, and me. We talked about the good times, and they were few. Trips we had taken to Florida before Mom got really bad. Time spent at the beach. Family barbecues.

When it was time to take Graham back to the hospital, I went with him and got him settled back into his hospital room. I spent the rest of the evening with him, having a late snack from the cafeteria vending machines instead of dinner.

We sat in his hospital room and talked quietly about Hunter and whether he was guilty and what would happen if he was.

"He told me he wasn't guilty. He didn't kill Spencer but his prints were on the weapon. It makes him look guilty. He says he was set up by Sergei Romanov."

"I hope he's not guilty," Graham said, his eyes distant. "We were friends once. So Romanov did it because of the sex ring connection?"

I nodded my head. "There must be some connection and Spencer was silenced when the connection was in danger of being exposed."

"Hunter said he'd kill Spencer if he ever hurt you again. Spencer hurt you again, remember? I'm not so sure he didn't do it. He had a motive."

"He didn't mean he'd really kill Spencer. That was just something he said in anger."

"Hunter was a soldier. He killed people in Iraq and Afghanistan."

"He *was* a soldier," I said firmly. "He isn't one now. He didn't do it."

I said it, but of course, I wasn't entirely sure myself. I only knew I wanted him to be released and to come back to the warehouse and stay with me.

I said goodbye, kissing Graham on the cheek, and went to find

James waiting besides the SUV. He opened the door for me and squeezed my arm softly as he helped me in.

"How are you?" James asked, glancing at me as he drove off.

"Tired. Any news on the Hunter front?"

"I got a text from George. Nothing new. Grand jury meets on Wednesday. I guess we'll have to wait for them to hear the evidence."

As we drove through the quiet backstreets to the warehouse, I leaned my head back and hoped against hope that Hunter was innocent, and that the grand jury would send him home and back to me.

I slept most of the next day, rising only to have a shower.

That night, I finally felt like getting up. My stomach grumbled – I had barely eaten anything, wondering about Hunter and when he'd be released. I rose from the bed and went to the bathroom. George was at the door when I finished.

"You're feeling better?"

I nodded. "I'm hungry. Have you heard anything about Hunter?"

"Nothing. Come, I get you some food." George went to the kitchen and waved me to the island. "Lawyer will call tomorrow after grand jury."

I sat at the kitchen island and watched as George opened the fridge and looked through the items inside.

"I bought some borscht. Maybe you like, heated up with some good black bread."

"Whatever you fix will be fine."

George poured the container of borsht into a pot and put it on the stove. Next, he took a round loaf of black bread – caraway pumpernickel – and started slicing it up.

Suddenly I heard an explosion of automatic gunfire outside the apartment door.

"What was that?"

George stopped what he was doing and drew his gun. He motioned to me. "Go hide in bedroom under bed."

I complied, watching as George slid along the wall to the doorway. I hurried to the bedroom and turned to watch as George peered at the video feed. "Go!" he said, waving his gun at me. But before I could, the door exploded open and several men in SWAT uniforms entered, throwing in a grenade of some kind.

"Hide!" George shouted. He fired his weapon and leapt behind the desk. I turned away, but was unable to go far. A blast knocked me off my feet and into the wall. As I lay on the ground, sparkles of light dancing before my eyes and my hearing dulled, I wondered if I'd die.

My vision cleared and I watched as a dark figure entered. One of the uniformed men grabbed the gun from George's hand and knocked him in the head, and then in the neck. George collapsed once more to the ground.

One of the black-uniformed men ran to me and knelt. Before I could say anything, he pulled out a roll of duct tape and covered my mouth. Next, he pulled out a black hood and covered my head, then he fastened my hands behind my back with plastic ties.

"You're coming with me."

IVAN HAD TREATED me with respect when he brought me to his club, but Sergei Romanov was completely different. His men were rough, handling me like I was nothing, throwing me into the back of a van, where I lay on my side, my face pressed against a filthy carpet on the van's floor. Every bump in the road jarred me, knocking me around. My arms ached from the position I was in and I felt my lip swell from where I'd hit it when I fell.

We drove for what felt like an hour, but I heard traffic all around us when we stopped at lights and so I wondered if we were driving around Boston. Maybe throwing someone – Hunter's people? – off the track.

Finally, we stopped, the tires screeching, and I was roughly dragged out of the back of the van. I was thrown over someone's shoulder and carried up a flight of stairs. In all the confusion, I tried to take note of the smells and sounds of my location in case I survived and was questioned by police. I hoped I would survive. Even that thought sent my pulse racing, so I shut it down. I shut off my worry and just went with what was happening, not trying to second guess or predict what they would do to me.

When I was finally thrown down onto a sofa and my blindfold taken off, I found myself in a large warehouse, the walls brick, the ceiling lined with ductwork, and the floors hardwood. The place looked like it was used for storage, and there was plastic sheeting hanging, like the place was being renovated.

A man came to where I lay, and I glanced up at him in fear.

Sergei Romanov.

I recognized him from news reports of his crime family and he'd been to Spencer's memorial service. His beefy face was bearded and he wore his longish dark hair slicked back. A large gold chain hung around his neck. He wore a cream sweater and dark jeans, and looked to be in his forties with a touch of grey in his hair.

"What am I going to do with you?"

His voice, rough-sounding, had a thick Russian accent.

"What do you want?"

"I want Hunter. That's what I want."

"He's in jail."

"Not anymore."

That made my heart rate increase. "He was let out?"

I heard the man snicker.

"So, what *will* I do with you? You're a pretty thing, and Hunter needs to be taught a lesson."

Adrenaline surged through me, and I wondered what that meant. Would they kill me to punish Hunter?

There was nothing I could say.

"Please don't hurt me."

"Leave," he said to someone else behind me.

I tensed when I heard footsteps and a door close. Then silence.

Sergei walked over to where I lay. The look in his eyes said everything I needed to know. When he grabbed his belt and began to unfasten it, I closed my eyes and tried to shut off.

Shut everything off.

CHAPTER 39

Hunter

MY STAY in the local jail in Alexandria was turning out to be much more difficult than I anticipated. I'd been in so many bad places in my life that one might think I'd be inured to the local lockup, but I wasn't.

I'd been in dozens of hellholes around the world: bullet-ridden mud-brick houses in Basra, half-destroyed palace rooms in Baghdad, two-bit fleabag hotels in Amman, flop houses in Syria, opium dens and dens of iniquity in Indonesia, straw huts in far-flung war torn tin-pot dictatorships in Africa.

Timbuktu, for fuck's sake.

I'd been used to being busy from the start of the day to the end, and being in cells meant an endless monotony from which I could not escape. It reminded me of when I was in Afghanistan – the long calm before a battle, when I'd lie under our armored vehicle and wait for the fighting to begin. We hated that wait because we knew a battle would come eventually, and would rather get it over and go back to base than sit in the darkness and wait. It was better to be doing rather than waiting. Battle was scary as hell, but it was also an adrenaline rush.

So the cells were tame compared to what I'd seen while deployed.

From the time I was a child, I was either fighting in the ring or active in sports. After I joined up, I spent a tour of duty in the hellhole that was the Persian Gulf during the rise of the ISIS insurgency, patrolling the streets of Fallujah, calling in air strikes, clearing streets house by house, protecting civilization from the scourge of terrorism by capturing and killing bad guys.

I'd seen so much shit, done so much shit, escaped so much shit, that if I didn't hear incoming, if I wasn't dodging IEDs and RPGs and cheating death, I wondered if I were still alive.

In cells, I felt dead. Sitting in a cell all day drove me nuts. The only entertainment came when the they'd bring in a new prisoner and we'd hear their story and try to figure out what was a lie and what was the truth.

I lay on my mattress and covered my face with an arm, wondering when they'd finally bring my info before a grand jury and either indict me or let me go.

Burning in eternal hellfire would be preferable to this.

I tried to divert my mind from thoughts the case to Celia, wondering how she and Graham were faring now that Spencer was dead. Although I had seen her in person, I wasn't sure she was being honest. I figured they'd both be relieved that Spencer was dead. I thought Celia was starting to warm up to me, but would she be secretly hoping I was indicted so she could forget the debt? It seemed like she wanted to be with me, but I wasn't sure.

I needed to be with her to know the truth.

ABOUT AN HOUR before my scheduled visit with McNeil, two guards came to my cell and escorted me to a conference room tucked away in one of the admin wings. McNeil sat inside.

Once the door closed and we were alone, I turned to him expectantly. "What's up? Why are we meeting early?"

"They're dropping charges."

"What?" I said in shock. "I thought the grand jury had to convene first."

"Usually," he said. "The coroner narrowed his time of death estimate, and you were in Boston or on the flight to Washington when Spencer was already dead in Alexandria. There's no way you could have killed him. And your prints weren't on the trigger. It had been smeared by something, which suggests that although you may have handled the weapon, someone else pulled the trigger."

I leaned back and ran my hands through my hair, relief flooding through me.

"So when will I get out?"

"In a few hours, once the paperwork goes through."

"Thank God," I said and sighed. "What took the coroner so long?"

"Seems he had to be convinced to go back and redo his calculations. Spencer died a lot earlier than he initially thought."

"Who convinced him?"

"Someone at the FBI."

"Well, whoever it was, I'd like to buy them a beer or two dozen."

"I thought you'd be happy."

"I am, believe me," I said, smiling broadly. I was thinking that, very soon, I'd be able to make good on my promise to Celia to make her pay. In a very pleasurable way. "Very happy."

Then he folded his hands on the table and looked down at the surface like he had something difficult to tell me.

"What's up? You look like someone died."

"George was shot and is in Mass General undergoing surgery."

Adrenaline surged through me. "What?"

"And Celia's gone. She was abducted after George was shot."

"*Fuck*." I covered my eyes with a hand and tried to grasp what he just said. Obviously, Sergei Romanov had Celia. "Jesus fucking *Christ*." I leaned forward, my head in my hands.

Celia...

I glanced up at him. "What happened? How did his crew get past my security? I had that place protected like fucking Fort Knox."

"Someone inside must have been working with Romanov. Apparently, one of the guards on the perimeter was called off to help with some problem and they got in that way. They took out two of your men guarding the rear entrance. Both dead."

I shook my head slowly, anger flooding through me that Celia was now in danger.

Serious danger.

It was my fault. I should have insisted she leave town once the Romanovs took an interest in her. I had known Sergei might go after her but I thought we were on good terms...

"What do you want to do?"

I sighed and considered. "I have to get her back. As soon as I get out, I'll have to meet with Sergei and see what he wants."

I also knew I'd have to talk to Millar and get his okay. I didn't tell my lawyer that, however. He couldn't know I was working as a black operator for the FBI.

"He won't hurt her," he said, making a doubtful face. "Will he?"

"He won't as long as he gets what he wants from me," I replied, my muscles all tense at the prospect. "Is George going to live?"

"I just got an update from the hospital before I came over. He lost some blood and is in serious condition, but they think he should be fine."

"Thank God."

I leaned back, my legs stretched out straight in front of me, the heels of my palms pressed against my eyes. Celia was in danger but Sergei knew enough that he wouldn't hurt her unless he wanted outright war between us.

He wanted something. Probably my willingness to run guns for him.

"When exactly am I getting out?"

"You should be processed in an hour or so. You'll be a free man."

I took in a deep breath. "What are the police saying about Celia? "

"She's Spencer Grant's stepdaughter. They're wondering if her abduction is connected to his death."

"Of course it is." I frowned. "Sergei killed Spencer, and now he's got Celia. He's killing two birds with one stone. He gets rid of Spencer to shut him up so his ties to Sergei's little underage sex ring won't be exposed. He takes Celia and forces me to comply with his demands to run guns for him."

I leaned forward, my elbows on my knees, and ran my hands through my hair. I looked up at him.

"Do the police know Sergei is involved?"

"Don't know," he replied. "They've said that the murder and Celia's abduction are connected but they have no suspects at this time."

I kicked the chair across from me, anger finally overflowing.

I SPENT the next hour pacing my cell like a lion in a cage, worrying about Celia, planning my response, impatient for the wheels of justice to turn and let me out of the local lock-up.

Finally, guards came to my cell and I was escorted to processing, where I signed the release forms and was given the rest of my street clothes and my personal property – my wallet, my keys, my cell, my money clip, and my shoelaces. Since I had a permit to carry a concealed weapon, my gun was returned along, with my holster. I took the unloaded pistol from the guard and holstered it, feeling complete for the first time in a long time. My jacket went over top, and I was ready.

The guard led me to the front entrance, where James waited with my SUV.

"Welcome back," he said as he opened the passenger door.

"How's George?" I sat and fastened my belt, then turned to him, waiting expectantly for an update. My cell had died while I was in custody so I couldn't still couldn't check my messages or make a call.

"He's still in ICU but should be released in twenty-four hours if his stats are stable."

I leaned back and closed my eyes as we drove from the jail to the gym. The first thing I was going to do was have a shower, then go to the hospital and check on George. After that, I'd call my men and we'd put out feelers to find out where Celia was being held.

When Stepan's brother Ivan took Celia, he'd contacted me directly to let me know he had her. I expected a message from Sergei to let me know he had her and wanted to meet. He wanted something from me and cooperation with his plan was the price I would pay to get Celia back. I wished I had George with me to discuss options.

While I showered, my cell charged, and by the time I was finished and was dressed in fresh clothing, it had enough juice that I could check my messages.

There were a dozen, several from George letting me know how things were, obviously before the abduction. A couple were from my stepmom, telling me to call her as soon as I could and let her how I was. My dad called and left me a very heartfelt message, saying he knew I was innocent and that I'd be out soon. The rest were from Donny's sons, checking in from the gym and letting me know how things were going with the clubs.

The final message was from Sergei.

"Hunter. I want to meet at my club as soon as you're out. We have unfinished business to discuss. By the way, your little bird is very delicate. I would hate to see any of her feathers plucked or her spirit crushed by captivity. Call me so we can arrange a time and place suitable to us both."

Like hell.

I was going in with as big an army as I could. I called up my contact in Romanov's business.

"What have you heard about Sergei abducting Celia Parker?"

There was a pause on the line, as if he were deciding to whom he should be loyal.

"I'll pay you very, *very* well if you give me her location."

"He's keeping her at one of his safe houses. I can give you a couple of addresses but I don't know which one for sure. You'll have to monitor activity to decide which one."

I called a few security experts I knew and asked them to do some sleuthing for me. They agreed to set up a couple of sentries to watch the two properties my informant had given me. We'd find out sooner rather than later where she was, based on the kind of movement into and out of the locations. These security experts were skilled in surveillance and I knew I'd get usable intel, and fast.

Then I drove to Mass General to see how George was doing.

GEORGE WAS STILL in ICU recovering. He was being cared for by a pretty young nurse when I entered the room. She turned and seemed almost fearful when she saw me. Did she recognize me from television coverage of the murder? Whatever the case, she patted George on the hand and left quickly, skirting beside me like she was afraid I'd hurt her while she passed.

"How are you, you old bastard?" I went to George and leaned over, giving him a squeeze on the shoulder without a bandage and kissing his cheek.

"What? You kissing now? So glad to be out of jail and see old Russian?"

"Yes," I replied. "A thousand times yes."

He smiled at me while I sat on the chair next to his bed, scooting closer because he sounded a bit hoarse, like talking was hard.

"So, tell me. Have you heard from Sergei?"

"Yes," I said. "He wants to meet to discuss 'unfinished business.' It's the guns."

"What is your plan?"

I sat back, crossing my arms. "I'm going all in. I'm going to take her back."

He shook his head. "No. Don't go all in. Negotiate. He might hurt her."

I glanced away, barely able to keep my emotions in check when I thought of him abducting her, shooting George, and killing several of my men.

"I'll talk to my contact in the FBI."

"Good," George said and he seemed to relax. "Let them handle. Don't let anger make you reckless. He will kill Celia. He doesn't care."

"He needs to be taken out," I said, anger welling up inside of me again.

"Use FBI. Don't be vigilante. They want him. Work with them to take him down. Get her out first. Agree to anything. Don't do it. Get Celia out."

Of course, George was right. As much as it would please me, I couldn't go all in, guns a-blazing. That might kill Celia and that was not my goal. I wanted her out alive. I wanted her safe.

I wanted her in my bed, night after night, but I knew that so long as Sergei was free and his family was powerful, she would always be a target.

I'd have to send her away.

I sighed. "I'll talk to my handler. Maybe they can get her a new identity in return for the evidence she can provide about her abduction."

"Would be best," George said, his eyes closing like he was too tired to continue talking.

I stood up and squeezed his hand. "You're tired. I'll go for now and come back later."

He nodded without opening his eyes, obviously exhausted by even this much talking.

I left the ICU room and found my way out to the parking lot, glad I'd spoken with him and had come to my senses.

Then I took out my cell and texted Millar, asking for a meet.

THE WATERFRONT a few blocks away from downtown had been rejuvenated in the past decade, but farther down the coast, the buildings were still rough, with the rusting hulks of old warehouses and lots of deserted back alleys. Millar and I met without much chance of being observed.

I pulled up to his car and opened my window as he did his.

"How are you? How was your time in the cells?"

"I've been in worse in Afghanistan," I replied.

"I bet you have. So, what's the purpose of this meeting? I take it you want to go and get your girlfriend from Sergei."

"You got it. I know he wants me to run guns for him. I said no before, but obviously, he didn't like that answer. If I agree to his request, he'll return Celia."

He nodded and surveyed the water. "If we can build a case against him on guns, we can take him out on a RICO warrant."

"I won't wear a wire," I said. "It'll have to be some other way."

"We'll see what we can do. We have some nifty ways of overhearing conversations. Micro drones, hacking electronics, that kind of thing. We may have to put a GPS chip in you so we always know where you are when you go to meet him, get him to give you orders that way."

I nodded, willing to do whatever it took to get Celia out safely. I'd read about some of the FBI special surveillance tech before, and was sure the FBI had access to a lot of great gadgets. Sergei was an expat Russian. He would be a target of surveillance for sure.

"You guys aren't already listening in to him?"

He smiled at me. "That's a whole other branch of government, Hunter. We'll have ways of getting evidence on what you two discuss. That's all I'll say."

"Okay with me," I said. "I just want to get Celia out and then nail the bastard."

"You meet with him. Let me know where and when, and leave the rest with our little friends in the NSA."

"Will do."

He rolled up his window and then drove off. I sat in my car for a few moments, considering. Then I took out my cell and called Sergei.

The number rang several times and then a man answered. It wasn't Sergei, but I didn't expect it to be.

"Hunter Saint for Mr. Romanov."

There was a pause. "Mr. Romanov is unable to take your call. What is your message, please?"

"Tell Mr. Romanov that I'll do whatever he wants. Let me know when and where I can pick up Celia. Tell him I said please don't hurt her."

There was another pause. "I will call you back with time and place." Then the line went dead.

I drove back to the gym, waiting to hear from Sergei's assistant when and where so I could get Celia back and find out how much I was going to pay for the privilege.

I said I'd do anything to get her back. I meant it. I wanted to kill Sergei Romanov for everything he'd done to me and my family – and to Celia. But if I had to work with the FBI and NSA to take him down legitimately to get Celia back alive and in one piece, I would.

HOURS LATER, as we drove to the old warehouse near the waterfront where Celia was being held, I was on an adrenaline high and thought how good it felt just to act. After being in cells for a week, I realized action was in my blood – planning and executing operations. I felt best when on a mission, however dangerous it might be, for it meant I was doing something, creating my own reality, rather than sitting by passively letting events simply happen. I had decided, after Sean's death, that I would never again allow other people to determine my fate.

As the buildings whizzed by, I realized that Celia had become too important to me, and that there was no way she could stay in Boston any longer. Until Sergei was gone, Celia was too much of a risk in my dealings with the Boston mob. My wanting her was a whole other matter – a distraction from the bigger goal – requiring more self-control on my part. My desire for her would have to be kept in tight check. Desiring anything outside the mission too much was a liability.

If you desire nothing beyond the mission, nothing else matters. The only thing that really mattered to me was vengeance. I tried to keep Celia restricted to a small corner of my thoughts, meant for physical gratification alone. A good sweet fuck on my way to revenge.

Only I was finding it more difficult than I anticipated. She occupied too much of my mental life. Her closeness to me made her dangerous and made it even more of a necessity to for her to leave and start a new life somewhere else. I didn't want that, but I would have to make that sacrifice. I'd pick her up, take her to the FBI, and demand they gave her a new identity somewhere beyond the reach of the Romanov brothers. The thought of losing her after I'd had her to myself for the past few weeks was upsetting, but it was necessary to get her out of the equation.

Once she was gone, there would be nothing left but taking down Sergei Romanov.

CHAPTER 40

CELIA

WHEN I WOKE UP, I tasted blood.

I lay on the hard concrete floor in a dark room. It was nothing more than a cell with bars on the walls. The only light filtered in from a tiny window near the ceiling.

A basement. I had no idea where.

When Sergei came at me with every intent to rape me, I fought back. I always fought back, even when Spencer threatened me. It just wasn't in me to let someone hurt me or humiliate me without resisting. That resistance probably brought me more punishment and pain, but at least my pride was intact.

Sergei was so much bigger than me that my resistance only brought on more anger, but whatever he did when I was unconscious was lost to me. For that I was glad, although the ache between my thighs and in my rear suggested it hadn't been gentle.

The last thing I remembered was fighting him, and the feel of his skin beneath my nails when I raked them over his face. I kicked him, I hit him, and finally, when he was unable to control me, he hit me, breaking my nose, the blood running down over my lips and chin. That was the last thing I remembered clearly. The rest was blurred images, sensations, sounds.

Whatever he did to me, whoever he let do things to me, I didn't remember much of any of it. Thankfully. I remembered waking while lying face down with Sergei – or someone else – grunting over me. When I cried out, he pressed my face against the floor.

"Zakróy svoy rot, súka!" Shut your mouth, bitch!

I had fallen back into unconsciousness as pain overtook me once more.

Now, I lay on my side and licked my lips, tasting coppery blood. I ran my tongue over my teeth and was glad that they were all still intact, at least. My lip had been cut, though, and was swelling, the flesh raw. Nothing else seemed broken, so I'd gotten off lightly.

The door opened, and light flooded into the room, illuminating it for the first time since I arrived there. It was filthy, with a rotting mattress on a platform, stained from who knew what. I didn't want to think.

A man stood in the doorway, his face hidden in shadow.

Now what?

More rape? More pain?

"Get up."

I struggled up to a sitting position and hid my eyes from the painful light. A man came into the cell and I closed my eyes, waiting for whatever hell he was going to administer, but he only slipped his hand under my arm and lifted me, pulling me to a standing position. I wobbled on my feet, dizzy, my muscles aching.

"Your boyfriend is coming to rescue you," the man said with a chuckle. "Too bad. I could use you in one of my brothels. Some men like to fight with a woman before they fuck her. I get extra money for ones like you. He's going to have to pay a lot to get you back."

He dragged me out of the room and up a set of stairs. We entered a warehouse with brick walls, duct work, and hardwood floors. Shelves of boxes filled the space. It looked like some kind of storage unit. He threw me back down and I landed on my knees, my hands preventing me from hitting my face, but only just.

"Take her," he said to another man who stood a few feet away. I glanced up and took him in. Younger, dark haired, goatee. Prominent tattoos on his face and neck and wrists.

Bratva. Vor. The Brotherhood of Thieves. I'd read those terms before – the Russian mafia in the U.S.

"Should we clean her up first?"

"No," the man said. "Let him see what happens to his women when he crosses me."

I glanced back at him, wondering who he was. He had the same dark hair and beefy face as Sergei, and I wondered if he wasn't Sergei's son or some other relation.

"Go, *pizdá*. It was fun. Maybe some other time if your boyfriend doesn't cooperate, we'll meet again. You got nice tits."

I stood and saw there was an open door leading outside. Hunter must be out there. Why didn't he come inside and get me?

I limped to the door, barefoot, wearing only a thin bloodied t-shirt and my jeans, which were wet between my thighs.

"Hunter?"

I got to the door and felt exhausted, but hope filled me when I saw him standing in a group of armed uniformed men, their weapons drawn. When he saw me, his face blanched and I could see his body tense.

"Let me go to her," he said, his voice low, almost a growl.

One of the black-uniformed men pointed a weapon at Hunter's head. "You stay." The soldier turned to me and waved me forward. "You come," he ordered.

I leaned in the doorway, my legs wobbling, tears of relief in my eyes.

"Hunter," I whispered and fell, my legs finally giving out. Hunter pushed past the soldier and came to me, kneeling beside me, hooking his arms under mine and picking me up. He kissed my cheek, my forehead, and I sobbed, so relieved he was there. I slipped my arms around his neck while he carried me down the stairs and tucked my face into his neck. He took me to the waiting SUV where James stood, his hand on the door, holding it open. His face was grim, his expression one of horror.

I must look pretty bad.

Hunter placed me gently into the back seat and I lay down, lacking the strength to do up my seatbelt. Hunter did it for me, adjusting it so I could recline. He got in beside me, and I lay my head in his lap.

"Let's go," he said. I caught a glimpse through the darkened windows of men holding up their weapons, the warehouse disappearing as we drove off.

"Where to?"

"Mass General emergency."

"No," I said, shaking my head. "Take me to your safe house. I don't want doctors poking and prodding me."

"You need a rape kit, x-rays, blood tests," Hunter said and stroked my hair. "Don't argue with me."

I didn't have the strength to argue and so I closed my eyes and tried to let everything go.

I was safe now.

Hunter had come to rescue me.

"What did he make you do?" I managed to ask.

"Shh," Hunter said and stroked my cheek. "Don't you worry about anything but recovering."

"He made you do something bad," I said, unable to keep the man's words out of my mind. "Tell me what I cost you."

"I'd pay anything," he said softly. "You have to know that. *Anything.*"

I finally relented, and tried not to think of what had happened to me. Instead, I thought about being safe – finally safe.

I was taken right into a room in the ER when Hunter carried me inside and told the triage nurse I'd been raped and beaten.

A nurse came in with us and did a preliminary exam, then an ER doc came in and did his assessment, telling me I'd be getting a rape kit, x-rays to check for broken bones, and a CT scan of my head to check for concussion. I was taken immediately for several x-rays and the CT scan, after they checked my blood pressure to make sure I wasn't bleeding internally. When that was finished, a special nurse did the rape kit, which I had no idea would take so long and involved plucking out dozens of pubic hairs, swabbing me, examining me, and taking photographs. She explained everything to me and advised me to get some counseling because of the trauma I had experienced.

"Even if you don't remember everything now, you may have vivid dreams and at times, you might remember parts of the rape that you don't recall now. It will help if you have someone to talk to who knows how to deal with this. We have resources that you can use when you get out."

I thanked her. When it was all over, I was taken back to my room and a lab tech came to draw blood. Finally, I lay on a gurney in an examining room, Hunter standing beside the bed, my hand in his.

He leaned down and kissed me tenderly on the mouth. "How are you?"

"I'm fine," I said and smiled. "Just a bitch of a headache."

The ER physician came in and stood at the side of my bed, checking my file.

"You have a concussion as well as some minor contusions and abrasions. Your nose was broken, but fortunately you won't need any surgery. You'll have swelling and two black eyes for a while, but everything should be back to normal in about six weeks. We'll turn the rape kit over to police and you should know soon about any exposure to HIV or other sexually transmitted diseases when the lab reports come back. The nurse talked with you about it?"

I nodded. "When can I go home?"

"We'd like to keep you overnight, just to be sure. That's quite a concussion you have so I'd feel better. You can stay in an observation room. It's semi-private, but that's all we have for now."

I turned to Hunter. He nodded. "You should stay."

I turned back to the doc. "Can he stay for a while?"

The doctor turned to Hunter. "Are you immediate family?"

"Yes," Hunter said. "I'm her fiancé."

The ER doc nodded. "You can stay, but there isn't much room for chairs. No more than one visitor at a time and only immediate family."

"That's okay."

Hunter turned to me, his eyes meeting mine, a sparkle in his eyes. I smiled, amused that he'd played the fiancé card.

When the doc left, I turned to Hunter. "So, I'm engaged, am I?"

"They're not going to kick me out of here," he said and kissed me again. When he pulled back, his expression was serious. "I'm so sorry this happened to you. It's all my fault. Everything. If only I'd just paid off Graham's debt and left it at that, none of this would have happened to you."

"It's Graham's fault," I replied, shaking my head. "If he hadn't lost all our money, we would never have had to come to you, involve you in our trouble."

Hunter nodded and stroked my cheek.

"But then," I said softly. "We wouldn't have met again."

"No, we wouldn't. You wouldn't have been abducted – twice. You wouldn't have been harmed."

"We can't go back," I said and squeezed his hand. "No use crying over spilled milk. All I want is for things to go back to normal. Now that Spencer's gone, Graham and I don't have to worry about him. I'll finish my law degree, and life can go on."

Hunter shook his head. "Things will never go back to normal, Celia. Not now that Sergei did this."

"We can try to make them normal," I said, frowning. "Won't the police charge him with my abduction and rape? They did a rape kit. There's evidence."

"Celia," Hunter said softly. "They're not going to charge him with rape."

"But he raped me. He abducted me."

"He's the head of the Russian mafia in Boston. He's not going down on a rape charge. They want to get him on something bigger. Racketeering. Money laundering. Gun running."

I frowned, angry that despite the fact he'd abducted and raped me, as did his henchmen, they wouldn't press charges.

"But the rape kit…"

"It'll go where the majority of rape kits go – on a shelf in the police station. Celia, Sergei is a big fish. They'll wait until they have enough to arrest him and keep him. They'll wait until they have a rock-solid case of racketeering before they take him in. A rape charge, an abduction charge..." He took my face in his hands. "They don't want to waste their effort. Most rape charges are never even prosecuted."

"That's not fair," I said, unable to accept that what Sergei did to me would mean nothing for him. Then I nodded, realizing what Hunter said was true.

"I understand." I sighed and closed my eyes, tears springing to them. I was suddenly overwhelmed with emotion and couldn't hold it back.

Hunter slipped his arms around me, holding me tightly while I cried.

"I'm so sorry," he whispered, kissing my cheek, wiping tears from my face. "I promise you that nothing else will happen to you. I promise you."

I let him hold me, for his arms were the only comfort I knew.

LATER, Amy and then my Aunt Diane came to the hospital to see me. Even Graham used a wheelchair and dropped by and so my overnight stay in Mass General's observation beds passed quickly. Hunter stayed until after midnight, not letting go of my hand unless he had to leave to let someone else visit.

Strangely, the police didn't come until later in the evening. I expected it was because of what Hunter told me. They weren't going to do anything. Still, the two police officers, one female and one male, took my statement and then left with a promise to call me if anything happened with the case.

I knew nothing would.

"He *will* get justice, Celia," Hunter said to me before he left that night. "I promise you. He'll pay for what he did to you. He'll pay for everything."

I nodded and closed my eyes. Hunter leaned down and kissed me, his kiss tender. He lingered over me, adjusting my covers, my pillow, stroking my cheek.

Then he left me.

And that was the last time I saw him.

I WOKE EARLY the next morning. Hospitals were so noisy, with nursing staff and cleaners bustling around at all hours. Even when they shut off the main overhead lights, there was still activity so my sleep was broken.

Still, they gave me some Tylenol for pain and I managed a few hours of sleep. A nurse came in the morning and asked if I wanted a shower, and I did. I'd had one after the rape kit had been finished, but I felt like I needed another one. I stood in the bathroom and stared into the mirror, at my two black eyes and swollen nose. Luckily, my nose hadn't been broken too badly and I'd show no long-term consequences. I didn't want to look like a boxer, and the ER doc assured me I wouldn't, but it would take weeks for the swelling to go down completely.

To my surprise, Aunt Diane arrived and brought me some clean clothes she got from Hunter.

"Did you talk to him? Why didn't he come himself?"

She nodded. "Yes, sweets, I talked to him. He said to tell you that he had to go out of town for a while. That you should come and stay with me until things get cleared up."

"What?" I frowned and texted Hunter.

CELIA: Hey, why aren't you coming to pick me up?

I waited and waited, but didn't get an answer.

CELIA: Why didn't you tell me you were going out of town?

CELIA: Hunter, please respond. Tell me where you are. Why am I staying at my aunt's place? It can't be any safer than your place.

No answer.

"What did he say to you?" I asked her. "Tell me!"

She had a guilty expression on her face, and avoided my eyes. "He said he was going away, and that you were going to have to as well.

436

The FBI is going to come by today and talk to you about moving somewhere safe." Then she turned and faced me. "Celia, the truth is that you're not safe here anymore. Not as long as Sergei is free. You have to move away. Get a new identity. Start over."

"What?" I sat dumbfounded, on the verge of tears. "I'm not leaving. What about Mom? Graham? I'm in Harvard Law! You don't just walk away from that."

"Everything will be arranged for you. New ID, new name and Social Security number. You'll have to have a cover story. You can apply to go to law school wherever you relocate. You were accepted at Stanford so you could always go there. You'll have papers that should help you get in."

"When did you discuss all this?"

"While you were sleeping. Hunter talked to his contact in the FBI and he agreed. You're in danger. Sergei Romanov hurt you once and he won't hesitate to do it again. He was likely the one who killed your stepfather. When he's in jail, we can re-establish contact, but there's no way to know how long that will take. He's a big fish. It takes longer to hook them and pull them in. Maybe a year or more."

I stared at the wall, tears in my eyes. "So Hunter hates Sergei so much, he's willing to send me away so he can catch him?"

My aunt took my hand and squeezed. "No. He cares for you so much that he has to send you away for your own safety."

I wiped my eyes, emotion overwhelming me. I didn't want to leave. I didn't want to leave Boston, my mother and brother. Harvard. *Hunter...*

"Can we visit? Can you guys come out to wherever I live?"

"No contact is allowed, Celia. Not while you're still in danger."

"But that may mean a year or longer..."

"I'm sorry, but I agree that it's for your own protection."

I closed my eyes and cried.

CHAPTER 41

Hunter

"You know I'm right."

Celia's Aunt Diane stood in front of me, her hands on her hips. She had this expression in her eyes that said she wouldn't accept no from me. Of course, she was right. I'd been nothing but bad news for Celia since she had come to me and begged me to save Graham's life. If I had been a man instead of a big piece of suck, I would have paid off the debt and walked away.

But I hadn't.

I would be a man now, when Celia needed me.

"You're right."

She nodded and pointed to the exit. "Leave now, and don't come back. I'll let you know how she is, but if you care about her, Hunter, you'll leave her for good."

I turned and left, my eyes blurring at the truth of it.

I had to leave her.

She'd have to leave Boston.

I'd talk to Millar and get him to make the arrangements. Then, I'd

439

extract myself from Celia's life for good. She'd probably be upset, but in the end, she'd thank me when she restarted her life free from the danger that still existed for her here in Boston.

A FEW DAYS LATER, I went to the hospital to check on George.

"How is Celia?" George asked, sitting up on the edge of his bed, dangling his feet to improve his circulation. He was slowly recovering. If he kept improving, getting stronger every day, he would be released in a week. Maybe ten days.

"She's much better, I hear."

"You are not seeing?"

I shook my head, a catch in my throat at the thought I wouldn't see her again.

"Is for best," George said and squeezed my shoulder as I helped him stand. "You know."

"I know, but I still don't like it."

I walked George to his bathroom and waited outside while he took a piss, listening to make sure he didn't fall. I heard the flush that signalled he was done and then the water running in the sink. The door opened and he came out once more.

"Should I walk? Get exercise?"

"Yes, you should. Come on, old man. Get your ass moving or you'll never get out of here."

We got his walker, and together we walked the hallways, his pace a bit faster today than it had been. He truly was on the mend but his docs said he'd still need to use a cane. The bullet had damaged nerves in his spine and he'd probably be weak on one side for the rest of his life.

Despite it all, he was happy to be getting up and walking. I was happy to have him back with me, although he would never be the same soldier he had been before the attack.

That, too, was on me. My fault.

I should have let Celia remain just a memory, but I couldn't. When she came to me, I couldn't resist her.

I could never resist her.

Even though I knew I shouldn't, I spoke with Millar and was filled in on the plans to get Celia a new identity and new location until Sergei was taken down. It would never be entirely safe for her, but once Sergei and his family went down, she'd be able to re-establish contact with her family. Until then?

She'd have to become lost to us all.

Millar took care of everything, promising not to talk to me about her until after it was done. I didn't know where she'd go, and I didn't know what her name was.

I felt sick about it, but it was for the best. She'd been hurt enough for one lifetime. First it was the loss of her father, then her mother's disability, then Spencer abusing her and Graham all those years. Finally, me taking advantage of my power over her to get what I wanted. Sergei's abduction and her rape was too much.

I had to let her go, no matter how much it hurt.

GEORGE CAME HOME about a week later and went to a special room I'd had hastily constructed with everything he'd need to recover over the coming weeks. A special chair that raised and lowered so he could get in easily. A bathtub that had an easy access. I hired an occupational therapist for him, who would get him back into as good a working shape as possible, given the damage to his nerves.

Four weeks passed, and then five.

Six weeks after I rescued Celia from Sergei's warehouse, I entered the space with my crew, weapons at their sides.

For two weeks, I'd planned the op, meeting with Sergei's competitors, finding my way into their good graces. I'd established a relationship with a man who wanted to take over some of Sergei's business in Boston.

I'd agreed, in a meeting with Sergei's capo, to store his shipments of guns at my warehouse on the waterfront and we were going to pick them up – or so the story went.

When we walked in, the guards checked us out but our weapons were expected because we were transporting the guns and needed protection. I was unarmed and went up to Sergei, shaking his hand.

"It is good you finally came around to my way of thinking about this matter," he said coolly.

"What choice did I have?" I replied, smiling.

"There was no choice, I agree. I hear your little bird was plucked and flew to a better nest. It is sad. I love a happy ending but there are other birds."

"There are."

"Yes, there are many pretty birds and they are very sweet," Sergei said, then waved at the boxes of guns. "But money is sweeter."

I nodded, not letting on how I really felt, smiling like Celia meant nothing to me.

Of course, Sergei knew she meant something to me – a lot. Enough that he could manipulate me to get what he wanted.

"So, you take my guns, and hold them until I have a buyer. You get a cut, I get them out of my warehouse."

At that moment, two more armed men entered. They were a few of the lower-level guards from one of Sergei's competitors, who I'd promised could take over the gun-running biz in Boston once I took Sergei down. It had taken a great deal of finesse to get them to trust me, but they finally did, having as much hatred for Sergei as I did, but for different reasons.

"What the fuck is this?" Sergei glanced at the men.

"Some backup," I said. "Just in case I needed them." I gestured to the men, who were dressed in swat gear. They stood at the ready. The lead man nodded at me. His name was Alexei – the son of one of the Russians in Boston who had fallen at Sergei's hands but he was wearing a mask that covered the bottom of his face so Sergei didn't recognize him.

"We're here with a truck, ready to go," Alexei said, holding his hand up to calm Sergei.

Sergei looked wary, but then he relented. "Be my guest." Sergei pointed to the boxes of guns. "I'll let you know when my buyer is coming to pick up."

"You heard the man," I said to Alexei and his man. "Take them."

That was the signal. Both men turned their weapons on Sergei's guards, who fell to the ground in a hail of automatic gunfire. I watched Sergei, who was cool as a cucumber. The only sign he was upset was the muscle pulsing in his jaw. He turned to me, reaching for his weapon, but I was faster, kicking away his hand before he could draw his weapon. Then I punched him in the head, easily knocking him to the ground. I knelt over him and took the weapon from his holster.

"This," I said holding the gun to his chin. "This is for Celia."

EPILOGUE

CELIA

MY NEW HOME a few miles north of San Francisco in Duncan's Cove was unlike anything I'd known. I knew it was Hunter's doing. The FBI witness protection program didn't provide oceanfront beach houses for their protectees.

I spent my days walking the coast, collecting shells, and waiting for everything to heal so I could move forward with my life, such as it was. I recovered from my concussion, the headaches slowly subsiding, and my bruises all faded. My memories of the rapes were sporadic, coming back now and then when I least expected it. With nothing else to do, I spent my time reading and watching Netflix, taking my first real holiday since I started college.

I heard nothing from anyone back in Boston except a short email from Monique, my contact in the FBI's witness protection program. She said all was well and everyone in my list of contacts was fine. All alive. All living their lives without me. They could only communicate with me via her so no one knew where I lived or what name I had taken.

For the first week after I arrived in Duncan's Cove, I cried every night, sad that I had been forced to leave everyone I loved, and that Hunter had agreed to it. I really thought he cared for me enough to want to keep me in Boston. I argued with my aunt, I argued with Graham, and I argued with my mother, but they all agreed that it was the right thing to do. Hunter wouldn't even see me, no matter what I did.

In Duncan's Cove, I didn't have to get a job. Money was deposited in an account for me once a month – more than I had ever earned before, and more than I needed. I knew that was Hunter's doing as well, and for that I was grateful, but I hated him for letting me go without even saying goodbye.

Then, out of the blue, six weeks after I left Boston, I was watching CNN and saw a headline on the ticker tape at the bottom of the screen.

BOSTON MAFIA BOSS SERGEI ROMANOV, brother Victor Romanov killed in gangland assassination.

THE NEWS WAS SORDID. A rival Russian gang had fought with the Romanovs over a shipment of guns. Sergei and his brother Victor were both shot dead, as well as three of their underlings. Two men from the rival gang were also killed, their bodies left at the scene.

The news coverage displayed a bloody scene, blue sheets covering the bodies in an old warehouse along the waterfront.

It was the warehouse where I was raped.

One of Sergei's relatives from New York City, Semion Romanov, came down from New York City for the funerals.

I called Monique to ask if that meant I could come back to Boston, but she assured me that I was still not safe. She told me to be patient, forget Boston, and focus on my application for law school at Stanford. That no matter what, I had to make a new life because my name would still be on the Romanovs' list of enemies.

I was assured that since I already had been accepted at Stanford when I initially applied the previous year, I could re-apply and would likely be accepted. The fact that I was in the witness protection program would be known to only a few of those involved in approving applications. The confidentiality of my real identity would be assured.

Resigned to my lot, I went out and sat on the deck overlooking the ocean and tried to get excited about starting law school in the fall, but it was hard. I still had months to wait until I could begin again. Bored, I got a job at a local bookstore and spent my time stocking shelves and helping customers find their books, even though I didn't need the money.

Every day I went to work, my name tag reading Emma Jones instead of Celia Parker. It was hard at first to adjust to using a new name, and I often failed to respond when my boss or one of my neighbors called out Emma, because I forgot who I was supposed to be.

Then, one day as I was walking along the beach, I got a text on my new cell. My new number under my new name.

JDOE: If you want to see me again, meet me at 7152 Cliff Avenue.

A surge of emotion swept through my entire body and my eyes teared up. J Doe? John Doe... It had to be Hunter. But how could I know? It could be one of the Romanov thugs come to kill me...

EMMA: How do I know who you are? Give me evidence to prove it's you or I'm calling the FBI.

JDOE: The first time we kissed, you rolled on top of me while we were supposed to be watching the stars.

Hunter. He was here, in Duncan's Cove. Cliff Avenue ran up the coast a few miles from my place.

I texted him, unable to hold back.

EMMA: Hunter! Why didn't you contact me all this time? It's been two months and I haven't heard anything from you. Why didn't you contact me sooner? You just expect me to come running to you after not even saying goodbye?

I cried after I sent that, torn between being angry at him and wanting to go right away.

JDOE: I know you're angry but I had to do it for your safety. Come to me.

EMMA: Why should I? You expect me to just run to you when you call me up?

JDOE: I remember that night so well. I tried to be a gentleman but you were brazen and insisted I kiss you.

EMMA: I was a foolish young girl.

JDOE: I protested, because I was supposed to be protecting you, not trying to seduce you. You kissed me anyway. It got me in trouble with Graham. And made me fall in love with you. Come to me. Whenever you want.

EMMA: Do you have permission to visit me? My handler didn't say anything about this. I'm not supposed to contact anyone from my past. I'm going to have to think about this.

JDOE: Take as much time as you need. I'm not going anywhere.

I wiped my eyes and walked back to the house, unsure of whether I should go to Hunter and see him again. My handler told me I couldn't go back until I had their approval and that I couldn't be in contact with anyone or I might lose their protection.

I sat in the house and stared at the fireplace, trying to decide what to do.

AFTER SEVERAL HOURS OF DITHERING, I got in my SUV and drove up the coast to the address despite my misgivings. I found the house and parked in the driveway, noting that there was a single SUV parked there – a black Mercedes. It had to be Hunter's.

I climbed up the pathway to the house, which was fantastic – maybe a couple of thousand square feet in all with an amazing deck, which was lit up by patio lanterns hanging from the rafters. I knocked at the door and waited.

The door opened to reveal George and I squealed with delight when I saw him.

"George!" I hugged him. He seemed surprised at my show of affection, but I felt real joy at seeing him.

"Miss Celia," he said, his voice thick with emotion. "I am so glad to see you."

I stepped back, my hands on his arms, and looked him over. He was the same old pug-faced Russian with a salt-and-pepper brush cut and a pale blue button-down shirt and jeans. His face was weathered, with deep lines in it above his eyes, beside his nose. His piercing blue eyes were just as I remembered. He put a hand to them, like he was overcome with emotion.

"What's the matter?"

He pulled his hand away and smiled. "I am so sorry," he said, extending his hand. "I am very glad that you are okay."

"I'm fine, " I said and took his hand. "It's you who was seriously injured. I was just roughed up a bit. Nothing serious."

Of course, that was a lie, but it was the one I told myself. I wasn't "just roughed up" and George knew it by the look on his face. I smiled, trying to pretend everything was fine, and followed him. He struggled up the stairs, using a three-pronged cane as he climbed the five stairs to the main floor.

"Where's Hunter?"

"He is in garage trying to fix car. Please to come in. Make yourself comfortable."

I smiled at his accent. It was one of those endearing traits of his. I hadn't realized how much I missed him.

We entered a huge great room with vaulted ceilings, dark wood beams, and an enormous stone fireplace. Two floor-to-ceiling windows overlooked the ocean.

"Sit," he said, waving to the sofa. "I tell Hunter you are here."

I went to the window, glancing around at the cabin, amazed at how fantastic it was, with huge windows overlooking the Pacific. While my place was nice, this was spectacular.

Just then, Hunter entered the living room from the back of the house.

He stopped when our eyes met. "Celia…"

"Hunter," I said, my throat closing, stopping me from saying more.

He came right over, a soft smile on his lips. He pulled me into his arms and kissed me, the kiss soft at first, then growing more passionate. He pulled me closer and finally, I threw my arms around him, kissing him back with abandon.

George cleared his throat and we broke the kiss and turned to him, both of us smiling.

"Sorry," Hunter said. "Got carried away." He turned back to me and touched my cheek, then stroked my hair. "How are you?"

"I'm fine," I said, feeling like I was far too close to tears. I *still* wanted Hunter. No matter what had happened to me, even if it was his fault, I wanted him.

"I'm so glad you decided to come."

"You thought I'd say no?"

He nodded. "I did," he said softly. "I thought you'd hate me. It was because of me that you... had to leave."

I said nothing, just looked at him, drinking in his face, his body. Finally, I spoke, my voice wavering with emotion.

"I could never hate you," I whispered.

Hunter smiled. "George packed a picnic basket for us. I thought we could hike along the trail along the cliffs and have lunch."

"Sounds nice," I said with a sigh. "I don't really know anyone here so it'll be nice to have some company for a change."

He nodded, his eyes lingering on my face. "I'm sorry. It must have been hard, being all alone for so long."

I nodded. Finally, he turned to George. "I'll take that."

George held out the wicker basket. "I pack good Russian food, " he said, a grin on his face. "Vodka, caviar, sour cream, blini. Fruit, too."

"Caviar?" I said with a laugh and stood up. "That's not picnic fare."

"Is in Mother Russia," George protested, a mock-hurt expression on his face. "Each year we go to dacha on Black Sea and eat caviar, drink vodka around fire."

I turned to Hunter. "Do you eat caviar? "

"It's really quite good, " he said and grabbed the basket. "Try it. You never know you like something until you try."

"I'll try for George's sake, since he went to so much trouble."

Hunter patted George on the back. "We'll be a while."

George nodded, smiling. "Have nice time."

We left the house and made our way along the cliff that overlooked the coast. While we hiked, I talked about the area and about my time there since I'd left, and he filled me in on news from Saint Brothers Gym and the whole business with Sergei and Victor.

I stopped him, my hand on his arm.

"Did you kill Sergei?"

He said nothing and started walking along the path.

"I take it that means you did, but you can't admit it."

He smiled at me. "Classified info. Let's just say I'm happy he and Victor are gone. Now the FBI has to take down his cousin Semion. He's a really bad guy."

We reached a clearing after hiking along a winding trail that cut along the face of the cliff with a few trees on one side, a sharp drop on the other. Below was a rocky shore where the waves crashed into white foam. The air was cool and a bit damp, the scent of pine and salt sea air strong. It was refreshing and kept me from overheating.

A couple of trees had been felled and the clearing was dominated by a huge tree stump where Hunter stood.

"Here's our table." He turned his back to me. "Do you like the view? I scouted this place out when we arrived and thought this would be a great place for a picnic."

I nodded, then frowned.

"How long have you been here?"

"A week." He glanced sideways at me, a guilty expression on his face.

"A week? And you didn't contact me?"

He shook his head. "I promised your mother and your aunt that I'd never see you again."

Anger bubbled up inside of me at them both for making Hunter promise.

"They shouldn't have made you do that. It's none of their business."

"They were afraid you'd be murdered, Celia. Murdered because of me."

I said nothing and watched while he placed the basket on the stump, which must have once been a massive tree. It was as big as a dining room table. He opened the basket and took out a blanket with ornate red, white, and black stitching.

"Is that Russian? It looks Slavic."

"Thanks to George. He bought the picnic basket and the blanket at this little Russian store in San Francisco."

"Really? There's a Russian store in San Francisco?"

"There is." Hunter took out dishes and glasses and a bottle of vodka. "I wouldn't know how to fix a picnic if my life depended on it." He opened the bottle of vodka and poured two shots into the tiny crystal glasses with delicate lacy etching. "Luckily, it doesn't or I'd be dead. That's why I have George. He, unlike me, actually had a life in Russia and learned all these things."

Hunter sat on the stump and I sat beside him, wanting to feel his body next to mine.

"So," I said as I leaned back. "Tell me about George. How is he?"

"George?" Hunter fished out a small insulated container from the picnic basket. He opened it and revealed a collection of small pancake-like items. He eyed them. "George is the kind of man who believes in going all out. These," he said, "are blini. Little Russian pancakes."

I smiled. "Yes, I know those. You put caviar on them and sour cream."

Hunter glanced up at me. "They're good. Salty and creamy and savory." He took out a small dish of black caviar and one filled with sour cream. He fixed a blini for me and handed it to me on a napkin.

"You should be drinking a shot of vodka when you eat this, to be truly Russian."

I laughed. "You didn't tell me why George was so emotional."

"He was afraid for you, that's all."

I smiled, affection for George filling me.

"After what happened in Boston, I'm quite happy to never see another Russian again, but I have a soft spot for George. As for the vodka, hit me." I popped the blini in my mouth and chewed. I didn't mind it. "Tastes like the ocean." I watched as Hunter ate one as well.

"How is he?" I asked. "He was hurt badly when they abducted me. He almost died, right?"

Hunter nodded and fixed me another blini. "George is tough," he said and leaned back. "He's recovering. He needs to use a cane, and probably will for the rest of his life but he's alive."

"I'm glad." I said and took the glass of vodka from him.

"To your health," he said and held up his glass once he'd filled it.

"To your heath," I repeated and we both downed the vodka. I squinted but enjoyed the sensation as it burned down my throat.

"So, tell me why you're here," I said. "Why bring George with you? It must have been hard for him to travel."

"I've been thinking. You know what they say – everything happens for a reason and for the best. To teach us life lessons."

"I don't believe that." I shook my head. "What reason was there for Sean to die?"

He frowned. "Because I was stupid. I should have pushed harder to get my family out of the business. I should have insisted and I should have stayed in Boston and taken over instead of going into the Marines. I was being selfish."

I was silent. "Maybe you wouldn't have succeeded. Sergei was a monster, as was his brother. You couldn't have escaped them very easily."

"No, you're right. But maybe if I had, the FBI would never have come that day to arrest Donny, and Sean would still be alive, and you wouldn't be in witness protection across the country from me so the bad guys can't find you and hurt you."

"Can't cry over spilled milk," I said. "That's what my counselor says."

A silence passed between us. "You start law school in the fall?"

"Yes," I said and sighed. "I wanted to start right away, but my counselor said I need time off to process everything."

He fixed another couple of blini and handed me one. "Any psychological problems as a result?"

"Yeah," I said. "My counselor tells me I have PTSD. I get panic attacks. I get panic attacks because I'm afraid of getting panic attacks. When my stress gets too high, I have them. Feel like I'm dying. That's why I can't go to school yet, I guess. Too much stress. Too much responsibility."

"That makes sense," he said. "What happened to you..."

I took a sip and changed the subject, not wanting to remind myself of what had happened.

"I'm working at a book store, if you can believe it," I said with a smile. "Shelving books, filling orders, that kind of thing."

Hunter said nothing, but he was frowning as he chewed his blini.

I reached out and touched his arm. "I'm fine, Hunter. I'll adjust eventually."

"No." He glanced at me. "You're not fine. You had a serious trauma. It's all my fault."

"Stop," I said. "It's in the past."

He nodded but I knew he was still upset.

"You must be lonely."

I shook my head. "Not really," I lied, and took a sip. "I'm just trying to get by." I closed my eyes. "I'm getting better, day after day. I'm just glad that Sergei and Victor are dead."

"I am, too."

I glanced at him, at his handsome face, his longish hair falling in his eyes in that sexy way.

"I'm glad you killed him. I wanted you to kill him, but I was afraid you'd go to jail for murder and I really wouldn't see you again."

A silence passed. Hunter fixed some more blini and handed one to me.

"Do you have any friends here? Boyfriend?"

"Boyfriend? Hunter, *no*," I said with a frown. "I'm still trying to recover."

"Just checking." He said nothing for a moment and the two of us glanced out over the ocean. Gulls flew overhead, no doubt aware of the food we had.

We sat in silence again. I felt a hole in the pit of my stomach. Finally, Hunter leaned over and poured me more vodka.

When he spoke again, his voice was low. "Do you remember what happened to you?"

I said nothing for a moment. "I have these vague memories," I said, anxiety filling me at the mention of that time. I did remember being raped. I remembered men, I remembered pain and humiliation.

"I'm so sorry."

"I wish I could forget but the memories come back, any time of the day or night." I covered my eyes, biting my lip to stop my tears.

Then I felt a panic attack coming on. I stood, dropping my napkin, the vodka glass falling from my hand.

"I have to leave," I whispered. I turned back and began walking down the path. I had gone about a hundred yards before he caught me, grabbing my arm, turning me gently around.

"Celia, I'm so sorry." He tried to pull me into an embrace but I struggled, turning away, panic rising in me as grief and fear over-whelmed me, making it hard to breathe.

I covered my face, gasping for breath as the panic attack kicked in and I felt as if my heart would explode, as if I would pass out. He grabbed me, his arms around me, and just held me as I fought to regain control.

"Just breathe," he said, his voice calm in my ear, his breath warm on my cheek. "Breathe in slowly. Count to six, then out through your teeth for six."

I tried, knowing the whole deep breathing exercise by heart, and in a few moments, the tingling in my arms and legs subsided and my chest stopped heaving. Soon, I was breathing almost normally, and the anxiety dissipated. I let him hold me, still needing his comfort to soothe my fears.

"You have to give yourself time." He kissed me and wiped my tears away. "Come back and sit down."

I turned and he took my hand, leading me back to the picnic spot. I sat on the stump and stared at the ocean. Hunter sat beside me, his thigh pressed against mine.

He put one arm around my shoulders. "You have to create new memories."

I struggled to speak. "I have new memories." I wiped my cheeks. "They don't delete the old ones."

He took in a deep breath. "Let me tell you a story. There was this beautiful princess who was forced into being a slave girl to a pirate. She tried to escape him, but he took advantage of her. Because of him, she was hurt very badly."

"That's not what happened."

"It's pretty much that." He looked away. "I should have paid off Graham's debt and let you live your life. Everything would have been different if I hadn't been so greedy. I remember the day I first saw you at college. You were so beautiful and I wanted you so much, but you were Graham's sister. I *always* wanted you. When you threw me over, I was hurt. I was jealous. I should never have taken advantage of your situation."

"I didn't throw you over. I let you go. I was afraid Spencer would get you in trouble. He threatened to if I didn't stop seeing you. I wanted you, too."

"It doesn't matter now," he said but he gave me a soft smile. "You were so smart and fun and I wanted to be with you. When you started seeing Greg, I felt like such a failure."

I said nothing for a moment. "I never saw Greg. That was just a lie to get you to stop coming by."

He shook his head like he didn't believe me. "I felt so – tarnished – compared to you. You were smart, really smart. When we got together that one night? I thought it was the start of a real relationship." He held my hands in his. "When you came to me and asked me to pay off Graham's debt, I had already decided to. I should have turned you away and never seen you again. What an idiot. I put you in danger. It was because of me that you were hurt. That you had to leave."

"I had to leave because of Spencer just as much as you."

He looked away. "In the end, I couldn't protect you. I promised I'd protect you and I failed."

"You were in jail falsely charged with Spencer's murder. It wasn't your fault I was abducted."

"I want to apologize for everything."

I glanced away, my emotions building with all the talk about the past.

"Is that why you're here? To apologize for not saying goodbye?"

He nodded. "Your Aunt Diane talked to me after I left the hospital that night. She told me I'd been nothing but trouble for you and I should man up and leave you to start a new life. I thought if I gave you time, you'd get a new life and move on. Both of us would be better off."

"Are you better off?" I asked, watching his face.

He shook his head. "Are you?"

"I'm alive," I said, thinking about my new life in Duncan's Cove. "But there's just this big hole, this emptiness. I miss Graham. I miss Boston."

What I wanted to say was that I missed him as well.

But I didn't.

Hunter stood and began packing the picnic things up. I watched, wondering if I could say it – that I missed him. He folded the blanket and tucked the empty glasses away in the wicker basket. When he was done, I followed him back down the trail. We talked about life back in Boston, and I tried to process everything.

When we finally emerged from the path back at the house, we stood in the yard at the door.

"Will you come in?" he asked. "You should probably have a drink of water, rehydrate after drinking the vodka."

I nodded. When we entered the house and climbed the stairs, George met us, his face wary.

"Can you excuse us for a while?" Hunter handed him the basket.

"Is everything okay?" George asked.

"I don't know." Hunter shook his head, rubbed his eyes. "How could it be?"

I frowned, wondering what he meant. George put the basket down on the island in the kitchen and went into the back of the house.

Hunter pointed to the huge overstuffed couch and chair. I sat on the sofa while Hunter went to the kitchen and took out two bottles of water from the large fridge. He handed one to me and then slumped down on the couch beside me. I opened my bottle and took a long drink from it.

An awkward silence passed between us and I fought with myself over how honest to be with Hunter.

I was so glad to see him, my heart felt like it could burst. But I didn't know what he wanted from me. I only knew what I wanted from him.

Then I made a decision.

"Hunter?"

He'd been rubbing his temples but pulled his hands away and looked at my face. "Yes?"

I climbed over and straddled him, one knee on either side of his hips. When I slipped my arms around his neck, he exhaled heavily, his breath shaky.

"I missed you," I said. "I've been so lonely without you."

I kissed him and was rewarded with the sharp inhale of his breath. When I pulled away, he brushed the wetness from my cheek.

"I missed you. I can't stand to be apart from you any longer," he said, his voice thick with emotion. "I tried to stay away, but I couldn't do it."

"I can't go back, Hunter. Even though Sergei's dead, he has family members."

"I bought this house," he said. "I've got a job as a civilian instructor at the Marine Corps Mountain Warfare Training Center in Bridgeport. I'll work training Marines several times a year. The rest of the time, I'll work from home, maybe being a digital day trader."

"What about Saint Brothers Gym?"

"I sold it to Donny's sons. I'm out completely. I'm staying, if you'll be with me. "

I glanced over his face. "As what? Your fuck toy? I can't be that anymore."

"No," he said, frowning. He took my face in his hands. "You never were. Celia, I love you." He kissed me softly. "Don't you know that by now? I'd do anything for you. Anything. I even let you go. I want to be your whatever you want me to be."

"Whatever I want you to be?" I said, unable to keep a grin off my face. "Pool boy?"

He laughed. "I could be that, if you want. I had something more permanent in mind, like," he said and hesitated. "Your fiancé."

I stared at him, my mouth open like an idiot.

"*Hunter*," I said and looked deeply into his eyes.

"Well, I did pretend to be in the hospital so…"

I smiled. "This is so out of the blue."

"Is it?" he said, frowning. "I've wanted you practically all my life."

"I wanted *you* practically all my life," I said, my throat closing with emotion.

"You don't have to say that just because I did."

"No," I said and cupped his cheek. "It's true. Ever since that first time I saw you standing in the ring with your hands wrapped in tape, kicking that punching bag."

I kissed him and it felt so right, it felt so familiar, as if finally, I was where I should be. Hunter took my hand and pulled me into the bedroom, closing the door before putting his arms around me.

We kissed again, our bodies pressed together, and it surprised me how much my body responded, despite what had happened to me. In fact, I had been afraid I would never want to be with a man again, but I didn't feel that way.

Not with Hunter.

I wanted him.

"Do you want to?" he whispered, kissing my cheek. "I can wait if you're not ready."

I didn't know if I was ready, but feeling Hunter's arms around me, feeling the intensity of his desire for me, and mine for him, made me want to try.

So I did.

. . .

I woke and glanced around the bedroom. Night had fallen and the bedroom was dark – Hunter's bedroom, in the huge house on the side of a cliff overlooking the ocean. The king-size bed covered in grey and burgundy satin beside me was empty. I was naked under the covers, and my body felt good. I had been afraid that when we fucked it would bring back memories of the rapes, but somehow, it didn't. It only brought back memories of Hunter and our times together *before*.

Hunter came back in through the open doors and went to a closet. He was wearing a pair of boxer briefs and nothing else. My gaze moved over his body with appreciation.

He retrieved a men's dress shirt and came to the side of the bed. "Here," he said and held it out. "Come out here. I have a surprise for you."

I complied, pulling his shirt over my nakedness, following him out the doors and onto the deck. Perched on a tripod was a telescope – a Celestron. Hunter stood on the deck beside it and peered into the eyepiece. He fiddled with the controls and then smiled at me, motioning me closer.

"I got this in the hopes that you'd come and live with me. I thought you'd like this. When it gets dark enough, you can see some pretty great things."

I glanced through the eyepiece and saw a blurry object in the field of view.

"What is it?"

"That's Andromeda, or M31. It's our closest galaxy outside the Milky Way. It's in the constellation of Andromeda."

"It's beautiful."

I stepped away from the telescope and leaned against Hunter, my eyes slowly adjusting to the darkness. Above us was the Milky Way Galaxy, the stars so bright where we were after midnight.

Then I closed my eyes.

"I always wanted to live in a house by the ocean," I said, happiness filling me.

I turned and slipped my arms around his neck, pulling him closer. Tears stung at the corners of my eyes.

He buried his face in my neck, kissed the skin beneath my ear.

"Never leave me again," he said, and pulled back, looking deep in my eyes.

"I won't."

I didn't.

THE END

NEWSLETTER

Sign up for my Newsletter and get all my news about upcoming releases, sales and preorders. I hate spam and will never share your email.

S. E. LUND NEWSLETTER SIGN UP

ABOUT THE AUTHOR

S. E. Lund writes new adult, contemporary, erotic and paranormal romance. She lives on the side of Burke Mountain in beautiful British Columbia, Canada, with her family of animals and humans. She dreams of living in a place where snow is just a word in a dictionary.

For More Information:
www.selund.net
selund2012@gmail.com